Caroline Bridgwood was bor⟨...⟩
in 1960. As the daughter of a diplomat, she lived in Norway,
Israel and Laos. She was educated at Badminton School, Stowe
and Oxford, where she read English. After graduating in 1982,
she worked in London for two years before turning to writing
full time. *This Wicked Generation* is her first novel.

*Caroline Bridgwood*

# This Wicked Generation

**Pan Original**
Pan Books London and Sydney

First published in 1986 by Pan Books Ltd
Cavaye Place, London SW10 9PG
9 8 7 6 5 4 3 2 1
© Caroline Bridgwood 1986
Photoset by Parker Typesetting Service, Leicester
Printed and bound in Great Britain by
Hazell Watson & Viney Limited,
Member of the BPCC Group,
Aylesbury, Bucks.

# ACKNOWLEDGEMENTS

With grateful thanks to my family, for
all their help and support. And to Caroline,
my editor, for her encouragement.

This book is dedicated to I. W. B.
'by her who best knows his value'.

'When an unclean spirit comes out of a man, it wanders over the deserts seeking a resting place, and finds none. Then it says, "I will go back to the home I left". So it returns and finds the house unoccupied, swept clean and tidy. Off it goes and collects seven other spirits more wicked than itself, and they all come in and settle down and in the end the man's plight is worse than before. That is how it will be with this wicked generation.'

*Matthew 12:13*

# PART ONE

'Cruelty has a Human Heart,
And Jealousy a Human Face;
Terror the Human Form Divine,
And Secrecy the Human Dress.'

*William Blake*

# PROLOGUE

## September 1910

A great shadow passed over the lawn as the sun momentarily disappeared behind a cloud. The croquet players sent up a unanimous cry of disappointment; the white-washed walls of Graylings, a gentleman's residence in the heart of Somerset, faded from gold to grey. And then the sun reappeared with the special late afternoon warmth of summer and the game continued, as the wood-pigeons called in the fading light and the long-discarded teacups were cleared onto trays and carried, rattling, up the steps.

George Colby was sitting in the lengthening shadow of the cedar tree, playing with his father's dog. He did not really like the dog, or want to play with it, but he had been told to do so. It was an old, mean-looking spaniel that did not wish to play any more than he did. They eyed one another resentfully. George glanced up and saw that his father was watching, leaning against one of the white pillars on the circular porch. He seized a stick hastily and began to wave it above the dog's nose in what he hoped was an enticing manner.

The dog took no notice. George waved harder, tapping the end of the stick on the dog's nose. The jaws lashed open this time, and closed again. Not on the stick, but on George's hand. George yelped.

'George, *mignon* . . . what have you done?'

His mother dropped her croquet mallet and ran towards him. Drops of blood splashed onto the pale yellow of her dress.

When George looked up again he saw his father shake his head slowly and walk back into the house.

Two miles away, at Heathcote House, Lady Henrietta Steele was opening her parasol. The retreating sun was forcing her to shade her eyes in order to watch the spectacle before her. On the lawn of the small, grey manor house, her son was attempting to mount the horse that she had just bought for him,. The thick-set grey stallion had not been fully broken, and she was eager to see how he would solve the problem.

He steadied the horse and mounted, but it threw him. He

trotted it in a ring and leapt on its back while it was moving, but when it felt his weight it stopped in its tracks and threw him again.

The sun blazed on dusty windows bedraggled with ivy. Lady Henrietta adjusted her parasol, unperturbed. She was confident that ambition would get the better of brute strength in the end. Her son was looking around him thoughtfully. He went to the bushes that flanked the grey stone wall and tore off a long switch. He approached the horse and she noted how his deep-set eyes were black with concentration, how energy was trapped in his every step. He mounted the horse again, and this time when it reared he gathered the reins tightly in his left hand and with his right rained down blows with the switch. The horse reared again; he beat it harder, struggling to balance himself with one hand. Eventually the horse stood still and lowered its head, foaming slightly. Sweat dripped from the boy's forehead onto its neck.

Lady Henrietta smiled. She had known that he would succeed in the end, if he wanted to badly enough.

For after all, that was how she had raised him to be.

# 1

Brittany Colby was going to ride the new bay mare: the horse her father had forbidden her to ride.

The evening before, the evening of 1st February 1911, Gerald Colby had delivered a rare address. 'The new bay mare arrived today,' he had said, 'but I don't want any of you children going out on her. Not yet. She needs a bit of schooling first.'

The next morning Brittany rose earlier than usual and crept down to the stables.

*The new bay mare*. The words had an enticing ring. Bluebell, her own plump, indolent pony, was dull. The accommodating broadness of his back and the resigned look in his eye were unwelcome reminders that theirs was a partnership dating from her early days in the nursery. There would be no escape for either of them for a few years yet.

But this creature was different. Brittany had noticed her elders' fondness for allotting people a Station in Life and liked to apply a similar scale of status to the horses in her father's stable. If Bluebell had always reminded her of the fat verger who trimmed the grass edges outside the church, then this very well bred animal was . . . Lady Steele? She laughed aloud at the thought. The new horse was certainly prettier. She had a small, tapering head and intelligent eyes that looked back at Brittany with simultaneous curiosity and disdain.

Brittany hitched her skirt above her boots and scurried over to the tack room to fetch a saddle and bridle. It was not that she wished to defy her father with direct disobedience, just that she was accustomed to disregarding what he said. She was not Frederick, his favourite, or George, his scapegoat, but something in between, a something which did not interest him. In her pert and outspoken way, Brittany had once asked Nanny Wynn why Papa behaved as though she was not there. First, she had received a sharp slap across the back of her legs. Then, softening slightly, Nanny Wynn explained that it was natural for a gentleman to take more interest in the upbringing of his sons, while the daughters were a mother's concern.

Of course, this was not true. Papa could scarcely bring himself to look at George. He liked his horses a great deal more than poor George. And as for Maman . . . On the rare occasions when they were alone together, Maman treated her with an indulgent sweetness that was almost as intense as the cloying tenderness reserved for George. But in company, Lucienne Colby shrank like Alice in Wonderland until she was only a tiny figure on the landscape, peering out through a fence of embarrassment. She would glance sharply, guiltily, at Brittany from time to time, as though fearful of being responsible for her daughter's words and deeds.

At the age of twelve and a half, Brittany had learned to accept this strange world where everything was divided into halves and each half lent a contradictory perspective. Indeed, she rather liked it, for it left her to make her own rules and impose her own interpretation on events. Her abundant naughtiness could go unchecked. She would take the bay mare now, and ride her, and if Papa ever discovered that she had ignored the previous day's injunction, he would say nothing to her. He eschewed confrontation, unless to chastise George. Besides, it would ruin his pretence that Brittany did not exist. If he cared sufficiently about the bay mare, he might ask Maman to speak to her, which would entail a mild, apologetic reproof. Or Maman might ask Nanny Wynn to deal with it. Which would mean another of the interminable slaps across the back of her legs.

As she humped the saddle back to the stable she was greeted with a cheery 'Morning, Miss Brittany' from one of the grooms and returned the greeting with as bright a smile as she could muster in her breathlessness. Her cheeks were flushed, her lips pursed and she blew up at her fringe with the effort. She was tall for her age, and strong, but it was difficult to balance the awkwardly distributed weight of the saddle *and* prevent the girth strap from trailing in the freezing, muddy puddles that collected in the uneven cobbles of the yard. The groom narrowed his eyes and watched her anxiously, and Brittany renewed her efforts before he could move to help her. She did not wish to have to explain why she was up so early, or to have him see her near the bay mare, for involving the servants in disobeying orders was something she wished to avoid. The twenty or so servants who worked in the house and the stables were her friends and it seemed far more natural to side with them than with her parents. They were

6

*comfortable* to be with, willing to listen and amuse, even if they did have to *Know their Place* in the end.

Twelve years and nine months on this earth, she reflected, as she buckled the brow band above the rolling, suspicious eyes. In twelve years and nine months her parents had not shared one single experience with her. She longed for someone to share things with. There was George, of course, but his opinions were only pale shadows of her own. Fräulein Lehrendorf, the lonely, buck-toothed Alsatian governess would probably have been glad to share, but Brittany would not let her. She had a horror of the dandruff that collected in the parting of Fräulein Lehrendorf's straight black hair. Every time they played cards, Brittany accused her governess of cheating. She never did cheat, but her consternation was a source of great relish to Brittany and George.

Once a friend of Frederick's at Harrow came to visit in the school holidays. He had lovely curly hair and wild, laughing eyes. Brittany would have liked to share her experiences with him but he never came again, not after that one time. Frederick spent all his time with the friend and Papa did not like it.

Brittany waited patiently until there was no one in sight, then rode the bay mare up the gently ascending drive and away from the house. She passed the green lake of a lawn, the brooding blue cedar, the path on the right that led to the beech copse and the bench that Maman had arranged to give views of the house . . . As the drive levelled off and joined the lane to the village, the bay mare sensed her exhilaration and quickened its pace. There was a surge of power quite unlike anything Bluebell could muster and for a brief, terrifying moment Brittany felt herself losing her balance. The world broke into a series of images rushing past her. Pale, frosted countryside. Trees huddling together against the cold dawn. The final, dwindling clumps of snow with fawn edges like baked meringue. Rooks scattering across icy furrows. The crest of the lane approaching rapidly beneath flying hooves. And behind her, below her, there it lay. Graylings.

The white house was set in a hollow like a pearl pin in a jewel case. Undulating lawns before it and a dark line of trees behind. Even today, with its backdrop washed wintry brown and grey, it exalted man's harmony with Nature. Order and proportion, authority, clarity and concord. The cool neo-Greek façade needed no adornment or animation. The Ionic pillars of the semi-circular portico rose cleanly from their stepped base to the triangular pediment above. Brittany still felt a sense of awe when she looked down on the house that her family had occupied for over a hundred years. It is like Valhalla, she thought. Home of the heroes. The myth of Valhalla had inspired her in the schoolroom and she pictured the ghostly Vikings stepping up between the brave white columns of her home and entering the domed marble hall to the sound of trumpets.

She sighed a gusty sigh and turned the bay mare towards the village again. Her destination was Nether Aston's squat, square-towered Norman church, not because she was moved by piety but because she was fascinated by its graveyard. It was bounded by a stone wall on one side and tall, dense bushes on the other. Dark, brooding yew trees flanked shaded, grass-covered paths between the gravestones. Brittany tied up the bay mare at the gate and wandered between the plots, tapping her crop thoughtfully against her thigh. She revered the majestic self-sufficiency of death. In her life a day rarely passed without argument. George, Nanny Wynn, Maman, Fräulein Lehrendorf – she argued with them all. But death was something you could not argue with.

The Colby family plot lay in the shadow of the church wall where the verges were most assiduously tended. She stood and looked at her grandparents' graves: *Frederick John Ratcliffe Colby, 1839–1905. Charlotte Evelina Colby, 1845–1907.* Brittany was named after her paternal grandmother. She only ever remembered her baptismal name when she visited the graveyard and contemplated her own end in this mysterious, shaded place. *Evelyn Margaret Colby, 1898– . . .* No one but Papa called her Evelyn. Everyone else, even Fräulein Lehrendorf, used the nickname that had been coined by her homesick French mother.

Try as she might, when she pictured her grandparents now, in the earth below her feet, she could only see them as they had been in life. Grandpapa vast, granite-jawed, dour, dressed in a dark suit. Grandmama tiny and timid in a rustling silk gown and lace cap. Smelling of peppermint oil. She had wanted to look at Grandmama's corpse, but Maman had said no, it will frighten you. Brittany had peeped round the library door and seen the coffin surrounded by candles, and the tiniest, most tantalizing glimpse of stiffened silk and waxy features. Then Aunt Georgina's steely hand landed on her shoulder and pulled her back, announcing that she had no business to be there and that naughty little girls like Evelyn Colby needed a Good Hiding and some Proper Discipline. Aunt Georgina . . . ah yes, she had forgotten . . . There *was* someone else who called her Evelyn. That had been the worst aspect of her grandparents' departure from this world: the descent of Papa's sisters from their marital homes.

Brittany's favourite grave stood by itself in one corner of the graveyard. A child's grave. The inscription read: *Here lies our beloved only daughter, Maria Padbury, who departed this world the fourteenth day of April, 1812, aged four years.* Above the unfortunate Maria's head hovered a white marble angel who wore a look of intense concern on her alabaster features. Brittany liked to close her eyes and imagine the funeral procession coming to a halt here, huddling around the grave in their ghastly black, the young mother wailing, swooning perhaps, as the tiny coffin was lowered into the grave . . . As she opened her eyes the clouds shifted and a ray of pale sunlight pierced the heavy branches of yew and fell vertically onto the battered, chipped marble. The figure of the angel glowed brilliant white and her wings were tipped with gold. And there, at the angel's feet, Brittany saw a clump of tiny, fragile snowdrops. The first flowers of the year. She bent and touched their petals wonderingly.

She was unaware of the dark eyes watching her.

The thick-necked grey that was standing in the lane shifted its weight impatiently beneath its rider. Brittany had moved forward until she became part of that pool of trapped sunlight, and her thick, straight hair was turned from golden brown to bronze. She tilted her face slightly, and beneath the fringe the horseman could discern the features that were almost, but not quite, pretty. Sallow skin, full-lipped determined mouth, quizzical brows and the strangest eyes he had ever seen, so drawn out at their corners that they took up the whole width of her face and would have made her look Egyptian had they not been an Anglo-Saxon blue. It was a pity she was still so young. He was impatient for her to grow out of the schoolroom and fulfil her promise. Adrian Steele smiled a proprietorial smile and turned his horse back towards the centre of the village.

By the time Brittany returned to Graylings it was eight thirty and there were several grooms moving about the yard, carrying buckets of water and bales of hay. Brittany waited in the shadow of the courtyard wall until they were out of sight before she led the bay mare to her box. Then, with hurried, haste-muddled movements, she untacked the horse, rubbed down with a handful of straw and covered her with a rug. Apart from the need for concealment, she had a good reason for hurrying. It was George's birthday, and she wanted to give him his present before he went down to breakfast. She and George still breakfasted with Nanny Wynn from trays in the nursery, but there was a tradition that on their birthdays the younger children would go down and share their parents' meal and receive their gifts. It was a gloomily formal ritual, an ordeal that had to be got through before the rest of the birthday could be enjoyed.

She passed Frederick on the stairs and he smiled broadly.

'Brittany, old girl,' he said, and squeezed her shoulder as he went by. Brittany watched him go down to the hall. She liked her brother, but could she say she knew him? No, of course not. He lived on the other side of the looking glass, in that mirror world that was the same as hers and yet not the same. How could anyone *not* like Frederick? He was self-assured, but as the same time so easy, so affable. At seventeen years old he was no longer a schoolboy, and the difference in age between him and Brittany had always been sufficient to divide their activities when they were young. It seemed that Frederick had always belonged with the adults while she and George were the property of Nanny Wynn. Frederick was patient with George and treated his sister with jovial civility, but he had never, not once, asked her a question about herself. He did not seem to want to know what she was *like*. When he talked about his schoolfriends, it was the same. One never received an impression of what they were like, only of what they did. 'Monty's no end of a chap; bagged thirty birds at his first shoot' . . . 'You should see Devereux on the playing field, runs like the wind' . . .

Brittany was excessively interested in what people were like. She suspected that Frederick was a little stupid. She did not know him well enough to be sure, but sometimes when she looked at him, his handsome face wore an expression of complete blankness. Brittany watched as he reached the bottom of the stairs and turned in the direction of the dining room, but there was no sign of stupidity today. He looked exceptionally cheerful, and Brittany knew that it was because he was looking forward to the shooting at the weekend. He pushed back the chestnut hair that sprang in thick, dramatic waves from his forehead, and put his hands in his pockets. He bunched his wide, curving mouth and started to whistle. He had his mother's high forehead and his father's long, square jaw, and it was as well that he was handsome, for this combination provided a very large area of face for the observer to take in. A maid scurried past, dropping a hasty curtsy, and Frederick stopped whistling to give her his open, easy smile. It was the sort of smile, Brittany reflected, that would have the maid re-enacting the moment in the servants' hall. *'And then the young master smiles at me like this, see . . .'*

She found George in the nursery. Nanny Wynn was on her fat knees, remorselessly fastening a stiff collar around his throat.

'George, happy birthday! Look – I've brought you this.'

She kissed him on the cheek and thrust a small parcel into his hand. George was unable to speak, but he rolled his eyes in reply above Nanny Wynn's white head.

The parcel contained a small wooden replica of a dog of Papa's that George was particularly fond of, a Jack Russell terrier called Barley. One of the estate workers had a reputation as an excellent carver and had willingly undertaken Brittany's commission.

'Brittany, it's lovely!' said George when he had been freed, his cheeks flushing pink with embarrassment at the start of the day's unwelcome attentions. 'It's Barley, isn't it?'

Brittany smiled down at George and patted his hair. It was Frederick's hair exactly; thick and waving and chestnut coloured. Visitors always exclaimed over the similarity between the two brothers, but intimate acquaintance taught that the resemblance was really an eerie parody. Where Frederick's face was large and open, George's was round and puffy; where Frederick's curved bow of a mouth was youthful, George's was weak and womanish. Frederick's grey eyes were ingenuous, George's tremulous and cowed. Two sides of the same coin.

'George, you'll never guess what I saw in the graveyard!'

He looked up at his sister, puzzled. 'The graveyard?'

'I rode there this morning. The first snowdrops! Oh George, I wish you could have seen them, they looked so *brave*, struggling out of the earth like that . . .'

George's eyes widened. The rotund figure of Nanny Wynn loomed between them. 'Enough of your nonsense! I want you out of that muddy skirt, Brittany, before you eat your breakfast. Your mother's got company later and I can't have you looking like that.'

As Brittany went to the door, George held the carved dog aloft. 'Th-th-thanks for this, Brittany.'

He was starting to stammer. He always did when he was nervous. Closing the door behind her, she pitied him. She pitied the misery the day would bring.

The dress that she was to wear lay stretched out on her bed, its arms opened beseechingly. She frowned at it. It was not a dress she much cared for: scratchy navy blue serge with a white piqué sailor collar. A fire was wheezing and coughing in the grate and Brittany moved closer to the hearth as she removed her muddy skirt and blouse and lifted the dress over her head. She had occupied a room of her own for several years now, while George still slept in the night nursery with his weak chest and Nanny Wynn. Her room was on the nursery floor, between the attics where the servants lived and the first floor where the eight principal bedrooms were arranged. Brittany had no wish to descend a floor and dwell among the high-ceilinged, elaborately draped chambers that were sunk in a stiff, cold stillness, even in summer.

Her own room was simple and cheerful. The walls were papered in faded cream scattered with roses and embellished with a sampler admonishing *I have oft heard defended, Least said is soonest mended*. A print of an exemplary Victorian child called 'Little Wide Awake' looked down on the bed with dewy-eyed disapproval. Old porcelain dolls with rattling eyes squatted on a white wicker chair in the corner. The two best things in the room, in Brittany's opinion, were a window seat that looked out onto the front lawn and an inlaid escritoire, a small replica of Maman's writing desk, sent by Tante Eugénie from Paris.

Brittany went to the mirror and started to brush out her thick mane of hair. She caught herself smiling, and laughed at her reflection. 'What are you grinning at, idiot?' she asked. The eyes that smiled back were keeping a secret. It was a wonderful secret and she had hugged it to herself all week.

Uncle Teddy was coming.

Uncle Teddy's real name was Charles Anstey, 3rd Earl of Teasdale, and he was the most wonderful person on earth. He had visited Graylings only once before, on Christmas Eve 1903. Nanny Wynn had told Brittany that if she was a good girl, Father

Christmas would come that night, and it seemed that even as she wished, Uncle Teddy had burst through the front door in a flurry of melting snowflakes and laughter. The coincidence made a deep impression on the five-year-old Brittany. Uncle Teddy's hair had been bright gold and his eyes were blue and he had swung Brittany up in his arms and said 'What a pretty young lady!' and laughed again.

Brittany had been amazed. She had never known an adult behave like this. Uncle Teddy had a wonderful new thing called a motor car which had brought him right up to the door, and he said he was just passing and thought he would call in anyway, which was strange. Nether Aston was not a corner of Somerset that people passed on their way somewhere else.

Aunt Alice, Papa's sister, and Uncle Walter were there for Christmas, and the Morgans, who were neighbours, and Maman's cousins, the Langbournes. And Uncle Teddy had said 'Oh good, enough people for a party' and Papa had scowled. At this point the children were despatched to bed, but Brittany crept down again and watched through a crack in the drawing-room door. Aunt Alice thumped out one of Chopin's waltzes at the piano. Brittany could remember the tune. She could remember the haunting, falling cadences, and Uncle Teddy guiding Maman around the room in slow circles. He seemed to lift her as they moved, so that her feet could barely make their own steps. Papa was very, very still, but his eyes never left Maman's pale, pale face. She seemed at once embarrassed and highly excited.

As she peered into the crack of light, into that enchanted grown-up world, it occurred to Brittany that Uncle Teddy looked at Maman as though he thought more of her than all the other ladies present. She was not surprised by this, since Maman was the most beautiful. But in the years that followed, by reading Maman's novels in secret and overhearing the maids' chatter, she learned that married ladies sometimes knew a man that they loved more than their husbands. So *that* was who Uncle Teddy was! The discovery excited her enormously, but Uncle Teddy never came again. He just sent her birthday presents on which he signed his name in huge, flourishing letters.

George and Frederick did not receive presents, nor were the presents ever mentioned in front of Papa.

Then, on Monday, she had been sent to the housekeeper's room on an errand for Nanny Wynn and had seen his name. There it was – on the list of guests for the weekend shooting party. Charles Anstey, Earl of Teasdale. And Viola, Countess of Teasdale. There was a note saying they were coming in the party of Roland and Lady Henrietta Steele.

Brittany felt a scorching disappointment as she stared at the name next to his. Viola, Countess of Teasdale. So that was what had happened. Uncle Teddy had acquired a wife.

It wasn't *fair*! She wanted him to be in love with Maman and go on giving presents to *her*, not to some little girl of his own.

But then Tuesday brought a far more interesting discovery.

It was Maman's habit to write letters after breakfast, seated at her desk inlaid with mother-of-pearl and ivory in the first-floor sitting room. The children were allowed to sit in the room with her as long as they were quiet. On this Tuesday, Brittany noticed that her mother was taking a very long time over one particular letter, putting her pen down and sighing frequently. Before she had finished the letter Mrs Masterman, the vicar's wife, called unexpectedly on parish business. Maman went downstairs, leaving the letter on her writing desk.

Of course, Brittany read it. She did not consider her action as an invasion of privacy. Indeed, it was almost a duty. If she was doomed to live in a world where no one ever told her anything, then she had no choice but to find things out for herself.

The paper that Maman wrote on was thick and crinkly-edged, the colour of anaemic lilac.

'*Mon cher ami*' (Brittany read),
'*I have just had a note from Henrietta Steele to say that you and your wife will be staying at Heathcote for the weekend, and intend to join the shooting. My darling Teddy, I am quite overcome and my poor brain aches from being turned this way and that. After all these years. I keep wondering "Does he long to see me as I do him?"*

*I felt I must write to you before you come, so at least you will know what I am thinking. But oh, my darling, it will be so difficult! After the last time, when Gerald was so cross that you came here like that. (Thank you for the* petits cadeaux *for darling Brittany. She is a lovely child, didn't you think?, and is turning out quite how I had expected and hoped she would.)*

*Perhaps now that you are a respectable married man yourself, Gerald will be easier. I read about your marriage and often wonder*

14

*what your wife is like. Are the two of you* vraiment amoureux *as we once were? For all our sakes I think it is better if we say nothing, and show nothing, so if I seem a little distant, it is for this reason and not because my heart no longer—'*

Brittany had felt very clever when she read this letter. First, she had already deduced the state of affairs for herself. Second, she had found evidence which substantiated her theory. A visit from Uncle Teddy was exciting enough in itself, but this made it doubly so. Her cheeks flushed as she thought about it and she laughed at her reflection again. The blue serge sailor dress made her look a little prim, and that was not how she felt at all. She felt quite wicked for knowing all this. What if Maman and Teddy still loved one another and the others found out? What if Papa ordered Uncle Teddy out of the house? How much did Viola know about Maman? . . .

Then a small voice at the back of her head said *'It is dangerous to think these things.'* Her breathing quickened and she felt faint with the dizzying power of secrets. It was as though thinking these dangerous things would make them happen.


George descended the curved staircase to the hall with two fingers jammed under the blade-like edge of his collar. He rubbed them back and forth, trying to loosen it from his sore, red flesh. He prayed that no one was watching his descent. He hated people seeing him come down these opulent marble steps. They were so broad and so subtly curving that he found it impossible to walk straight down their centre. He veered drunkenly from one edge to another every time.

It was nine o'clock. There was still time for him to go out and fetch the flowers, since his parents never ate breakfast before nine thirty. A raw, cold wind pulled roughly at his Norfolk jacket and he clenched it around his plump chest as he crossed the front of the house. To the left of the classical façade lay the flower garden, bounded by a sloping wall and accessible by an ornate iron gate. Jennings, the head gardener, was crooning to the empty flowerbeds, burying his fingers in the numb earth. He was a tall, thin man with a skeletal head and wet, blue eyes, and when he stooped over the ground he looked to George like a hairpin bent neatly in the middle.

'I'm looking for the snowdrops,' George said abruptly, and blushed.

The pin straightened and a head bobbed up.

'So, Master George,' Jennings said, with infuriating slowness. 'It's snowdrops you're after, is it? And why would that be?'

George blushed again. 'They're such brave little flowers. I want to show them to my mother.'

Jennings's face softened. 'Well, I reckon you might find some underneath the big cedar,' he said weightily. 'Reckon I've seen some over there.'

George found the flowers hiding near the bole of the tree. Their petals felt cool, the stalks rubbery. When he had gathered a small bunch he stood up, smiling at them benignly.

A jewel for the crown, that's what these were. For had not Nanny Wynn said to him, 'Every time you're naughty, a jewel falls from the crown your Mama will wear in heaven.' He wanted Maman to have the most beautiful crown of all and dazzle the angels with her long neck and white shoulders and her large, gentle eyes. But all too frequently he was hounded by the tinkling, splintering sound of falling gems and his mother's woebegone face beneath a circlet of rusty metal.

Still clutching the flowers, he climbed a little way up the drive so that he could look down on the house. He thought it resembled a large sugar lump. The fluted pillars at the front looked sweet and delicate enough to eat, like white, crumbling Edinburgh rock. All the same, he was glad that it would belong to Frederick and not to him. If one could simply live in the house it would be all right, but people noticed what you did if you were the owner of the estate, and there were so many things to remember, so many things to get right. Nanny called them responsibilities. Responsibilities terrified him. He did not give much thought to what he would do when he grew up, and no one seemed to expect him to. He would have some money and he would probably use it to buy a house nearby. Perhaps Maman would come and live there, once Frederick had a family of his own. And perhaps Brittany as well, if no one married her. And Papa might be dead by then . . . He squeezed his eyes closed in prayer.

And if he could come and stand here sometimes and look down at Graylings, just *look*, he would be quite content. He would have liked to stand and look all day and pretend that February 2nd was not his birthday, but it was cold and if he was late for breakfast, Papa might come looking for him. Besides, he had the snowdrops to give to Maman.

*

Breakfast in the dining room was a formidable affair. Silver chafing dishes sizzled above spirit-lamps, groaning with plump kidneys and sausages, eggs presented in a confounding variety of ways, pungent kippers, steaming kedgeree . . .

All this was on one sideboard. On the opposite sideboard cold dishes of York ham, glistening tongue and cold turkey jostled with cold guinea-fowl, grouse, partridge and homemade brawn. George glanced from one sideboard to the other, his eyes wide with panic. How on earth was he going to choose?

His parents were already seated but there was no sign of Frederick. The room was dominated by a terrifying long slab of mahogany and two dozen Chippendale chairs, but breakfast was always eaten at an oval library table arranged in the window alcove. Maman insisted that she would not break her fast in the gloom, and could sit at the oval table, under the east-facing window which provided plenty of early morning light. It reflected in the silver teapot, and made Maman's skin more pearl-white than ever. She rose when she saw George and the lace ruffles on her gown spilled over onto the edge of the table.

'Darling, come over here! What will you have? Some porridge?'

'Yes,' said George.

Papa's face was hidden behind *The Sporting Life*, but Papa's voice said 'Happy birthday, George'.

'M-Maman, I've brought you these.' He handed over the crushed and slightly sweaty flowers.

'Oh darling, how lovely! Aren't they pretty! I'll ring for Annie to put them in water.'

George beamed.

Maman watched him eat his porridge, smiling so much and leaning so close that George trembled and could hardly swallow. When he had finished, she produced a parcel that she had been hiding on her lap, and handed it to him. She looked as excited as a child herself. Inside the wrapping there was a flat wooden box, about a foot long. George lifted its polished lid and found tubes of paint neatly laid out in rows, with brushes.

'Paints! Lovely . . .'

'Yes, and they're real paints too, darling. Oil paints.'

George stroked the tubes tentatively with a plump finger.

'. . . And Papa has *un petit cadeau* for you too . . . Gerald?'

The newspaper twitched and Papa's head appeared: massive,

immobile, the jaw shaded finely with graphite. 'Yes, yes I have,' he said gruffly. 'I'll go and fetch it.'

They waited in tense silence while he was out of the room. George was frightened. Papa did not usually give birthday presents. What could it be? *What would he be expected to do with it?*

Papa returned, holding a wriggling, squirming mass at arm's length. George blinked, disbelieving.

'My best pointer bitch has just whelped. Thought you'd like a dog of your own.'

A dog of his own! If only Papa knew how he'd longed for a dog of his own! Frederick had two already.

Papa waved the furry bundle at George's face. 'Well, go on – you'll have to choose one, you know!'

George could not even tell how many puppies there were. Three? Four? Paws and heads seemed to protrude everywhere from the brindled clump, but it was impossible to determine which body they belonged to. They were squealing pathetically, which made it worse.

'How about the brown one?' murmured Maman encouragingly.

Brown? But they were all brown. If only Frederick would hurry up and come to breakfast. He would know which was the best one to choose. What about that little head in the middle? It looked rather small, though. Or perhaps . . .

'*Come on,*' said Papa, through clenched teeth.

He pushed the puppies under George's nose, his grip tightening, fingers sinking into fur. The frightened squealing was growing louder . . . Drops appeared on the carpet as one of the creatures emptied the contents of its bladder over Papa's wrist. Eyes widening in horror, George watched the thin yellow stain seeping up Papa's immaculate starched cuff.

'I-I-I . . . Th-the . . '

*Dear God, please*! He had started to stammer.

Papa turned round abruptly and walked to the door.

'You will get nothing as a result of such feebleness,' he said quietly.

George turned away, so that Maman would not see his tears. He did not wish her to know that he had wanted a puppy far more than a box of paints.

Gerald Colby walked across the stableyard, holding the puppies at arm's length. His gait was tight with anger and exasperation. God damn the boy! He was only trying to be kind to him.

The kennels stood in the back corner of the yard, farthest away from the house. He returned the puppies to their straw-lined box and stooped to fondle the ears of the pointer bitch, who whined expectantly when she saw him.

'It's all right, old girl, you've got your babies back,' he murmured. 'All of them,' he added bitterly.

The horses would calm him. He always went to them when his nerves were jarred, or he had suffered a bad run on the cards. Touching their smooth, strong limbs soothed him, their smell revived him. He moved vigilantly from one box to the next, holding out his hand to be snuffed, slapping their warm necks, checking their condition. The Colby stable was one of the finest in Somerset, and Gerald had created it himself. His sober, parsimonious father had ridden out to hounds occasionally, but only kept one ageing hunter, a lady's hack and a couple of carriage horses. He did not like spending money. Like the line of prudent, scrupulous men who had gone before him, he considered his purpose in life the guardianship of the estate purchased by one Samuel Colby, London merchant. The dream of a lifetime for a simple man who had made sensational gains in the South Sea Bubble. He spent what was necessary to maintain the 15,000 acres, but no more. Fancy horseflesh was not considered necessary by the late Frederick Colby.

But Gerald Colby itched for it, burned for it. When his father died, his frail, submissive mother looked on in dismay as he bought two new mounts. Then three more. Then still more . . . By the time she, too, was stretched out beneath the yew trees in Nether Aston churchyard, he had built twelve new loose boxes and employed several more grooms. Now there were nearly as many grooms as horses.

The last box belonged to the new bay mare. Gerald unlatched the door and went inside, making quiet crooning noises. Horses were rarely nervous in the presence of this monolithic and motionless man, but his latest acquisition was highly strung and he intended to build up their relationship slowly. He stood square to her flank, lifting the rug and running his fingers over the smooth coat, savouring the contours of the muscles beneath the skin. It was very slightly damp, and a few small wisps of hay were sticking to it. He sniffed his fingers and frowned.

'Tom!' He called the head groom over to the bay mare's box.

Tom put down the bucket he was carrying. 'Yes, Captain Colby?'

'Has any of your lads been exercising this mare? I thought I gave instructions that no one was to take her out yet.'

Tom looked back blankly. 'That's right, sir. She's not been out, sir, not that I know of.'

'Well, she's sweating a bit. Get someone to come in here and give her a good rub down, will you?'

As he stepped round the horse to reach the stable door, his foot crunched on something. He bent down and picked it up. Small, light and flexible. Evelyn's riding whip.

The charm worked by the horses evaporated. The dissipated anger returned. He walked back to the house in the same way that he had set out, as taut as the whip in his hand.

Gerald went to his study and laid the whip down on his desk, staring at it. He would ring for the butler and ask him to have Evelyn sent down. He had, after all, expressly forbidden her to ride the new horse, for the reason that it was very valuable. His hand moved to the bell pull, then he hesitated. He had to admire her courage, taking the beast out alone like that. If only George had half her guts. Even Frederick was not always as quickwitted as she.

He reached for the bell pull again. She had been deceitful; she would be punished. Yet . . . the only effective punishment for her sort was to learn the hard way. The expression 'riding for a fall' came to his mind. Eventually she would pick a mount that she could not handle, and be thrown. Yes, that was the best way to punish her.

Relieved, he sat back in his chair and picked up the whip again. He had a very good reason for wishing to avoid disciplining Evelyn.

She was not his child.

He considered it imprudent to dwell on this fact. He had seen how a horse that wore blinkers could sometimes make better progress on the straight. So he wore his own blinkers, cutting from his vision things which he did not wish to consider. What he did not like, he did not see. His wife Lucienne had briefly been included among the things he liked, but had now faded out of his line of vision. (George occasionally had the misfortune to blunder into it.) He disliked the fact that his wife had received the attentions of a young aristocrat several years his junior, so he shunned it as best he could.

He had met Lucienne de Vesey in 1892, when he was thirty. She was very beautiful, very sensitive, very well-groomed. He coveted her as he would a thoroughbred mare. He set about acquiring her in the same way. The French girl was penniless; that she was 'up for the highest bidder' was one of the more polite jokes that was made about her plight. She had been sent to visit Engish relatives in the hope that her exotic looks would sway some Anglo-Saxon heart, for the French *bourgeoisie* were far too fastidious to consider the daughter of an impoverished count, while the aristocracy had no choice but to look for a large dowry to enhance their own estates.

Gerald might have paid less attention to Lucienne had his father not become seriously ill at the same time. It was a bout of rheumatic fever from which Frederick Colby eventually recovered, but not before Gerald had been given cause to consider the continuity of the male line. He had never thought much about marriage before that time. He disliked his father and distanced himself by spending as much time as possible in London or shooting with friends, but when his inheritance seemed imminent he realized that he did not wish to live at Graylings with only his mother for company.

It was time for him to find a wife. He had spent five years, with the army, as an officer of the Somerset Yeomanry, travelled a little in Europe, practised indiscretion with one or two older woman. He had no title, but his two brothers had died in childhood and only sons with large estates were always a 'catch'. He left his father's sickbed full of these thoughts, went to a ball in London and there she was. It was all too easy.

Lucienne was twenty-one and had been a guest of her cousins, the Langbournes, for well over a year. It was an uncomfortably protracted visit and she seemed pathetically grateful for Gerald's attentions. Her Catholicism had discouraged several would-be husbands.

'But she's a *Roman Catholic*!' hissed Gerald's sister Georgina when Lucienne was taken to Graylings for the first time. 'Look at that jewelled cross she's wearing around her neck. How *vulgar*!'

But Gerald did not care what his family thought. Lucienne was beautiful, she was feminine, she was amenable. She readily agreed to convert to the Church of England, and the Colbys were silenced.

A year later, when Frederick was born, the wisdom of Gerald's choice was proved to his own satisfaction. But Lucienne did not like horses or outdoor pursuits and Gerald felt a waning of interest in her. Neither of them cared for the physical rites of marriage and they stayed in the separate bedrooms that they had occupied during Lucienne's confinement and lying-in. The baby thrived and Lucienne seemed quite content.

Then she met 'Teddy' Anstey.

Gerald tolerated the affair at first. He was even flattered by Anstey's interest in his wife, in a narrow, snobbish way. After all the Earl of Teasdale was the noble scion of one of England's most distinguished families: brash, brilliant and popular. He lent the Colbys a certain social cachet. There was also an unwritten convention, emanating from the Marlborough House set, that once a married woman had done her duty and produced a son, she could indulge in discreet affairs with impunity.

But Lucienne did not appear to know the rules and when he learned that she was pregnant, Gerald cursed the day that he had married a witless foreigner. There was not the slightest possibility that the child was his, but Gerald was not going to give the world the satisfaction of knowing as much.

He named the girl after his mother.

In the end, Gerald managed things to his satisfaction. Anstey had the good sense to disappear before the child was born; the child had the good sense to be a girl and thus avoid rivalry with the five-year-old Frederick. It irked him that the sharp-eyed and sharp-tongued would gossip about his 'daughter', for she resembled no one more than the boy-wonder Anstey, and for this reason he could not bring himself to feel affection for her. All the same, he was gratified that he had acquired a child who loved horses as much as he did.

And he had gained an important hold over his wife. She would never dare to question him about his own affairs now, never ask him anxiously how much he had lost when he returned from London. They never mentioned 'Teddy'.

Except once in May 1899.

Evelyn was still a baby. Henrietta Steele had asked the Colbys to dine at Heathcote House and had been unable to resist revealing that the Earl of Teasdale was among the guests. Lucienne was desperate to attend; Gerald had refused point blank to allow it. Later that evening he had heard her sobbing in her room and knocked at the door in a clumsy attempt at apology. He was afraid of driving her back to her relatives in France, for she might take Frederick with her.

He found her half naked and disturbingly beautiful. Lust was far simpler than apology. Nine months later, George was born. He was a sickly child and Gerald did not expect him to live, but this only seemed to endear him to Lucienne the more. She devoted herself to George and was content again.

The morning's post had been neatly arranged on a tray on the desk. Gerald opened the first letter and frowned. It was from his bank. Just as well there is no wife inquiring into my financial affairs, he thought.

'Dear Captain Colby,' he read, 'I refer to your request of the twentieth January instant, for monies to be made available in the form of a mortgage on your property. I would seek to remind you that you have already followed such a course of action with regard to 5,000 acres of the Graylings estate. In view of this, I feel that it would be advisable for us to meet and discuss your financial position before we proceed . . .'

Gerald flung the letter down on the desk with a sigh. His horses were expensive, but his other passion was more expensive still.

Gambling.

On one corner of the desk stood a set of baccarat cards and counters. He stroked them lovingly. The counters, indicating denominations from five shillings to ten pounds, were of embossed leather. He had bought the set as a gift to himself after winning some money from the then Prince of Wales, at *baccarat banque*. His Royal Highness was very fond of baccarat and he, too, had an embossed leather set, sporting the three feathers. Of course, he could afford to fund his habit. Gerald could not.

Nor could he stop gambling. Why was it that a man normally so slow to have his passions roused should find his blood heated and his spirit quickening as the stakes were raised over and over, to breaking-point and beyond? Gerald had often asked himself that question. The weaker his hand, the more his cheeks flushed, the more his heart pounded, the more he wallowed in his surrender to elusive Chance. Oh, he loved it so! It was seduction of the most blatant kind. The odds might fade, but there was always that tiny chance remaining, and as long as he clutched the cards in his right hand, his left would go on pandering to it, pushing the counters into the centre of the table. He was irredeemably in love with that one chance. When it failed him, it was like the betrayal of a fickle mistress.

And like a smitten lover he would always return.

Gerald read through the contents of the letter hastily and put it back into its envelope.

'Papa!'

He looked up at the small window to the right of his desk. It looked out onto the gravelled arc at the front of the house where Frederick was standing, waving and gesticulating, his breath making white circles around his face. He could not help but smile at the sight of his beloved elder son, especially after Evelyn's disobedience and the unrewarding encounter with George. Thank God Frederick was the heir, and not George! He had tried to be patient with George and he had suffered guilt, too, for his own harshness, but the boy was so slow, and he would not *learn*. If only he had been eager, Gerald could have tolerated the infuriating clumsiness. As it was, he felt mocked by the grotesque outward resemblance to Frederick.

He raised his hand in a peremptory salute, then strode out onto the portico to greet his son.

'Papa! Good morning!' Frederick gave his open, easy smile and was about to speak, then his eyes flickered and he fell silent for a second.

Gerald waited, watching him closely, anxiously.

'Papa, Forrester says you're riding out to Coombe Farm this morning. Can I come with you?'

'Of course. We shall have to try and recruit some beaters while we're there, for the weekend.'

Gerald descended the steps heavily and put a massive hand on his son's shoulder. 'Frederick, the pointer pups are weaned now. Perhaps you'd like to pick one out for yourself?'

He was rewarded with another of the smiles. 'Thanks, Papa! I'll go and take a look now.' He started to run towards the yard.

'Oh, and Frederick,' Gerald shouted, relenting as the warmth of good humour returned, 'choose one for your brother, will you?'

Lucienne Colby lifted the hem of her skirt with one hand and started her ascent of the curved marble staircase. She did so slowly, carefully. It was impossible to go up or down this staircase unnoticed. The domed skylight above it had a circular window like an eye, illuminating the smooth white steps and anyone who happened to be travelling on them. They were so heavy and broad that they dwarfed their passenger, exposing more than deportment. Lucienne watched strangers on this staircase in order to learn more about them. Nervousness, arrogance, cheerfulness were all revealed by the time they reached their destination.

Lucienne went into the first-floor sitting room and closed the door. It was a square room with tall, north-facing windows admitting a bleak light, but nevertheless it had a restful, feminine atmosphere. The elaborate moulding on the walls was picked out in gilt, the armchairs were covered in faded pastel silk and over the fireplace was a portrait of Gerald's grandmother wearing a large leghorn hat with pale blue ribbons. The delicate inlaid writing desk stood beneath one of the windows.

George was underneath it.

Lucienne stooped slightly so that she could see his face.

'Aren't you going to use your paints, darling?'

'Later. Brittany said she'd show me how to use them, later.'

'Very well, darling,' said Lucienne with a sigh. She sat down at the desk with George at her feet reading *Our Empire Story*. He often came and curled up beneath the desk when she was writing, drawing himself into a tight ball as though he were trying to retreat into insignificance. Lucienne indulged him shamelessly in this, as in everything, spreading her skirts about the chair so that if Gerald came in, he would not see his son's hiding place.

Truly, George was the only child who had ever belonged to her. Frederick had been dominated by Gerald's plans for him from the start. And Brittany, her love-child . . . she saw in her daughter all the qualities she had loved so passionately in Teddy. Even her nickname served as a reminder. Lucienne's family owned an ancient, decaying farmhouse in Brittany, and it had been her favourite place as a child, a place of mystical memory. When she and Teddy fantasized forlornly about escape, Brittany was to be their destination. A rustic haven. And after Teddy was gone . . .

Brittany, Brittany. She liked to remember the way he said it. The word became a comforting symbol, and it had a pretty ring to it, far nicer than the stiff, strait-laced Evelyn.

She loved her daughter so much . . . But she could not show it.

There always seemed to be someone watching, watching her shame eat into her. Besides, Brittany had a wilful, independent nature. So the love that was hers by right was poured like a stream of treacle into the innocent George.

She worried constantly about George. He was eleven years old now, and in two years time he would leave Graylings for his incarcertion at Harrow. Lucienne had suggested that in view of his poor health he should continue his studies at home, with a private tutor, but Gerald insisted that Harrow would be good for him and she dared not argue. She did not see how it could be 'good', though. A lonely George wheezing miserably on a muddy playing field. 'Good'? The English educational system was very hard to understand. The boys *had* to go to school, but when Lucienne made known her opinion that Brittany should attend a girls' boarding school, she was told that it would not 'do'. It was inappropriate to send her away from home, Gerald said, when home would be her lifelong environment. Sport and learning would not only be useless, but positively dangerous. They might turn her into a tomboy or bluestocking, and therefore render her less attractive as a future wife and mother.

It was all so contradictory. Brittany must not become a tomboy, yet while Lucienne tried with feeble good intention to prevail on her children to prize gentleness, tolerance and an appreciation of beauty, Gerald gave no thought to ethics or behaviour as long as his children could sit a horse well and shoot straight. George was doomed a failure because he could do neither.

Her own childhood had been very different. Maman had died when Lucienne was a baby, and she and her elder sister Eugénie had been raised by an aged, toothless family nurse for the first few years of their lives. Thereafter they were left to their own devices, while their quiet, disinterested father retired with his butterfly collection and his books. The family château had long since been sold to pay off bad debts, and until Lucienne was twenty, 'home' was a shambling apartment in St Germain des Prés, crammed with relics of the de Veseys' former glory: ornate gilt and ormolu furniture and large, dirty oil paintings from which aristocratic faces peered like cats out of coalholes. When she was twenty, her father died and a scheming godmother selected Lucienne to be the recipient of hospitality from the Langbournes, who were cousins of her mother by marriage.

She was selected in preference to Génie for the sole reason that Génie was plain and she was not. The motives for the trip to London were entirely mercenary and there was an unspoken understanding that she would come back as a married woman, or come back in disgrace.

It was terrifying.

The ambitious French godmother had failed to account for the anti-Catholic atmosphere and the complete lack of tolerance among the English. English Catholics banded tightly together and the Langbournes were not of their number. At the dances Lucienne attended, little programmes were issued, with matching tasselled pencils, and were used to trap partners in advance. Lucienne's programme always filled quickly, but if someone discovered that she was a Catholic, quite often he did not come back for the next dance, even if he had reserved it. It was a prejudice rendered doubly exasperating by Lucienne's complete lack of personal faith, and it was with a sigh of relief that she abandoned her Catholicism in order to marry Gerald Colby.

She married him without thinking. She had done many things in her life without thinking. Suddenly, there he was, and it seemed the obvious thing to do. When young Englishmen were being witty she did not understand what they were saying, and here was a man who seldom spoke, a tall, massively built man with stubble so dark it was almost blue. She thought the warm, safe feeling inside her was love, but it was not. It was only gratitude. She realized that as soon as she met her darling Teddy . . .

And now Teddy was coming. She glanced down at the cursory note from Lady Steele which asked politely if she could bring her house guests, the Earl and Countess of Teasdale to take part in the Graylings shoot, and saying that she would call to discuss Lucienne's plans for the weekend's entertainment on the afternoon of Thursday, 2nd February. If Lucienne had thought harder about it, she would have concluded that Henrietta Steele wanted to gloat over Lucienne's consternation and her own cleverness, but her mind was too agitated and excited by thoughts of seeing Teddy again. Did Gerald know? Had he seen the list of guests yet? She had not dared to discuss the weekend with him, for fear he said something, for fear he . . . stopped Teddy coming, somehow. But not *now* surely, not now he was married? And what was she to wear?

27

There was something she *must* wear, if only she could be certain of finding it . . .

She pushed back her chair and left the room, quite forgetting that poor George was exposed to public view through the open door. She went into her bedroom. Soft satins, scented silks. Rows and rows of ruffles. Swagged and draped bed piled high with lace-edged cushions. Sheer, heavenly self-indulgence. The small carriage clock above the fireplace beat time to her excited heart as she rummaged through drawer after drawer of hand-embroidered underwear, ribbons, buttonhooks, uncoiling silk stockings and pairs of gloves until she found what she was looking for. A small black velvet-lined box.

Inside the box was a pair of diamond ear-rings like twin drops of water, each stone clasped in its setting by a pair of tiny gold hands, perfectly sculpted with tiny fingers, even fingernails. Teddy had given them to her. Lucienne stood in front of the mirror and held one of them up to her ear. Impossible to tell what they would look like when she was wearing this high-necked morning gown . . .

She unbuttoned the dress and pushed it down so that her shoulders were bared. That was better.

Like many women who are natural beauties, Lucienne was not vain. She stared at her reflection with equanimity. Her hair was a rich brown and simply dressed, accentuating her high forehead and grey eyes so heavily laden with lashes that her eyelids seemed to droop beneath the weight of them. Her long neck and her shoulders were snow-white, milk-white, pearl-white . . . all of these, and better. A whiteness with the warmth of flesh, a whiteness rendered pink by the cold light of the diamonds. But look again and the pink had vanished, it was a trick.

Lucienne sighed with satisfaction. She had never worn the ear-rings before.

She would wear them when Teddy came.


## New York, 2 February, 1911

David Stein looked out of the window onto the street below. The traffic of Fifth Avenue trundled past in its clockwork fashion; horse-drawn omnibuses, the occasional motor car, a stream of well-dressed pedestrians. It must have been noisy, but the windows on the street side were always sealed shut, and thick velvet curtains muffled any sound.

Then he turned and looked in at the mausoleum of a mansion, cavernous and over-stuffed, dark despite its brash décor of gold and blood-red. The room was spotless – with an indoor staff of twenty, how could it fail to be? – yet it smelled dusty. Was it because of the morass of ornaments and objects which *would* collect dust if they could?

Money, that is what the expensive clutter was saying. Money. *We have money and we care to show it by buying priceless Fabergé and Limoges as though they were cheap trinkets.* And power. Signed photographs of statesmen and royalty in every corner, reminding the ignorant that Jewish moneylenders might never head governments, but they had the ear of those who did, and that meant power.

Whenever he looked out at the street, David felt as though he were looking at it from a cage. Watching the world go by . . . but this *was* the world, this four-storeyed treasure chest of a house. This and the grey stone building on Wall Street from which the money and power were generated. Papa took them to see it from time to time, in case they were in danger of forgetting. David's elder brother, Jake, was at this very moment being treated to one of these empire tours. David wished that Jake would hurry up and come back, and then maybe they could find something to do. His sisters were so dull . . . *There was nothing to do.*

He decided that he would go and find his mother. He often relied on her to distract him. He wandered down wide corridors beneath endless chandeliers. From one room came a scrape–thump, scrape–thump. Sixteen-year-old Sarah in the throes of a dancing lesson. From time to time the sound was drowned by inexpertly played Mendelssohn from yet another echoing room. Eighteen-year-old Leah practising the piano.

Hannah Stein was at the centre of one of the formal drawing rooms, a solitary figure beneath a ceiling densely populated with cherubs, dwarfed by the pink damask sofa on which she perched.

'Ah, David . . .' She patted the sofa beside her, appraising her fifteen-year-old son with gentle eyes as he walked across the vast space that separated them. 'You've missed Rachel. She came to call, but she has just left.'

David was relieved. Rachel was his oldest sister, newly married and expecting her first child. He found her bulging stomach and swollen breasts alarming.

'I'll ring for some tea, dear. I've had mine, but perhaps you'd like a cup?'

David nodded and lay back on the sofa to look at his mother as she gave a brief authoritative peal on her brass handbell. He approved of what he saw. After all, the fine-boned face was a little like his own. He had seen bankers' wives, friends of his father's, who dressed themselves up like French poodles. His mother was dressed, as usual, in dark silk with black velvet frogging. She did not like to show off.

A uniformed footman came in to receive the order. He bowed very low.

'My son would like some tea.'

'Indian, Ceylon or China, madam?'

David laughed aloud.

'Indian,' said his mother firmly. 'Darjeeling.'

'Milk, cream or lemon, madam?'

'Milk, I think.'

When the footman had gone, David sat up and said with mock inscrutability, 'Jersey, Hereford or Shorthorn, madam?' He let out a whistle, then laughed again. 'Glory be, Mother! What a performance. That guy would do better in vaudeville.'

Hannah Stein looked hurt. 'Don't patronize, David. He has to feel he's doing something important. Anyhow, it's all your father's idea. He thinks people will be impressed by that sort of—'

She broke off and flushed slightly.

David's green eyes sparkled. 'Go on, Mother. "That sort of nonsense" – is that what you were going to say?'

'Don't tease, David,' said his mother severely. Then she laughed at the sprawling figure next to her and patted his leg. 'You're a good boy, David.'

She often said that. Why did she think he was good, David wondered? Because he didn't do the wicked things that Jake used to do when he was young, like sliding the length of the central staircase on a tea tray? But David *wasn't* good, not inside. It was Jake who thought banking was wonderful and wanted to join Papa. David didn't. He wanted to be . . .

What did he want to be? Something different.

Perhaps his mother thought he was good because he liked *her* so much? But she ought to know what he was like. She ought to know that he was only coming to see her, and charming her and cracking jokes because he was at a loose end and had nothing better to do. She obviously didn't care. Maybe mothers always thought their youngest child was 'good'.

'So . . .' Hannah said, pouring the tea expertly. 'No more lessons today?'

David shook his head.

'What are you going to do, then?'

David yawned. 'There's *nothing* to do. I've—'

'You could read, dear.'

He sat up suddenly. 'Read? Sure, I could read. But in books it's all happening to somebody else, isn't it? Think of all the exciting things that are going on in the world at this very moment, Mother. But why aren't they happening here? *Nothing* ever happens here.' He flung himself down on the cushions again and crossed his arms.

Hannah smiled wisely and proffered a cup of tea. 'Perhaps it's better that exciting things are confined to books, David. The Steins have seen trouble and danger already. We have a peaceful life now, and that's the way we like it. You should thank God, David.'

He frowned, and she added placatingly, 'What about your Conan Doyle stories?'

'I've read them all.'

'All? Are you sure?'

David had received a full set of Conan Doyle's works, bound in gold-embossed morocco, for his fifteenth birthday.

'I can assure you that it took no time at all, Mother,' he said gravely. 'I love his stuff. Mystery, mistaken identity, a trail of clues . . . Perhaps you could pay Conan Doyle to write me some more?'

Hannah Stein was anxious to humour her favourite son. 'I'll tell you what, dear. We'll do better than that . . .' She turned to face him, folding her hands neatly in her lap. 'We'll write a detective story of our own. Where shall we start? A stolen heirloom? A missing will? Or, or,' she frowned and put a finger to her lips, 'someone vanishing into the London fog . . .'

'No, no,' said David. 'It has to start with someone finding a body, in a place they wouldn't expect to find one. In . . . in . . .'

'I know!' said Hannah, clapping her hands. 'In the back of a hansom cab!'

'Yes! That's just right! You're learning fast, Mother. And the only clue to its identity is . . .'

'. . . it's in full evening dress, of course.'

'Of course. And the only clue is . . .'

'A locket containing a single golden curl!'

'Perfect, Mother! What a wonderful game. Why didn't we think of this before?'

Jake Stein followed his father up the steps of the Stein building on Wall Street. The doorman bowed deferentially, and although Jake was two steps behind Isaac, he was so much taller than his father that the bow seemed to be aimed at him. He blinked, and smiled at the man slightly. He had entered the bank many times before, but this time felt different.

Isaac Stein's small, rotund figure positively bounced as he led Jake up the thickly carpeted stairway. *He's up to something . . .* thought his son. He waved Jake into his office with a plump, freckled hand, and sat down at his desk. The seat of the chair was cunningly raised so that he could look down on the occupant of the chair opposite: even so, his figure was small and squat. His light blue eyes were glowing with pleasure.

'Well, Jacob, why do you think I've brought you here?'

That was just like Papa, opening with a question that caught you unawares.

Jake looked back at him blankly. 'I have no idea,' he said honestly. 'Something about the bank?'

'Not about the bank, about your life.' He pointed a finger accusingly into the centre of the room. 'This is a pretty smart building, isn't it?'

Jake looked at the carpeted floor, the Herculean proportions of the desk, the expensively framed portraits of Jewish patriarchs who looked on at the conversation with shrewd interest. 'Yes, yes it is.'

'This is nothing,' said Isaac Stein simply. 'Pretty soon I'm going to tear this place down and build a bank that makes this look like a greengrocer's shop. Everyone's going to be doing it, the whole city will look different in ten years' time. Only I'm going to do it first. And I'll tell you something else . . .'

'Yes, Papa?'

'Banking is still only in its infancy. People are going to wake up to all the different ways they can turn money into money, and then—' He blew onto the palm of his hand. 'Whoosh! We're going to have operations everywhere. Paris, London . . . I'm going to need you, Jake.'

Jake smiled at his father and ran his hand self-consciously through his thick, straight hair. 'I always knew that, Papa. I always said, didn't I, that I wanted to join the bank—'

'I'm making you a partner.'

'What – now?'

'Yes, now, why not now? You're twenty-two years old. Do you know what I'd done by the time I was twenty-two years old? No matter, I've already told you . . . So, you're twenty-two. You've had the best education I could buy for you. You've travelled in Europe. It's time.'

'But a partner, Papa, I—'

Isaac stood up abruptly and waddled to the window. 'Why not a partner? Do you want to go and join my clerks and sweat it out from the bottom, adding up rows of figures? That's the way *I* did it, because I had to. But why the hell did I work so hard? *So you wouldn't have to!*'

He bellowed the last words, then sat down with his hands resting against each other lightly, as though in prayer. This was a sign that he was about to make a speech. Other men would have remained standing, but Isaac Stein was so short that it would have no effect.

'When I was young, the only thing I could think about was making something of myself. But the fancy house on Fifth Avenue was a long way off, believe me . . .'

Here we go again, thought Jake wearily: Frankfurt, the Judengasse, the ghetto . . .

' . . . Forty years ago I was working in a money-changing bureau in the Judengasse in Frankfurt. Making a profit, sure, but treated like filth by the other people in the city, herded into a ghetto where we had to live on top of each other. And being a moneylender you were doubly unclean. But I got together enough money to come over here to New York, where I could be somebody . . .'

Jake stared straight ahead. *Enough money to dam up the Hudson,* he was thinking.

'. . . And now when people visit my house, they get treated as though they were royalty. I've got enough money to dam up the Hudson, and nobody's going to say that Isaac Stein's a jumped-up little *yeki* who doesn't know how to behave. And what's more . . .'

Jake blinked and shook himself slightly. This postscript was a new development.

'. . . They're going to see how the Steins stick together and put up a united front. So you're going to be my partner. And you're going to work goddamn hard!' He looked out of the window again. 'The car's waiting for us. Come on, I've got something to show you before we leave.'

He led Jake onto the front steps of the narrow, grey building and pointed up at the carved stone letters over the lintel. 'You must have known what our trip was about when you saw that.'

The I. STEIN & CO had been changed to STEIN AND SONS.

'I didn't see it,' confessed Jake. A freezing east wind whipped at his hair.

'Well, you're going to have to do better than that, Jacob.' said Isaac drily, placing his top hat on his balding head and seeming smaller than ever as a result. 'I'm going to have to rely on you to be observant.'

'But, Papa,' said Jake, squinting up at the sign, 'Why does it say "AND SONS"? Surely it should be "AND SON"?'

Isaac paused, his gloved fingers resting lightly on the frame of the car door. The chauffeur stood staring impassively ahead, holding the door open. 'Do you think I'm going to waste money paying for it to be done twice? David's going to be joining us, remember? It's not time for him yet, but it will be.'

'Papa, I don't think David *wants* to,' said Jake anxiously, as he slid into the seat beside his father and muttered a polite 'thank you' to the chauffeur.

'Of course he wants to!' scoffed Isaac. He gave his son a wintry smile and pulled the fur-lined **rug** across their knees.

'. . . But he'll be joining us whether he wants to or not.'

## Somerset, 2 February, 1911

'I just hope Anstey has the sense to bring his own gun!'

Roland Steele was muttering to himself as he shambled about

the darkened landings of his home in his stockinged feet. He often muttered to himself, since there was no one else at Heathcote particularly interested in talking to him. And especially not today, when his wife was desperately trying to marshal the house into order before her weekend guests arrived.

He headed for the gun room. A maid jumped as he passed her, almost dropping the tray she was carrying. 'Oh sir, it's you!' she gasped with relief.

'Well, who did you think it was?' he muttered angrily. It was true, he was wearing no shoes, but then any sane person would leave their boots at the door if they were caked in mud. He had forgotten that he was given a wild appearance by his wet hair, which was dripping onto his shirt and waistcoat. His thinning red locks had fallen from their usual arrangement on his balding pate and were clinging to his neck and shoulders like the shag of some river god. He had been riding about the muddy lanes, more to keep away from the house and exercise the dogs than for any constructive purpose, and on his return he had rinsed the mud splashes from his face by immersing it under the pump in the yard. Not the sort of behaviour he would indulge in while his wife was looking. Or his son Adrian for that matter.

His son was a damned snob. Roland had allowed it to happen. When the child was born, Henrietta was so keen to model the red, screeching lump of clay that he had tactfully bowed out and left her to it. He looked on it as an experiment, really. Expose a child to a sole parental influence and see what happens. The answer was depressingly obvious. Their only son took after his mother in every way.

The gun room was more of a cupboard than a room. It was situated behind the stairs and crammed with boots, hats, sticks – anything but guns. There was one gun, resting on a wall-bracket, and Roland took it down, smiling at it. Adrian had a gun, of course, a very decent gun that his mother had given him, but he did not deign to keep it among this dirt and clutter. God knows where he *does* keep it, thought Roland as he stroked his own gun. In his room, probably, hidden. Furtive, secretive boy.

Roland foraged for the tin containing rags and grease which he used to clean his gun. He bent to his task, but the room lacked both light and air and hampered his movement. He decided he would take the gun outside, eschewing the yard at the back for the reason that his son was there talking to the stable lad. He went instead to the square lawn at the front of the house, enclosed within a high stone wall that ran along the edge of the village street. Heathcote House was a fine place and he eyed it with satisfaction between bouts of poking and peering down the barrel of his gun. The façade of greyish Somerset stone was square, as were the windows and the thick stone lintel around the front door. Inside, the rooms were square, aligned predictably with the four corners of the house. It was a plain house, a yeoman's house, but since Roland had never lived in any other it did not occur to him to find fault with it. His wife, however, had found fault with it from the day she first arrived as a somewhat elderly bride.

*Then what did she marry you for?*

Sometimes he ignored the familiar question. Today he decided to answer it. Because no one else would have her, of course. Because she had held on for nearly two decades for the proposal from a member of the aristocracy that never came. And in the end, Lady Henrietta Dysart, daughter of an earl, was forced to settle for a plain 'Mister' with a small, square manor house, a few nonde-script farms and a collection of debts.

*Wouldn't it have been preferable to remain an unmarried earl's daughter than to descend to all that?*

She makes it quite obvious that it would, were it not for the existence of her precious son, conceived during a honeymoon that has proved to be the only marital congress we've ever known.

*And why didn't the titled young men want her?*

Because she was haughty, sharp-tongued and intolerant, that's why.

*And why should you put up with all that?*

Because I needed her money, damn it. Greed. And because I was young and impressionable enough to think that she might take me up with her. But she stays on her level, and I stay on mine. Probably happier that way, anyway . . .

Roland conducted this dialogue as he cleaned his gun; half in his head and half out aloud. It acted as a substitute for quarrelling with Lady Henrietta, and he would scourge himself thus for his foolishness in marrying her, then allow himself to forget her for a while.

'Roland!'

It seemed he could not forget her yet. Lady Henrietta's figure appeared in the doorway. She hesitated for a moment, shaking her head, then crossed the balding winter lawn. She had clearly decided that it would demean her to shout her message from the house.

'This is hardly the place to clean a gun,' she said in her cold, still voice before briskly turning on her heel. 'In full view of the house. I see no reason why one of the men shouldn't clean it for you, but if you must clean it yourself, please do so in the yard.'

Sighing, Roland carried the gun round to the yard and continued to clean it there. Lady Henrietta was being more sensitive than usual, he knew, because Heathcote would be 'on show' that weekend. 'Damned stupid idea!' he exclaimed out loud, referring to his wife's decision to invite some people they hardly knew and spoil what would have been a peaceful weekend's shooting with a neighbour. He had met 'Teddy' Anstey a few times at Graylings, and by some ghoulish coincidence the new Countess Teasdale was some long-lost cousin of Lady Henrietta's. She was possessed with a sudden urge to see her again, despite not having laid eyes on the girl for years.

'Damned foolish woman!' he mumbled as he carried the gun back to the house. Even *he* could see that Heathcote would be a bit of a disappointment after what the Teasdales were used to, and they didn't really have the staff to cope with house guests. But when he suggested that the Teasdales might be better off staying up at Graylings, Lady Henrietta had replied with her most withering look. She took it hard, living in only the second most imortant house in the district.

'The woman's just a snob!' he said as he put the gun back in its bracket and wiped his blackened, greasy hands on his trousers. She had taught Adrian to be far too acquisitive for a man whose expectations were meagre, whose social position was lowly. It made Roland feel uncomfortable.

Still, the shooting would be enjoyable. Roland had used the thought of it to cheer himself up all week. Whistling tunelessly, he ambled to the billiard room to practise his game. Gerald would put on a good show, he always did. He and Gerald Colby had known each other since boyhood, and they respected one another. Some people found Gerald cold and stand-offish, but Roland was immune to that sort of reserve after eighteen years of marriage to Lady Henrietta. He had come to quite like Gerald Colby. He certainly envied him.

'I'll bet Gerald Colby's wife never tells him where to clean his guns!' he said to his billiard cue, with a heavy sigh.

Lady Henrietta Steele was wielding a garden trug on one arm, in defiant attitude like Britannia with her shield.

'Only forsythia and winter jasmine, I'm afraid,' she said imperiously to the terrified maid who stood before her, 'but we shall just have to do our best with them. We don't have access to hot-house flowers at this time of year, like some people I could mention . . .'

She laid out the tangle of branches resolutely on the dining room table. '. . . but then again, too many gaudy colours look vulgar . . .'

She cast an ironic glance around the dark, cheerless room. At either end of it were two oval mirrors set in the walls in Victorian fashion and surrounded by a macabre frieze of black cherubs carrying garlands. The figures were raised and moulded and shone dully. A clock ticked from a sidetable. It wasn't always easy to console herself by assigning the luxuries of others to the realms of bad taste. But she could not bear simply to let people *assume* that she knew the difference.

'I think we'll confine ourselves to three arrangements.' she continued, ignoring the maid, 'the drawing room, the main staircase and the guest bedroom. So arrange them in a triangular shape with the width at the bottom . . . do you understand me?'

The girl nodded quickly.

'Right, off you go, then.'

The maid waited until her mistress had reached the door, then gingerly thrust some of the branches into a crystal vase.

'No, no, no!' said Lady Henrietta without turning round. (She *has* got eyes in the back of her head, the girl said to herself.)

'Here! You'll never do it that way! Don't you see? The weight of the thing is all going to slump to the front. Even my son could make a better job of it. In fact he has quite an eye for these things . . .'

The maid watched sulkily as her handiwork was corrected, and rewarded her own patience by sticking out her tongue at the door as Lady Henrietta slammed it behind her. One of the cherubs fell off the wall.

Really, there's very little I can do with this charnel-house, this *morgue*, Lady Henrietta told herself as she swept up the stairs to change for her afternoon outing.

Many brides would have burst into tears as soon as they saw Heathcote House, arctic and uncomfortable, with only one bath. Lady Henrietta's reaction had been one of sheer fury. She had been led to believe that the house was 'pleasant'. It was not. She had allowed *herself* to believe that she would be lady of the manor, in the fullest sense of the word. She was not. She found that, since the 1780s, Heathcote had merely squatted in the shadow of a palatial Georgian mansion owned by a family of *parvenu* gentry whom she had never even heard of. The eighteen years of her marriage had been conducted as an elaborate revenge on all fronts. She defied sceptics by conceiving a child straightaway, at the age of thirty-five, and promptly locked her booby of a husband out of her bedroom. He had served his purpose. And while she plotted and schemed to propel Adrian up and out of Heathcote, she looked for every opportunity to humiliate Lucienne Colby.

In her room, she unbuttoned her dress briskly and stepped out of it. The energetic, angular frame did not belong to a fifty-two-year-old woman, but it had never been a young body either. No plump, young curves; no voluptuously yielding flesh. Her limbs had always been sinewy, her breasts flat and scrawny. She thrust herself into an afternoon gown of lavender wool and spent a few moments before the mirror, bullying a small, felt hat into place. She saw a handsome, disappointed face, slightly buck-toothed and marred by too many frown lines. The eyes were a hard cornflower blue and the black hair that was coiffed in an impregnable turret had a faint blue sheen, like the plumage of some great crow. She had never quite lost the mannerisms of one who is used to being revered and admired, tossing her head and opening her eyes unnaturally wide when someone paid her a compliment.

Before she left the room, she practised the smile that she reserved for Lucienne Colby. It was one of her masterpieces, at once disarmingly friendly and blatantly patronizing. What a piece of luck that Anstey had married the daughter of her own second cousin! A heaven-sent excuse to put Lucienne Colby in her place. The woman was a perfect fool! It was one thing to indulge in a little tasteful adultery, but quite another to bring a child into it. The Frenchwoman had completely mismanaged the affair. The girl was quite obviously Anstey's; you could tell just from her bones.

Breeding will out, as the late Countess of Dysart had always said. The only people who appeared not to notice were Roland, who was hopelessly naïve about such matters, and Gerald Colby. And he was just being stubborn. It was a pity the girl was not old enough to notice the resemblance herself. Then the arrival of her house guests really would put the cat among the pigeons . . .

There was one more thing to be done before she set out for Graylings. Riding up to the big white house like poor relations was a sore affliction for which Lady Henrietta had the perfect remedy, and she dosed herself without fail every time she went to visit her neighbours. She went into the water closet that she had insisted be built next to her room, and crouched down on the floor. The floorboards were slightly dusty. No one ever came in here, which was exactly why she had chosen this spot. One of the floorboards was loose. She lifted it with her fingernails and there it was.

Money.

There may not have been hot-house flowers in the ridiculous profusion that Lucienne Colby favoured, but it was not because she could not afford to buy them. It was simply that she was saving her money – *her* money, not Roland's – for a purpose. That was what Lady Henrietta had to tell herself every time she saw the Colbys. *I have money. I have money and, what's more, they do not.*

Most of the time, her plans were confined to thought alone. There was little that she could actually *do*. That was up to Adrian. But she countered this role of cipher, by gathering information; watching and listening. She had always known about Gerald Colby's squander-lust. You only had to look at his face when someone mentioned a round of cards or a bet on a horse. His skin colour intensified in that purely pleasurable way of an adulterer anticipating a clandestine meeting. And she had her sources at London's tables who, when she casually mentioned Gerald's name, assured her that he was losing. And losing, and losing . . .

He had to find the cash somewhere to continue playing, and while outwardly his property was intact, Lady Henrietta had a shrewd suspicion that the Colby inheritance was slipping through his fingers like sand.

While *her* money grew, carefully invested, reinvested, saved. Oh yes, she could have deposited it all in a bank, kept it in shares or property. But she preferred it like this, at her fingertips. She looked at the neat piles of white banknotes and cloth bags containing gold sovereigns. This was *real*. And for her own sake she needed to keep it here where she could hold it and touch it, and remind herself.

That it could only be a matter of time.

Adrian Steele sat in the brougham and waited for his mother.

He suppressed the tremor of excitement that he felt at the prospect of a trip to Graylings, dismissing it as childish. But there had always been an air of inviolability about the place, so that when the carriage turned sharply right and it lay below him, cool and secret in its green hollow, he felt his heart beat faster. He also felt a sense of injustice, since Mama had impressed on him from an early age that *he* should be living in a house like that.

Mama crossed the courtyard sedately, her hands thrust into a large grey muff. She removed one of them so that Adrian could help her into the brougham, and the touch of her fingers was cool and firm, her grip as strong as a man's. Father was watching them from one of the ground-floor windows, but she did not wave to him. She put her hand back in her muff and turned away.

It seemed quite natural to Adrian that he should accompany his mother on her social calls, and not Father. Ostensibly he was going to Graylings because Frederick Colby was the same age and they were friends, but he knew that it was more than that. Mama seemed to derive pleasure from his being there, inside that gracious house, in contact with all those beautiful things. Father would be quite useless on such occasions, anyway. Adrian could see that it was difficult for other people not to like this simple, unpretentious man, but from childhood he had been taught to despise his father and to blame him for everything that was unsatisfactory. When the school he attended turned out to be pedestrian and second-rate, it was Father's fault. When the plumbing failed, it was Father's fault. And all the while Father seemed to crumble, to grow more vague and distracted, as though Adrian's thoughts were eroding him.

The old brougham creaked out of the village and into dispirited countryside, bleached and muddied by weeks of winter. Mama was smiling to herself, as she often did when she had something of importance to say. Adrian waited for her to speak.

Eventually she leaned forward and pressed a cold hand on his wrist. 'Be nice to Brittany. You know what I'm talking about, don't you?'

'I'd always rather assumed you wanted her to marry me.'

Adrian made the statement baldly, because that was how it was between them. No pretence. But he did not mention that he had already seen Brittany that day. The hot, fierce longing generated by a half-grown girl was one feeling that would be kept private.

Mama ignored the undignified way the jolts of the carriage were sending her bony rump from one end of the seat to the other. She patted her sleek hair and lowered her eyelids at him in a gesture that was faintly flirtatious.

'That's where assumption comes to an end, I'm afraid. You can't *assume* she'll have you. You have to work at these things, Adrian.'

'I intend to.'

'Good.' Mama's eyes glittered like bright blue stones, but she kept her voice as calm as ever. 'I have every faith in your ability to achieve your ambitions, my dear. And there are already certain things in your favour, you know. Under the circumstances, I doubt that Gerald Colby will want to make a lot of fuss over Brittany's coming out. He'll be content to marry her off quickly and quietly, and he has quite a high opinion of you, in his peculiar way . . .'

The brougham approached the bend in the lane and Graylings was just visible, a thread of white woven through burnt ochre.

'As long as he gives her a sizeable chunk of Colby money.' Adrian's flexible mouth spread into a long, vulpine grin.

'Their main asset is the house, of course,' said Mama airily as they rounded the bend and the subject of their aspirations sprang into view below them.

'Pity Frederick will get the house.'

'Sometimes it's strange the way things turn out . . .'

He narrowed his eyes suspiciously on Mama's face, and then he laughed, tweaking playfully at the grey muff. 'Come on, old girl, you've got that look in your eye. Tell me what you're talking about.'

'Well, one hears gossip . . .' Mama sighed wearily, as though hearing gossip was an indignity that she was forced to suffer. 'There's a history of illness in the Colby family. Only among the males. Gerald Colby was one of three boys, but the other two both died of this complaint in childhood . . . You only have to look at that child George to see how sickly he is. Not that *he* would ever try and prevent Brittany living there if the house came to him. He wouldn't say 'Boo' to a goose. And he worships the girl. You could *start* by getting on *his* right side.'

'But that's absurd! Frederick's as right as rain,' said Adrian.

Nevertheless, when he saw the house, he looked at it long and hard.

'Luci*enne*,' drawled Mama as she alighted from the brougham and exchanged one cool kiss on the cheek for Mrs Colby's two.

'. . . And I've brought Adrian with me, to pay his respects to Frederick.'

'I'll call him,' said Mrs Colby nervously.

Frederick duly appeared at the top of the marble staircase and came bounding down it, his knees lifting loosely and easily, the doomed skylight bestowing a halo on his chestnut hair.

'Adrian – good to see you!' He clasped Adrian's hand in a firm handshake but completely avoided meeting his eyes as he said, 'Papa's just given me the most splendid pointer pup. Come over to the kennels and take a look at her.'

Adrian picked his way fastidiously through the pools of dank, dark liquid that punctuated the cobbles of the yard. He paused every now and then to admire the occupant of a particular loose box. He shared Gerald Colby's covetousness of fine horses. Mama had recently bought him a new hunter, a grey stallion, choosing the meanest and most powerful brute that she could find, so that every ride would be a challenge, a goal to reach . . .

He caught sight of Brittany in one of the loose boxes, patting and stroking the pretty bay mare that had been tied up in the graveyard.

'Frederick!' he called abruptly after the figure striding ahead of him, 'I'll join you in a moment. There's a horse here I'd like to take a look at.'

Brittany had her back to him when he came into the loose box, so that the first thing he saw was a white sailor collar with hair tumbling over it like liquid butterscotch. Instinctively he reached out a hand to touch one trembling lock, but at that moment she started and turned round, so that he was left with his hand poised awkwardly in the air between them. He reached up and scratched his nose with it.

He had been about to suggest that the clean bib and tucker were not the ideal clothing for playing about in a stable, but she looked annoyed, so instead he pointed at the bay mare and said, 'She's very pretty.'

'Yes. She's Papa's latest.'

'And he let you ride her?'

Brittany turned and looked at him sharply.

He raised his eyebrows quizzically. 'Well?'

She said nothing, turning back to the horse again.

'I saw you in the graveyard this morning.'

'Good for you.' Her back was still turned provokingly, her hair glistening at him.

'What a strange girl you are! What on earth did you want to go *there* for?'

He had not meant them to, but the words came out with a half sneer, half laugh. He felt hot. He wanted to pull her hair hard, twist it through his fingers.

'I'll go where I please!' Brittany said crisply. 'And it's no business of *yours*, Adrian Steele.'

She turned round and brushed him out of her way with one arm as she left the stable. 'If you don't mind, I've got better things to do than stand here and be insulted.'

*Be nice to Brittany* . . .

She walked back to the house, turning only once to fix him with her strange, inscrutable eyes.


Lucienne was feeling distinctly uncomfortable. Half an hour, and still no mention of Teddy! She began to think about how she despised Lady Henrietta for being charming without really being *charming*.

Perched at an imperious slant across the seat of her chair, Lady Henrietta was despising Lucienne Colby for trying to appear thoughtful without ever thinking.

'That's a lovely dress, Lucienne,' she said through her crocodile smile, leaning in the direction of the striped pink and cream silk which accentuated the intense fragility of Lucienne's beauty.

'Oh? You like it? It's nothing, really, it was terribly cheap.'

You see!, Lady Henrietta told herself triumphantly. She said that without thinking. She doesn't even know how to lie properly. Anyone with sense would have attributed the gown to Lucille, Worth even.

She put her cup down with a clatter, so that drops of tea spilled on the carpet in front of Lucienne's tiny kid-shod feet.

'It doesn't matter,' she said mildly, but her limpid, extravagantly lashed eyes were full of annoyance. Lady Henrietta let this be her cue.

'Now, about the weekend. You know the Earl of Teasdale very well, of course . . .'

She had intended to use the word 'intimately', but decided that there was nothing to be gained by lack of subtlety.

'We are old friends, yes.'

'But you've never met Viola? Lovely girl. Charming. She was a very pretty child, and I believe she's grown into a beautiful—'

There was a loud shriek and a crash. Both women turned to stare at the drawing-room door.

'I wonder what . . .'

Lucienne glanced at Lady Henrietta in alarm as she opened the door.

George was standing at the centre of the staircase with his hand to his mouth and a velvet cloak around his shoulders. There was a heap of clothes on the floor at the end of the banister. It groaned, then laughed, then Brittany's head appeared, crowned with a large, fringed lampshade. The pool of brocade she was lying in appeared to be a bedspread.

'Brittany . . . what are you doing?'

'Playing at dressing up. The Queen of Sheba, see?' She waved her robe majestically. 'Then I asked George if he dared me to slide down the banisters. I fell off.'

'Take that ridiculous thing off your head at once! And put it back where it came from. Why can't you play something quiet? Go and play with the paints I gave George.'

Lucienne quivered indignantly at her daughter and she felt herself blushing when she saw Lady Henrietta examining Brittany's face as though she were a rare exhibit in a zoo.

'I do apologize, Lady Henrietta,' she murmured as Brittany heaved the heavy bedspread upstairs, clutching the lampshade to her head with her other hand.

'On the contrary, Lucienne, I think such high spirits are an admirable quality.' She followed her hostess into the drawing room and resumed her seat.

'You must wonder where she gets them from . . .'

*

Brittany looked down at the paintbox doubtfully.

'But they're oil paints, George. We don't really have the right sort of paper.'

George looked sad. 'Does that mean we can't use them after all?'

'Oh, I didn't say that . . .'

Brittany was looking around the nursery thoughtfully. It had a dark, polished floor covered with a threadbare Turkey carpet that did not quite meet the skirting board. A rocking horse with a vicious eye stood in one corner. On either side of the fireplace there were bookshelves, but the facing wall was bare and painted off-white.

'. . . We can paint on the wall.'

'On the *wall*? Brittany, we can't do that.'

'Why not? They do it in churches, in Italy. Fräulein taught me about it. The painters were called Fra Angelico and Della-Robber-Something. It'll improve the look of the place, you'll see.'

'But what will Nanny Wynn say?'

'She'll be pleased. Why shouldn't she? We won't show it to her until we're finished . . .'

Brittany pushed the nursery table and chairs away from the wall to make a space.

'. . . it'll be a surprise.'

'We'll have to use the lid of the box as a palette.' She picked up a tub of bright yellow paint and squeezed out a large blob. 'I'm going to start with the sun.'

George crouched next to her, his eyes wide with fascination. He reached out a fat finger and pushed it into the yellow paint. 'Mmm, feels lovely.' Then he looked at his yellow finger and without thinking wiped it on his Norfolk jacket. The knobbly tweed was laced with yellow. George stared at it helplessly.

'Doesn't matter,' said Brittany. 'Have a brush. What are you going to paint?'

'Can I do a sun too?'

'Don't be silly, there's only one sun in the sky. Do a tree.'

Brittany's sun sent out its rays, which tangled rather awkwardly with the thick brown branches of George's tree.

'You've done your tree too close,' she complained.

'Well, I can't move it now. Can't it be a setting sun? Put some red on it.'

George had his tongue out in concentration as he squeezed a

tube of green paint for the leaves. Some of it went on the carpet, but he was far too absorbed in the task to stop.

They were not discovered until dusk, by which time the mural was no more than a dusky blur against a grey wall. It was not the Renaissance masterpiece that Brittany had envisaged. They had tried mixing colours, but found that everything was reduced to a common denominator of purplish sludge. And the wall was a lot harder to fill than they had anticipated. There was no pastoral scene blazing from one corner to another in shades of aquamarine and indigo, vermilion and topaz. Instead, there was a dark, mud-dled smear with a lot of white space around it, as though someone had thrown something unpleasant at the wall. Brittany had just decided to surround it with a blue sky and fluffy clouds, when Nanny Wynn opened the door.

She did not say anything at first, she just looked. She looked at the uncelestial branches of the trees and the bleeding sun. She looked at the paint on the carpet and on George's best suit. Then her face began to turn red, the exact shade of carmine that Brittany had struggled all afternoon to create.

'You wicked children!' she said, pointing a disbelieving finger at the work of art. 'Those are your new paints I suppose, George?'

He opened and closed his mouth, but no sound came out. Nanny Wynn was already retreating.

'I shall have to tell your father,' she said, then she was gone.

In a flash Brittany scrambled to her feet and ran to the top of the stairs. 'But Nanny *Wynn!*' she shouted. 'It was all my idea, truly. Nanny *Wynn!*'

Nanny Wynn did not turn round.

'You can't do this – it's his *birthday!*'

The white head disappeared down the narrow staircase.

Brittany sat miserably with George until he was sent for. He was white with fear and clutched at her arm. 'I'll come down with you and explain,' she promised.

Gerald was standing in the doorway of his study as they came down the staircase. In his hand he was holding Brittany's riding whip, tapping it slowly against the palm of his left hand, beating time to their descent.

'Papa, it was my idea to paint on the walls.'

'I don't want to hear any excuses. Come in here, George.'

Then Brittany recognized the whip he was holding in his hand.

'No, you *can't*!' she said shrilly, reaching out to take it. 'Not with that!'

Gerald ignored her, propelling George towards the desk.

'*Give it to me!*' roared Brittany. She snatched at the end of the whip, but Gerald pulled it roughly away. 'Give it to me, it's mine!'

'Then you shouldn't leave it lying around where other people will find it.' He looked directly into her eyes and she felt herself grow faint with a sense of injustice. She had unwittingly baited the trap, but as usual it was poor George who had blundered into it.

'Go to your room, please, Evelyn.'

She knew then that it was useless. She only hoped that she could get to the top of the stairs before the noise began.

Later George came to find her and they huddled together on Brittany's bed while he cried. Affected by his misery, Brittany cried too.

'Can you forgive me, George? I should have known this would happen. It was my fault.'

'No, it wasn't,' said George stoutly. He wiped his nose on the back of his hand. 'It wasn't your fault that Papa got so angry.'

'That wasn't your fault either.'

'No.'

'Then whose fault is it?'

But neither of them could answer that question.

---

## 2

### Somerset, 4 February, 1911

'Adrian, that was quite a display you put up at the last drive,' said Captain Colby. 'You outshone the rest of us.'

Adrian flushed slightly, aware of Mama's hard blue eyes burning into him. 'Thank you,' he replied calmly. 'It was kind of you to let me take part.'

'You've shot before?'

'A little, with schoolfriends.'

'I expect your father's given you a few tips. Is that right, Roland? . . .'

'Eh?'

This time Adrian coloured with embarrassment. Father was dreaming over his mulligatawny.

'. . . Frederick's keen to improve his aim, but I keep telling him I'm not the man to ask. There are only a couple of days' decent shooting here each year, and we don't go in for these sophisticated pheasant-rearing techniques. Hunting's more my sport, as you know.' Captain Colby fingered his soup spoon with brisk, impatient movements. 'I meant to ask you, Adrian, about that magnificent dappled grey I've seen you out on . . .'

Adrian answered his host's inquiry politely, but he felt uncomfortable at all the unwonted attention he was receiving. Mama would have attributed it to Captain Colby's liking for him, but even so, it was not like Colby to be so talkative. He was distracted, nervous even, glancing every so often to the end of the table where his wife was seated.

There were twelve for dinner at the end of the first day's shooting. The Graylings dining table had a surface like dark water, and the faces that were reflected in it should have worn a look of relief. The first hurdle had been cleared, the first awkward hours' shared activity with virtual strangers passed, and though they were an ill-assorted group, now was the time for them to be settling to their roles. But it was not so. There was a tension in the air; it moved among the stiff, waxy petals of the arum lilies at the table's centre, it moved the candle flames to and fro with the ladies' breath, it shimmered on the surface of crystal and silver.

As soon as Adrian had set eyes on his mother's guests, he understood why. It was there on the face of Charles Anstey Earl of Teasdale. He had seen eyes like that only once before, as wide as a clown's and fearlessly blue. They were the eyes that had gazed mournfully at the statue of an angel in the graveyard. Adrian had looked from Anstey's face to Mama's and her expression had answered his unspoken question.

Brittany's eyes.

Though he understood the cause of this underlying tension, he remained aloof from it. Mama had hinted about Brittany's progeniture so often that resemblance to Teasdale aroused no more than initial surprise. And his mind was already taken up with the preposterous task of winning the affections of a twelve-year-old girl. However, this melodramatic secret appeared to be affecting even the innocent members of the party.

Adrian observed them furtively as champagne was served with dessert, running his finger down the ice-dewed crystal glass, leaving a wet and dripping streak. There was Richard Langbourne and his immaculate blonde wife, Maud, wealthy shipowners and cousins of Mrs Colby's. Richard Langbourne was pulling unnecessarily at his moustache and repeating a shooting anecdote for the third time, though no one seemed to notice. Maud Langbourne was pretending to discuss Rudyard Kipling with Henry Morgan, cheerfully dismissing his opinions as nonsense while her eyes roamed unhappily to the Earl of Teasdale's face.

Henry Morgan's wife, Ruth, was sitting directly opposite Anstey. She was a great friend of Mrs Colby's, but boycotted by Mama because she had divorced her first husband. Her wordly, bird-like dark eyes stared quite shamelessly at the features on the other side of the candle and from time to time she smiled to herself. Anstey appeared undisturbed by this rampant curiosity, telling endless jokes and laughing uproariously . . .

Adrian listened carefully. Wasn't that laugh a little too loud? Anstey's wife Viola had the pretty head of a drooping flower. She looked nervously from her husband's flushed countenance, to the grim-faced Colbys on the dark, panelled walls of the dining room, to . . . her husband's former lover.

And that lady was deathly white, a pallor accentuated by the diamond drops that clipped and chafed her swan's neck. She did not seem to dare look anywhere except straight ahead.

Apart from Father, who was cramming Bath Oliver biscuits into his mouth as fast as possible, showering crumbs onto bare arms over a radius of several feet, the only person who enjoyed a state of blissful ignorance was Frederick Colby. As the port entered and the ladies vanished, he leaned across to Adrian.

'Adrian – game of billiards?'

His good-natured face was damp with perspiration. He appeared to have drunk too much.

Adrian nodded and followed Frederick out to the billiard room.

'Let's undo our collars,' said Frederick as soon as they were clear of the dining room. 'It's so hot, don't you think?'

Adrian did not. He found the house chilly. But he unfastened his white piqué bow-tie and removed the stud from his wing collar, so as to appear agreeable.

The cavernous billiard room seemed quiet and empty after the dining room. Wall-mounted gaslights gave only a dim light, a welcoming haze. Frederick arranged the balls in their neat triangle and squinted down his cue.

'Hate sitting over dinner so long, don't you?' He yawned then turned his beaming smile on Adrian.

Adrian smiled back.

Suddenly Frederick's billiard cue fell to the floor with a clatter.

Adrian stared down at it, then up at Frederick, who had fallen slightly, awkwardly, against the table. His skin was very pale; a sickly, mauve pallor. When Adrian looked closer, surprised, he saw that the eyes that had been smiling a few seconds earlier were now staring rigidly ahead. Adrian's brain was telling him that he should help Frederick, do something, but he did not move at first. He stood still, thinking. After what seemed a long time but could only have been seconds, he reached out and put a hand on Frederick's shoulder.

'I say, Frederick . . . are you all right?'

Frederick blinked and his wet face became limp.

'What?'

'I said "are you all right?" You dropped your cue.'

'Perfectly all right, thank you. Just felt a bit dizzy. So hot in here, isn't it?'

He smiled weakly at Adrian and began to line up his first shot.

Adrian replayed the strange scene in his mind and was shocked. For as he stood and watched his friend, he had not been thinking *'Frederick must be seriously ill; I must tell someone'*.

He had thought *'How clever Mama is'*.


He embraced her so tightly that she could feel her ribs straining.

'Ah . . . I thought that wretched meal would never be over.'

'Teddy, *Teddy*.' At first Lucienne could say no more than that. She said it over and over again.

'Oh God, I've been so lonely . . .' The full extent of her plight began to sink home and her eyes filled with tears. 'So lonely. Seven years, Teddy . . . seven years.!'

He rocked her in his arms, kissing her hair roughly and burying his nose in it with a strange, animal sound.

'I knew, as soon as I saw these, I knew . . .' He fingered the diamond ear-rings, clasped in their golden hands.

'Teddy . . . darling . . . what are we going to do?'

He stepped away from her, frowning. '*Do*? Nothing. There *is* nothing. What *can* we do? Even if you were to make a complete break . . . it's impossible now, anyway.'

He thrust his hands into his pockets and strolled over to the shelves of leather-bound books, peering sideways at the titles. He looked boyish, Lucienne decided, a tall boy with a moustache. A stuffed owl looked on dolefully from a glass case.

'But *why*?' burst out Lucienne, winding the folds of her skirt into anguished whirlpools of silk. 'Why? Why does life have to be like *this*? Do you know what it's like here? I eat my breakfast in silence, I sit down and write my letters, I see to the flowers and the meals . . . and no one cares. For seven years! And all this time, you and I love each other . . .'

Her mouth crumpled into an ugly line and she began to cry loudly, her lower jaw falling down and inwards like a child's.

Teddy held her until she had composed herself. She sniffed.

'Tell me about your wife,' she said quietly.

The pacing began again. He resembled an actor trying to remember the lines of a play. 'She's a good woman, she *is*, Lucie, but . . .'

He looked up and his eyes were troubled. 'There's nothing to say. She's a nice girl, a very nice girl—'

'But it's not like us?'

'No.'

'Thank God.'

Lucienne smiled and reached out her hand. 'You look so young, darling, you haven't changed.'

Teddy's heavy gold hair glittered in the firelight, and as he bent down to stoke the blaze he pushed it back impatiently from his forehead. His blue eyes were black in the moving shadows.

There was an uncertain note in his laugh. 'Neither have you. You're as beautiful as ever.'

'I feel as though I've lived a hundred lives since . . . I *feel* old.'

'How about Brittany?'

'Brittany? Ah – Brittany! She's very well. But I didn't allow her to come down tonight. I thought it better. I didn't know . . . your wife.'

'Is she so very like me?'

'Very,' said Lucienne flatly. There was a large, gilt-framed mirror above the fireplace and she began to smooth her hair into place and dab her eyes. 'Come, we had better go back. The others are bound to have counted heads by now.'

'I'd like to see her.'

'Later, perhaps. Kiss me.'

They kissed hungrily.

'What a pity you're staying at Heathcote tonight . . .' Lucienne laughed at the expression on Teddy's face. 'Well, it would be nice, wouldn't it? Just one last time . . .'

'Perhaps there will be other chances. I'll try and think of something.'

'Will you?' Lucienne was surprised.

'I will. We'll talk about it tomorrow.'

The repercussions of the painting episode had been severe.

As a punishment, Brittany had been debarred from accompanying the ladies to the shooting luncheon on Saturday, and from meeting the guests before dinner that evening. She found her deprivations harsh. On any other weekend, both rituals would have been tedious, but this weekend Uncle Teddy was among the guests and she so terribly wanted to see him . . .

Nothing daunted, she set about doing just that. At midnight she crept down the staircase, a small and ghostly figure moving silently down the vast marble slabs, her bare feet squeaking slightly on their cold surface. Her white cotton nightgown was warmed in the pinkish glow of the gaslights.

Brittany was not yet sure how she would entice Uncle Teddy from the creaking, guffawing, cigar-smoking horde in the dining room, but so far her plan centred around finding Frederick and asking him to pass a message on to Uncle Teddy, secretly. It was easy to see that Frederick thought highly of Uncle Teddy. She had heard him recounting his sporting exploits at length earlier that day, using the same tone he reserved for friends who were 'good chaps'.

She drifted, sylph-like, down the passage, enjoying the sense of danger that pressed thumbs against her stomach. If someone appeared, Papa for example, she would pretend that she was sleepwalking. The nightgown would provide corroborating evidence, but she was unsure how convincing her acting would be.

There was a distant 'rumble–clack' from the billiard room. Frederick might be there . . . But on her way down the passage, Brittany was distracted by a quite different sound coming from the library. She stopped beside the door and listened. There were two voices, a man's and a woman's. She pressed her ear against the white paint of the door.

'. . . *and all this time, you and I love each other!*'

Maman.

There was an anguished sobbing and the man was murmuring something. Uncle Teddy. He was in *there*. And they still loved one another!

The door of the billiard room opened and Frederick came out.

'Brittany, what are you doing there? And dressed like that – in your nightgown!'

Frederick seemed embarrassed. Then she saw Adrian Steele leaning in the doorway, resting on his tall billiard cue. He was staring at the suggestion of girlish breasts and hips beneath the outgrown gown.

'I wanted to see Uncle Teddy . . .,' she began automatically, then stopped, reddening. She must not give them away! Frederick might go and look in the library . . .

'You wanted to *what*?'

'Nothing I—'

'You want me to find him for you?'

'No, no. I'll see him tomorrow, I'm sure.'

Brittany turned and hurried back to the hall. When she heard footsteps coming after her, she thought that it was Frederick, but it was Adrian.

She paused on the second of the marble steps and looked down at him. Adrian's really rather handsome, she decided. He had an angular, athletic body, rather too long for its legs. His hair was black and very straight, the sort of hair that greys prematurely. His eyes receded so deeply beneath their brows that it was difficult to discern their colour, and the brows themselves were crooked: inverted diabolic 'V's.

'Who's "Uncle Teddy"?' he asked.'

Brittany felt foolish. 'He's staying at your house. He's an earl really.'

'And he's your uncle?'

'No.'

'Well, why d'you call him "Uncle" then?' Adrian was tenacious.

'He's a friend of my mother's,' said Brittany with finality, and turned to go. Adrian reached up and tweaked the plait that hung over her shoulder.

'You'd look a lot more grown up if you didn't wear your hair in pigtails.'

Brittany stared back at him. Adrian was so difficult to understand. He followed her around as though he liked her, and then when he trapped her, he worried her, like Barley worrying a rabbit. What would happen if she were friendly to him? That would surprise him! She felt little desire to be nice to Adrian, but perhaps it would be fun, just to *tease* him . . .

'Let's see, shall we?' she said softly, raising her eyebrows at him. As she lifted her arms, her small breasts swung up and pressed against her nightgown like buttons. Adrian's eyes followed the movement, darkening with curiosity. He appeared to be holding his breath, and she knew that he would not speak until she had finished. She was starting to enjoy herself . . .

Her fingers moved expertly among the thick ribbons of hair, unravelling them. And when they had all been loosened and combed with her fingers, she lifted her chin slightly and shook her hair so that it drifted around her shoulders in a cloud, its fine, brittle ends tinged with gold and blush rose under the gas lamps.

'It made a noise.'

Brittany looked at Adrian quizzically.

'It made a noise, your hair, when you shook it. A sort of clicking noise. Do it again.' He was insistent. 'Do it again, please.'

Brittany hesitated, but the sense of power was proving too heady and she whipped her head around even harder this time, sending her hair out in a crackling circle. Strands of it whipped Adrian's cheeks and eyes.

'Did you hear it?' he asked eagerly.

'That noise? Nanny Wynn calls it . . . what is it? . . . Something like . . .Static. Yes, that's it. Static. It happens when you brush your hair a lot. Have you really never heard it before?'

'No, I never have.' Adrian sounded almost humble.

'What – you haven't ever seen your mother brushing her hair?'

'Of course not. She does it in private.'

'Well, so do I, of course, only you *did* ask me . . .'

'So I did.' The ambitious glint had returned to Adrian's eye. 'And now I'm going to ask you for a goodnight kiss.'

Brittany laughed. 'Certainly not!' she said primly and began to walk up the stairs, pulling her nightgown in tightly so that it hugged her behind.

'But it's a hostess's duty to kiss her guests goodnight!'

'Maman's your hostess, not me. Ask *her* to kiss you!'

'You *are* the daughter of the house, though.'

'That's true.' Brittany put a finger to her lips as though she were considering the matter. She was enjoying herself hugely. This was as good as being in a play. She descended a few steps and put a small, sallow hand on Adrian's black tailcoat.

'I'll tell you what . . . *perhaps* – only perhaps, mind – perhaps if I'm in a good temper, I'll kiss you tomorrow!'

Adrian's long, mobile mouth lurched into a grin. 'I'll remind you that you said that!'

He disappeared in the direction of the dining room.

Brittany was about to start up the staircase again when she heard a door being quietly opened and closed in the passage. She saw Maman emerging into the hall and behind her the tall outline of a man, moving in the shadows.

'Brittany, what's the matter? Are you ill?'

Maman's face and dress were both crumpled.

'I was sleepwalking,' lied Brittany, capitalizing on the fact that Maman was too distracted to perceive a lie.

'Sleepwalking? But, darling . . . You've never—'

Maman blinked hard, then pressed her palm against Brittany's forehead.

'Are you ill? Should I call Nanny Wynn?'

'No, no. Not ill. Just a strange dream.'

'Well, go upstairs at once, before—'

It was too late. The drawing-room door opened and Lady Henrietta marched out, her corseted body like a clothes peg in its nutmeg satin. Behind her cowered a woman whose heart-shaped face reminded Brittany of the fragile wild pansy. Heartsease. How she loved that word . . .

'Ah, Lucienne. There you are, my dear. Viola and I were just—'

Viola. She was Viola. Teddy's wife. Maman had just enjoyed a lucky escape! Brittany's breathing quickened.

'But you're with your *daughter*, Lucienne . . .' Lady Henrietta emphasized the word with great relish.

Viola was staring.

Nanny Wynn had always said that it was rude to stare at strangers, and Viola was staring right at her, at her loosened hair. The pretty heart-shaped face had taken on a stricken look and she stepped backwards.

But not once did her gaze leave Brittany's hair, hair that fell about her shoulders like a mantle of burnished gold.

The ladies joined the gentlemen in the drawning room.

Lady Henrietta was at the piano, like Boadicea at the helm of her chariot. The two wall candelabra on either side of her head were the Roman torches lighting her way, deepening the blue shadows of the tortuously erected column of her hair. She was not sure if anyone was listening to her cunningly executed *lieder*, but she considered it necessary to play at least once, to demonstrate the extent of her accomplishment. In case anyone dared think that she had let these things slip while she was incarcerated in her marital dungeon. She played with her head on one side, a desiccated replica of what had once been a fetching gesture. And as she played, she remembered the old days at the castle, when eager young men had gathered beneath the tapestries to hear her subdue the ancient harpsichord, while feudal fire burned in the massive stone grate . . .

Roland Steele, Henry Morgan, Maud Langbourne and Viola Anstey were gathered for a half-hearted rubber of bridge. Roland Steele yawned occasionally and looked at his fob-watch.

Maud surrendered her trick to Henry's trump with a sigh.

'I'm entirely in your hands, Henry!'

'Really! I shouldn't let your husband hear you say that!'

Maud blushed and dimpled becomingly.

'Is it over yet?' asked Roland Steele.

'Oh Roland, you old time-server! It's Henry to lead now. We'll never stop him if you don't look sharp . . .'

Gerald Colby was challenging Adrian Steele to a game of black-jack. They were seated in front of the fire and Gerald was dealing cards onto a petit-point footstool between their knees, while nearby, Teddy Anstey demonstrated card tricks and told tall tales to a rapt Frederick.

'In my opinion, this gets going better if we have a small bet,' Gerald was saying in his curiously still, cold voice. 'Just enough to keep us awake – farthings, say. Agreed?'

Adrian nodded.

'Do you enjoy staking a bet, Adrian, taking a chance on . . . on the outcome?'

Adrian smiled slightly, baring his teeth. 'I do,' he said, looking directly into the older man's eyes.

'As I thought. Two of a kind.' Gerald appeared to speak to himself.

'Papa!' exclaimed Frederick from his corner. 'Papa, did you hear that?'

'What?'

'Teddy's shot at Sandringham!'

'Oh? Really?'

*'So he's Teddy now, is he?'* he murmured under his breath, but did not look up. The game continued, both players watching intently the growing heap of coins.

'Papa, look, Teddy's making the ace rise out of the pack!'

'Frederick,' replied Gerald drily, still not looking up, 'I believe I showed you the trick with the rising aces when you were George's age.'

'Yes, but Teddy's better than you!'

Gerald glowered. The game continued in taut silence until Gerald flung down a winning card and claimed the large pile of coins that had accumulated.

'Well done!' said Adrian loudly, helping to gather up the jangling, slippery mass. 'I didn't stand a chance.'

Pleased, Gerald looked up to acknowledge his son's approval. But Frederick was taking a card from Teddy's outstretched hand, his eyes sparkling with adulation.

At first Brittany thought she was dreaming.

He stood in the silver shadow of the curtains, stroking his moustache thoughtfully.

Brittany stirred her heavy limbs, trying to reach out and see if he was real.

'Don't uncover yourself,' he whispered. 'You might catch cold.'

'It's Uncle Teddy,' she said, half to herself.

'Yes, it is.'

'You've come.'

'Yes, I have.'

He sat down on the edge of the bed and patted her hand. 'How's my favourite girl?'

'*Am* I your favourite?'

'Of course. Couldn't you tell from all the presents I lavished on you? You did like them, didn't you?'

'Well, that depends.'

'On what?'

'On whether I'll always be your favourite.'

He laughed, a happy, abandoned laugh. 'Now you're flirting with me!'

'Well, *will* I?'

'Of course you will. Always. I can see I shall have to continue sending presents to young ladies. It gets me in their good books.'

'Now *you're* flirting!'

'Am I? Both of us flirts, fancy that!' Teddy bent and kissed her gently on the cheek. Far away a clock struck one. 'You go back to sleep now. I just came to tuck you up.'

'No one's tucked me up for years.'

'Really? Not even your mother?'

'No.'

Teddy hesitated, stroking the faded counterpane with a loving movement. There was a woollen stocking lying loose on the floor and he picked it up and laid it gently on a chair. The dolls stared out from the shadows of their secret corner with blank, accusing eyes.

'What about your father?'

'No, never. He never comes up here.'

Teddy studied her face, and though the darkness hid the colour of his eyes, Brittany could see that they were thoughtful and a little sad.

He sighed. 'Well, I must vanish. The carriage is waiting.'

'Like Cinderella.'

'Just like Cinderella.'


## New York, 4 February, 1911

It was snowing. Loose, damp blobs of snow moved past the window as though they were in a hurry to reach the pavement, even though they might melt when they reached their destination.

David Stein watched them fall, wondering whether it was truly possible that each snowflake was different from its neighbour. Surely if enough snowflakes were studied, two identical ones would be found? People were exactly like snowflakes, but only if you didn't count twins. Perhaps there were twin snowflakes out there somewhere?

Downstairs the praying had started. It sounded more like a moan than a prayer. But David ignored it and returned to the neatly stacked papers on his desk. He liked his own handwriting. Firm downstrokes and no messy loops. He was left-handed, and Isaac Stein had predicted gloomily that he would never be able to write properly. It was a source of great satisfaction to David that his father had been proved wrong. It was a rare occurrence.

'*The Mystery of the Blue Urn*', he read, '*by Hieronymus Shand*'.

He was pleased with the pseudonym. *David Stein* had a mundane ring to it.

The clock on his desk said a quarter to eight. Oh dear, he really was very late. He would go down in a minute, as soon as he had finished the sentence . . .

He picked up his pen.


After the introductory prayer, Isaac Stein glanced around the table and hissed to Jake, who was on his right, '*Where's David?*'

Jake shrugged. 'He hasn't come down yet.'

Isaac's eyes bulged angrily. '*But we have guests!*'

The Stein family were assembled in the dining room for their sabbath dinner. It was a vast catafalque of a room, decorated in the colour scheme of red and gold much favoured in the Fifth Avenue mansion. The ox-blood walls were crusted with gilt mouldings, bubbling and swelling like some diseased growth. There were mirrors everywhere, dark tarnished mirrors that seemed to absorb the light from the hot, airless room. It was at the centre of the house and there were no windows, and no lamps, only a forest of perfumed candles, giving off a dusty, musky scent. The table was so laden with gold plate and ranks of engraved crystal spreading fine lacy shadows, that its surface could scarcely be seen. At its centre stood a striking gold menorah, the ritual candlestick. Each of the seven branches was scaled with precious stones and filigree.

The group seated at the table was made up almost entirely of women. In Isaac Stein's view this did not matter at a sabbath dinner, which was strictly a family occasion, but on the other hand it made David's tardiness even more obvious, and that angered him. All three of his daughters were present, dressed in their best lace and velvet. Rachel sat opposite her young husband, Shimon, smiling contentedly as her pregnant stomach bulged against the edge of the table.

Also present were the Abelsons, a family with three daughters of their own. Joshua Abelson had once been a tailor and now owned an endless chain of cutting-rooms and clothing factories. His eldest daughter, Miriam, was just twenty and would make a perfect wife for Jake. It was a pity that the other two were not sons, then perhaps Leah and Sarah . .

Hannah Stein was seated opposite her husband at the head of the table: too far away for him to speak to her. They could not eat before she had blessed the candles and Isaac had blessed the wine, and that could not be done until everyone was present. The introductory prayer had been a delaying tactic, but now an awkward silence fell. Isaac Stein caught his wife's eye and led it meaningfully to the empty chair on her right. She reached out to ring for the footman, but Isaac Stein shook his head. He coughed.

'I'll just go and see what's keeping David,' he said, and everyone turned to stare at him, as people do when no one has spoken for several minutes.

'Tell me, was it snowing when you arrived?' Hannah Stein asked Joshua Abelson bravely, and by the time Isaac Stein reached the door, the hot, hazy room was filled with the murmur of polite conversation.

Isaac flung open the door of David's room and stood there without speaking. He was still wearing his yarmulka, and his shoulders shook with indignation causing the fringes of his prayer shawl to quiver. It looked ridiculous on his small, squat figure, as though someone had thrown a tablecloth over a piece of furniture to mask its ugliness.

David looked up from his desk and smiled his careless smile. 'Just coming, Papa!'

'*I should say you are!*' barked Isaac. He planted a freckled hand on his son's shoulder and pulled him roughly to his feet. Then he twitched the sheaf of papers scornfully. 'And what's this?'

'I'm writing a book, Papa,' said David smoothly, 'A detective story. Perhaps you'd care to read it sometime?'

'If you want to waste your spare time with fairy stories, I can't stop you. But not today. It's *sabbath*, David! The Lord forbids us to work on *sabbath*. Besides, we have guests.'

'Work, Papa?' said David with a wicked glint in his eye. 'You describe this as work?'

'I didn't say that!' snapped Isaac. 'You know better than to put words in my mouth. Get downstairs.'

David stood at the centre of the dining room and bowed elaborately to the assembled company.

'I do apologize', he said, 'for my excessive lateness. I have no excuse.'

He swept the curious faces with a graceful smile. *That should make Papa mad as hell* he thought cheerfully, as he slipped into his seat beside Hannah. She caught his eye as they bent their heads in prayer.

The regal battery of gold plate housed a simple meal: boiled chicken and vegetables, a rich paste of almonds and dried fruit and the sweet, cloying sabbath wine. David was the most cheerful person present, picking hungrily at his chicken and flinging friendly inquiries at the Abelson girls through mouthfuls of meat and large draughts of wine. He saw at once through Isaac's artful introduction of Miriam and Jake, and was amused.

'. . . I've just started work at my father's bank,' Jake was saying in his slow deliberate way, staring shyly at his plate. 'I've got a lot to learn, but already—'

David interrupted.

'Don't listen to him, Miriam, he's just being modest. He's a partner! Up there with the gods!'

'Really?' Miriam showed a fraction more interest. She was a haughty, high-bred Jewess, with sleek, sable hair, liquid dark eyes and a long neck.

'Sure, he is! He's been a partner for ten years. There's nothing he doesn't know.'

'Ten years?' Miriam appeared to be calculating hastily. 'But Papa said he was twenty-two.' She blushed slightly. 'I mean, he looks—'

'He *looks* twenty-two, but we Steins all look young for our age. Take me, for example. I look fifteen, but I'm really twenty-five.'

He winked, and Miriam's look of disbelief changed to one of fury.

'Don't listen to anything David says,' pleaded Jake, and then he laughed too, unable to help himself when he saw the look on Miriam's face.

David was gratified. He had only done it because he wanted to make poor Jake laugh. It was always worth the effort, to hear that loud, uncontrolled, joyful laugh, a sound that made him feel glad to be alive.

Isaac Stein sat up long after the Abelsons had left, thinking. He had a room reserved especially for this occupation, a study on the second floor. Its walls and ceilings were covered with panels from a sixteenth-century English manor house, painstakingly removed, shipped across the Atlantic and reconstructed in New York. The expense had been high, but Isaac considered it cheap for a piece of English heritage. The room would not have deceived a member of the English ruling classes – the surface of the panels was a little too highly polished – but the warm honey colour of the wood was inviting and the thick slate blue carpet restful on the eyes. There was very little furniture in the room, and at its centre stood a vast leather night-chair, replete with rows of leather studs, originating from a London hotel. Isaac was dwarfed by the tall back, and if he sat well to the rear of its seat, his feet did not touch the ground.

He heard movements on the other side of the walls and knew that his wife was going to bed. The study occupied the central position in their private apartments and had two connecting doors, one leading to Isaac's dressing room and one to his wife's.

'Hannah!'

'Just a moment.'

A door opened in the glossy, yellow wood, and Hannah appeared, in a low-cut satin wrapper. She saw Isaac glancing inquisitively at the shadow of her cleavage and pulled the front of the wrapper more tightly closed. Even after twenty-five years of marriage and five children, she and her husband never treated one another with intimacy.

'You look very fine in that . . . er . . . thing, Hannah.'

A hand appeared out of the recesses of the night-chair and pointed at the ivory satin. 'You look like a bride.'

'Thank you,' said Hannah without smiling, worrying that this might prove to be a prelude to one of Isaac's infrequent visits to her room. Not on the sabbath, surely?

'David was late for dinner because he was writing a story,' said Isaac in his abrupt manner. 'I saw it there in his room.'

'Yes, I expect that would be his detective story.'

'You *knew* about it?'

'Yes. It was my idea.'

'Your idea? Hannah, what sort of nonsense are you putting into that boy's head?'

'It's harmless, Isaac. He's very bright, his lessons bore him—'

'Well, let him have more lessons then! Before we know it, he'll be fancying himself as a writer, or a detective. And he's a banker. You've spoilt that boy, Hannah. Now, I can quite understand the way you feel about your younger boy, I'm not blaming you, but we must think of what David's turning into . . .'

Hannah put her hand on the door as if to go.

'Will that be all?' she asked quietly.

'Hannah! Didn't I just say I'm not blaming you!' Isaac was becoming over-excited.

'. . . But I tell you, I've seen it happen to other people's children when they're allowed to . . . drift off. They end up marrying *goyim* . . .'

He watched his wife's face change, knowing that he had hit a weak spot. 'You don't want that to happen, do you, Hannah?'

'No, I don't,' she admitted.

'Good, so we're agreed then. We'll try and discourage this detective business. The boy's got too much imagination for his own good . . .'

Hannah Stein did not reply. She raised her hands in a submissive gesture, but her green eyes were unrepentant. Then she left the room.

Isaac waddled to the walnut cabinet that housed a supply of alcohol, with the intention of pouring himself a brandy, but the decanter was empty. Swearing, he stepped out onto the landing. Perhaps he could intercept one of the army of servants he employed, before they retired to bed.

Footsteps approached but it was not a servant. Jacob. *My favourite son* . . . The son who bore no resemblance to either of his parents. Isaac's pale, bulging eyes feasted on the tall young man. He would never know where the sad, square face came from, and the expressive eyes. Nor would he ever fully know the mysterious person behind them.

'Did you like Miriam Abelson?' he asked bluntly.

Jake looked lost. He flapped his long arms vaguely.

'Yes, I liked her, Papa.'

It was not exactly a lie, but his memories of the slanting eyes that looked disdainfully down the fine, Jewish nose, were less than warm.

'Don't play games, Jake! You know what I'm talking about. I thought she'd make you a good wife.'

'But, Papa—'

'Her father's a very prominent man.'

In Isaac's vocabulary, 'prominent' meant rich.

'He'd do anything for his daughter. So, why not?'

Jake considered his answer carefully.

'I'm sure she'd be as good a wife as any. It's just that I wasn't thinking of marrying yet. I wanted to concentrate on learning the business . . .'

Isaac smiled warmly and reached up to pat Jake's arm.

'Of course, of course. I forget how young you are. Plenty of time yet. No need to hurry . . .'

. . . Because there's always the possibility that a richer girl might turn up, thought Jake cynically.

'But at least promise me you'll think about it?'

'I'll think about it,' said Jake, banishing from his mind the unwanted image of Miriam's coldly voluptuous body.


### Somerset, 5 February, 1911

A thick coating of frost furred twigs and leaves. The sun that smiled shyly through the pink-white mist promised a clear, cold day and blue skies.

A bell tolled insistently from the square church tower and Nether Aston began to stir. The village was perched on the craggy edge of the Mendips, thickly wooded and threaded with steep, twisting lanes. But the hills dropped away abruptly, and below, the landscape was very different; the undulating quilt of the Wedmore plain. The horizon stretched unbroken for miles, almost to the sea, and once the lake of Avalon had been its glittering heart.

The Glastonbury Tor, rising from the centre of the marshland, served as a reminder of its mystical past.

Lady Henrietta Steele, who had no time for mysticism, was in the kitchen at Heathcote, imposing on her servants with more than her usual energy. A decent breakfast must be offered to her guests before the shooting, and a decent breakfast included kedgeree, even if the cook, a simple-minded village woman, invariably burnt it. After throwing away the first attempt in the pig bin and ordering the cook to try again, she went in search of the under-housemaid, to ensure that a fire was laid in the dining room. There was a lingering smell of old meals that she was anxious to banish.

At Graylings, Lucienne Colby rose earlier than usual. She had spent a fretful night. She emerged from the tangle of lace pillows, catching impatiently at the great swatches of material that dropped from the circular polonaise above the bed. It was too early for the maid to bring hot water and a towel, so she splashed her face with the ice-cold dregs that remained in the china ewer on her wash-stand. It toned down the puffiness of her eyes, but her skin still looked grey. She slapped at her cheeks angrily, trying to force some colour into them. Today of all days, she must look alluring, she *must* . . .

She would arrange for her maid to boil water and pour it over some herbs so that she could steam her face. Then she would apply packs of ice, then more steam, and so on. Eventually a healthy glow would creep into her cheeks. It was a trick taught her by her godmother, who was a very resourceful woman, and it never failed. Then she would apply a little almond oil to her hair, to make it shine, then she would buff her nails, then add a little charcoal to emphasize her eyebrows . . . but first she would brush out her hair.

As she set to work with the heavy silver-backed brush, Lucienne was trying to picture Teddy as he had looked the night before, stirring the library fire and looking down into the flames. She remembered that precise moment because it had captured perfectly something about his dear face, the essence of his vulnerable charm.

She had felt a bursting of joy within her at that moment, until she remembered that it was not, after all, something that she could keep. If only one could freeze such moments and hold onto them for ever. She grieved for it already, as though it were long gone.

Already the picture had faded, so that she could not quite see his features. She tried hard to picture Teddy's face, but it was elusive. At least she would have another chance to memorize it today.

There was a knock at the door.

'Come in, Ellen,' Lucienne called, expecting the hot water.

It was Brittany.

'Maman, can I come with you to the lunch today?'

Lucienne looked at her daughter and sighed. 'Why not? What harm can it do?' She was resigned.

Brittany's blue eyes widened with eager pleasure, and Lucienne could suddenly remember how Teddy looked. She stroked Brittany's hair carefully.

'If you come, *chérie*, you can't dress in that old skirt. You will have to find something more suitable. Go and tell Nanny Wynn.'

As Brittany reached the door, Lucienne twisted on her dressing stool and called over her shoulder, 'I hope you slept well. No more bad dreams?'

Brittany remembered the 'sleepwalking' and hastened to give a reassuring smile.

'No, quite the opposite, Maman. I had the most wonderful dream. A man came into my room, and he turned out to be the man I love best in the world!' Lucienne pretended to be shocked.

'A man! You're far too young to dream about such things!'

But she laughed all the same.


'Only a cold collation, I'm afraid. I don't like to put the servants to too much trouble.'

At this utterance of Lucienne Colby's, Adrian Steele looked up. He was intrigued by the naïvety of the remark. Mama would never *dream* of saying such a thing. After all, what were servants there for, if not to be troubled?

As the morning had worn on, Adrian found it increasingly difficult to concentrate on shooting. They had started to the north of the Home Farm, from a patch of heath that was richly purpled with heather in the summer months, and had moved up into a belt of woodland. The season was far advanced and only a few cock pheasants flew out of the dark stripped trees. Adrian had moved stealthily in the wake of Frederick's noisy enthusiasms, his thoughts straining more and more towards luncheon and the light relief of conversation with the ladies.

67

On the far side of the wood there was a flat, grassy terrace, before the land dropped away in a stony slope and thick cushions of bracken. This plateau provided the perfect resting place and the ladies contrived to arrange themselves on it so artfully that it seemed almost natural to stumble on a table covered with glazed white linen and awaiting wineglasses.

The table was of solid oak, borrowed from the servants' hall and transported to the clearing on the back of a farm cart. Cushions and rugs did little to conceal the catholic assortment of chairs, ladder-backed kitchen chairs with rush seats, wicker chairs rescued from the summer house, and a refectory bench. The fact that no one was at the same height as his neighbour did not detract from the formality of the meal. Wine trickled into crystal glasses with a chill, ceremonious sound, a sound that reverberated provocatively in the empty outdoors and drowned the crunching of frozen twigs underfoot.

Heaping his plate with slices of raised game pie, stuffed eggs and chicken in aspic, Adrian noticed that the men seemed at ease at table, their blood warmed and appetites sharpened from the sport which brought them naturally to the clearing, while the ladies were at pains to justify their existence there, asking polite questions about the morning's progress and valiantly pretending not to be chilled to the bone.

The most uncomfortable person of all was undoubtedly George Colby, too young to shoot, but as conspicuous among the ladies as a fat duckling among swans. He was seated between his mother and his sister on a chair with uneven legs, so that whenever he reached out to take food, the chair wobbled uncertainly and sent him dipping down into one corner of its seat. Adrian watched with mingled fascination and revulsion as George crammed pieces of pie into his mouth, adding the latest while its predecessor was still a porridgy, unswallowed pulp. His timid eyes stared self-consciously as his jaw struggled to crush its load, but soon they were looking around for more food.

In recent years, Adrian had found it difficult to be civil to eleven-year-old George, repulsed by his complete lack of self-assertion and irritated by his slowness. But he quelled his feelings now, when he saw Brittany answer George's querulous looks with an indulgent smile, patting his plump hand absently as it continued its nervous quest for food. When the meal was over and the party was beginning to disperse, he cornered George and put a hand on his shoulder in what he assumed was a paternal manner. He did his best to ignore the fact that the lovat green Norfolk jacket, a little tight around the middle, was smeared with gravy from George's unrestrained attack on the pie.

'So, George, how long before you're out there with the guns?'

George started, frightened by the unexpected show of interest.

'I . . . I . . . d-d-don't know.'

'Know how to use a gun?'

'No.'

'Well, I'd like to teach you sometime. How about starting with some instruction on the working parts of the gun, and keeping it clean? Would you like that, George?'

'I suppose so.'

Adrian's eyes narrowed. Ungrateful little sod, he thought, and was about to retract the offer when he saw Brittany looking at him suspiciously.

'It's up to you, old man,' he said, excusing himself with another brief and insincere squeeze of George's shoulder.

It was agreed, though Lucienne had no memory of active consent, that the carriage would stop at Heathcote House and leave the Countess of Teasdale, who wished to rest quietly in her room, and then it would continue to Graylings, where Lady Henrietta would assist Lucienne in the preparations for tea.

Lucienne was displeased with the arrangement. She was desperate for her chance to talk to Teddy, and had hoped that if she followed the guns after lunch, he might hang back and they might find themselves falling behind the others . . . But when she suggested that she might stay, there had been an atmosphere of unspoken disapproval in the air, as though Lucienne were too fragile and pretty a creature to do anything more than receive the returning sportsmen in her drawing room. She did not dare insist, because she so rarely took an interest in the shooting that her motives were already in question. And George had looked so miserable at the prospect of returning to Graylings without her, under the critical chaperonage of Lady Henrietta, that she had abandoned the idea. It would have to be this evening.

Reluctantly, she admitted to herself that she would be glad when the weekend was over. The constant surveillance was beginning to wear at her nerves. At lunch she tried to maintain cool composure but was aware that there was an exceptional degree of radiance about her. It was enhanced by the sparkling silver fur at her throat and drew attention to her when she spoke. She had been forced to ignore Teddy, and yet she could not deny herself a tiny peep at him every so often. It was as necessary to her as breathing. She *had* to look at him. Yet every time she raised her eyes in his direction, masking the movement by reaching for the salt or turning to answer a query from one of her guests, she saw Viola Anstey watching her. It was a stiff, unwavering gaze, and the unambiguous accusation in the pretty eyes filled her with scorching shame.

Brittany and Ruth Morgan had stayed to watch one drive, so after Viola had returned to Heathcote, only Maud, Lucienne, Lady Henrietta and a queasy-looking George remained in the carriage. Lady Henrietta fussed anxiously like a hen with a chick as Viola was handed down to the pavement and escorted into the house by one of the maids. When they trotted away up the village street and Viola was just a speck in the distance, Lucienne leaned back in her seat with relief.

But Lady Henrietta was smiling self-importantly, her angular body quivering with admonitory joy.

'Viola's delicate, you know,' she said, turning to smile at Maud, but addressing the remark to Lucienne. 'Especially now, in her condition.'

Lucienne paled. 'Her condition?'

'Oh yes,' Lady Henrietta could hardly contain herself in her excitement but she managed to lower her voice in deference to propriety. 'She's *enceinte*.'

'I didn't know.'

Lucienne's voice sounded thin and far away. She clutched at the side of the carriage, looking over the edge at the ground flashing past beneath the wheels. The rhythmic rattling became deafening. She felt sick.

'She's only just told me. Last night, in fact, after we dined at Graylings. She was looking a little pale when we got home, and when I commented on it, she and Charles broke the happy news . . . Are you all right, Lucienne? You look unwell, doesn't she, Maud?'

Lucienne straightened.

'Perfectly all right, thank you,' she said coldly.

'. . . Only you looked so green, one might be forgiven for thinking you were in a delicate condition yourself!'

Lady Henrietta refrained from looking into Lucienne's eyes, but there was no mistaking the ugliness of irony in her high, throaty laugh.

After lunch, the guns proceeded down the stony slope and up again into a beech copse. Although the paths were wide, their surface was uneven, and Brittany felt hampered by her long, grey flannel skirt and the nipped-in waist of her jacket. And she wished Ruth Morgan wouldn't stroll and dawdle so, plucking gaily at passing branches as though they had all the time in the world. She felt she had to stay with Ruth, and yet she wanted to keep up so that she could watch Uncle Teddy.

When he arrived for lunch he had smiled and winked at her, but thereafter paid no attention to her at all, even though she had tried desperately hard to catch his eye. She supposed it must be because he was in love with Maman and she was present, but it really was most exasperating.

And then there was Frederick. She admitted to herself that she was jealous of the attention Uncle Teddy was lavishing on him at lunch, comparing notes about their morning's bag. She felt a sulk coming on, muttering to herself, 'It's not *fair*, just because he's a boy . . .'

Then she remembered Uncle Teddy's visit to her room and she checked herself. It gave her a warm, comfortable feeling inside her stomach.

The sportsmen had completed their first drive, and now things had come to a standstill while they discussed how to proceed. The path narrowed considerably and descended into a gully, and Papa had decided that the guns would have to reposition themselves. He wanted Roland Steele at the front, where he could keep an eye on him, presumably, and two people standing side by side at the back of the line, to take advantage of their higher position on the path. Papa proposed that those two should be himself and Frederick.

'Oh *no*, Papa!' exclaimed Frederick, in the tones of downright rebellion. 'Can't it be Teddy and I? Please? I want to stand next to Teddy . . .'

You *fool*, Frederick, thought Brittany. How could he be so

stupid? He didn't even seem to notice the reddish stain, the colour of wine, that rose to Papa's grey face. Frederick obviously knew nothing of Teddy's association with Maman, and therefore could not be expected to appreciate the precariousness, the delicacy, the *danger* of Teddy's position in the shooting party, but he could use his own eyes for once, couldn't he? He ought to know by now that Papa could not bear to let anyone near his precious son.

While the argument raged, Ruth grew more restless.

'Just *listen* to them, darling,' she drawled to Brittany. 'Like little boys! I'm not going to stand here and listen to this.' She handed Brittany her shooting stick. 'Here, hold this for me. I'm going to go and pick some of those delightful snowdrops we just passed. Let me know when something happens . . .'

She scurried off into the thicket and Brittany eased herself onto the leather shooting stick, planting her feet squarely apart in an unfeminine pose. Adrian Steele broke away from the men and sauntered over to her, his gun on his shoulder.

'We'll be here all afternoon if they don't make up their minds!'

His voice was hard and impatient and Brittany found herself remembering the sight of Adrian controlling his big, bellicose grey mount, his mouth pulled into that same tight, impatient line.

'Still,' he added, with his terrier's grin, 'it gives us an opportunity to talk, doesn't it?'

'I suppose it does.'

Brittany reached up and rubbed her nose with the back of her gloved hand, not meeting his eyes. The shooting stick wobbled. When she finally did look at Adrian, his gaze was so concentrated and calculating that she feared he was about to mention the kiss. She was quite unprepared for what he was about to say.

'Heard the good news, then?'

'What news?'

'Your *Uncle* Teddy is about to become a father. The Countess is going to have a baby soon. They were talking about it at breakfast this morning.'

Brittany quivered with indignation. How could he! He had promised her. Only last night, he had said she would be his favourite girl, *always*. What if this new baby was a girl, though?

72

Then *she* would be the favourite, wouldn't she, because she would be his daughter.

'Will it take very long for the baby to come?' she asked eventually.

'About the usual time, I expect!' Then, slyly: 'You do know how babies are made, don't you, Brittany?'

Brittany did not. Once, she and George had taken off all their clothes, and after examining their bodies they had come to the conclusion that one of them must be hideously deformed – but which? She had still not found out, but she was not going to give Adrian the satisfaction of knowing that.

'Of course,' she lied. 'Of course I do!'

'Then you'll know . . .' Adrian affected a casual pose, leaning on the butt of his gun, 'you'll know that having a baby starts with kissing.'

Brittany smiled back knowingly, but she was appalled at the idea. She'd assumed that it had something to do with getting married. Then her mind raced back to a parlourmaid they'd had once, called Bertha. She had seen Bertha kissing a footman under the mistletoe at the Christmas party in the servants' hall, and then, some time later, when Bertha left Graylings, the maids were whispering about her having a baby. So that was where it came from, the kissing. But other people kissed under the mistletoe, and *they* didn't have babies. Why Bertha?

The discussion about stands was coming to an end. Papa had not got his way. He would stand at the back, with Teddy and Frederick in front of him.

'We'll just try it this way to begin with, Frederick.' She distinguished Uncle Teddy's ringing voice. 'And if you come and stay at Bellingham for the October shoot, we'll be able to stand together every day . . well, let's just see how it goes this time, shall we?'

If anyone other than Uncle Teddy had said that, she would have thought they were trying to annoy Papa. She could not see Papa's face because he had his back to her, shouting to Sir Roland to carry on down the path. They were off.

But Adrian hung back.

'I haven't forgotten that kiss you promised me, either.' He leaned closer. 'You could give it to me now, while nobody's looking.'

'Certainly not! I only said "perhaps".'

Brittany jumped off Ruth's shooting stick and it fell with a clatter onto Adrian's foot.

It all happened terribly quickly.

That was how it seemed to Gerald when he thought about the incident in the years that followed. It was all so quick that it was as though nothing had happened at all.

Oh yes, he had seen how Anstey was looking at his wife. Making jokes for her ears alone, laughing in her direction. He had noticed them both mysteriously disappearing after dinner last night. Who hadn't? Lucienne had always been a clumsy stage manager. Left to her own devices long enough, no doubt the two of them would be tumbling into bed, fumbling to remove clothing, heaving, groaning . . .

But it was not the role of cuckold that was angering Gerald as he trudged through the frozen wood on that sharp February afternoon. Not that. He had long since lost interest in Lucienne as a possession. Taking Frederick was a far more serious offence. A woman could be replaced but not a son, not the fine, healthy son he needed so much.

He had watched Frederick's schoolboy infatuation growing all weekend. It had goaded him more deeply, more bitterly than seeing Anstey with his wife ever had. And Anstey, the shameless adulterer, was exploiting it to the full, encouraging him until it was 'Teddy this' and 'Teddy that' every hour of the day. Before long Gerald had found himself looking for a way to teach Anstey a lesson.

It was the repositioning that started it all. He ended up just behind Anstey, so that every time he raised his sights he caught a flash of the loose-limbed aristocratic stance and the glittering gold hair moving under the sunlight. After a while he found the barrel of the gun wandering in line towards the golden head. It was a tempting idea. Not to shoot the man, of course, just to send a cartridge whistling past his ear, give him a bit of a fright . . .

It had happened to Gerald himself once, years ago when he was in the army. He had been standing in front of some half-blind, senile colonel and had nearly taken a bullet in the neck. The sound of the shot had terrified him so much that his bowels had turned to water and he had disgraced himself.

He decided that he would do it if he could pick a choice moment. After all, there was no one behind him who might guess his game . . .

His obsessive fury at Frederick's treachery had grown so great that he had forgotten Adrian Steele, now bringing up the rear after hanging back to make sheep's eyes at Evelyn.

There was something in this form of revenge that appealed deeply to Gerald's gambling instinct. The outcome was uncertain. Even his own intentions were ambiguous. He had assured himself that he just wanted to give Teasdale a fright, but some dark part of him . . . was not entirely sure what he wanted to happen. The chance of his target standing still at the moment he chose was not great. Not great at all, in fact tantalizingly small . . . If Anstey moved his gun to the right, the shot would go wide. If he moved to the left . . . but that would never happen, since Anstey took aim from the left shoulder.

When the moment came, Gerald had never felt happier, or more powerful. His senses sang, the blood rushed round his motionless frame with such force that his wrists pulsed visibly and he found it difficult to steady himself. He waited for the cue from in front: the deadly crackle of guns firing in sequence.

Then Frederick cried out.

*'My God, Teddy – look at that! Three dead in the air at once!'*

Frederick had forgotten the cardinal rule *never* to speak above a whisper when someone is about to shoot. At the sound of Frederick's squeaky exultation, Anstey turned in surprise to look at him.

And in doing so, he stepped to the left.

Gerald had already made his surrender to Chance. The shower of shot had already left his gun as Anstey moved, and it tore away the left side of his head above the ear. He fell to the ground before the expression on his face had time to change, and his face rested there, white against the black soil, its right side still looking pleased for Frederick.

As people began to shout and run, casting the corpses of the birds aside as they did so, the only thought allowed entry to Gerald Colby's numbed brain was *'Thank God I was at the back of the line and no one saw me take aim.'*

It took Adrian very little time to calculate that he was the only person to see what happened. The Graylings keeper, Richardson, who acted as Captain Colby's loader, was standing to one side and a little in front of him. Not in the right place to see that Colby had had his sights trained on the Earl of Teasdale's head half the afternoon. And Brittany and Ruth Morgan were at the top of the slope, where they had been advised to stand when the shooting started. Too far away to see clearly.

Adrian did not move forward when the others did. What was the point when he knew that Teasdale was already dead? He remained in his position at the back of the line, his gun pointing down, and watched the others crowd around like flies on raw flesh.

Then he saw his father looking up at him. He was at the far end of the line, and the last to find out what had happened. He had let his gun fall, and he was standing with his shoulders drooping and his mouth hanging slackly open. But he was not staring at Earl Teasdale, he was staring at his son. Could he have known?

Adrian was to have two clear memories of that terrible afternoon. The first was Father's behaviour. Never before in his life, not once, had Father told him what to do. But he loped up to Adrian's side as they followed the makeshift stretcher through the woods, and started muttering 'Poor Gerald, what a terrible thing to happen. He'll never be allowed to forget it.' He stopped, removed his deerstalker and scraped his straggling red hair onto his bald pate. Adrian moved on, but his father snatched at his arm and pulled him to a halt.

'Whatever happens,' he hissed, 'you must *never* speak to anyone about what has happened today. Do you understand?'

Adrian nodded. He had no intention of speaking to anyone about the Earl of Teasdale's murder until it suited him to do so.

The second memory was of Brittany. When Teasdale fell, she flew past Adrian, pushing him brutally aside. He had never seen anyone run so fast in a skirt. A deafening sound went up, so loud and so piercing that birds started from their branches and circled the sky above, crying a desolate chorus.

It was the sound of Brittany screaming when she saw that her father lay dead.

Out of respect for the feelings of Viola Anstey, the Countess of Teasdale, they took her husband's body to Graylings and laid it in the library. When it was dark and they had all gone, Brittany went down to look at it.

Could he really be dead, as Grandmama and Grandpapa were dead and rotting beneath the turf in the churchyard? Was the laughter that lurked round the edges of everything he said stilled inside him for ever? When she looked at him she could not believe it. From the right he looked as though he were only sleeping; he even wore a delighted smile. The golden brown hair had not lost its brilliant gleam, even in death. Only the white sheet that had been hastily draped over the other side of his head betrayed the terrible secret.

She, too, was betrayed. For the first time in her life. She bent and kissed his forehead gently.

'I loved him,' she said out loud. She spoke to no one in particular. It was a bare statement of fact. As long as she looked at him, he seemed real, he existed and she found she could not leave him.

They found her there in the morning, asleep in a chair.

Brittany was not allowed to go to the funeral, but Maman went. Brittany walked out onto the white steps of Graylings to watch her departure. She was dressed with stunning elegance, swathed in long black veils which swirled from her black ostrich feather hat. As she reached the waiting carriage she slowly drew off her long black gloves and, raising white hands covered with diamond rings, put back her veils. The sun glinted on a pair of diamond ear-drops, and on the beautiful, pale face.

She looked up at her daughter and Brittany saw the mirror image of her own grief. Their eyes met fleetingly in acknowledgement, then she was gone, the black veils fluttering in the wind.

## 3

### Somerset, 23 December, 1912

Aunt Georgina was coming to the Christmas party, which would probably spoil it.

Nevertheless, as Brittany toured the kitchen, dipping her fingers into bowls of cake mixture when the cook was not looking, and stealing nuts and raisins from the large boxes of fruit that were waiting in the larder, she felt a certain satisfied anticipation. Graylings had been a gloomy place since what was now referred to as The Shooting Accident. Papa more or less disappeared. He spent longer and longer periods in London, and when he returned he vanished into the stables, coming in after dark and eating supper from a tray in his study. Maman seemed to have lost all interest in visiting or receiving friends, retreating behind a tight, white mask of self-pity. Brittany could not help but be glad that the house would be full of people again, and though aunts and cousins were visitors of the worst kind, the Langbournes might provide some compensation. They were bringing their children this time, among whom was a daughter slightly older than Brittany.

It was impossible not to gravitate towards the kitchens. After hours of broiling, roasting and baking they were the warmest place in the house. Steam trickled slowly down walls and windows and there was sweat on the upper lip of the scullery maid as she peeled and chopped her way through a mountain of onions. The smells were rich and pungent pervading the house with warm waves of ginger and cinnamon like some wind from a Middle Eastern climate.

In the drawing room a Christmas tree stood waiting like a virgin bride, its clean, glossy branches trembling beneath a mantle of candles and silver streamers and white satin rosettes. The fireplace was half obscured by a waxy wreath and festoons of red ribbon. Later, candles would be lit and carols sung around the piano, and the flickering candle flames would multiply in the shining surface of the silver punchbowl. It would be full of mulled wine, steaming patiently on a side table while the guests sang and the slices of orange turned purply red.

And then there would be dances and party games and Maman would sing French cradle songs in a quavering voice and Papa would drink a decanter of port and smoke a cigar and say nothing. And George would eat too much and go off quietly to be sick and Frederick would drink too much and laugh until everyone grew bored with the sound. At least, that was how Christmases had always been in the past.

Had those Christmases always been crisp and snowy, or was that just the invention of story books, along with the bearded, jovial

Father Christmas and goodwill to all men? There was certainly no snow to be seen now, only a mean, grey December gloom that had the maids lighting lamps at two in the afternoon. And rain, lashing angrily at the windows and hissing down chimneys.

Brittany went upstairs and curled up in front of the fire in her room, with a book. It was one of her mother's Seton Merriman romances, a very silly tale about a very silly lady and a very silly gentleman. From time to time Brittany would lay the book down and try to picture Uncle Teddy's face, as she often did when she was alone. And behind the chintz curtains, rain knocked spitefully against the panes and spat in the grate.

The door opened abruptly and Nanny Wynn walked in. She did not knock; she never did. Having handled her charges from the first hours of their life, the concept of their privacy quite escaped her.

'Get yourself up off the floor, you great ninny. Look at you, you great scarecrow, crushing your dress like that.'

She pulled Brittany up by her elbow and began to brush down the skirts of her cherry red dress. It was not a dress that Nanny Wynn approved of. The colour and the clinging fabric, both Lucienne's choice, had been condemned as 'unsuitable'.

'Mr and Mrs Seaton have arrived,' said Nanny Wynn, as though that were a fitting punishment for idling before the fire and crushing a best dress. 'Now you get downstairs and show them you've got some manners.'

Faced with the prospect of Aunt Georgina, Brittany wondered whether she had any at all. There was something about Aunt Georgina that made her want to behave as badly as possible. Even at the age of fourteen, she felt an urgent need to stick her tongue out the moment her aunt's back was turned. There was little or no love between Georgina Seaton and her elder brother Gerald, and her periodic appearances at Graylings were more like the visits of a sanitary inspector than an embassy of familial detente.

She was a large woman with the square Colby head, iron grey hair and steely grey eyes that glinted ferociously when she saw Brittany descending the staircase into the hall with as much insolent nonchalance as she could muster.

'So here's *Evelyn*!' she said, in the way one might say 'typhoid' or 'diarrhoea'.

Brittany ignored her aunt.

'Happy Christmas, Uncle William,' she said to the unfortunate Mr Seaton, a sad-eyed man with a drooping moustache who was trying, ineffectually, to brush the rain from his cape. It had drenched the mountains of luggage that footmen were piling up, and trickled damply over the eyebrows of the two Seaton children, seven-year-old Arthur and ten-year-old Leonora.

Uncle William looked around dolefully at the circle of forced smiles.

'Well . . . here we are again, then . . .'

Those were Brittany's precise thoughts as she sat in the drawing room, while tea was brought in and there were polite murmurs about the efficaciousness of the blaze in the grate and the exquisite arrangement of the seasonal decorations. Here we are again, thought Brittany, drumming her heels against the back of her chair and counting the crumpets that George demolished as she might count sheep.

Papa had, of course, absented himself to attend a sick horse, leaving Maman to do the work. She twisted her diamond rings nervously while Aunt Georgina licked the melted butter from her lips with relish. Having got them quite clean, she wiped them on a napkin and proceeded to pat and fuss over her daughter, smoothing her dark hair, which hung in old-fashioned ringlets about the child's head. She picked up a curl between finger and thumb with the delicacy she might have devoted to a dying butterfly, unrolled it and let it snap back into place. Then the long-awaited question:

'Now, Lucienne, tell me all your News . . .'

Last year poor Maman had been forced to include The Shooting Accident in this grisly catalogue, and her hand had trembled so violently that she dropped her teacup. This year, however, salvation was at hand.

The butler came in.

Mr and Mrs Richard Langbourne are here, madam.'

'We're early, I'm afraid, Lucienne.'

Maud bustled into the drawing room, her pretty blonde curls a-quiver. 'But I see we're in time for tea!'

The drawing room began to fill with people, giving George his opportunity to creep away unnoticed. Richard Langbourne was there, stroking his moustache and rocking back and forth on his heels. He laughed jovially, but was he remembering his last visit to

Graylings, Brittany wondered, when human blood had drenched his expensive tweed plus fours?

The three Langbourne children stood in the centre of the room for inspection and admiration. Johnnie Langbourne was Frederick's age. He was a handsome, slender boy with a lovely complexion and beautiful straight teeth, but his responses to the ritual round of questioning were so dull and conventional that Brittany dismissed him at once. Claudia was little more than a baby: a plump, engaging child, all round eyes and curls, creeping behind her mother's skirts.

But Susannah was perfect.

Brittany wanted to reach out and touch her, to make sure she was real. Her hair was gold, not Brittany's rusty, brassy gold, but pale white-gold like a child's. She had large, benign brown eyes and cheeks with high, delicate bones, like seashells. She wore a sophisticated dress of lavender wool, and the fashionably tight skirt revealed grey kid boots with pearl buttons. Pearl buttons! Brittany almost fainted with covetousness. And her jewellery! Turquoise and diamond rings and a gold bracelet of exquisite delicacy.

Maman was obviously so relieved to see Maud that she relaxed and started to smile.

'Brittany, *chérie*,' she said warmly. 'Perhaps you would like to show Susannah to her room, and then give her a tour of the house. And take Leonora with you too.'

Lucienne pouted. Susannah, yes: Leonora, no, certainly not. She disliked her cousin, who was a spoilt, petulant child with affected manners and a sly gleam in her eye. Besides, she was only ten. How could she learn all she wanted to know from Susannah with a ten-year-old child dogging her heels? But there was always a solution to the problem of the unwanted guest. A little hard on George, perhaps, but he would survive.

When they were in the passage, Brittany took Susannah determinedly by the arm and turned to look down at Leonora, who was hovering in the shadows, pulling her curls.

'You don't want to see the house, do you Leonora, so you run along now. Go and find George. He's got a new puppy, and if you're lucky he might let you play with it.'

Leonora looked mutinous. She did not like George.

'Perhaps Leonora would rather come with us?' said Susannah gently.

'I would.'

Brittany glared at her cousin. 'Nonsense! She's seen the house already, haven't you, Leonora? And the puppy's lovely, all soft and playful. Now go on! He's probably in the nursery.'

She pushed Leonora towards the stairs, exerting a warning pressure on her elbow with a finger and thumb. Leonora stomped up the stairs, turning once to reaveal a sulky lower lip.

'She'd just be a nuisance anyway,' said Brittany hastily.

Susannah turned her madonna's eyes unwaveringly on Brittany's face. A crucifix glinted reproachfully at her throat.

'I don't think that was very kind, Brittany.' There was such compassionate sadness in her voice that Brittany shuddered with guilt.

'The puppy's heavenly, though. She'll love it.'

'I hope so.'

Susannah looked up at the small retreating figure with a sigh. Her sincerity made Brittany feel wicked inside, just as she used to when she was a small child and pushing Nanny Wynn to the limits of her endurance, goading her into administering a slap and unleashing the cathartic flow of tears. She found herself wondering idly how far she could push Susannah before she became angry.

She also realized that she had miscalculated. She had been granted the friend she so wanted, but it had never occurred to her what she would do if the friend turned out to be one of Nanny Wynn's 'good children'.

If Nanny Wynn was to be believed, Susannah Langbourne was already guaranteed a place in heaven.


'At least *you're* pleased to see me, boy.'

George sat on the nursery floor and hugged the puppy to his chest, squashing it clumsily so that it struggled to get free.

It was the second puppy he had owned. The first was the pointer given to him on his eleventh birthday. The unhappy day had provided an inauspicious start and the puppy Frederick had picked out sickened and finally died from enteritis only a few weeks later. The new puppy was a sheepdog and more robust. George dragged it everywhere with him, and recently had begun to tell it things. It had two advantages as a confident: it was uncritical and consistent. You knew where you were with a dog. He would have liked to tell it about Susannah, but he was afraid that Nanny

Wynn would hear him if he spoke out loud. And then he would be sent downstairs again, promptly . . .

So he spoke the words in his head instead, the words he would have spoken to the puppy.

*She looks just like an angel. Like one of the angels who will crown Maman in heaven.*

As the horrible ritual of Being Polite to the Guests had worn on, George had felt an uncomfortable crushing sensation in his lap, manifesting itself gradually as the need to empty his bladder. He also found himself thinking wistfully of the puppy's clumsy paws and soft vulnerability, and longed for a chance to hold it and stroke it and feel the warmth of its frantic little body through his clothes.

The two ideas started to flash before his eyes in monotonous rotation: dog, water closet; dog, water closet . . . He tried looking to Brittany for help but she seemed miles away, drumming her feet against the chair and staring at the ceiling. How could he raise such a sensitive topic in the company of Aunt Georgina?

Then more people came into the room, with wet and cold still clinging to them. While the drawing-room door was still open, he had tipped his stiff body off its stool and escaped into the cool of the hall. He scurried blindly, awkwardly round the curve of the staircase, blinking in the dim light, deafened by the sound of the wind battering the skylight, and it was then that he saw her.

She stepped underneath the glass skylight and the light from the gas lamps reflected down from its dome, illuminating her pale hair and white, even teeth. She was following the others into the drawing room, but she caught sight of him cowering in the arc of the stairs and stopped to smile. A warm, confident smile. George had fled up the stairs wheezing loudly, pictures of a hundred blonde-haired angels bursting in his brain.

He stayed there in the nursery, savouring his solitude, and weak with relief that in the future Christmas gatherings would be Frederick's responsibility and not his.

After what seemed only a short space of time there were footsteps on the landing and the door opened. It was Brittany.

'George, where on earth have you been? People have been looking for you all over!'

George was smitten with fear. Had Papa sent her?

'Why, what have I done?'

'Done? Nothing, silly. Lady Henrietta and Adrian have arrived and the party's starting. We're about to play the flour game.'

The flour game! George's heart sank to his shoes. The awfulness of Christmas reached its zenith with the flour game.

'Games before carols, I think,' said Lucienne Colby. 'But we'll light the candles anyway, it's more festive.'

She rang for a footman, and after she had whispered in his ear, he returned with a taper and solemnly processed round the room, lighting candles as though he were performing the Stations of the Cross. There was a tense silence as the gaslights were extinguished and the expectant faces receded into a shadowy orange light.

Adrian Steele's eyes wandered automatically to Brittany, sitting beside the Christmas tree, picking destructively at its needles. Anyone near the tree could not help but draw attention to themselves, for it made a beacon in the corner of the candlelit room, its tiny lights blurring into one great arc light. From Brittany, Adrian's eyes moved to the plump cluster of mistletoe berries hanging from the ceiling. This time he had Christmas as an excuse . . .

'Gerald's not here yet . . . Perhaps one carol while we're waiting? Henrietta – I mean *Lady* Henrietta, would you oblige?'

Mama gave a condescending nod and picked her way to the piano. She insisted on the use of her title, even from old acquaintances. Adrian believed that it was her way of setting herself permanently above Father, and the habit persisted even though they were rarely together now. Father had been so looking forward to the Christmas celebrations at Graylings that deception had been necessary before he and Mama could set out that evening. Such measures were unavoidable, though. He seemed to have worsened so much of late.

Adrian found Frederick at his elbow as they all grouped around the piano and Mama struck up a chord to give the singers a key.

'Why isn't your father here?' he asked, as though he had been reading Adrian's thoughts. Only Frederick was too naïve for that.

'He couldn't come. He's unwell.'

'I'm sorry to hear that,' hissed Frederick through the introductory strains of 'The Holly and the Ivy'. At the end of the first verse, he looked at Adrian strangely and said:

'But didn't I see him in the village this morning, in his dogcart? What's wrong with him?'

'It's his chest,' whispered Adrian hastily. 'He disobeys the doctor's orders from time to time.'

'Oh.'

Frederick smiled radiantly, more than satisfied with this explanation.

At the end of the carol, there was some self-congratulatory clapping and then people returned to their seats.

'Look, Mama, mistletoe!' shrieked Leonora Seaton, whom Adrian had already dismissed as a most objectionable child.

'Indeed,' said her mother drily.

'Mistletoe!' Mama had mock gaiety seeping around the edges of her cleverest smile. 'And who will lead the way? I think it should be Brittany, as the daughter of the house.'

There was a universal chorus of agreement, and Adrian hoped that they were all too preoccupied with conviviality to notice Mama's hard blue eyes directed meaningfully, first at his face, then at Brittany's. Her eyebrows were raised in exhortation.

There was an empty patch of carpet below the mistletoe, and Brittany stepped onto it. Shadows came and went in the flickering amber light, making it impossible to tell if her sallow face was blushing, but her long eyes glittered as she tossed her hair back, laughing self-consciously. She turned in a slow circle and there were murmurs from the others of 'Who will it be?' . . . 'Hurry up and choose' . . .

Adrian felt his blood quicken in anger as she passed him by and stopped in front of Richard Langbourne, smiling invitingly. But it did not occur to him to admit defeat, especially now that Mama was watching him closely, just as she had once watched him school the horse she had chosen for him. This would be a little like leaping on the horse while it was still rearing, turning resistance to advantage. He jumped to his feet.

'Since the lady is taking so long to choose,' he said boldly, stepping into the circle of Turkey carpet as though it were a fairy ring. 'I would like to take this opportunity to deliver the first Christmas kiss.'

There were nervous sniggers as Brittany turned to face him, barely concealing the anger in her eyes. She was trapped, unable to resist without a severe breach of manners and Christmas spirit, but the look in her eyes was unyielding. Good, thought Adrian smugly, the victory's the greater if they're unbroken. As Mama always says.

*Perhaps the silly girl still thinks kissing will give her a baby . . .*

The thought amused him and his mouth broke into a grin as he reached for hers. Brittany surrendered to the kiss with tightly clenched lips and broke away, breathing hard through her nostrils, to the sound of laughter and applause. The impotent fury in her eyes would have convinced even Mama that being kissed by Adrian Steele was not something she considered a privilege. But fortunately Mama's attention was directed elsewhere. She was contemplating the blonde Susannah Langbourne, no doubt weighing the joint advantages of prettiness and an extremely wealthy father.

When the laughter had died down, and silver cups of fragrant mulled wine had been handed round, it was decided that the time was ripe for the flour game. Captain Colby had arrived, his hair still wet with bath water and smelling faintly of oil of cloves, but a search for George had to be initiated before the game could begin.

It came as no surprise that George was missing, since in previous years he had always been the first to lose the flour game. Generous imbibing of mulled wine invariably turned the trivial contest into a battle of nerves and was traditionally accompanied by a great deal of shouting and laughter, all of which reduced George Colby to a quivering jelly. He crept into the drawing room now, preceding the ceremonial plate of flour like an unhappy gladiator.

The plate was carefully set down on a table at the centre of the room. It held a shining white pyramid of flour, skilfully compacted, with a glass marble on top. The players would take it in turns to slice the pyramid with a knife but if, in doing so, they caused the marble to fall from its crowning position then they were forced to remove it from the pile of flour with their teeth.

All except Claudia and Arthur were to play, and the space around the table became so crowded that the light from the candles was entirely obscured. It was agreed that a candle should be placed on the table next to the flour, and it illuminated the eager faces from beneath, like flames from a campfire. Once preparations were complete, there was an inevitable argument about who should go first. The more slices that were cut from the 'cake', the greater the chance of the marble toppling when the knife was inserted.

Susannah Langbourne, speaking calmly over the hubbub, had a suggestion: 'Who picked up the marble on the last occasion you played?'

'I did,' said George miserably. The look on his face suggested that he was reliving that moment now, the flour in his hair and nostrils, the look of utter contempt on his father's face . . .

'Well, then, surely George should go first this time?' Susannah's voice was so smooth, so eminently equitable, that there were general murmurs of concurrence. George looked up at his saviour adoringly, then blushed and turned his gaze instead to the crucifix around her neck, as though it were a sacred relic he might kiss.

Susannah handed George the knife and he cut slowly and carefully, his tongue protruding between his lips. The marble stayed intact, and both Susannah and Brittany applauded loudly. Adrian had never seen George look so happy. His plump face, damp with exertion, shone in the candlelight.

Leonora Seaton took her turn next, as a concession to her age, then Maud Langbourne, then Brittany, then Adrian, then Captain Colby. The marble wobbled slightly as his slice of flour crumbled to dust, and there was a catching of breath from the audience. But the marble remained precariously in place, and with a flourish Captain Colby handed the knife to Frederick.

'See what you can do with that!' he challenged, slapping his son on the back.

Frederick was known for his dexterity in the game, and Adrian leaned forward with the others to watch more closely. An expectant hush had fallen. Surely even Frederick would not be able to extract the blade without toppling the marble? As Frederick extended the knife towards the plate, Afrian noticed that his hands were trembling. And his face looked very strange . . . Intrigued, Adrian found himself remembering the dim light of the billiard room. *That* was where he had seen the strange look before, on the eve of Charles Anstey's death. Even in the candlelight, his skin looked grey. Perhaps Adrian ought to say something? He glanced quickly around the circle of faces but no one seemed to have noticed. They were all watching the marble reverently.

The blade entered slowly, but Frederick's hand shook and the marble fell. There was much laughter, cries of 'Forfeit!' and 'Pick it up!'. Smiling bravely, and with his hands behind his back, Frederick bent his face into the flour.

Then Adrian heard it. Above the chuckles and cries of

encouragement came a sound of distress, a strangled, gasping sound.

'*Get back*!' Adrian shouted, pushing wildly at the crowd of people. 'All of you, get out of the way!'

They stared back at him uncomprehendingly, as though the sounds that were coming from the heap of flour were all part of the fun.

'*Frederick's ill!*' he shouted, and in the confusion there was a cracking sound as Frederick's skull hit the plate and he collapsed. Lucienne Colby screamed, a thin, disbelieving sound.

'*Adrian – come and help me!*'

Gerald Colby had rushed forward and was pulling Frederick's shoulders back from the table. A fine cloud of flour drifted through the air. Lady Henrietta's eyes narrowed as she watched her son lift Frederick's ankles and help Captain Colby carry him towards the drawing room door.

'He only needs some air.'

Adrian said nothing, but he felt that air would not be enough. Frederick's body was twitching violently, muscles rigid, and there was a froth of saliva on his flour-powdered lips.

Outside the drawing room, the air was thin and cold, the light grey in contrast to the glow of the candles. They laid Frederick gently on the ground. His body gave a final, desperate convulsion and then he lay still.

His tongue was protruding, just as George's had done when he was cutting the cake, and Adrian was struck by Frederick's overwhelming and eerie resemblance to his younger brother. Only tonight George had succeeded and Frederick had not. And George's face had been pink and healthy, while Frederick's was the whitened face of a sad clown.

Captain Colby knelt on the ground and touched a lock of chestnut hair, turned as grey as an old man's by the white flour. Then, still kneeling, he turned and looked up at Adrian. He did not speak. Adrian had expected to see shock in his eyes, but found only bitter despair.


## New York, 26 December, 1912


David managed to slip down the stairs unnoticed.

The noise was deafening: a string orchestra playing in one room, the babble of conversation and laughter beneath a rising cloud of cigar smoke.

Once he was in the street, he leaned against the front door and heaved a sigh of relief. The cold, empty air embraced him.

He began to stroll down Fifth Avenue, briskly and with a distinct spring in his step. He had escaped! The annual Christmas party was definitely a chore, not a diversion, one which he and Jake had often plotted to avoid. The Steins did not celebrate Christmas themselves, of course, but every year Isaac Stein threw a large, ostentatious party for his non-Jewish clients and any other of New York's well-heeled Gentiles whom he wished to impress. There were crates of vintage champagne, plates seeping with wet, shiny Beluga caviare, syrupy candied fruit, majestic iced *bombes* and dusty-looking truffles.

And when they were younger, silence would be called for at a choice moment and the five Stein children would be herded in. They stood beneath the gargantuan, jewel-encrusted Christmas tree, dressed in identical German folk costumes and singing German carols.

Even at a tender age, David could tell that this act was a severe transgression of taste, as well as offensive to his Jewishness, but the guests seemed to like it, nodding their expensively coiffed heads and lavishing sugary applause on the reluctant, velvet-clad minstrels.

But this year – no singing and no party either! David walked faster, even though he did not know where he was going. He wanted open air, he wanted space, he wanted to *move*. His unofficial departure had meant going out without a coat, and a tailcoat and embroidered satin waistcoat were insufficient protection against the sharp, frosty night. He pulled the jacket tightly about him and stopped every few paces to blow on his fingertips.

An old-fashioned carriage drew up at the kerb beside him.

'No overcoat on a night like this? You must be quite a man!'

It was a woman's voice. David looked up and saw a middle-aged woman riding alone. It was too dark to see her face properly, but even the yellowish street-lighting could not disguise the brilliant red of her hair.

'Where you walking to all alone, No-Coat?'

She had a deep southern drawl and there was a mocking edge to her voice.

'Nowhere special,' said David truthfully.

'Well, why don't you jump up and ride with me a little way? Reckon you might be warmer!'

She patted her heavy sable rug invitingly.

'Thank you, ma'am.'

As David clambered into the carriage he could not resist a smile. He felt happy, excited. A few seconds ago he had been alone. Now he was not. All that was missing to make it perfect was the fog. A larger-than-life character appearing out of nowhere to take him to . . .

'Put your arms under here, honey – there! Now we're cosy.'

The harder David looked at his companion, the more extraordinary she seemed. It was impossible to tell how old she was – forty at a glance, but it could have been as much as sixty if the skilled application of make-up was taken into account. David's mother and sisters did not wear cosmetics, and he was fascinated, peering hard into the darkness. Her skin was wrinkled a little round the eyes, but the rest appeared to have been smoothed over with a sort of clay. When they passed a lamp-post he could see a layer of pink powder on top of the clay, with grains clearly visible around her nostrils. Her mouth was a deep, wide gash of carmine red and her eyes, beneath artistically drawn brows, were ringed with thick, stiff black lashes of exorbitant proportions.

David had seen eyes like that only once before, at the Metropolitan Ballet. He had borrowed his mother's opera glasses and examined each ballerina in turn, more interested in the feminine mystique than in art. He had directed the glasses at their faces: their exotic, painted, slant-eyed faces and then, at the bidding of a more pressing whim, he had studied what was visible of their breasts in their *décolleté* dresses, and the line of their muscular thighs as they raised themselves on their *pointes*.

But this woman could not possibly be a ballerina. The clue was her hair. Ballerinas had smoothed-down hair, brown and worn in a discreet chignon. This woman's hair was a brilliant flame red and piled into a nest of curls. When she moved her head, the curls stayed still. Perhaps it was a wig? This fiery mass was crowned with a sealskin toque, to match the muff on her lap, and her costume was fuschia pink, trimmed with gold braid. Lumpy jewels were everywhere that bare flesh showed – wrist, neck, fingers – and they flashed each time the carriage rolled past a street lamp.

'Well, now . . .' the woman sat back and patted his thigh. 'Ain't this grand?'

She seemed as pleased as David with their unexpected meeting.

'Oh, but we're forgetting our manners, aren't we? We haven't introduced ourselves. I'm Ginnie. Ginnie Cassidy. Pleased to make your acquaintance.'

She extended a plump, jewelled hand.

'David Stein.'

'Now, David, I want you to tell me what you were doing walking down Fifth Avenue *away* from the party I could hear damn near two blocks away. You should be in there with the rest of them; such a big fancy house and you all dressed up in a penguin suit! Who lives there anyhow?'

'I do.'

'Oh.' Ginnie was temporarily silenced. 'What d'you say your name was?'

'David Stein.'

'Stein, huh? She nodded slowly, as though the name alone was ample explanation of everything, including his flight down the freezing street.

'Well, now, what do you say to a drink to warm you up? We're just near my house now.'

'I'd be delighted.'

The carriage came to a halt outside a flat-fronted town house on East 55th Street. As Ginnie swayed decorously up the front steps, David saw that her body was much younger than her face, trim and flexible, and cunningly moulded by her bright pink suit to emphasize a full bust and neat waist.

David looked around him in astonishment when he stepped inside the house. He had expected flamboyance and stylishness, but not the barefaced opulence that stared back at him. There was no hint of it from the quiet, discreet façade of the house. Chandeliers cast a sparkle on highly polished satinwood and outsized oval mirrors. To the left, double doors were thrown back to reveal a piano – not only a grand piano but a *white* grand piano, standing beneath a window draped in tasselled velveteen.

But this was not the cold grandeur of his Fifth Avenue home. The house felt, warm, intimate, alive. It had a clean, feminine smell: a combination of sandalwood, beeswax and gardenias, with the papery overtones of folded dollar bills. A white Persian cat stretched indolently across a chair.

Ginnie handed her muff and hat to a negro footman and pointed to the room with the piano.

'That in there's where I usually entertain my guests, but because I like you I'm going to take you up to my private parlour.'

She smiled mischievously at David and beckoned him up the carpeted staircase. From behind a closed door on the right of the hall came a rumble of conversation, punctuated by high, girlish laughter, but Ginnie offered no comment on the noise as she led David into a small room on the first floor, facing out onto the street. The floor was carpeted with silky Chinese rugs, and above the fireplace hung the largest oil painting that David had ever seen. He looked at it – then looked again, blinking in disbelief. Before his eyes was a very naked lady, lying in abandoned pose on an ottoman, like a pale pink snapdragon, while above her glowered a turbaned blackamoor whose intentions were clearly dishonourable. He would have liked to look closer at the plump, pinky white limbs and the suggestive patches of shade, but he did not want Ginnie to think that he had never seen a naked woman before, so he stood with his back to it.

'Now – a drink!'

Ginnie settled herself on a sofa. It was the colour of purple orchids, in startling contrast to her red and pink plumage.

'Champagne?'

David shook his head violently. 'Back there . . . too much champagne!' He jerked his head in the direction of Fifth Avenue.

Ginnie laughed. 'Why, you poor little rich boy! Brandy, then?'

She poured two glasses of brandy from a decanter, pausing to croon at a white cockatoo in a cage near the window.

'This is a very nice house,' said David politely. 'Do you live here alone?'

Ginnie threw herself down on the purple sofa with a raucous laugh.

'Alone? Don't you know *anything*, boy? This is a *whore*house. What fancy folk might call a brothel.'

It was David's turn to laugh.

'Well, what's so funny about that?'

'I was just thinking that I ought to know a whorehouse when I see one. An unkind visitor to our house on Fifth Avenue once described it as a cross between a French *château* and a brothel.'

'Well, you'll feel right at home then.'

'Is it expensive?' asked David. 'I mean to . . .'

'Well now,' said Ginnie with the aplomb of an experienced businesswoman, 'that depends. We start at about 200 dollars, but then my girls are the best. I won't have any rubbish. We've got all types: blondes, redheads, mulattos . . . I've even got an Eskimo girl. I'll wager you've never seen one of *those* before!'

David was calculating rapidly on his fingers. 'But that's a great deal of money. If they come often, of course. *Do* they come often?'

'Some do.'

David's face took on a sly look. He decided he would tease Ginnie a little.

'Forgive me asking this, ma'am . . . but wouldn't it be a great saving if these gentlemen . . . well, if they paid their attention to their wives?'

He had expected Ginnie to laugh, but she looked serious. 'You've got a lot to learn yet, David.' She took a gulp of her brandy. 'A wife can be expensive too, you know. Very expensive. Some of my best customers are the ones who've been married, sometimes more than once. But they swear to me 'never again'. Nine times out of ten the woman makes off with a generous share of the family jewels, which probably end up being sold to feed, house and clothe another man's piece of . . . well, you know what I mean. At least here they know what they're getting. They pay for their pleasure and that's an end to it. They walk away free men.'

'That sounds a very sensible arrangement.'

David was still standing in front of the painting, warming himself in front of the fire that crackled and spat in the grate. Ginnie was chewing her large, red lower lip and looking at him thoughtfully.

'How old are you?'

'Eighteen,' lied David.

'Mmmm. Reckon you're a little younger than that, but old enough all the same. What d'you say to going upstairs and having yourself a little entertainment?'

David was astonished. 'You mean . . . with you?'

Ginnie clasped her hands and rocked back and forth, laughing so hard that tears came to her eyes and the cockatoo became excited, screeching and hopping frantically along its perch.

'Bless you, no! But ain't that the sweetest thing I ever heard? I'm a little too old for that sort of thing, but in my time . . . No, I was thinking of one of my girls.'

'The Eskimo?'

'I'm afraid she's not available. But I have just the one.'

David looked disappointed. 'I don't have any money with me.'

'Never you mind that. This one's on the house. On account, shall we say?'

She took David's hand and led him to the top floor of the house. She pointed to an empty bedroom and said, 'You wait there while I see to it. And come and see me before you go. I've enjoyed your company.'

The bed that David sat down on was a four poster with a heavy canopy of green brocade. The walls were covered with finely pleated, watered silk of willow green. There was a bow-fronted dresser with a green valance, on which brushes, combs, powder and pins were laid out. In one corner there was a washstand and a conspicuous chamber pot.

After a few minutes the door opened and a girl came in, carrying a towel. She had frizzy yellow curls and sparkling dark eyes and she did not look much older than David himself. She sat down beside him on the edge of the bed and with a playful movement dragged expert fingers over his smooth boy's jaw.

'You're a young one,' she said, matter of fact. 'Does your mother know you're here?'

Mother. He could see her gentle green eyes in the green room, full of shock and disappointment. He had better stop thinking about her, quickly, before she spoiled things.

Before he had a chance to reply the girl took his face in her hands and kissed him. Her mouth was wet and open on his and he struggled like a drowning man to grasp what was happening, his nerves aching with a newness of sensation.

Her hands were reaching down and unbuttoning his fly, touching and caressing him with a thrilling intimacy. She pulled off his satin waistcoat, cream, embroidered with gold thread – David's pride and joy – and dropped it on the floor.

'Come on, then.'

She picked up the towel and spread it on the green bed and then lay back on it. What David saw both delighted and terrified him. She had her skirts and petticoats flung back, and she was not wearing any bloomers. He had expected to have to fumble with garments that buttoned in obscure and difficult corners.

He thought he might faint at such a sight, and at the warm, animal smell of her, but he did not. He reached out trembling fingers and touched the forbidden toy.

'Come here.'

She guided him towards her, and at the first miraculous contact he felt a tugging at the root of his brain and an exquisite pleasure flooding secret places he had not known existed.

When he regained consciousness he was slumped across the girl's thighs and she was dabbing them with a towel, saying, 'It's often like that with beginners.'

Then she was gone.

For what seemed like a long time he lay on his back, half naked, staring at the green silk canopy above his head. He found it difficult to recall how the evening had started or how he had come to be in the house on East 55th Street. With his eyes still closed he heard the clock over the fireplace striking midnight. Then he remembered.

The Christmas party.

He dressed quickly and ran downstairs to the parlour to say goodbye to Ginnie. She kissed him affectionately on the cheek and patted his hand as though he had merely called for a cup of tea.

'Delighted to make your acquaintance. Next time, don't go out without your coat. And bring your pocketbook!'

There had been no offer of transport for the return journey, so David set off down the street at a run. His body felt numb and warm on the inside even though a light snow had begun to fall. As he reached the corner of Fifth Avenue, he heard a car's horn and recognized the lamps of the Stein Daimler looming out of the fine mist of snowflakes.

Jake was at the wheel.

'Where the hell have you been?' he shouted as David slipped into the front seat beside him. 'I volunteered to go out and look for you. Mother's sick with worry.'

'I didn't think they'd notice . . . the party—'

'Of course they noticed. People kept asking where you were. And where *were* you? Are you going to tell me?'

'I've been to a whorehouse,' said David smugly.

Jake rolled the car to a halt and stared at his brother, his hands still on the wheel.

'Only by accident,' David added hastily. 'I went out for some air, and got talking to this very nice lady, and she asked me home for a drink. Only home just happened to be a whorehouse.'

'*Just happened?* And I suppose you took advantage of the facilities while you were there?'

David nodded, smiling broadly.

'David!' cried Jake. 'When are you going to grow up? Don't you know that you might . . . You're going to get yourself in some trouble one of these days, you know. You may be only seventeen, but your father's Isaac Stein of New York. You can't dodge that forever. One day you're going to have to—'

'Oh yes,' cut in David angrily, 'I was forgetting! I have *you* to live up to, don't I? And you're quite Papa's little golden boy, aren't you? Going to marry that slant-eyed bitch Miriam Abelson, aren't you—?'

He stopped when he saw the look on Jake's face, full of pained concern.

'I'm sorry, Jake. I guess you meant to help.'

Jake took out his handkerchief, wetted it and scrubbed at the crimson smear of Ginnie's lipstick on David's cheek.

'Look, we'll say no more about this, and I won't tell Mother and Papa what happened. We'll say you got lost. Okay?'

'Okay.' David patted his brother's shoulder happily.

'. . . Only there's one other thing,' said Jake with a gleam in his eyes as they waited for the front door to be unbolted.

'Yes?'

'. . . What was it like?'

### Somerset, 29 December, 1912

'Bloody rabbits are like the plague!' said Roland Steele. 'They're all over m'land. Can't shoot 'em fast enough!'

He received no reply, for there was no one to give him one. Heathcote House was empty, the ashes of the morning's fires settling in piles of white dust on chilly hearths. Roland trudged to the kitchen, where the remains of the Christmas turkey were congealing in the meat safe. He removed one emaciated wing and took it with him on his aimless journey, sliding slightly on the polished wooden corridors, as he wore stockings but no boots. His breeches had been thrust on over his nightshirt, and a jacket on top of that. It had tails, which flapped uncertainly above the trailing ends of the nightshirt. His red hair hung in tendrils round his neck; he rarely bothered with scraping it onto his head now, and it was so long since his whiskers had been trimmed that they formed a ruff round his face, giving him the appearance of a large ginger tomcat.

He went into the drawing room and sat down in one of the armchairs, still chewing the turkey bone. A portrait of his brother-in-law, Robert Dysart, looked down distastefully from the wall.

'Rabbits, Bertie,' said Roland to the portrait, licking the grease from his fingers, 'just don't know what to do about them. What would *you* do, Bertie?'

In the distance, a door slammed and there were voices, but Roland did not hear them. He had already sunk back into his reverie.

Lady Henrietta and Adrian stood in the hall, waiting for the housemaid to come and remove their rain-soaked wraps.

'She's probably fast asleep, the lazy creature,' said Lady Henrietta bitterly. 'And I particularly asked her to keep an eye on your father. Go and see where they are, will you?'

Adrian disappeared dutifully and she waited in the hall, shaking the rain from her black umbrella and brushing drops from her black skirt. Then her son returned.

'He was in the drawing room.'

'Well, he shouldn't have been in there. Did you find Deborah?'

'Yes, she's taken him up the back stairs and she'll sit with him for a while.'

'Good. I have something to show you.'

Lady Henrietta sailed regally up the staircase, the damp hem of her black gown rippling over each stair. Adrian walked behind her like a squire behind a knight.

'You know . . .' she said, without turning round to look at him, '. . . I think that was the worst funeral I've ever been to. Worse even than my sister's, and she died at fifteen. All that rain, and the crying. And when they threw the earth on the coffin, I really thought Gerald was going to throw himself in after it! And he was only the same age as you. How frail is the flesh!'

She turned and fixed her son with her hard blue eyes, as though dying were evidence of weak character.

They went into her bedroom. She led the way into the tiny room next to it and placed herself on the mahogany seat of the commode. Then she pointed imperiously at the floor. 'Now, lift that floorboard.'

Adrian lifted the board and looked inside. He picked up one of the small cloth bags, shook it and looked inside it.

'Money, Mama? I don't believe it! How did it get here?'

'I put it there, of course! I'm going to tell you all about it. We're going to have a little talk. But not here in the water closet. We'll go down to the drawing room.'

The drawing room fire had long since died, and the room was uncomfortably cold and damp. It was decorated in rose and grey, faintly evoking the grandeur of times past. It was here that Lady Henrietta displayed a collection of eighteenth-century furniture that had once belonged in her father's baronial home.

'Sit down,' she said, pointing to an armchair.

She walked to the window and looked out. The panes were smeared and greasy and the film it left on her bony fingers made her frown at them in disgust.

'Really, I must get something done about this! It only needs a bucket of hot, soapy water, surely they can manage that? In the old days, one never had to request such things as clean windows, it was all done as a matter of course. And that's how its going to be for you, Adrian!'

'Explain, old girl, explain! This is getting too mysterious.' Adrian grinned impatiently. Then he frowned as his foot encountered something on the floor beneath his seat. Reaching down he retrieved a chewed turkey wing and stared at it in amazement as his mother snapped: 'Pay attention! That money is mine, but I'm going to give it to you.'

'You never mentioned it before, not even—'

'Of course I didn't! Letting people know you have money can be as imprudent as revealing that you're penniless. Anyway, for a long time I was forced to keep it a secret from your father. Not that it matters now . . .

I lied to him. I let him believe for years that what came with me as my marriage settlement was all I had, when in fact I had a great deal more. It was a sort of precaution at first, and then later I had definite plans for it. It was a mercy that by the time I was married they had changed the law that would have made my property the property of my husband. I simply had to arrange for the trustees to keep it in my name.'

'But keeping it *here*, Mama, under the floorboards. It's hardly—'

Lady Henrietta laughed and patted her dark hair coquettishly. 'Why, Adrian, you don't imagine I'm such a fool, do you? That's only part of the whole, kept here to remind me. What one might call 'tangible assets'. The rest of it is still tied up in land and property, but I can release it when I choose. And I'm going to give it to you.'

A smile of sheer pleasure lurked in the recesses of Adrian's dark eyes. 'And what do you intend me to do with it?'

'It's for Graylings, of course. I've wasted years here, and I've watched that place being wasted too. It *ought* to be yours, Adrian.'

She turned to face her son, and in her passion, her vigorous past shone through embittered beauty.

'How did you know Frederick was going to die, Mama?' Adrian absent-mindedly passed the turkey bone from one hand to another.

'*Know*? I didn't *know*. It was an informed guess and, in the end, a piece of luck. I knew about the epileptic disorders in the family, but as you said yourself, Frederick seemed healthy enough. Perhaps it was Gerald Colby's attitude that alerted me. He was always very protective. But even he might not have known for certain . . '

Adrian was silent, remembering the look on Gerald Colby's face as he touched his dead son's chalky skin.

'Explain how the money comes into it.'

'Easy. Gerald Colby has spent all his. As things stand, I imagine he has raised a mortgage on the land and the place will have to be sold to repay it when he dies. It's certain George will never be able to raise the money to hold the estate together. Unless Brittany marries someone with money . . .

Graylings will go to George when Gerald dies, but *look* at him, I mean, it won't be *his*, will it? It will be hers.' Lady Henrietta sighed loudly. 'Alas, you won't have enough to buy the estate outright. I tried, but it just wasn't possible. Fifteen thousand acres . . . But you should have enough to pay back what he owes. So go to Gerald, tell him you're willing to marry Brittany and put your own money into Graylings. He's bound to see the sense in it, and he likes you. And with Frederick gone . . . Take Porphyrus and ride over there now. Speak to him.'

'Now? Directly after the funeral? Hardly the time for dynastic matches, old girl.'

'It's precisely the time. That's when people feel most insecure. There's a very good argument against waiting until tomorrow anyway. Tomorrow Gerald will probably be on the train to London, panting to lose more money.'

Adrian shook his head admiringly. 'You have thought about this a great deal, haven't you, Mama?'

'I just keep my eyes open, notice what's going on around me,' she said tersely. 'Any fool could do as much. After that shooting accident, Gerald Colby had a veritable spree at the tables. It seems reasonable to expect him to do the same now.'

Lady Henrietta looked down at her son, and her face softened.

'I've spent a long time preparing for this, Adrian. Don't let me down now.'


On a dark drizzling afternoon in late December, a black-clad figure on a large grey horse rode out of Nether Aston, heading North.

Porphyrus was in a mutinous temper, and would have liked to gallop hard down the rain-steeped lanes, but Adrian deliberately checked his pace. He wanted to spin out his journey because he needed time to think.

He had not argued with Mama; she would only have accused him of being without ambition. And that was not true, he *did* have ambition. Perhaps more than she realized. But he knew that Mama's scheme would never work.

He pulled Porphyrus to a walk as they mounted the lane that curved towards Graylings. His feet were not in the stirrups and his legs hung easily against the horse's massive flanks as he rode, his black-gloved hands on his thighs. How could he even begin to explain to Mama what the reality was? There was no room in her world for things she did not wish to believe. If he had said 'But Mama, don't you see, Brittany doesn't *want* to marry me!' her reply would have been 'Nonsense, you just have to persuade her!'

He doubted Brittany's susceptibility to persuasion. And there was something about her that made him feel ugly and unpleasant when he was near her. It made his belief in himself seem entirely unfounded and brought him face to face with . . . with the things he disliked in himself. They stared out at him through her strangely hypnotic eyes. Dislike was a more potent obstacle than hatred. But Mama could not, *would not* see that her son might not be an acceptable husband by virtue of his person alone. He thought she was probably afraid to do so. After all, she had built her whole life on his clambering up into the social niche that had once been hers.

Don't worry, Mama, he said to himself. I'll get Graylings, don't you worry. He smiled the smile of a wolf; greedy, hungry.

*I'll just have to do things in my own way* . . .

He could be certain now, at least, that he was the only one who knew. For a while he suspected that Father had been able to see. From his position in the leafy hollow, he might just have been low enough to see Gerald Colby raise his gun, if he had happened to glance back at that moment. It would have explained the hurried injunction to silence, as an attempt to protect Gerald Colby, the only friend Father had . . . But whatever Father saw or did not see, he posed no threat now. The events of that day were lost in his muddled brain. Even since Christmas, only a few days ago, he had deteriorated still more.

Porphyrus stopped instinctively when he reached the bend in the lane, as if to prompt the rider's admiration.

Adrian needed no prompting. Instead of the envy he usually experienced as he passed this place and looked down, he felt joy. The stately white house in its protective mantle of trees, would be his. *He* would decide whether to fell a tree or plant one, *he* would park a motor car on the gravel forecourt, *he* would choose the first summer's day warm enough to open the French windows onto the lawn . . . no one else but him. If Brittany cared about the place enough to overcome her dislike and take up her place in the scenario his fervid imagination depicted, he would be pleasantly surprised.

If not, Graylings would be enough on its own.

He knew he could not stay in the stables all day, yet dreaded going into the house.

Gerald Colby made another tour of the loose boxes as it started to grow dark. He ignored the rain that was soaking him, pressing his wet face against the faces of his horses, willing them to offer comfort. Tears mingled with the streaks of rain that ran down his blue, unshaven jaw. Finally, he turned and walked across the yard to the house, his hands thrust into the pockets of his black overcoat. Inside it would be waiting for him, the smothering blanket of bereavement, the grief that sucked at him like a hungry, demanding child.

The butler hovered solicitously, apologetically, explaining that Madam had gone to her room and would not be down that evening. Gerald grunted in acknowledgement and whistled to Frederick's dogs. They were sitting in the hall, waiting. Their whining tore into him.

'Come in here,' he said to them, opening the door to his study. A fire had been laid and he sat the dogs in front of it, running his large hands over their quivering limbs, to comfort himself as much as them. The expectant look on their faces made him feel guilty. You couldn't explain to a dog. They might, in their own way, understand that someone was never coming back, but you couldn't explain *why*.

He asked himself again if it was his fault. If there was something he should have done. Perhaps he should have taken Frederick to a doctor in London . . . But no, he had done nothing. He had been too afraid to face the truth of something he had dreaded so much. That his perfect son was flawed. He had ignored the signs – the blank looks, the momentary dizziness – and had looked for them in George instead. Waiting for George to grow ill, as his own brothers had. But George was still here and Frederick . . . extinguished suddenly like a bright candle flame.

He broke off from petting the dogs and poured himself a tumbler of whisky. A game of cards would cheer him. Roland Steele always used to be happy to play, in the old days. Perhaps if he rode over to Heathcote now, they could have a game.

The butler put his head discreetly around the door.

'Mr Adrian Steele to see you, sir.'

Gerald was too weary too evince surprise.

'I was just thinking of riding over to see your father,' he said to Adrian. 'Have some whisky.'

'Thank you.' Adrian accepted a glass and stood drinking it in front of the fire. 'I wouldn't bother with Father if I were you,' he said briskly.

'Why not? Is he too ill for a game of cards?'

'Not ill exactly. Demented. 'Senile dementia' is the term, apparently.'

'This afternoon your mother said it was bronchitis.'

'Well . . . the sake of pride, you know.'

'I see . . .'

Gerald went to sit at the chair behind his desk and the dogs followed him, whining. 'Good of you to come and tell me about it.'

'That's not what I'm here for, Captain Colby.'

Adrian's eyes were bright beneath their peculiar pointed brows and he wore a half smile that just revealed the tips of his teeth. There was a restless energy radiating from him that seemed to demand attention, blocking the heat of the fire and leaving Gerald tired and cold.

'Well, what do you want then?'

Adrian and Frederick had been friends. Perhaps he was after some keepsake.

'I want Graylings.'

Gerald laughed drily. 'I see. And I'm to go and camp in a field?'

'Not now. I mean I want you to leave it to me in your will. In place of George—'

Gerald raised his head and looked coldly at Adrian. He was in no mood for wild schemes and Adrian's presence made him yearn to be alone with his grief.

'No, I won't,' he said curtly. 'Would you mind leaving me, Adrian? I want to be on my own.'

Adrian did not move. He smiled, baring his teeth fully.

'You've obviously forgotten. *I saw what happened.*'

Gerald did not understand.

'I saw you shoot Charles Anstey. I was standing behind you. I was the only one who saw.'

The cold, clear February day came to life in Gerald's mind. He could hear the shot, the horrified cries; feel the sticky blood on his fingers. And Frederick . . .

*It was an accident . . .*

Those were the words that came automatically to Gerald's lips and he wanted to say them. But he found that he could not. Not with Adrian Steele staring at him like that. Still not moving.

'Just tell me. Just tell me, that's all I want. I saw what happened, but I want to know what you intended. I want to understand you.'

103

'You'll never understand!' Gerald was sweating now, on his brow and on the palms of his hands. He thought of Frederick smiling at Anstey, smiling . . .

*'You'll never understand!'*

'What was it, something to do with your wife? The cuckold's horns weighing heavy, eh?'

*Frederick, walking briskly through the frozen wood, whistling. Frederick. Alive, whole, perfect. Coming to a halt at Anstey's side. And himself. So afraid he might lose his son . . .*

*Frederick. Dead. Lost for ever. His body a cold useless thing, stiff in its coffin. The deep earth piled above him . . .*

*'No!'* Gerald shouted. *'No!'* He sent his chair hurtling backwards, catching in the folds of the Turkish carpet. 'Just leave me the hell alone. Can't you see——.' He wiped the sweat from his forehead with his cuff. There were tears in his eyes. 'You know that I can't talk about that today. For God's sake!'

'Very well.' Adrian was cool. 'Let's talk about Graylings. I want to help. To save Graylings, if you like. Just tell me what will happen to the place when you die.'

Gerald straightened his chair and sat down again. He seemed relieved to be diverted by material considerations.

'Nominally it will pass to George. But I've mortgaged nearly 10,000 acres and the whole thing would have to be sold. Unless I find a way of repaying it during my lifetime . . .'

'But even if you could,' said Adrian in an even, reasonable tone, 'what would George make of the place? How would he keep it going? You don't *want* George to have it, do you?'

His dark eyes bored into Gerald's face and his angular body, still emitting its exhausting energy, leaned closer.

'No I don't,' admitted Gerald. He sighed heavily, and was silent for a moment. 'It was to be Frederick's, of course. I would have saved it for him somehow, but now—'

'Now I have the money. Money of my own, from my mother. Enough to keep Graylings going and run it as it ought to be run. It just requires your solicitor to change the will in my favour—'

Gerald gave a dry laugh. 'I know I'm not exactly a young man. I'm fifty. But I might live another thirty years.'

'Do you remember asking me once if I liked gambling? I'm prepared to take a chance on . . . the outcome.' Adrian smiled.

'And if I don't do it?'

'There's no need to think about that, Captain Colby. It's the obvious answer. You can forget George, you can forget about the mortgage . . . but I should advise you against losing too much more of the estate. My resources are limited.'

Gerald looked down at Frederick's dogs and could no longer rouse himself to feel anger. There was no reason to care now.

'Very well,' he said slowly, head still bowed. 'You win.'

'Good.'

Adrian stepped back from the desk abruptly.

'When your solicitor has redrafted the will, arrange to have a copy sent to me. Then no more need be said. And there'll be no mention of Anstey either. Goodbye.'

He was walking to the door as he spoke, and was gone before Gerald looked up.

---

# 4

## *Somerset, 23 July, 1915*

In Lucienne Colby's room, a patch of sunlight sparkled on the satin surface of the bed as it would on a sea. With drifts of Nottingham lace for foam.

Lucienne was making the final adjustments to her *toilette*, then she would go down and join the young people.

She liked calling them 'the young people', setting herself apart. At forty-four she was now irrevocably ensconced in middle age and secretly enjoying the role of the dignified matron. It was safe, more comfortable than any she had filled before. People expected less and forgave more. She could preside over the uncertainties of youth with a self-satisfied calm, knowing that her own struggles were over. They had died with Teddy, and in the four years that followed, she had learned acceptance of the ending of love. This acceptance was fuelled by the strange justice that had decreed Teddy should be denied to all women and not only Lucienne. In some unknown place, out of sight, Viola Anstey was bringing up Teddy's child, a girl, alone.

Lucienne had decided on dove-grey chiffon and pearls and a wide-brimmed straw hat which, when viewed in the full-length cheval mirror, gave her a decidedly jaunty air. She felt guilty about enjoying the war. Zeppelin raids had not reached Somerset and so far any food shortages were minor. People were sociable and less inhibited, and there had been an air of celebration after each Allied victory.

And she enjoyed having Graylings to herself. Only a few days after war had been declared, Gerald had arranged to let one of his grain stores as a recruitment office, overseeing the process himself. He had then been requested to go to a camp on the south coast to train new recruits, and from there he had been recommissioned by the Somerset Yeomanry and had sailed for France.

He did not write to her. For years they had circled around one another, avoiding even the most formal of contact. It had started when Teddy was killed and Gerald had sensed that there could be no forgiveness on her part, even though it was an accident. Then, when Frederick died, it was Gerald who withheld forgiveness, silently blaming her for giving birth to a son who would not survive, discounting *her* grief as inferior to his own disappointment and gall.

Gerald had lost interest in Graylings long before he handed it over to a temporary wartime agent, and most of his horses had been sold. To Lucienne, however, Graylings felt like home for the first time, and she could spoil both George and Brittany shamelessly with no one to watch her.

After she had perfected the carefree angle of her straw hat, Lucienne spent several minutes searching for her parasol. Several of the indoor staff had volunteered to fight or, in the case of the women, work in munitions factories, and Lucienne's personal maid now doubled as a parlourmaid. Consequently, her room had become a little untidy and she had to rummage at the bottom of her wardrobe before she located the parasol, faded from the sun and stiff with long disuse.

The young people were sitting on the lawn on the area of grass where baking sun met shade from the low branches of the cedar.

Lucienne stood inside the open French windows and studied them, as a lepidopterist might study a group of rare, brightly coloured butterflies on a particular shrub. The girls were

106

protecting their pale, gauzy dresses by sitting on a rug; all except her own daughter, who was sprawled indolently on her side like some queen from the East. She waved a daisy stalk in an imperious circle above her burnished bronze head. George squatted, eunuch-like, at her side. Adrian Steele was the pasha, sitting at a short distance from the others with his legs crossed, inscrutable. (Lucienne felt glad, not for the first time that day, that his mother was away visiting her grand relatives.)

Eight-year-old Claudia Langbourne had her short legs sticking straight out in front of her on the rug, and she was tousling the ears of one of George's dogs. Maud's son was at the front and Richard was away supervising his factories' adaptation to wartime production, so she had brought the girls to stay at Graylings for a few days. She had also brought two guests of her own, whom Lucienne had never met before. Jennifer Bladon was sitting on the rug next to Susannah Langbourne; demure in a dress of cool, mint green. Her cousin, Randolph de Beer, was obviously considered an ideal marriage prospect for Susannah, and Lucienne suspected that he was at Graylings as part of an underhand series of field trials that Maud was instigating before she pushed her daughter firmly in the right direction. He was a South African, as rich as Croesus and with what Maud primly described as 'financial interests' in the war.

But when Lucienne walked out onto the steps and raised her parasol, thereby shading her eyes from the glare of the sun, she could see quite clearly that Mr de Beer was not paying the necessary attentions to Susannah. He was lying on the grass facing her own daughter, and even from a distance of thirty yards it was possible to see that his eyes were directed at Brittany's face. Then he raised them and saw Lucienne picking her way delicately across the patches of sun-bleached grass.

'Here, comes your mother.'

Lucienne heard him speak, and when she saw his expression as he waited for Brittany's response, she shivered, despite the heat, with vicarious pleasure.

George had tired of listening to Brittany talking to the South African. His own attempts to attract her attention had failed and he was too shy to talk to the others. He did not even dare to look at Susannah.

He put his hands in his pockets and ambled away with the sheepdog at his heels, whistling self-consciously. At fifteen he was tall and had lost some of his plumpness, but his eyes had a permanently worried look. Now, as he walked up the slope of the drive and looked back at the house, he did not see a tempting white sugar lump of a house, but a responsibility that would one day be his. He still felt the quivering of fear in his bowels when he remembered that Frederick was dead.

I won't think about that now, he told himself, I'll think about it later. He stood waiting for his dog to extract itself from the thicket it was rooting in. Then he followed the narrow path that led away from the drive on the righthand side. It led to a small beech copse where Maman had arranged for space to be cleared and a wooden bench placed in strategic position overlooking the house. For both George and Brittany it was a favourite place; but they rarely, if ever, went to the beech copse together. It was a place of private contemplation.

But not today. As George watched the shadows made on the warm wood by the moving beech leaves, and thought about nothing in particular, he heard someone approaching on the path.

It was Susannah.

'I saw you walking up the drive. I hope you don't mind,' she said apologetically.

'No, not at all.'

George's voice was faint. He closed his eyes and held his breath as Susannah sat down only inches away from him, feeling the seat sink slightly under her weight. By the time he opened his eyes, he had been holding his breath for so long that he dared not let it go for fear of making an unseemly gasping noise. He waited for her to speak, his cheeks puffing unnaturally with the effort.

'What a lovely spot this is!' Susannah seemed happily oblivious to his discomfiture. 'I love the way the trees make a screen behind the house. And so many different shades of green!'

'Yes,' said George, releasing his breath in a snort.

'We were discussing what we ought to do this afternoon. We thought we ought to stay out of doors, since it's so fine. Randolph suggested a game of croquet.'

'Are you going to marry him?' asked George, allowing the words to escape before he had a chance to check them, and then wishing he hadn't spoken. He blushed violently.

Susannah turned to look at him, moving her head into the light so that her hair looked almost pure white, and the sun sparkled fiercely on the gold crucifix at her throat. She did not seem offended.

'I'm only eighteen, George. And besides,' she added soberly, 'I don't think this is a time to be thinking about such things. Perhaps when the war's over . . .'

'But they think it could go on a long time now, don't they?'

'Yes, they do.'

Both fell silent. Susannah was thinking of her brother Johnnie, and of the slaughter at Neuve Chapelle in March of that year, by which time half of the men who had enlisted were reputed to be either dead or wounded.

George was wondering what he would do if the war was still being fought when he reached his eighteenth birthday, and which was worse, the responsibility of the estate, or being a soldier.

'So, what do you think, George?'

'What?'

George looked up, embarrassed. He had been staring at the fragile gold bracelet on her tapered arm. Several times during the silence it had fallen down over her wrist, and he abandoned his thoughts of inglorious war to watch the replacing of the bracelet, watched it tightening her soft flesh as she pushed it impatiently up her arm again and then waited for it to loosen . . . and for the inevitable fall.

'What do *you* think we should do this afternoon?'

'Oh. A picnic.'

'A picnic! What a good idea, George!'

Susannah took hold of his hand and the bracelet rubbed against his skin. 'Come on, let's tell the others about your idea.'

'I'd rather you told them,' he said desperately.

Susannah laughed. 'Very well. I'll put it to them. On one condition: if they agree, then you have to confess that it was your idea.'

George followed her meekly down the drive, quaking with dread at the prospect of being the instigator of a Good Idea.

Brittany held out her napkin and wiped a smear of custard from George's chin; absently, as though he were a child.

They had carried the hamper, the rugs and cushions and the

precious gramophone to one of the meadows that lay between the house and the Home Farm. The girls' skirts had made an intimate little sound as they brushed through the waist-high stalks, a sound barely audible above the humming of insects in air choked with the ugly-sweet smell of cow parsley. A white linen cloth had been spread on a patch of stubble, and on its uneven surface were bottles of lemonade, the remains of a cold chicken and a bowl of sherry trifle.

Brittany sat in the shade of a chestnut tree at the edge of the meadow and watched Adrian Steele throwing a ball for George's dog. Everyone else was resting in the hope of combating at least some of the effects of rich food and strong sunshine. But Adrian was throwing the ball with all his force, dodging from side to side to deceive the animal, sometimes running impatiently to retrieve the ball himself. The sleeves of his flannel shirt were rolled back, and the muscles of his forearms were visible as he drew back his shoulder to throw, shifting slightly under the skin. The harsh light of early afternoon masked the white that was beginning to appear in his black hair and turned him into a boy again; a boy intent and serious in his game.

Brittany could never understand Adrian's odd combination of vitality and destructiveness. All that energy. It should have been infectious. Yet it only made more obvious the traits she did not like, and left her oppressed by a negative feeling she could never entirely shake off. Earlier that day, for example, Maman and Maud had been discussing improvements that Maman could make at Graylings while Papa was away, and Adrian had interrupted with a suggestion of his own. He had insisted that Maman should install the new automatic gaslights, lecturing at length on their convenience and the attractive appearance of the little chains which were pulled to make the light come on. There had been an assumed authority in his voice that annoyed Brittany. Why should he care what Maman did in the house, and what business was it of his, anyway?

'I hope you're not planning to spend the whole afternoon staring at another man?'

Randolph de Beer was at her elbow.

Brittany sighed. 'I was just wishing I could like him better.'

'Cousin Jennifer seems to like him well enough. And she's in need of a husband.'

Randolph's laugh sounded cruel. Brittany looked at him thoughtfully but did not reply, turning instead to consider Jennifer. She was a few years older than Brittany; tiny and pretty, with dark hair and dark skin so even in texture and tone that she appeared to be modelled from pale clay. Since her arrival at Graylings she had said very little above conventional pleasantries and Brittany had dismissed her as dull and insipid. Now, seeing the determinedly proprietary look in Jennifer's eye as she watched Adrian's endeavours, she was not so sure.

'It's unbelievable, isn't it, all this?' Randolph made a broad gesture with his arm, which encompassed the leaf-laden chestnut tree, the basking meadow and the Somerset wetlands in general.

'Unbelievable?'

'That England is at war. But, of couse, it's a characteristic of your national *hubris* not only to think that England is the best country in the world, but also that wars are distant things, fought by other people in other places. When I see a sight as beautiful as this, it's easy to see how that smugness came about.'

Brittany opened her mouth to retort angrily, then hesitated, lowering her heavy lids at him.

'That's a pretty speech coming from a *profiteer*.'

She mouthed the word lightly, delicately, as though it were a cake offered at a vicarage tea party.

Randolph looked amused.

'Oh, so I'm a "profiteer", am I? If your experience of the war were not so limited then you might side with the people who see us profiteers as necessary.'

'My experience of the war has been pretty feeble,' said Brittany honestly. 'And I wish that weren't the case.'

'Surely there's work you can do?'

'I wanted to go and work in France, but I'm not old enough. I asked if I could go and help in the nearest military hospital and Maman couldn't decide on her own, so she said she'd ask Maud what she thought. Maud said that she would never hear of Susannah doing that sort of work; that it wasn't suitable for 'girls of our class'. So I have to be content with helping Maman at the Good Works Group and the Hospital Committee. It consists mainly of bandage-rolling and listening to the women capping each other's stories about their wonderful, brave sons.'

Randolph put a hand on her wrist.

111

'Don't frown like that. You look so attractive when you smile.'

Brittany obliged him. She found *him* attractive too. He was handsome, quickwitted and, despite his cynicism, charming. But it was more than that. He reminded her of Teddy. He had the same tall, loose-limbed build, the same golden blond hair. His eyes were paler than Teddy's and his skin was tanned to a dark brown by years in the African sun.

'Brittany, come on – we're packing up to go back now!'

Susannah beckoned urgently. She was kneeling on the ground, folding the white linen cloth into a neat square. Brittany's smile was returned, but her own was cool and tight-lipped, and she was looking in Randolph's direction.

That evening, Brittany slipped away from the after-dinner revels and went to sit alone in the arcane shadows of the conservatory. She was thinking about the pressure of Randolph's hand on her wrist, and about the look on Susannah's face.

On many occasions since the beginning of their friendship, Brittany had been tempted to offend Susannah's coy prudishness. Encouraging Randolph de Beer's attentions had been a part of that irrepressible urge. But it was becoming something different. It had been there on Susannah's face. She wanted Randolph.

And Brittany realized *she* wanted him too.

It had nothing to do with marriage. But once, when he passed close to her, she thought she could smell him, smell the faint warmth of his flesh, and when she thought of that now, she felt her pulse quicken.

There was no mystery about it now. Ruth Morgan had lent Maman a copy of Elinor Glyn's scandalous *Three Weeks*, and when she and George had finished reading it, they were no longer in doubt about the things that had puzzled them. And now *she* wanted to lie on a tiger skin, like the queen in the story. She laughed aloud at the thought, leaning back in her wicker chair and hooking her feet up on the rim of the window seat in front of her, so that the skirt of her dress fell back at an indecorous angle. She laughed at the moon, hanging in the sky like a silver coin, so bright it appeared to quiver.

Then he came into the conservatory and stood in front of her.

112

Moonlight was thin gruel after the rich, burning July sun, but it made him shine the way Teddy did when he came into her room on the night before he died.

'You've come,' she said, just as she had said to Teddy, and reached out her arms to him. His cheek was cool against her own, then his lips warm as he kissed her.

She laughed again, this time at Randolph's surprise when she whispered, 'I'm sorry, there's no tiger skin.'

It was all George's fault.

Adrian had intended to follow Brittany as soon as she left the room, but at that precise moment, George asked him if he would play billiards and he could find no excuse, even though his days of buttering up George Colby were over.

As soon as he could, Adrian contrived to end the game. He started to search the house for her, with a methodical thoroughness befitting a future owner of the property.

She was in the conservatory.

He caught sight of her dress first, a shimmering column of light among shiny dark leaves. It was made from pale crêpe de chine the colour of magnolia flowers, and sewn all over with tiny crystal beads. He was so preoccupied, so *impressed* with the way it moulded to her figure that at first he did not even notice that she was not alone. Until her back arched in pleasure.

He watched them through the glass door of the conservatory. She was standing with her back to Adrian, but her movements betrayed pleasure and he knew that her mouth would be as hungry as de Beer's, just as he knew that de Beer's hands were pressing and moulding her breasts, teasing her nipples. The hands started to touch her hair. She wore it 'up' nowadays, a rather precarious arrangement due to its weight. But now the pins were being loosened and the whole shining mass, the colour of polished brass, was slaking the thirst of those fingers.

Adrian moved his hand out, as though the glass were not there and he could touch the two people on the other side. He could hear the thin metallic sound of hairpins falling on the Italian mosaic floor. He could breathe the thick, warm air of the conservatory, scented with orangeblossom and stifling dampness.

Then Brittany began to shake her hair in a cloud around her

113

shoulder's, the brittle ends flying out. *Stop!*, he longed to say, *Stop, don't do that!*'

Instead he turned and ran blindly in the opposite direction, shaking with anger and violent lust.

He found himself under the eye of the dome in the hall. There was someone standing on the staircase.

Jennifer.

He had barely noticed her all day. But now he saw that her evening dress was cut low to reveal small, haughty breasts.

'I, er . . . where are you going?' he asked stupidly.

'I was on my way up to bed.'

'Oh, I'm sorry, I—'

*Let me touch you,* he wanted to say, *please let me touch you.* He was so hot, and her pale brown skin looked so smooth and cool.

Then she said the most surprising thing he had ever heard.

'Were you thinking of coming up there with me?'

She looked at him expectantly. He found himself walking up the stairs and kissing her roughly, pressing his mouth down until his teeth were tearing at the edges of her lips. But she lost none of her composure. She took his hand and led him up to her bedroom.

As soon as he had closed the door she locked her arms around his neck and pushed her doll-like face into his, opening her mouth, teasing with her tongue. There was a look of determined concentration on her face which did not go away, even when he pushed her onto the bed and began to fumble desperately under her petticoats, sliding his thigh over hers.

'I had no idea,' he gasped afterwards. 'Today, I mean. I had no idea that that was what you wanted.'

'Oh yes,' she said, smiling for the first time, 'that's exactly what I wanted.'


## New York, 23 July, 1915

'It's really going to be something, isn't it?' Isaac clapped a plump hand on his son's shoulder.

'Yes,' agreed David. 'Yes, yes it is. Really something.'

Christ, he thought, I wish Papa would hurry up. He must be doing it on purpose . . .

They were inspecting a plot of land on Wall Street that was to be

114

the site of the new Stein bank building. At the moment it was just a heap of rubble where an old warehouse had been demolished. David had followed Isaac over the uneven ground for a weary hour and a half, listening to his plans for the site, pandering to his grandiose vision in the hope that he would be finished all the quicker . . .

The paternal hand on his left shoulder seemed heavy, oppressive. He couldn't move without Isaac feeling the movement. And he couldn't glance at his watch, which was on his left wrist, without Isaac noticing:

He was going to be late . . .

'This area will be the reception hall,' said Isaac, waving his free hand at a heap of stones, tightening his hold on David with the other. 'And behind that, a formal entertaining area—'

'Papa, oughtn't we to be getting back now. Mother—'

'Why the hurry. Do you have another engagement?'

They left the site at nine o'clock, returning to Fifth Avenue as it was growing dark. David stood in the hall and waited for his father to climb the stairs to the first floor, and to call for a footman to bring him a drink in his study. Then he opened the front door as quietly as possible and ran down the steps into the street.

*Halleluyah*! he wanted to shout, *Free at last*! He felt as jubilant and light-hearted as a schoolboy escaping the classroom. Without glancing back at the house, he headed for East 55th Street at a brisk trot.

Ginnie Cassidy was holding a soirée, what she liked to call a 'little party'. David had been to them before, and they were always the same. Lawyers, politicians and civic dignitaries huddled in sheepish groups, trying to look anonymous. And *she* would be there. Dulcibel.

The party was in full swing by the time David arrived. Ginnie was sitting at the white piano playing a whimsical popular song. She was dressed in olive green silk, with a confection of brilliantly coloured plumage in her vivid red hair. When she saw David she stopped playing and came towards him, waving a Spanish fan to and fro over her broad expanse of bosom. It was a humid evening and her powdered skin looked warm and damp.

Isaac's procrastination had left David burning with impatience. 'Where is she, Ginnie?'

Ginnie's fan fluttered. 'My, my, we're in a hurry, aren't we?

115

This is supposed to be a party you know, *select*, not—'

But David was already searching the groups of white-gowned girls who were helping the maids to hand round glasses of champagne and trays of cakes. And there she was.

She called herself Dulcibel, but it was probably not her real name. She was the girl who had enjoyed David's virginal embrace on his first visit to Ginnie's and he had asked for her again when he returned with a wallet full of dollars, out of curiosity. When he stepped into the green bedroom for the second time, he had been determined to acquit himself well and make more of an impression. He had succeeded, but his thirst for this most unimpressionable of girls had not been quenched and he had returned again and again, giving way to physical infatuation. Ginnie did not foster a system of favourites, but because David was so young she relented, encouraged by the seemingly endless supply of dollar bills that he brought. Hannah Stein had opened a bank account for him on his eighteenth birthday and paid money into it regularly, quite innocent of the fact that the payments were being continually called upon to satisfy her son's lust.

Dulcibel greeted David with her usual reserve. Although she regarded him as her own special property, it was not in her nature to be demonstrative, and her playfulness was all acquired, a skill of her trade. She was secretly glad that he had come, but would not have dreamed of saying so. She was proud, and all too well aware that as client and employee, they would only meet when it suited David.

Tonight he was appraising her so frankly that she forgot the desired *hauteur* and met his gaze with her lop-sided grin. She was not exactly pretty, but there was something self-contained about her face which excited his imagination. Her eyes were such a dark shade of brown that he could not see into them to read what she was thinking, and her dyed blonde hair waved about her head with a life of its own. She was dressed in white eyelet lace, fastened tightly about her midriff and cut away at the front to expose most of her large breasts. David felt hot as he glimpsed tiny circles of naked flesh through the holes in the lace. They seemed to press and strain to escape confinement.

*Christ! How long is it since I've been here? Two weeks? Three weeks? How on earth have I managed to do without her . . .*

It was always like this. He could go for weeks without giving

116

Dulcibel a thought, while she waited patiently for his visits. And yet when he was here . . .

'Dulcie,' he said urgently, 'we're going upstairs now.'

'But you've only just arrived!' She feigned indignation. 'Miss Ginnie does have some rules, you know. At these affairs you're expected to stay around for a while and talk nicely, just like we was at a real party, you know, a polite affair . . .'

Still protesting, she followed him out of the room.

Their lovemaking was every bit as passionate as David had imagined it would be, but as he followed Dulcibel down the stairs afterwards, he knew that it had been curtailed too soon. His eyes were fixed on the tiny naked circles on her back and he still wanted her. When they reached the foot of the stairs, he made his wishes known.

'Not here, we can't—'

'Why not?'

'But Ginnie—'

'To the devil with Ginnie! I pay her for this, don't I?'

Dulcibel was delighted. 'My green-eyed Jew . . .' she murmured, pulling his face down to hers, kissing him voraciously. She liked David best like this; uncompromising, possessive.

She began to rock back and forth against him, busying her fingers in a teasing game, moaning slightly as her own impatience grew. David pushed her back against the polished wooden pillar at the end of the banister, and raised her skirts. The candles in the chandelier above his head burned down through the stiflingly still air, scorching the skin on the back of his neck as he bent over Dulcibel.

'No, we can't . . .'

'I thought we were in agreement about this . . .' David reached to unbuckle his belt.

Dulcibel's body tensed beneath him.

'David, there's a man there – behind you!' she hissed.

'Well, what does he expect in a whorehouse? He'll go away.'

'No, he's staring at you.'

David glanced over his shoulder and saw the man.

Papa.

Isaac did not speak. He gave his son a curt nod, and with a

look of utter contempt on his face he turned on his heel and walked to the front door.

David released his hold on Dulcibel so abruptly that she fell hard against the pillar and stared at him in anger and amazement.

'Wait there. I'll be back in a minute.'

David ran out into the street. Isaac was climbing into his car.

'Papa! What the hell are you doing?'

Isaac curled his lips in an ugly smile. 'Not sampling the wares, if that's what you think. Whatever else I may be, I'm not a hypocrite.'

'You followed me here, didn't you?'

Isaac shrugged.

'You were *spying* on me!'

'Perhaps. But that's not the issue here. The issue is this: do you want me to tell your mother what you've been doing? Spending her money, I presume? . . .'

David opened his mouth to protest, but Isaac ignored him and went on, '. . . Very well. In that case you will get in the car with me now. And you will never come here again.'

David thought about Dulcibel, leaning against the post at the bottom of the stairs, her skin oily with sweat and her lace dress in splendid disarray. His body was longing for her even now.

'What if I don't?'

'Then you will break your mother's heart. And you will cease to live under my roof.'

David sighed and walked down the steps to the car. They sat in silence until it drew up in Fifth Avenue. Then Isaac leaned across and covered David's hand with one of his fat, freckled ones.

'Look, David, if it's a woman you want, you should have told me. I would have understood. But not *there*. It's too well known. People will see you and talk, and it might get back to your mother. I'll tell you what . . .' He applied pressure with his hand. 'Next time you want . . . let me know about it and maybe I can arrange something, for both of us together . .'

David pushed his father's hand away and climbed out of the car, slinging his jacket over one shoulder.

'What's that, if not hypocrisy?' he asked levelly. 'Your suggestion disgusts me. But even if it didn't, you don't think I'd come to you, do you? You may control my public life, but you're not going to control my private life.'

'That's what you think,' said Isaac.


Jake Stein frowned as he knocked at his brother's door. He was very unhappy about the task he had been given.

David was sitting on the edge of his bed.

'You're here to talk me into it, aren't you?' he said straightaway.

'Yes,' said Jake, sitting down beside him on the bed.

'She's down there, isn't she?'

'Yes, they're all down there.'

David stood up abruptly and walked to the window, where darkness was closing in on the brilliant summer green of the trees in the avenue.

'Damn him, Jake!'

He slapped his hand hard against glass that was sealed tight against the dust. 'Well, if you've come to make a speech, I suppose you'd better get on and make it.'

Jake sighed.

'All right.' He looked around his brother's room. It had pale blue walls and handsome, expensive leather furniture. The desk in the corner was piled with books and papers. David was ostensibly studying languages before he started work at Stein and Sons, but Jake knew that he spent most of his time reading and scribbling.

'Very well,' he continued, opening a silver case and lighting a cigarette ponderously, 'I was asked to talk you into agreeing to become engaged to Rebecca Garber, and I said I would. But I want you to realize that it's not Papa speaking now, it's me – Jake.'

'So you're telling me you think this engagement is a good idea?'

'Yes, given your situation. The only way to win with Papa is by playing his game. Just look on this as a way to buy time. If you agree to marry Rebecca you'll have him off your back for a while. He'll leave you alone. You're only nineteen, and no one's suggesting that a marriage should take place for several years yet. Anything could happen. Engagements can always be broken . . .' Jake inhaled heavily on his cigarette and stared at the ceiling. '. . . So I think it's in your interest to agree.'

'Well, if that's the case, why haven't you agreed to marry Miriam Abelson yet?'

'Because I've never had to. I've never gone sneaking off to

Ginnie Cassidy's house, for example . . .'

'. . . Though you might have liked to,' prompted David.

'. . . Though I might have liked to.' Jake exhaled smoke through an ironic smile. 'I haven't had to marry Miriam because I've never made it look as though I'm in danger of doing anything else.'

'Yet.'

'Yet. So, what do you say, David? Are you going to give Papa what he wants this time?'

'I suppose so,' said David reluctantly. He walked to the mirror and straightened his bow tie. 'Did you say the party had already started? We'd better go down then.'

Jake stood beside him and looked at their two reflections: David's dark curly hair and impish expression and his own straight, sombre brown.

'We look a couple of real swells!' said David cheerfully. 'Come on, then, let's get it over with!'

Downstairs, the family and guests were gathered in the grandest of the formal reception rooms. Thick crimson velvet curtains had been drawn across the thirty-feet-tall windows, making the room airless and hot. According to family tradition, special occasions demanded candles, so the group who had gathered at the centre of the vast room were outlined by a faint, flickering light. A small forest of candles was banked on several silver trays that had been placed on side tables around the edge of the room.

As David and Jake approached, there was a scuffling and a few people began to clap.

'Champagne, everybody!' Isaac cried magnanimously, bouncing his short body on his heels as he beckoned to the footman to bring trays of champagne glasses. 'We have a very important toast to drink tonight, my friends. But first, where are the two young people in question?'

He beckoned to David to come and stand on his left, and then held out his hand to a girl who had been standing shyly at the back of the group, positioning her at his right.

David turned to look at his future wife with what amounted to little more than passing curiosity. Rebecca Garber was seventeen and excessively timid. David's first thought was that she could not have been more different from Dulcibel, and thereafter he could not get the idea out of his mind, comparing Rebecca's meekly girlish body to Dulcibel's voluptuousness; her red-brown hair and open, pleasant face to Dulcibel's furtively beautiful one.

'We are gathered here,' Isaac went on, beaming with self-satisfaction, '. . . to celebrate the betrothal of these two young people. It's a doubly happy occasion for me, since it not only assures a happy future for our youngest son David—'

He hugged David to illustrate his point, and Hannah Stein smiled tenderly.

'—but also it joins my family with that of Solly Garber here. Solly is not only my oldest and dearest friend, but a partner in my bank, and for this reason . . .'

As Isaac droned on, David stopped studying his shoes and looked to his brother, hoping to catch his eye. He saw Jake frowning soberly into his glass of champagne and then . . . there it was.

Barely discernible, but a wink, nonetheless.

## London, 30 September, 1915

'*My dear Adrian* . . .'

Jennifer frowned down at the words. No, that did not sound right. She screwed the piece of paper into a ball and took a fresh sheet.

'*Dear Adrian.*'

That was better. She continued.

'*You will no doubt be surprised to hear from me like this, but I have something that I wish to say to you* . . .'

Jennifer put the pen down carefully and looked around the room: a book-lined study in a fashionable part of London, furnished to imitate a room in a comfortable country parsonage, from the heavy brass fender with its padded leather seat to the eighteenth-century oil paintings of prize cattle. A pleasant room. But not hers.

Since her mother's death, three years ago, Jennifer had been living in the house of elderly relations, acting as a companion. And since she was thoroughly dissatisfied with her lot, she decided to take steps to amend it. Just as her mother would have done.

Mrs Bladon had been the daughter of a Jewish tailor, who transcended her origins sufficiently to marry a well-connected

Anglican clergyman with prospects of a bishopric. He died before attaining this end, leaving his wife to instil in Jennifer the evils of penury and the importance of the security of marriage.

Jennifer learned her lesson well. After her mother died and she moved to London, she wasted no time in finding out the whereabouts of her father's rich relations. To her dismay, she discovered that they had left England for South Africa, where they had bought mines. Undeterred, she wrote to them conveying good wishes and veiled hints about her plight. Her efforts were eventually rewarded. Two years later she received a letter saying that her cousin Randolph was visiting London and wished to make her acquaintance. He introduced the twenty-two-year-old Jennifer to the Langbournes, who generously invited her to join them on their trip to Somerset. And so she had met Adrian Steele.

Though stubborn and strongminded, Jennifer decided that it would be to her advantage not to draw attention to herself while she was in Somerset. She would then be able to watch and listen and make a decision about how best to take advantage of her situation. Accordingly, she said little above what politeness required.

She was instantly impressed by Graylings. Its classical lines had an effortless superiority that the late Mrs Bladon would have greatly admired. The heir, George Colby, did not share this virtue, however. He was still young, it was true, but even a brief acquaintance convinced Jennifer that he would never amount to anything, and was therefore not the sort of person she would have cared to marry. Besides, she did not have time to wait for a boy to grow up. Johnnie Langbourne had sounded very promising, but his absence in the trenches made him an impractical proposition, even for someone with Jennifer's letter-writing skills.

That left Adrian Steele.

The contrast with George Colby could not have been more striking. All his movements were generated by an impatient, suppressed energy. He was not given to sitting still. This pleased Jennifer, who was forced to spend more time than she liked sitting still and quiet, doing nothing in particular. She found him handsome, too, in an animal way.

By listening to the chatter of the others, she slowly built a picture of his circumstances, and was satisfied with the construction. He was the only son of a titled lady, living in a manor house and owning land. And he was unattached. The neatness of events was surpassed only by the ease with which he succumbed to her compromising invitation. This surprised her, but she accepted it as part of the satisfactory pattern.

She picked up her pen and turned her attention to the letter again.

'*I have no alternative but to tell you that I am expecting your child. I realize that this will come as a shock to you, as it has to me. My circumstances are that I am the dependent relative of an elderly couple, so you will understand that I have no choice but to rely on your support. Perhaps it would be possible for us to meet and discuss this matter . . .*'

## Somerset, 3 October, 1915

Lady Henrietta Steele had begun the day in a decidedly ill temper.

The patience that had sustained her for over twenty years was running out. Life at Heathcote House had deteriorated beyond her worst expectations. Not only was it damp and dreary, it was now dirty as well. She had lost almost all her staff to the war effort, and begrudged spending the precious money that she saved for Adrian on the high wages that were now demanded. Consequently she had only a cook and one maid, who was too busy chaperoning Lady Steele's confused and, by now, incontinent husband to find time to clean the house.

She made no comment when her son abruptly left the dining room with the letter he had just received. She sat in front of a yellowing and decayed-looking piece of smoked haddock and waited for him to return. She knew that he would before long, and that he would tell her about the letter then.

Porphyrus was often used to exorcize Adrian's anger. As the belligerent, square-shouldered grey had grown older, his temper had grown worse. Adrian had taken to wearing a pair of spurs on his riding boots, and he dug them cruelly into Porphyrus' sides as they left the lane for the open ground of the Mendips. He urged the horse to an insane pace, daring him to unseat his rider, and the clods of dew-sodden earth that the furious hooves threw up spattered his face and clothes. By the time the horse was exhausted, he had made his decision.

123

He would marry Jennifer.

He had no choice. If he impregnated her and then abandoned her, he would never win the acceptance of people like the Langbournes; Graylings or no Graylings. He had no wish to dwell there in splendid isolation, shunned by people who were willing to think the worst of his mistakes. Eventually he would need a wife, and it was increasingly obvious that the role was not to be filled by Brittany Colby. Jennifer Bladon would do as well as any.

He turned Porphyrus round and returned to the house to tell his mother the news.

'You've got mud on your clothes,' she said without looking at him, reaching up to her hair, which was now clouded with grey.

'Mama . . . I'm going to get married. Soon.'

'I see. I take it you've just been to visit Brittany?'

'Brittany? No – I'm not marrying Brittany, Mama.'

'Indeed?' Lady Henrietta's voice was cold now, and still. 'And who is the lucky young lady?'

'She's called Jennifer Bladon. I . . we met at Graylings in the summer. I've just heard from her, and you may as well know, since we've always been open with one another, that she's expecting a baby.'

Lady Henrietta recoiled slightly, blinking and pressing her lips into a tight line. But her peculiarly acid brand of sangfroid did not desert her for long.

'I'm surprised at this naïve attitude, Adrian, I must say. One doesn't necessarily *marry* the girls one gets into trouble. One provides them with money. It will make a dent in your inheritance, but I dare say there'll be enough for—'

'It's you who are naïve, Mama!' said Adrian angrily. He threw his crop onto the table and dropped heavily into a chair. 'I can't just buy her off! She's not that sort of girl. She comes from a decent family . . . and, anyway, they'll know.'

'Who will?'

'The Colbys. They'll get to hear of it eventually. Do you think Brittany would marry me then?'

'She certainly can't if you're married to somebody else, can she? And I'll tell you this, Adrian . . .'

Lady Henrietta stabbed vindictively with her fork at the offending piece of haddock.

'. . . If you think that after forgoing my comforts all these years

I'm going to let my money be wasted on raising a herd of brats . . .'

'There won't be a herd, Mama. Just one. I'll marry her and then sign up with the volunteer forces, as I intended to. Jennifer can live here and give you some help around the—'

'But that money was for *Graylings*! Don't you understand? For *Graylings*!'

Lady Henrietta's voice became a pitiful screech and she stabbed the haddock brutally for emphasis with each mention of the trophy now lost.

Adrian bent and tugged off one-splattered boot. He was smiling. Surprised at his confidence, his mother leaned forward to read the secretive depths of his dark eyes.

'Did you hear me?'

'Yes, I heard you, Mama. And I'm going to own Graylings, don't you worry.'

'How?' Lady Henrietta's blue eyes were glassy and unblinking.

Adrian threw his boots to the floor and the spur rattled triumphantly.

'There *is* a way, Mama. I've already found it.'

## 5

### Arras, 27 March, 1918

The rain was unceasing.

Gerald Colby trudged along a disused railway track, sliding occasionally on a surface made slimy with rain and mud. Were he to walk down the same track in a few months time, the air would be sweet with the smell of wild herbs crushed underfoot. It was difficult to decide which was worse: winter warfare, when they lived in the scummy, fetid, rain-filled trenches like rats in a sewer, or the pity of war in the summer when apples went unpicked, farms and barns were gutted and the sun blazed down on fields of corn that would never be harvested.

Gerald had gone out walking as evening approached. He often went out by himself, despite the rain, just to escape the smells and sounds of the support trenches and the constant demands of his men. Not that they would ever ask for his help out loud. But the combined trust and dumb suffering in their eyes tore at his nerves.

By the time he returned to the officers' dug-out, it was almost dark. He sank down in a chair with a sigh. Here, at least, there was a floor beneath his feet. And bunks, and a table; even a gramophone. Hendry, his batman, lit the camp stove with loving care and lifted the battered tin kettle as tenderly as if it were a baby.

'Shall I do you a cup of tea, sir?'

'In a minute. I want to do the rounds first. Is Lieutenant Gittings about?'

'I haven't seen him this evening, sir.'

'Well, if you do, tell him I was looking for him.'

Gerald put on his cap and set off on a routine inspection of his men. There was very little he could do to improve their living conditions, but he liked to think that their morale was lifted by his concern for their equipment, and their feet. Feet were highly regarded by the British Army. Usually the men liked to laugh and joke about the sacred nature of their extremities, but tonight as Gerald checked that their feet were oiled and dressed in clean socks, the men were subdued. There was a tense, unnatural silence hanging over them. They had heard the same rumours that Gerald had heard.

The Germans were about to launch a major offensive on their section of the line.

When Gerald returned to the dug-out, he found Gittings waiting for him.

Second Lieutenant John Gittings was twenty-four years old. He had a pale, freckled face with large, eager eyes and a thatch of sandy hair. His bride, Emma, had been left behind with a newborn son, but his stoic cheerfulness was never daunted. Indeed, Gerald had come to rely on it as a life-enhancing force.

He sprang to his feet when Gerald entered the dug-out.

'You wanted to see me, Major?'

'Yes, yes, I—'

Gerald broke off, suddenly aware that he too was affected by the terrible suspense that hung over his troops.

'Sit down, will you, Gittings. I thought we might have a game of cards.'

It had become a habit of Gerald's to ask his junior officer to play cards with him in the evening. He sensed that Gittings did not enjoy their games much, but was complying to humour him. Tonight, as they sat on either side of the small, square table, his pulse was throbbing.

'Let's have a little bet tonight, Gittings.'

Gittings laughed good-naturedly.

'I'm not sure what we can use as stakes. I've very little pay left. No cash, at least.'

'Well, we'll use what we have, and then we can put in personal effects: watches, trinkets.'

Gittings hestitated. 'Oh, all right then. A bit of sport before battle, eh?'

Hendry lit a lamp for them and they began to play. The game was five-card stud, and Gerald wasted no time in putting all his money to the centre of the table, confident in his greater experience as a card player, and warming himself in the cold, dank dug-out with the tawdry seduction of chance. Gittings quickly ran out of money and reluctantly put a gold watch on the table.

There was one last call before they declared their hands, but now Gerald, too, had run out of money. He searched the pockets of his uniform for something that he could use as a stake. He had a silver cigarette case, but it was old, battered and worthless; a mean gesture after Gitting's gold watch. That left only one thing. He looked at the ring on the little finger of his left hand. It was a gold signet ring engraved with the family crest. He had given it to Frederick on his eighteenth birthday, and Frederick had been wearing it when he died . . .

And what if Frederick had survived? He would have wanted to fight for his country, naturally. Would he have been mown down by the fire of German guns in some stinking trench?

He put the ring onto the pile in the middle of the table.

'Who shows first?' asked Gittings nervously.

'I will,' said Gerald. He laughed. 'But I doubt you can do better than this.'

He laid down a full house of queens and jacks.

Gittings looked at the cards with his wide, solemn eyes and a faint pinkness crept over his freckled face.

'I think I *have* done better.' He laid down a royal flush. 'Are aces high?'

They sat drinking brandy late into the night, talking, waiting for the burst of shell-fire. Eventually Gittings stood up with a sigh and walked to the door of the dug-out.

'Time I went to bed, Major Colby.' He rattled the coins that weighed down his pocket. 'This money . . . I'm not really supposed to keep it, am I?'

'Of course. Winner takes all. That was the understanding when we started.' He gave a short, dry laugh. 'Put it towards your son's education.'

Gittings reached into his pocket. 'This ring, though . . .' He held it out towards Gerald. 'It was your son's, wasn't it?' he asked gently.

Gerald nodded.

'Please take it back. I couldn't keep it.'

'It's yours now,' said Gerald gruffly.

'Well, in that case, I'm giving it to you. As a gift.'

He held out the ring.

There was a long silence. Light from the oil lamp glinted on the smooth, gold surface. Then Gerald reached out and took the ring, folding it reverently in the palm of his hand.

'Thank you, Gittings. That's very decent of you.'

It started the next day.

The smoke and the chaos, shrieks and groans, and the incredible noise of ceaseless bombardment. The whistle of shells and the thud as they hit their target. Mud on the floor of the trenches, curdling with blood and vomit . . .

The British forces were strong at Arras and the Germans failed to break the line, but the casualties were heavy. The men on the higher ground in front of the trenches, up to their knees in slime, were an easy target for the Germans. Gerald watched them rushing up against the barbed wire to be riddled with bullets and hang there, like rags on a clothes line. The dead did not fall off the wire. It's true, thought Gerald, clenching Frederick's ring into his fist.

Hell exists.

As it grew dark, he went out to hunt for his men. He made slow progress at first, staggering in the craters made by shells, temporarily deaf and stunned. The men he found were all dead.

He could not tell how much ground he had covered, or how many corpses he had counted by the time he decided to make his way back to the lines. He was only aware of a burning pain in his right shoulder, and a desperate need to rest his legs. Eventually he found a place, crouching behind a line of damp sandbags. As his eyes slowly grew accustomed to the darkness, he realized he was not, after all, alone in this silent, corpse-strewn hell. He could make out the shape of another man.

At the same moment, they both snatched their rifles.

Then Gerald went limp with relief.

'Gittings!'

'Major Colby! Thank God for that. I thought you were a German!'

'And I was about to blast your head off!'

'Here,' said Gittings, 'I've got some drink in my hip flask, and some rations. Would you like to share them with me?'

They ate in silence. There was nothing to be said about the day's events that had not been said before on other occasions like this. And silence seemed better suited to an unexpected moment of comradeship whose taste was sweet.

After they had eaten, they decided to make their way back to where the company was entrenched. But by now the firing had started again and they were forced to crawl on their bellies. As they lay side by side, Gerald was aware of Gittings peering solicitiously at his wounded shoulder.

'You're losing blood,' he whispered. 'We ought to rest, or you'll never get there.'

Gerald allowed himself to be guided to a mound of sandbags, just visible in the darkness, and fell into an exhausted sleep.

When he woke a few hours later, it was quiet again. And the moonlight was so bright that he could see that he was not leaning on sandbags, but on a bank of dead bodies. Gittings was still next to him.

'John,' he whispered, not quite sure why he was using the man's first name.

Then he saw what had happened.

They had lain down next to an unexploded shell. He must have been so deeply asleep that he did not hear the muffled explosion.

Gittings was lying dead, with his entrails hanging out.

\*

129

The wound that Gerald had sustained was only superficial. After it had been bandaged it no longer hampered his movement, and on the day after he returned to his company's trenches, he set about the cheerless task of repairing them in preparation for the next bombardment.

That evening, Hendry came into his dug-out, holding out a small packet rather self-consciously.

'Sir, these papers belonged to Lieutenant Gittings. I thought you might want to pass them on his widow, sir,'

When he was alone, Gerald sat down to look at the packet. It contained a curl of baby hair and a wedding photograph. The earnest, freckled face smiled out happily. And there was a letter. Gerald opened it and began to read.

*'My darling Emma. Thank you so much for your recent letter. I hope you won't believe too many of the dreadful things you hear. Life here isn't really too bad. Our men are some of the best, and Colby, our commanding officer, is a good chap.*

*But I hate the war, Emma. I hate what it does to people. The other day I found a doll lying in the mud. It had a drop of rain on its upturned face, just like a tear. I caught myself wondering whether it belonged to an English child or a German child, and then I realized what that meant. That in war, children suffer just the same, whatever side they're on. It made what we grown men are doing seem so meaningless.*

*I just tell myself that I'm doing it for you, and for baby John. So that there will be a future for you both. That continuity has become so important to me now; knowing that a way of life will be allowed to continue because we have fought for it. I worried about it at first, but now I'm so glad about the baby, Emma. And glad that he's a boy too, so I've done my bit to ensure that there'll always be a Gittings at Highclare . . .'*

The letter was unfinished, but at that moment, with the cold rain streaming down the walls of the dug-out, it made the young man seem vividly alive. Gerald sat and stared at it for a long time. How frail the flesh is, he thought, if a letter can survive its writer.

Then he summoned Hendry.

'Hendry, bring me some decent paper, will you? And a pen. And get one of the other men to come in here. I need two of you to witness what I'm about to write.'

130

## Armentières, 5 April, 1918

Adrian Steele could hardly believe what he was seeing.

Two of the walls of the dug-out were panelled with wood, the others were wallpapered. There were pictures on the wall, scenes of sunlit countryside, and bottles of wine on the table.

'Bloody Germans!' he said out loud.

But he was fascinated by what he had found. He walked slowly around the dug-out, his muddy boots silent on the earth floor. He touched everything gently, almost reverently, trying to remember the last time he had seen such things; the trappings of civilization. The past three years had turned his imagination to grey and khaki. He picked up a full bottle of wine, smashed its neck against the wall and drank deeply.

There was a box of cigars on the desk in the corner. He put them in his pocket. Then he opened the desk drawer. Amongst papers typewritten in German there was an ivory paperknife in the shape of a dagger, and a silver pillbox. Adrian hesitated. They had a name for what he was doing. Looting. And the penalties, if he were caught, would be severe.

But who was to notice? From above he could hear the sound of running, and hastily shouted orders. His company were returning to their trenches after a successful attack on the German line. He put the knife and the box in his pocket and went up to join the retreat across the rain-drenched fields.

The flat lowlands on the Belgian border were criss-crossed with little rivulets called 'beeks'. Over the months, constant bombardment had broken down their boundaries until their contents flooded into the fields and made a swamp. The men from Adrian's company had laid duckboards across the swamp to facilitate the movement of men and supplies from the base camp to the front line. The retreat over the duckboards was the final humiliating obstacle after hours of battle. It was like running on ice; progress was agonizingly slow and tortuous, and all the while the last vengeful shots from the German guns rained down behind them.

Adrian clutched his pockets to stop the ivory knife and the silver box from falling out as he slithered across the duckboards. On either side of him, shell craters formed deep lakes filled with fetid water and afloat with the broken bodies of men and horses. Like a tight-rope walker, Adrian kept his eyes fixed firmly on the damp

131

khaki back of the man ahead, trying not to look down at the treacherous lakes with their hideous debris of war.

Suddenly the duckboards trembled violently.

He closed his eyes, waiting. The man ahead skidded, slipped off the edge of the boards and fell into the mud. Adrian dropped his rifle and crouched down, trying to reach out and pull the man to safety, but he had already sunk to his knees, weighed down by the pack on his back.

'I'll get some rope,' shouted Adrian. 'Wait, I'll go for a rope.'

The man shook his head. It was too late. Adrian watched dumbly as he sank slowly into the foul water.

'*Shoot me!*'

As the water reached his neck the man began to shout, rolling his eyes wildly. '*In God's name, shoot me!*'

Adrian pulled himself carefully to a standing position. He closed his eyes, but the noise went on. He could not bring himself to go and leave the man, but he could not bear to listen to the terrified screams any longer. He reached for his gun and fired the shot.

'Better that than to drown,' he said out loud, as he scrabbled across the duckboards. But it was several hours before his hands stopped shaking.

The next morning the sun shone. It filtered apologetically through the thin layer of cloud, as though reluctant to cast its rays on so cheerless a landscape. There was no fighting that day, and the men sat outside to clean their guns, enjoying the sensation of warmth on their arms and faces.

Adrian indulged in a leisurely shave before the small, cracked mirror in his dug-out. Although the war had hastened the greying of his black hair, it had not dulled his eyes, as it had the eyes of so many men at the front. They were still alert, still watchful.

He washed his hands carefully and sat down at a small table to write home. Not to his wife, but to his mother. Jennifer would receive no letter of her own, only an inquiry after her health via Lady Henrietta. That was his way of punishing her. He was still smarting with anger that Heathcote House had not, after all, seen the birth of a child five months after their marriage. At least Jennifer did not stoop to pretending that she had miscarried. She merely wrote, with a gall that surprised Adrian, that at the time of her first letter 'evidence strongly suggested I was with child'. It turned out that she was 'mistaken'.

He took out his mother's most recent letter and re-read it. The usual complaints about domestic inconveniences: the poor quality of meat, the scarcity of fuel, the pilfering by the cook . . . *'These things must sound paltry to you who are so bound up in the glory of the war . . .'*

Adrian threw the letter down in disgust. The glory of the war! There was more glory in an abattoir, but his mother was too short-sighted to see it. The war had changed his attitude to many things, but most of all it had changed his attitude to Lady Henrietta Steele.

At first he had tried to keep himself aloof and apart. When he arrived in France in 1915, it had been 'their' war. His own had not started. When he looked at the muddied corpses that were strewn over the fields of Picardy, he felt no compassion, only a slight feeling of superiority at having survived. And he had remembered an admonition of his mother's, echoing from his childhood . . . *'It will end in tears.'*

But then he, too, was sucked in. He saw that there could be no superiority, no pride at a front where messages were still sent on horseback as though it were 1815, and where men lived in sewers like rats. There was only disillusion, and the realization that there was no such thing as 'their' war, only 'my' war. Whether he survived or died, each individual lived out his own wretched, muddy tragedy. Gradually the letters from his mother bored him, then angered him. He despised her narrowness, her meanness. The petty social games she cared about had lost their significance. He had once thought Mama knew everything. Now he realized she knew nothing at all.

He took up his pen and began to write. Quickly, fluently.

*'Dear Mama, Yesterday I killed one of my own men. I shot him between the eyes as he drowned in the mud. How could I do such a thing? Because I am a machine, Mama. And I'm part of a bigger machine. It eats live men and spews out dead and wounded. Today, as I write this, they're loading the wounded into ambulances to take them to the clearing station. They're filthy and ragged and covered from head to foot in mud. When the mud dries, it looks chalky and their eyes stare out like . . .'*

Adrian screwed up the letter and threw it angrily to the ground.

133

He was wasting his time. Words alone would never make her understand, or feel. He would write her the sort of letter she was expecting.

'*Dear Mama, Thank you for your letter. I am glad to hear that you are well. Everything here is much as it was when I last wrote. Yesterday we launched a successful attack on the German line, and it looks as though we're more than holding our own . . .*'

He might write that letter later. But he could not write it now. Thinking about his mother and Heathcote had induced the lethargy of despair. What was the point of all this anger? He was here today to think about these things, but he probably wouldn't be tomorrow.

He walked out into the sunshine, feeling slow and aimless. Patches of muddy ground were beginning to dry and crack. He strolled to the makeshift supply tent where the casualty list was pinned up and began to run his eye automatically down the list, not really reading, just filling the time, as one might browse through a magazine.

Then he stopped.

'*Colby, Gerald Ratcliffe (Major). Killed in action March 31st, Arras.*'

Major. So he had been promoted. Adrian smiled to himself and walked back to his dug-out. His pace was brisk.

Now he wanted to live. Now he wanted to return.


## New York, 12 September, 1918

Katherine was balanced on the very edge of the parapet.

'Don't sit on the edge of that thing, darling,' said Jake, 'it frightens me.'

'You have a perfect right to be frightened,' Katherine replied equitably, 'but why don't you come and sit down beside me, anyway? I'll be frightened too, and then we'll be quits.'

That sort of remark was typical of Katherine. She stretched out a hand to him, smiling. He sat down next to her and looked down at the lights in the street below.

Jake was in love. He had met Katherine Exley at the beginning of the summer. She was twenty years old, slim, blonde, athletic; the youngest daughter of an 'old' New England family living on

Long Island. She was also Anglo-Saxon and a Protestant: in short, the apotheosis of ineligibility as a Stein bride. And Jake had fallen in love with her immediately.

It was difficult for them to be together, but that only made them more determined. They had met, quite by accident, at a charity ball to raise funds for American troops. It was a large, self-important social occasion, the sort where hundreds of wealthy, well-dressed New Yorkers gathered in the ballroom of a large hotel and stood in groups with people they already knew, eyeing those they did not know with suspicion or envy. Nobody in Jake's circle knew anybody in Katherine's. Old money did not mix with new.

Jake had grown bored with Miriam's conversation, but was too shy to approach any of the pretty girls who glanced at him from a distance. He decided to find a quiet corner in which to enjoy a cigarette. The ballroom had three large French windows giving onto a balcony that overlooked the street: all but one were locked. Jake slipped out through this remaining door unnoticed, struck a match to light his cigarette, and found himself staring into the face of Katherine Exley. She had used the same escape route to find fresh air.

He had never met anyone like Katherine before. She had a simple self-assurance and directness that made Miriam Abelson look sly. She talked about herself and her feelings, and she questioned the feelings of others. To Jake she seemed a bright and shiny creature, a spark firing in the darkness like the match he had struck before he saw her face.

'I'm awfully sorry,' she had said, in her flat New England voice, 'but as you can see, I got here first.'

They had stood in the dark and talked until the other guests started to leave, tentatively arranging to meet again.

The next day, Katherine telephoned and said that she was being driven into Manhattan to do some 'shopping'. So began a series of meetings, aided and abetted by sympathetic friends, meetings which always seemed to Jake to be carefree and happy, despite the furtive plotting to bring them about. Katherine was quite sure that Hamilton Exley III would not approve of Jake.

'But we'll wait until January, when I'm twenty-one, and then we'll get married,' she said, with the unshakable confidence of youth. 'Then Daddy can go hang.'

Jake never mentioned Isaac, or the obstacles that he might put in their way. He felt sure that his father would already be spying on him, noting his absences from the bank in the afternoon, but Isaac, too, kept silent. Perhaps he was waiting for the affair to lose momentum and fade into nothing. Jake moved in this silent shadow of disapproval; uncomfortable, but resolving to resist at all cost.

He must have Katherine.

He was turning the problem over and over in his mind as he sat with Katherine on the edge of a terraced roof garden overlooking Madison Avenue. The broken strains of ragtime floated over them, and nearby there were couples dancing and talking. A schoolfriend of Katherine's had invited both of them to the party: both had lied about where they were going that night.

'Why so sad, Jake?' Katherine reached out and touched his hand gently.

'Oh, I don't know, I was just thinking.'

'About us?'

He nodded.

'I was thinking about us too,' she said quietly, staring down at the lights, hundreds of feet below. 'I was thinking that we'll have to make sure we die on the same day. Because neither of us could bear to go on without the other. And I've been thinking that we must have children, or a child, at least, so that we'll be joined together even after we've gone. What do you think, Jake?'

'Darling . . .'

'If we have a child, whatever happens, there'll always be a part of us that's together. Let's do it, Jake, please . . .'

There was a defiant note in Katherine's voice. Was she uncertain of the future, afraid even? Jake looked at her precise, angular little face and baby blonde hair, and her sun-tanned limbs, smooth and strong beneath her fashionable calf-length skirt.

'We'll do whatever you want,' he said gravely. 'But it's a little early to be thinking about children, isn't it? We've all the time in the world to worry about that. Let's dance.'

As they danced under the stars with the faint rattle of tramcars beneath them, like the sighing of a distant river, Jake said: 'How are you going to get out to Northport tonight. Do you want me to drive you to the ferry?'

Katherine tilted up her chin and gave her most confident smile. 'No need to do that. I told my parents I was going away for the night, to stay with Mary Rencombe's family at Cape Cod. I'm all yours.' She laughed self-consciously. 'What shall we do?'

They went to a hotel.

Jake felt guilty as he reserved a room for Mr and Mrs Stein, and he still felt guilty when Katherine peeled off the last of her undergarments and presented her smooth, tanned body to him, saying 'Well, here I am' in flat New England vowels.

She was astonishing light in his arms, and as he ran his fingers over the muscles of her shoulders, she pulled away slightly so that she could look into his eyes. The expression on her face was both one of intensity and of great clarity, as though she had seen a vision of something that she wanted with all her soul.

'You do want this, don't you, Jake? It feels right, doesn't it?'

In answer to her question, Jake folded her tightly in his arms, kissing her until the nagging guilt was forgotten.


The next morning they lay in bed late, then Katherine went to do some shopping and Jake returned to Fifth Avenue.

He met David on the staircase.

'Jake! I've been waiting for you. I've got something for you.'

He led Jake towards one of the sitting rooms, but Jake held back.

'I think I'd better just—'

'Oh, don't worry about *them*!' said David gleefully, 'They're out. Papa went to the bank to deal with some urgent business, grumbling about it being *sabbath*. Mother's calling on Rachel and the children. And there's no need to worry about last night, either. At breakfast I complained very loudly about hearing you come upstairs at two o'clock in the morning.' He grinned at his brother. 'In fact there's little chance I'd ever hear you from my room, with the door closed. But they don't seem to have worked that out yet.'

He led the way through double doors into the rose damask sitting room, as though he were a host and Jake his guest. At the far end of the room, next to the window, stood a table with an ice-bucket on it.

'You know, it's ridiculous, isn't it?' said David, walking to the table. 'How old are you? I'm twenty-two and you're . . . twenty-nine? And here we are, forced to sneak around like a couple of kids. It makes me *want* to behave like a kid.'

Jake reached into the ice-bucket.

'What's this? Champagne – at this time in the morning?'

'*And on the sabbath!*' rejoined David in a passable impersonation of his father, and they both laughed.

'It's a celebration.' He unwound the wire cage from the neck of the bottle.

'What are we celebrating?'

'We're celebrating your doing something that Papa doesn't like, for the first time in your life.'

'Not the first. The second. There was sliding down the staircase on a tea-tray, remember?'

'Of course, I was forgetting.'

David started to ease the cork expertly from the bottle. 'The second time, then. And I don't know who this girl is, but I can tell she's not Jewish, just from the way you're behaving.'

Jake watched as David slid the cork away with no more than a muffled sigh, and a wisp of white air as the gas escaped. Then he wrapped a linen napkin around the bottle and poured deftly into the two awaiting glasses. David noticed his brother's scrutiny.

'If you're wondering where I learned how to do this, the answer is at Ginnie's.'

'Do you still go there?'

'Only on special occasions,' said David with a wry smile.

'And Rebecca?'

'Rebecca? I hardly know she's alive. But the engagement keeps Papa off my back. You were right about that. In fact it's the best piece of advice you ever gave me. What about your . . . sweetheart? Do you love her?'

Jake smiled shyly. 'Yes.'

'And you're going to marry her?'

'Yes.'

'I'll drink to that!' David raised his glass. 'I really hope you succeed. And I wish you the best of luck!'


'Well, John, good to talk to you; and thank you for your hospitality to Katherine . . .'

Hamilton Exley frowned into the telephone.

'Oh, I see. I thought you would have seen her at your place on Friday night . . . You didn't? . . . She wasn't? . . . My mistake, John. Right, goodbye.'

He hung the receiver on its hook and stood looking out of the window. He was in the garden room, which projected from the main part of the house and had steps leading to the lawn. His youngest daughter was sitting in a deckchair in the middle of the grassy slope that led from the buttermilk mansion to the waters of Long Island Sound. She was dressed in tennis clothes, stark white against the cool green of the lawn, and her pale blonde head was bent forward as she petted the large tiger cat that wound itself round her ankles. An abandoned tennis racquet was flung nonchalantly onto the grass a few feet away.

Hamilton Exley was not a tolerant man. He believed in God, hard work and himself, though not necessarily in that order. By the time he had been born, the family that had arrived on the East Coast of America from Scotland was already rich. His chief duty in life was to see that it earned the respect of society by remaining so, and he considered that he had succeeded in this. His engineering firm on the mainland shore of the Sound was thriving. But Hamilton Exley believed that his family would only survive if they continued to behave in the same prescribed, rigidly self-seeking manner. There was no room for non-conformity. If children showed a natural rebelliousness, then it must be stamped out, before the smouldering became a blaze. Even the fact that Katherine was his favourite would not sway him.

He walked out onto the lawn.

'Katherine!'

She looked up, shading her eyes with her hand. The striped cat paced around her plaintively, trying to clamber onto her lap.

'I've just been talking to John Rencombe.'

She started visibly, and pinched her lips together, but continued to look steadily at her father's face.

'I was under the impression that you were spending Friday night at the Rencombe place, but he says he hasn't seen you. Where did you go?'

She did not answer.

'*Where did you go?*'

Katherine sighed and looked down at her lap.

'Katherine! Are you going to answer me, or am I going to have to put you over my knee and beat you? You're not too old, you know!'

'I was with a friend.'

'I suppose it was that Jew?'

139

'What Jew?'

'Don't play dumb, Katherine, you know who I'm talking about. I mean Jacob Stein. And look at me when I'm talking to you!'

Katherine peered up at him through her fringe. She took in the tall, heavily built man with greying hair and strong, hawkish face.

'How did you know about him?'

'I'm surprised at you, Katherine. Someone of your intelligence should have realized that these things always come out in the end. A friend of mine saw you together. He had the good sense to tell me about it before you could go sneaking off like some—'

He broke off suddenly, his leathery face darkening in anger. Then, with a great effort, he smiled and held out a hand.

'Come. I want to show you something.'

He pulled Katherine to her feet and led her across the lawn, with one arm around her shoulders. He led her past the gracious plane trees, whose leaves were just beginning to fall, and down to the jetty where the water sparkled with blinding brightness. He led her to the new tennis court, precise and pristine in its geometric neatness. Then he guided her back towards the house. The doors of the garden room were still open, and the breeze caught at the fine white muslin curtains, swelling them like sails.

'You don't want to lose all this, do you, Katherine?'

Katherine shook her head. It was true, she did not. She loved her home and she loved the island. She did not want to leave them behind unless it was absolutely necessary. But she had yet to test that necessity.

'If you carry on seeing this Jew, that's exactly what will happen.'

Katherine rounded on her father, pulling herself away from his encircling arm.

'Don't talk about Jake like that!' she exploded angrily. 'As though he were something beneath your notice. He happens to be a very intelligent man, and a kind one. And he's got enough money to buy Exley Engineering ten times over!'

'I see. You're interested in him because he's very rich?'

'You know it's not that, Daddy. I just thought it was a quality *you* would respect.'

She spoke bitterly.

'I have no doubt that this man would be able to provide for you quite comfortably, though we can't be sure whether the goose that lays the golden eggs is not really controlled by his father. But his people would never accept you, any more than he would fit in here. He would be breaking the laws of his religion, for example, if he married you. Such marriages usually cause nothing but unhappiness for everyone.'

The sun had sunk low in the sky, its rays deepening and mellowing. With a sigh, Katherine bent to pick up her tennis racquet.

'Daddy,' she said earnestly, touching his chest lightly with one hand. 'Look at me.'

He looked down into her eyes.

'Don't you see? How can anyone be truly happy if they can't be with the person they love the most? Don't you want me to be happy?'

'Of course I do . . .'

Hamilton Exley was offended. He had always prided himself on doing his duty by his three children.

'. . . But I know better than you where your happiness lies. So you won't be seeing Jacob Stein again as long as you're living under this roof.'

He walked back to the house.

Katherine sat in her room and calculated. In three months time she would be twenty-one. She would just have to wait until then. She looked out at the garden, and the tennis court, and the Sound. Was it worth leaving all this?

Then she smiled, remembering Jake's sad, serious face, and the reverent way he had held her . . .

But she would have to let him know. They had aranged to meet on Wednesday, and now she would be unable to go. She crept downstairs to the telephone and lifted the receiver, communicating to the operator in a stage whisper that she wished to be connected to Stein and Sons in New York.

'You'll have to speak up, ma'am,' said the telephonist at the bank.

'*Could I speak to Mr Jacob Stein?*' hissed Katherine.

'I'm afraid Mr Jacob is not here at present.

'When will he be back?'

'I'm afraid I don't know.'

Katherine went back to her room and scribbled a note.

'*Dearest Jake. I will be unable to come on Wednesday after all. Daddy has found out. Best to keep a low profile for a while and I'll contact you the day after my twenty-first birthday. Your own Katherine.'*

She ran downstairs with the envelope, but her mother had just come back to the house after visiting friends. She was standing in the hall; small, neat and smartly dressed.

'Going to post a letter, darling?'

'Yes, yes I was.'

'Well, leave it on the tray here and Willard will take it out later.'

'It's all right, Mummy, I've just remembered something I forgot to write in it.'

Katherine fled upstairs again, to begin her waiting.

Jake looked at his watch.

It was three o'clock, the time they had appointed to meet at the little café on Madison Avenue. Jake had arrived at a quarter to, and settled himself at a quiet table near the window. But there was no sign of Katherine. Jake ordered a second cup of coffee.

It was a beautiful autumn afternoon, and New York was at its best. Crowds of expensively dressed people strolled along its avenues, laughing and talking, the fresh light making carriages seem bigger and newer, and the horses that pulled them more sleek. Jake soon fell into a rhythm. He watched three or four people go by, trying to train his eye on their furs, their jewellery or the way they wore their hats. He looked at his watch again. Then back to the passers-by, forcing himself to pay attention to them. Back to his watch. He waited until half-past four before returning to Wall Street.

They had agreed that if one of them was unable to come, they would write or telephone. Katherine's letter arrived on Thursday. As soon as he had read it, Jake asked his secretary to telephone the Exley residence on Long Island.

Hamilton Exley answered.

'I'd like to speak to Katherine, please.'

'Who is this?'

'I'm Jacob Stein. I'd like to speak to Katherine.'

There was a short, tense pause.

'Mr Stein, I have told my daughter that she is to have no contact with you.'

142

'And she agrees with that?'

'Until she is twenty-one, she has no choice. I suggest you wait until then.'

Jake waited. He counted every hour, every day and every week of those three months. He sat staring at the black and white squares of the calendar that hung on his office wall, mentally deleting them. On her birthday, he sent twenty-one hot-house orchids to the house on Long Island. On the day after her birthday, he telephoned again.

Katherine wasn't there.

Once more, it was Hamilton Exley who answered.

'Katherine has gone away for a few months with my wife.'

His voice sounded strained.

'But where is she? How can I contact her?'

'You can't. She does not wish to be contacted by you.'

'But—'

'I believe it's called a change of heart. So I'm afraid I can't help you. Good day, Mr Stein.'

Jake did not believe him. He looked at the snowflakes falling rapidly past the window, then at the calendar. It was 4 January.

He waited. Every week he mailed a letter to the house on Long Island, pleading with Katherine to tell him what had happened, but the letters were never answered.

On 19 March, Isaac called Jake into his office. He was bouncing with pleasure.

'Exciting news, Jacob! Now that the war in Europe is over, we're opening up our first office there. In London. How would you like to be in charge?'

'I'd like it.'

'Good!' Isaac looked sly. 'Of course, there'll be a lot of entertaining to do. It's a pity you're not married . . .'

On 29 March 1919, Jake asked Miriam Abelson to become his wife.


### Somerset, 2 February, 1919

Brittany closed the door of her mother's room with a grimace and a sigh.

She hated Maman being ill. Her temperament was too impatient and restive for the role of sick-nurse. And the house was dull when Maman took to her bed. The servants instinctively lowered their voices and Brittany and George retired early without the distraction of the guests who frequented the house since Papa had been gone.

Brittany found herself smiling at the thought of the intimate little supper parties her mother loved to give, perhaps with a game of charades afterwards, or dancing to the music from the gramophone; the needle crackling on the record and the fire crackling in the grate . . .

There was a distinct shortage of young men, but Brittany had found her admirers among those who had managed to escape the war for one reason or another. She had never seen Randolph de Beer again after his visit to Graylings. After that weekend, it seemed he failed to find favour with the Langbournes and returned to South Africa. On St Valentine's Day in 1916 he sent her a small satin pincushion in the shape of a heart, trimmed with lace. All the way from South Africa.

His cousin, on the other hand, had stayed. She had surprised everyone by becoming the bride of the dogged Adrian Steele. Indeed, the wedding was so hasty that it was rumoured she was expecting a baby, but no baby came. Bland, pretty Jennifer Steele used to accompany her mother-in-law when she visited Graylings, but after Papa's will revealed that Adrian Steele was named as heir to the estate, the visits became too embarrassing to both sides, and they stopped. Maman seemed relieved not to have to be polite to Lady Steele any longer.

Brittany tripped lightly down the marble staircase, choosing a path directly through its centre. Bleached winter light filtered through the domed skylight, brightening her hair from brown to gold. She paused to look at herself in the mirror above the ormolu table in the hall. Her hair had darkened since childhood, but it still had a burnished, metallic sheen. The squareness of her face gave a pleasing clarity to her features, which were dominated by her eyes. If anything, they were longer and more sultry than before, a blaze of blue in that sallow, unEnglish skin. She was twenty-one. Perhaps, if there had been no war, she would have been presented at court, with white feathers and a great deal of fuss . . .

She pushed the thought from her mind and went in search of her brother.

144

It was George's birthday.

Even more surprising than her attaining the grand old age of twenty-one was the fact that George was now nineteen. She found him in the stableyard. It was not the brisk and pin-neat place that it used to be. All the horses save three had been sold, and there was only one ageing groom to care for them. George had taken over the duties of the kennel boy when he had left for France. The kennel boy now lay buried in the mud of the Somme, and George still came out into the yard twice a day to feed the dogs.

Brittany stopped a few feet away and watched him. With his tongue pushed out in concentration, he laid out the thick, chipped earthenware bowls so that they made a neat row on the ground. Then he ladled an equal amount of foul-smelling scraps into each. Only when he had examined them from a distance, with one eye half-closed, and was satisfied that the division of the spoils was fair, did he open the door to the kennels.

'Come on, boys – teatime!'

George was dressed in battered old corduroys and a collarless shirt. His face had narrowed and lengthened with age, and had a slightly weatherbeaten look now that he spent much of his time out of doors. Brittany thought that he resembled Frederick more than ever.

He smiled when he saw Brittany.

'How's Maman? Any better?'

Brittany shook her head.

'Is it one of her headaches again?'

Brittany nodded.

'Do you think she'll ever be completely better again?'

'I hope so.'

George bent and stroked the backs of the dogs, who quivered in ecstasy as they devoured their food. There was a peaceful smile on his face. Brittany could not fail to notice how much happier he had been since Papa went away.

She always thought of it as 'when Papa went away', not 'when Papa died'. He had not returned to Graylings once since the beginning of the war, preferring to spend his leave in the clubs and bars of London, so when the telegram came, announcing his death, it was difficult to feel differently. And there was no proof, except for the muddy, bloodstained uniform that had been posted back to Graylings in a parcel. Maman had consigned it to the attic without even unwrapping it properly.

'I came to talk to you about dinner.'

George looked blank.

'It's your birthday – you choose what we eat for dinner tonight, remember? I told Betty you'd go and discuss it with her.'

George hesitated.

'Can't you do it, Brittany, if I tell you what I'd like?'

Betty was the new kitchen maid. She had frizzy hair and very large breasts, and when George had been in the kitchen on his own, she had pressed close to him, touching him playfully, panting and laughing at the same time.

'Oh, all right then.' Brittany did not attempt to hide her exasperation. 'I'll speak to her. What do you want?'

'Steak and kidney pudding and spotted dick.'

As she walked away, George had his eyes closed in bliss at the thought of the steaming pudding. More than that, he glowed with content. It was not only Papa's absence which had changed him. He had been even happier since the will was read and tyrannical weight of responsibility for the estate was pulled abruptly from his shoulders.

And now all they could do was wait. For Adrian Steele's return.

Roland Steele coasted dreamily down the corridor of Heathcote House, resplendent in riding breeches, shirt tails and an embroidered evening waistcoat.

'The sun is over the yard-arm.' he said decisively. 'The sun is over the yard-arm.'

In fact the sun had set several hours earlier. Sometimes a word or phrase would get stuck in Roland's mind and rattle around in it for hours without any apparent reason. Occasionally, if the phrase expressed some powerful image, it might stay in his mind for days or weeks. This had been the case in 1914, when Roland overheard someone mentioning 'the war to end wars'. For several weeks this phrase – bold, dramatic, rapacious – had eaten up all other thoughts and whirled around his confused mind like a rat in a trap.

Lady Henrietta watched him go, with contempt. She felt an overwhelming urge to shout, 'No, the sun is *not* over the yard-arm, don't be so ridiculous!', but she knew that it was useless. He could not hear her. Of late he had been so restless, so uncontrolled in his

146

ramblings, that she did not dare invite people to the house. Had she been on her own, she might have resorted to locking him away in one of the rooms on the top floor of the house, but it would be difficult to justify such a course of action to her daughter-in-law.

Lady Henrietta turned and swept up the stairs, raising the front of her skirt daintily, like a débutante at a dance. She went into her room, shut the door behind her and smiled. Here everything was in readiness. The outfit she would wear on the day she moved to Graylings was hanging on the back of the wardrobe door. It had been made specially: a suit of plum-coloured gaberdine with a fashionably short skirt and a matching tricorne hat. The dressmaker had pointed out with as much tact as she could muster that the style was really intended for a more bosomy lady, but Henrietta Steele was undeterred. She wanted eveything to be exactly as she had always pictured it, and in her mind's eye she was stepping onto the white portico of Graylings in proprietorial plum-coloured gaberdine.

The table under the window was heaped with swatches of furnishing fabrics and samples of wallpaper. She had spent many happy hours alone in here, matching colours, planning. She walked to the table and fingered the materials, judging their respective merits. She had not quite decided on the material for the drawing-room curtains. The Regency stripe, or the cream brocade?

Thinking of Lucienne Colby made her laugh out loud. What would that poor Frenchwoman think, if she could see her now? It was a little shabby, not calling when Lucienne was ill. The reason was not that she wished to avoid the hypocrisy of proffering friendship when they both knew that she was about to take over as mistress of Graylings, but because she would be quite unable to contain her feelings of glee.

How had Adrian done it? She was still not quite sure, but somehow he had managed to convince Gerald Colby that whether or not he married Brittany, he was the natural choice of heir. The coup had earned him her increased respect.

And her attitude to Jennifer had changed too. At first, when she learned that there was no child, and that her son had fallen for a trick as old as history, she had written to him insisting that he divorce Jennifer. Adrian ignored her. Jennifer stayed.

At first Jennifer was as sullen as Lady Henrietta was sneering, but gradually they both thawed. Although she would scarcely admit it, Lady Henrietta was lonely for the first time in her life. The war had changed the pattern of daily existence, and she saw little of her old friends. Jennifer kept her counsel but helped with the running of the house in a compliant, uncomplaining fashion. Lady Henrietta came to respect her self-possession.

She arranged the samples of material in a neat pile in preparation for packing them. Then she took a piece of paper from her desk and swept downstairs into the drawing room. The fire was smoking, owing to blocked flues, but Jennifer sat patiently before it, her small brown hands weaving a needle swiftly through a piece of embroidery, blinking furiously to clear her smarting eyes.

'Well . . .' said Lady Henrietta. She held out the paper.

'A telegram?' Jenifer raised her eyebrows.

'Yes,' said Lady Henrietta with satisfaction. She sat down next to Jennifer and stretched out her hands to warm them before the unsatisfactory blaze.

'He's coming home tomorrow.'

The village of Nether Aston nestled in a hollow like a baby in the crook of its mother's arm. It was approached by a steeply declining road, which turned at several right angles, so that the village could never be seen or assessed from a distance. One simply found oneself in it. The houses were built from hard, bleak grey stone, standing separately on the outskirts of the village and huddled closely together at the centre. Approaching from Wells, from a southerly direction, the first building that caught the attention was a public house called 'The Lamb and Child', on the right, then a butcher's shop and a post office on the left, followed immediately by the strong, square wall of Heathcote House, raised slightly above the level of the street and accessible by a small flight of steps leading to an iron gate. Finally, on the right, there was the sturdy Norman church, whose most singular characteristic was its complete lack of architectural embellishment. At no point did the village open out onto a pleasing green or a patch of common ground which would provide a core, a heart. It simply straddled its narrow, undulating main street as though gripping it tightly.

Adrian Steele found the village tired and empty, its lifeblood drained with the men who had been slaughtered in France. Yet it also seemed tense, expectant, waiting for something to bring it to life again. As he rode a sloth-fattened Porphyrus down the street, he felt as though eyes were watching him behind moving curtains and half-drawn blinds.

He stopped at the church, dismounted and walked into the graveyard. He did so out of an old, forgotten impulse, hoping to find Brittany there. He wandered slowly among the graves, which were as neatly tended as ever. The yew and laurel still threw thick shadow over Maria Padbury's battered marble angel, and the branches of the fir trees smelled sweet, even though the ground was frozen and the air cold.

There was one grave that he particularly wanted to see again.

*Frederick Gerald Colby. Born 20 July 1894. Died 23 December 1912.*

Someone had laid a bunch of snowdrops in front of the tombstone. The first flowers of the year.

Adrian mounted Porphyrus again and followed the lane that rose out of the village on the north side, towards Graylings.

He did not go into the house immediately. Instead, he walked around it like an animal assessing its new territory, circling the dour cedar tree and finding himself, finally, inside the walled flower garden.

A winter garden. The bare earth, ready to receive new plants, had a special smell. Adrian picked up a handful of it and sniffed it. What had he known for the past four years, but mud? Yet this dark, loamy earth was very different from the slime of Picardy. It was cool to the touch, and clean. And here, too, there was expectancy. The soil itself had been waiting for his arrival. He would grow, create, command. He would cram this soil with phlox and lupins, wallflowers and asters, and when they came to flower they would remind him of his own ambition.

He stood up and walked to the front door of the house, patting his pocket. It contained his copy of Gerald Colby's will.

Adrian had called a meeting with Lucienne Colby and her solicitor, to discuss the future of his property. As he had expected, Brittany also attended. They sat in a circle in the library, with chill ceremony, while Mr Gamp, the solicitor, coughed and prevaricated. Lucienne Colby was even paler than usual, but neither she nor her daughter seemed disturbed. They sat calmly and waited. Adrian felt uneasy.

'I would draw your attention, Mr Steele,' said Gamp, coughing enormously, 'to the codicil at the end of the will. *'While it is my intention that Adrian Robert Steele should have control and management of the above named estate after my death, my wife Lucienne shall enjoy the right of occupation of the house, Graylings, for the remainder of her life.'*

'But—' Adrian felt himself grow pale. 'But there's no mention of that on my copy of the will.'

'Major Colby made the codicil at a later date. But it is valid, nonetheless. The appendix has been signed and witnessed.'

'I disagree!' Adrian sat up straight in his chair. 'It is contrary to the agreement between us. And you all know that I have already arranged to pay off existing debts with my own money!'

Gamp caught Lucienne's eye, and she nodded slightly.

'There will be no further discussion of this, Mr Steele. The meeting is at a close.'

In confirmation of this statement, Lucienne and Brittany both left the room.

Adrian stood up and paced angrily. 'I can't accept this, I'm afraid. I'll find my own lawyer, someone who can look into it—'

'I strongly advise you against that, Mr Steele,' said Gamp firmly, collecting his papers together and putting them in his case. He glanced at the closed door and then said in a quieter tone:

'I'm not sure if you are aware of this, but Mrs Colby has been in very poor health recently. No lawyer would wish to be involved in hounding a . . . someone so seriously ill from their home. I advise you to leave matters as they are – for the time being.'

He gave Adrian a meaningful look and left the room.

Adrian found Brittany retreating up the marble staircase.

'Brittany!' he shouted, unable to keep the desperation from his voice.

'What is it?' Her blue eyes were cold, but she turned and walked down the steps again, staring straight ahead. No one else could move on that vast gleaming structure with such confidence and composure.

'I just wanted to say . . .' He took a deep breath and went on '. . . that if you would consider marrying me, I would divorce Jennifer at once.'

Her only reply was a contemptuous glance somewhere in the direction of his feet. Then she turned and walked up the stairs without a backward glance.

Adrian returned to Heathcote and waited for Lucienne Colby to die.

# PART TWO

'What though the field be lost?
All is not lost; the unconquerable will,
And study of revenge, immortal hate
And courage never to submit or yield . . .'

*John Milton*

# 6

## *London, 12 May, 1923*

Brittany loved London.

Lucienne Colby had died in the winter of 1922. After the inevitable weeks of unpleasantness, with the funeral to organize, and Adrian Steele's lawyers banging on the door day and night demanding rights of possession for their client, Brittany had accepted the Langbournes' offer of hospitality with relief and gratitude. For six months now, she and George had been guests at the Langbournes' opulent mansion in Park Street, Mayfair; showered with trips and treats like spoilt grandchildren.

While Brittany enjoyed her new life in London, and was content there for the time being, she was not happy about Graylings. It had been a shock. Not the contents of her father's will, but what happened afterwards. Neither she nor George wanted to be encumbered with the running of the estate, so Gerald's unorthodox arrangement with Adrian Steele seemed a stroke of fortune. They were, after all, protected by Maman's right of tenure of the house for her natural life: they could afford to feel comfortable. Brittany had even rather enjoyed Adrian's blustering and energetic descent on the house when he returned from France. His disappointment at not being able to take over as lord of the manor had been all too obvious. And of course, he *would* resort to charging around like a bull in a china shop with preposterous offers of marriage.

They had thought Maman would go on for ever. Or at least until they had married and moved away to homes of their own. It had never occurred to them then, in 1919, that Maman's frequent headaches would do anything but go away of their own accord. Instead, they had worsened, and a doctor came all the way from Bristol and pronounced that Maman had a tumour on her brain. Even then, for much of the time, Maman seemed quite as usual, and they did not believe it, they simply did not believe that this invisible tumour was eating up her brain like a worm in a rose, and was going to make her die.

And all the while Adrian Steele continued to live at Heathcote with his silent wife, running the Graylings estate with an energetic and meticulous efficiency and waiting for the inevitable.

Brittany would not allow Adrian Steele the satisfaction of seeing how she felt about losing her home to him. She did not betray a flicker of emotion as their bags stood packed and waiting in the hall and Adrian watched from the marble staircase with one strong hand resting lightly, autocratically on the curving banister. She did not give any hint of displeasure as the car borrowed from Henry Morgan drove her and George to the station at Bath, nor when Maud Langbourne clucked over them tearfully as she welcomed them to Park Street.

It was only when she was alone in her new pink and white bedroom, a room so pretty that it made her feel uncomfortable, that she gave way to the surge of angry tears. She was angry with Adrian Steele for his ruthless and unpitying ambition; she was angry with Maman for deserting them. But most of all she was angry with Papa for his cold, implacable treachery. He had bartered them away like some debased coinage: Brittany because she was a girl and George because he was not Frederick.

It came as no surprise that Papa had not seen fit to tell them of his plans. That state of affairs had existed since the early days of Brittany's childhood: no one ever explained anything. At that time, she had tiptoed the corridors of Graylings in her nightdress, eavesdropping on her mother. Now she took matters into her own hands in a more sophisticated way.

She called it 'litigating'. When she received a letter from Adrian Steele's lawyer offering one of the cottages on the estate as accommodation, she furnished him with a curt reply, stating her intention to live at the main house, or not in Somerset at all. Then she went about discovering how London's resources could help her adhere to this intention.

She did not tell the Langbournes of her quest. They might think her ungrateful, and they certainly would not approve of such strident action. Their own simple view of the world prescribed a successful marriage as the solution to all her problems. With difficulty, she arranged unchaperoned 'shopping' sprees, feeling like an adulteress as she kept her illicit appointments with first one lawyer, then another. Each said that there was little that could be done, but out of kindness and sympathy for her plight, they always managed to provide her with the name of someone they knew who *might* be able to help her.

154

On that particular morning in May, she had been to consult with a barrister whose chambers were in the formidably imposing King's Bench Walk. He was a plump, fatherly man who sighed a great deal and chewed his lip thoughtfully, and told her that unless she was able to prove that her father had been of unsound mind, then she would have to accept defeat.

As Brittany strolled through Trafalgar Square and along the tree-lined avenues of the Mall, she did not feel at all defeated. She would find a way, eventually. In the meantime there was all London to be enjoyed. It was at its most appealing at this time of year, the trees in the parks weighed down with their damp new leaves and the scent of lilac everywhere. Blossom was scattered beneath her feet like confetti. London had thrown off the drabness of the war years and was coming to life again, with more dealing on the Stock Exchange, more drinking and dancing and more Dixieland jazz than ever before.

Brittany was wary of returning to Park Street empty-handed, so she headed for Bond Street, with its fascinating shop windows. She paused for a while outside Mrs 'Freddie' Cripps' brand-new hair-dressing salon, then pushed the door open and went inside. The interior was a gleaming palace of glass: glass-fronted cabinets, glass-stoppered bottles, cut glass bowls of face powder. Brittany fingered a silver and tortoiseshell compact, coveting it.

'Can I help you, madam?' asked the pokerfaced assistant. 'Some scent, perhaps?' She proffered a bottle of Patou. 'Or were you hoping to have your hair cut?'

'My hair . . .'

Brittany reached up and touched it. Her ineffectual chignon had slipped and was hanging heavily at the back of her neck. It was a sultry day and the weight of it made her feel hot.

'I'd like to have it cut,' she said rapidly, 'but unfortunately I don't have any money with me at present.'

The meagre portion left to her in her father's will had been invested for her by Richard Langbourne, who insisted on taking care of her living expenses, and told her that if she needed money to spend, she should go to him.

'Perhaps madam would like to open an account? Then the bill could be settled at a later date.'

Brittany nodded gratefully, and was guided to a large leather chair whose arms were soon littered with her glittering brown-gold locks. She was a little alarmed when she saw the final result in the mirror. Her hair had been cut in an Eton shingle: parted at one side like a boy's, with smooth, short waves over her ears and a ducktail at the back. She felt shiny, naked and newborn.

As she signed her name at the bottom of the chit that had been laid out for her on a glass-topped desk, she glanced enviously at a girl who had just received similar attention. She wore lipstick and a smart cloche hat and she carried a leather handbag which she clicked open with a flourish, producing a sheaf of banknotes which she handed to the assistant. Brittany did not even own a purse.

As she left the salon, she decided that she would find herself a job. It seemed such a wonderful idea that she almost laughed out loud with delight.

Brittany had visited London only once before, when she was eight, and Maman took them on the boat-train to Paris to visit Tante Eugénie. Her trips around the city were like voyages of discovery. There was such an astounding array of faces, and so many things happening all at once. Sometimes she glimpsed girls sitting at desks, or moving their fingers rapidly to and fro over fearsome-looking typewriters. Why shouldn't she become one of those girls? It did not occur to her that the work might be dull or routine, she simply saw a vision of herself as busy and interesting; a part of London's bursting life. And with money of her own to spend.

She would talk to Maud about it.


George hated London.

He hated the traffic and the bewildering clamour and the people who brushed against him as they walked by. He hated the constant round of social events which required him to change his clothes several times a day. And he missed the dogs terribly.

However, he did like living with the Langbournes. Maud's warm, motherly ways reminded him of Maman, and of course there was Susannah. Now that she was a graceful, elegant young woman of twenty-five, she seemed more like an angel than ever, and further from his reach. He blushed when he thought of her and trembled violently whenever she came into the room, yet being near her filled him with an intense feeling that he could only describe as happiness.

Happiness . . .

156

George looked around the room he had occupied for the past six months. He spent a lot of time in here, tidying things away, even after the maid had been in. He liked a room to be tidy. In one corner stood Maman's inlaid escritoire. The lawyers had decreed that Adrian's rights did not extend to the contents of the house, and the desk was one of the treasures that had been hastily salvaged. Space for storage had been offered by the Morgans and the Stanwyckes, old family friends who lived about ten miles from Graylings, and Aunt Georgina had descended in high dudgeon to carry off some of the more valuable trinkets in the house. The larger pieces of furniture and portraits had to be left behind.

George stroked the surface of the escritoire lovingly, remembering how he used to crawl underneath it while Maman sat down to write her letters. There was barely room for him to squeeze his knees under it now. Then, with a sigh, he turned back to the problem in hand.

What on earth was he to wear?

Clothes had become a constant threat, a responsibility. At Graylings no one noticed, nor did they care, so George dressed in outdoor clothes – a rough shirt and breeches – with the exception of occasions that required a black tie. This afternoon, for example, Maud was entertaining guests for tea, and had asked George to come down and meet them. Should he wear a suit? Flannels?

There was a knock at the door.

'Are you coming down, George?' It was Susannah.

George blushed furiously. 'Come in.'

He had lost his childhood stammer, but sometimes he felt as though he were still stammering inside.

'Did you enjoy your shopping?' he asked lamely.

'Shopping?'

'Brittany was going shopping this morning. I thought you would be going too.'

Susannah shook her head. 'No.' She forced a quick smile. 'She didn't mention it to me.'

George had noticed an uneasiness between his sister and Susannah, and it troubled him. He could not bear people quarrelling.

'Susannah . . .,' he asked hesitantly, not looking at her face, 'there's nothing wrong between you, is there? You used to be such good friends.'

'Of course not, silly!' She pressed his arm affectionately but

George was not entirely convinced by her assumed breeziness.

'Now . . .,' she went on hurriedly, as though sensing his doubt, 'you seem to have a great number of clothes laid out here. What's it to be?'

'I was going to ask you that question.'

'The flannels, I think . . .'


'Welcome to London!' Jake Stein embraced his younger brother. 'Come in. How was the trip? Miriam's through here . . .'

Jake led David into the drawing room of his house in Eaton Place. His wife was reclining against a pile of lemon silk cushions. She curled her fingers in an affected little wave, but did not stand up to greet her brother-in-law. Miriam Stein had grown from a rich, spoilt, ambitious girl to a rich, spoilt, bored woman with a fondness for diamonds. She and David disliked one another intensely.

'Sit down. I'll ring for a drink . . .' Jake was solicitous, but unable to hide his excitement. 'You can have a wash and brush-up here, and I'll have your luggage sent around to your new apartment. Then if you're not too tired, I'll take you down to Ironmonger Lane and show you how it all works. Our new Foreign Exchange department is really—'

Miriam yawned pointedly.

'. . . Well, we'll see how it goes.'

David could not keep still. He examined the room and its contents, then went to stand at the window and looked out at the tranquil street and the blossom that littered the pavements.

'It's so quiet here after Fifth Avenue . . .' He turned back to Jake with a grin on his face. 'London! I can't believe I'm here! When are you going to show me around, Jake? Tell you what, let's start tonight with a tour of the hottest nightclubs—'

'Well now, isn't David just too *artless*!' drawled Miriam, holding her laquered fingernails up to the light while she inspected them. 'There's poor Jake trying to get you to take an interest in the bank, and all you can think about is getting yourself a good time. You don't change.'

'Neither do you, honey. You're still pure poison.'

'There are some great shows on,' said Jake, ignoring them. 'When was it? . . . Tuesday, we went to the Shaftesbury and saw the Astaires in "Stop Flirting". They did this great dance called the "Oom-Pa Trot" and all—'

'Really, they have nothing to compare with Broadway.' Miriam countered. 'Why, they have to borrow Fred and Adèle because their own little shows are so drab and ama*teur* . . .'

'Who cares?' said David, refusing to let Miriam flatten his spirits. 'I'm here in a city with all the alcohol and all the jazz and all the girls I could—'

'Oh David! I completely forgot to ask!' Miriam's face broke into something approaching a smile, 'How *is* your fiancèe? How's dear little Rebecca? . . .'

Maud Langbourne looked around her and was satisfied with what she saw.

It was her habit to tour the house each day, making sure that all of its twenty-five rooms were in order, and that the vast, faceless army of servants were all busy at their allotted tasks. It was the influence of her middle-class background that was at work when she personally supervised the running of her household. She would have felt uncomfortable delegating control to a housekeeper.

Maud opened the door of a formal reception room and looked in.

'Hmmm . . .'

A flower arrangement the size of a small tree caught her attention. She looked it up and down and tweaked delicately at the waxen yellow roses, her little finger cocked. She rearranged the veil of trailing ivy.

'There . . .'

Satisfied, she continued on her journey down the carpeted corridor, her pale blonde curls bright in the sunlight, bouncing slightly as she moved. She was very light on her feet, despite her plumpness.

Maud was thinking of words to describe her home. 'Imposing' was one word that came to her mind. 'Luxurious'. It was unimaginatively symmetrical in design, but this did not discourage Maud, who enjoyed having four floors of corridors *with corners*, and a *lift*!

After the tour was completed, it was time to go upstairs and change in preparation for her tea party. Tea parties were wonderful things. So cosy. Maud held at least one a week. The rest of her time was taken up with anonymous Good Works, and organizing her daughters into meeting plenty of Nice Young People. She could no longer rely on the series of suitable friends that Johnnie brought home. Darling Johnnie had not been one of the lucky few who returned from the Somme.

Johnnie's death was hardest for Richard. There was no longer a Langbourne to inherit the Company. Langbourne and Sons had been founded by Richard's great-grandfather, Alasdair, son of a ghillie on an important Highland estate. The aristocratic owner of the estate had arranged a job for Alasdair as a clerk in a shipping company, and within ten years he owned his own business, including shipyards in the North West. With the boom in British ship-building, Langbourne and Sons had become an empire in true Victorian fashion. And now there were unprecedented opportunities in transatlantic travel and Richard was starting up a passage line, working with all the dry, burning dedication of the bereaved. He was a very wealthy man.

Maud knew that they were considered *nouveaux riches*, but she genuinely didn't care about this label. Her own father had been in trade too, supplying timber to the Langbourne yards, and what was more, he was a devout Christian, teaching his children to despise the pride that money incites. Maud had her little snobberies, but she kept them to herself. She was shielded against the outer world by a spotlessly nice life, and armed with the two-barbed arrow of amicability and affluence.

Maud sighed with pleasure as she entered what she called her 'boudoir'. It was a temple of pleasantness and good taste. She sat down at her dressing table and began to hunt for the right brooch to wear with her tea gown. There was a knock at the door.

'Come in!' she cried gaily.

'It's me,' said Brittany. 'May I ask you something?'

'Sit down, darling, sit down.'

Still looking in her jewellery box, Maud pointed to the perfect chair, covered in cream chintz and arranged next to a cream silk-shaded lamp and a bowl of cream roses.

Then she caught sight of Brittany's reflection in her mirror.

'Darling, your hair!'

She twisted round on her stool to look more closely.

'I had it all cut off, Maud.'

'So I see.'

Maud folded her plump hands in her lap, somehow turning this into a gesture of disapproval.

'And I've decided I'd like to get a job.'

'A job! Darling girl! What on earth could you possibly want a job for? Darling ridiculous child!'

She tried not to look at Brittany's hair.

'I decided I'd like to earn some money of my own. Please, Maud – I do hate depending on you and Richard. And I've nothing to do.'

'Nothing to do!' Maud looked as though she might faint. She raised her hand to her chest, still clutching the diamond brooch she had chosen. It was in the shape of a cross. 'But you're having a lovely time, aren't you?'

The diamond cross flashed at Brittany in accusation.

'Yes, of course . . .' Brittany admitted helplessly. She was not very adept when it came to dealing with Maud.

'Well, there's very little point in our discussing it now.' Maud turned back to the mirror dismissively. 'We're going down to Dorset next week, remember? We'll talk about it again when we get back.'

At first the visit to Dorset seemed set to be a success.

Early summer was the height of the social 'season' and therefore not the conventional time to take a house by the sea, but Maud did not care for such rules. The summer was already promising to be hot and sultry, and if Maud wanted to leave London for the country, then she would.

The servants went on ahead by train to prepare the house and the family travelled down in two motor cars, arriving on the coast at dusk. Brittany and Claudia laughed loudly all the way as their hair was teased by the warm, salty wind. There were trivial word games to pass the time, games whose content grew more frivolous and outlandish as the miles were covered, and by the time they reached the village of Charmouth and their destination, Roxton Grange, Brittany was feeling extremely cheerful. Only Susannah was quiet.

People were surprised when they discovered that the Langbournes had no country seat of their own, for weekends and sporting pursuits. They certainly had the means to buy one. But Richard's involvement in running Langbourne and Sons kept him in London for much of the time, and Maud preferred to be at his side. '. . . I would never want to spend time down there without Richard, so the place would be empty and the servants up to heaven knows what. And what would be the point of that?' demanded Maud, practical to the last.

Consequently they rented a series of manor houses, castles and shooting boxes whenever they wished to retreat from the city. These rented properties were often the extravagant follies of men forced to let them once they struck penury, or the English homes of maharajahs and Arabian princes, luxurious or bizarre; so that the outcome of the Langbournes' ventures could never be pre-dicted.

'It's always terribly exciting . . .' Claudia explained to George breathlessly, '. . . because we never know what we're going to find when we get there. Once we rented a sheik's house in Surrey. He only used it for Goodwood. And it had a handbasin made from a solid lump of onyx, with real gold taps. And there was a fountain *inside*, which pumped champagne! . . . Only it was empty,' she added ruefully.

This precarious and haphazard way of acquiring temporary homes was particularly surprising in the Langbournes of Park Street, for whom life was metiulously well-ordered at all times. Brittany decided that it was exactly like a game for them: an exciting and all-too-rare chance to surrender themselves to the random. They all seemed to relish the fact that they knew nothing whatsoever about Roxton Grange, like naughty schoolchildren with a treat in store.

Their excitement was infectious: nevertheless, Brittany was relieved to find not a jewel-encrusted replica of the Taj Mahal, but a very pretty Regency villa. It was painted palest pink, and wistaria trailed carelessly over its wrought-iron balconies. The garden was a delightful profusion of summer flowers and the lawn extended right to the edge of the limestone cliffs.

Their three weeks at Roxton Granfge seemed set to slip idyl-lically by in a round of punishing sets of tennis, picnics on the cliff tops and post-prandial games in the chintzy drawing room, fol-lowed by the oblivious sleep that only sunshine and fresh air can bring.

But it was not to be.

After breakfast on the first day, Brittany prepared herself for a walk on the beach, deciding that she would ask Susannah to accompany her, as a conciliatory gesture. She had noticed how different and withdrawn Susannah had been since she and George moved to Park Street, and she also noticed that this mood was reserved solely for herself. Towards the others she was her usual gentle, sweet-tempered self. Brittany had resolved at once to discover what was wrong, but it had proved impossible. Susannah simply avoided her.

'Where's Susannah?' she asked George, as she laced up her white deckshoes and arranged a limp sun-hat on her cropped head.

George blushed and looked uncomfortable.

'I don't know. I haven't seen her since breakfast. Perhaps she's playing tennis?'

'Don't be foolish!' snorted Brittany. 'With whom? I'm here, you're here and Claude's in the drawing room. She must be upstairs.'

She set out alone. Once she reached the sand-dunes, she took off her shoes and walked barefoot between the patches of vetch and the sea-pinks. The sand felt cool and velvety between her toes, bringing back memories of childhood summers at Filey; of Nanny Wynn's rotund form crammed into a deckchair like a cork into the neck of a bottle, gesticulating with her knitting and shouting at children too far off to hear, *'Don't you dare get those clothes wet! . . .'*

She wandered slowly down to the water's edge and climbed out onto the black rocks with the bobbing gulls and stared, mesmerized, into the glistening liquorice-dark sea. The sea had so much power. It even had the power to make you feel like a child again . . .

Then she saw Susannah.

She was perched on a large, square rock at the water's edge with her arms crossed over her knees and her head burried. She had removed her hat and it lay on the sand beside her with her discarded shoes and stockings, like amorphous flotsam. The breeze lifted the brim of the hat as though it wished to drag it out to sea, fluttering at Susannah's pale hair and the hem of her primrose yellow dress.

She did not look up as Brittany approached.

'Susannah?'

Susannah's shoulders heaved. She was crying.

'What's the matter? Is it Johnnie?'

Susannah did not move. Very gently, Brittany put her hand on Susannah's shoulder and pulled her upright. Her face was pink and damp. In her hand she clutched a battered photograph. Brittany prised it from her fingers and recognized at once the narrowed eyes and mocking mouth.

It was a picture of Randolph de Beer.

'It's all your fault!' sobbed Susannah. 'It's all your fault that he's gone away.'

'But Susannah! . . .'

Brittany was appalled.

'I had no idea that you cared for him so much. If I'd known there was an understanding between you, I—'

'There wasn't an "understanding"!' said Susannah bitterly. 'But if it weren't for you there might have been. When Mama saw him . . drooling over you in that revolting fashion she decided that he wasn't suitable and got rid of him!'

'But how did Maud know? I didn't think—'

'That's just it!' exploded Susannah, breaking into renewed sobbing. 'You didn't think! You could have any man you wanted. You only have to look at them. But Randolph was *mine*! And you had to take him too! The only chance I've ever had . . .'

'But Susannah!' Brittany straightened up to take in the lustrous brown eyes and white-blonde hair, dazzling in the light reflected from the sea. 'You're beautiful! Much more beautiful than I am.'

'That's not the point!' said Susannah savagely. 'They only have to look at you and I may as well not exist. And you always know the right things to say. I don't understand what it is you've got, but they all want it. And I haven't got it!'

She gathered up her hat, shoes and stockings and ran sobbing along the shore. Brittany stared after her, wondering what 'it' was, and hoping that now Susannah had given voice to her grievance, their holiday would be improved.


There was worse to come.

Susannah stopped avoiding Brittany but her participation in their shared activities was languid, desultory even. After they had been at Roxton Grange a week, Maud announced that she had invited some Nice Young People down for the weekend, conferring a meaningful look on Brittany and Susannah.

Maud was matchmaking again. The latest victim was a gentle-man farmer's son called Charles Whitlock ('more like "Witless"', Brittany hissed to George) and at first Brittany could not decide whether he was intended for Susannah or for herself. Susannah's recent outburst alone was enough to persuade her to keep her distance, but she also found Charles Whitlock deeply unappealing. He was very tall and as large as it is possible to be without being fat. His face wore a permanently disagreeable expression and his lips were full and pouting. He did not laugh or smile once during Maud's cosy little dinner party in the chintzy dining room. Indeed, he barely spoke.

Brittany's decision that he was the most objectionable person she had ever met coincided with the realization that he was not intended for Susannah, but for her.

The more Brittany avoided Witless, the more alarmingly unsubtle Maud became. After dinner, she shunted her guests around the room like counters on a draughts board, so that Brittany and her potential suitor always finished up alone together. Since Witless was disinclined to speak, and Brittany was rendered speechless with disbelief, they sat in sullen silence for most of the evening, both trying to escape when the assembled company were reshuffled, and finding themselves outmanoeuvred by one of Maud's firm 'Brittany-darling-over-here-I-think' requests.

After they had all retired to bed and she was on her own again, Brittany felt inclined to laugh about Maud's little games.

But then she made a discovery that did not make her feel like laughing at all.

She was passing Maud and Richard's room on her way to the bathroom, when she heard raised voices. This in itself was unusual. Maud was far too genteel for anything more than well-modulated articulation.

'I *know* she didn't like him!' Maud's voice was high and shrill. 'But what alternative is there? We don't want her on our hands indefinitely, do we? Who knows where it will lead!'

'But Maud, dearest, her bereavement . . . And the girl's homeless.'

'Fiddlesticks! She's a bad influence on Susannah. And she's becoming uncontrollable. Chopping off her hair! Demanding a job! I've no doubt that before long she'll be getting herself into worse trouble, and I won't have it, Richard. The quicker that sort of girl's settled in marriage, the better for all concerned!'

Richard made a muffled reply that Brittany could not hear.

'. . . Very well, dear, I'm willing to concede that Charles Whitlock isn't suitable for her, but there must be somebody else. We'll just have to keep on trying . . .'

Brittany crept away, trembling with anger and indignation

The next morning she announced that she was returning to London to find a job.

'But *darling*!' wailed Maud. 'You can't possibly! We've still got another week to go here. And we're all having such a wonderful time here, aren't we?'

She looked around the breakfast table for support.

Susannah stared fixedly at her plate.

Richard stroked his moustache nervously. 'I believe Maud promised that we would discuss . . . er, a job, after the holiday was over—' he began placatingly.

'I want to find one now,' said Brittany stonily. 'Please don't try and persuade me to stay. I'd be grateful if you could arrange for the car to take me to the station. If not, I'll walk there.'

She turned quickly and left the room. She could not bear to see George stare at her so beseechingly.

## Somerset, 20 May, 1923

'Kale! That has to be the answer!'

Adrian Steele was so excited that he spoke out loud and looked around the library triumphantly, even though he was alone in the room. Then he turned his attention to the magazine again, running a finger down the margin, his deep, black eyes flickering quickly from side to side.

When he had finished reading he looked round the room and smiled. Graylings. The only thing he had always loved, and been faithful to. He had lusted after it for so many years. Now it was like his bride, and as in the first unspoilt, heady days of marriage, it still seemed exquisitely desirable. Yet he woke every morning with the painful sensation of having an urgent problem to solve. He must win acceptance as master of the place.

Adrian was not a popular landlord. The tenants of the remaining two farms attached to Heathcote (one had been sold immediately after the war) claimed that he was no longer interested in them and accused him of neglect. The foremen on the Graylings estate had the opposite grievance: he was interfering too much in the day-to-day running of the farms, telling them to plant root crops in place of grain, to devote more land to growing cattle fodder, to use modern machinery.

At twenty-nine, Adrian was dedicated to prosperity. He visited all of his farms at least once a week, bullying his tenants into taking his advice, cowing them with his unrestrained energy. And his spare time was taken up with studying farming manuals, scientific tracts – any material that he could lay his hands on in order to satisfy his lust for success.

He enjoyed having the house to himself. Only when he was alone could he really feel that it was his. Even before Jennifer's impassive gaze he felt a usurper. There was something in the way she looked at him – the barest hint of suspicion, perhaps? – which reminded him that if he was not exactly an interloper, he had come to be master of Graylings by an extraordinarily fortunate series of events, not because he had been born to it.

He had insisted that Jennifer remain at Heathcote while the refurbishment of Graylings was carried out. The drawing room was being redecorated in accordance with a scheme of Mama's, and upstairs two new bathrooms were being built, with shiny tiles and sparkling chromium taps. Adrian had maintained that it would be unsuitable for Jennier to be left alone during the day in a house populated with uncouth workmen, but the real reason was that he wanted it to himself for a while.

He liked Jennifer well enough, and found her company tolerably pleasant. She did not prattle in the way that some women did. But he found himself losing interest in her. The early promise she had shown in the bedroom at the time of her unexpected and masterful seduction had not come to fruition. She was too mechanical, too tidy in her lovemaking. He would soon be in a position to try afresh in the marital bed, and he hoped that after a period of abstinence his wife would be more abandoned. The last of the builders had now left and Jennifer was to move to Graylings that afternoon.

Adrian tidied his books and papers and went to the tack room to collect his riding boots. He carried them to the edge of the curved portico, where shade met daylight in an abrupt glare, and sat down on the steps to pull them on. The rays of the sun which had long since dried the dew that collected on the lawn, blazed brilliantly on the blue branches of the cedar and on the wallflowers that Adrian had planted in the lee of the walled garden, dredging up their hot, sweet, musky perfume. Apart from the droning of bees in the flowerbed, it was very, very quiet.

Adrian sat still for a few moments, listening, waiting . . . The silence surrounding the house never failed to make him tense, but if someone had asked what he was waiting for, he would have been unable to answer. A footfall, perhaps, or an accusing hand on his shoulder, or the sound of a bubble bursting as he woke up and found that he had only dreamed that all of Graylings belonging to him . . .

His destination that morning was Coombe Farm, one of the largest farms on the estate and the nearest to the house after the Home Farm. He rode out on Porphyrus. The brutish grey was as bad-tempered as ever, but becoming older and slower and less inclined to make trouble. As he travelled the warm, fecund summer lanes at a sluggish trot, Adrian found himself thinking of Jennifer, and then discovered that his mind was drawing a startling parallel between his horse and his wife. Neither of them provided a challenge any longer.

Coombe Farm was occupied by a tenant farmer called Daniel Lester. The Lesters were a large and prolific family, and any Lester would have been glad to tell you that they were one of the oldest families in the area, citing a reference in the Domesday Book. Daniel Lester was a lazy, haphazard young man, who had recently taken over the running of Coombe Farm from his father and was largely content to let it go its own sweet way. For this reason Adrian Steele got on far better with Daniel than he did with any of the other farmers. Daniel was entirely tractable and quite happy to accept whatever innovations his landlord suggested.

After the tour of the decaying shed where Daniel 'stored' his rusty agricultural equipment, with Adrian talking very fast and gesticulating frantically with his hands and Daniel nodding sagely and saying 'Yassir' at the appropriate moments, Daniel invited Adrian to come into his house and meet his wife.

The farm kitchen was noisy and untidy, with traces of straw and manure on the floor and even on the battered old sofa where a

168

brindled cat had just given birth to a mass of squirming kittens. Adrian picked his way fastidiously to a seat while Mrs Lester hastily placed a half-consumed fruit cake on a plate and put the kettle on the hob. She could not have been much older than twenty and she wore a bemused air, as though she could not quite believe that the three grubby children crawling vociferously about the kitchen floor owed their existence to her. Her hair was loose, and beneath her floral print dress her legs were bare.

As Adrian gulped down the dark, pungent tea and the youngest child besmirched the shining surface of his riding boots with sticky fingers, the door opened and another young woman came into the room. She sat down in a chair in the corner of the room and, without speaking to anyone, took out a silver case from her pocket and lit a cigarette.

'That's Phoebe,' said Daniel proudly. 'My sister. She's living with us for the time being.'

Adrian looked more closely. He had never seen a woman smoking before, not even in the brothels of France. He judged Phoebe Lester to be about twenty-six, though there was a hardness about her face that made her look older at first glance. She had a broad, square face with a wide, clever mouth. Her chestnut hair, so bright that it was orange when the sunlight fell on it, was tangled at the back, as though she had just got out of bed. The top two buttons of her lace-trimmed blouse were undone, and when she leaned forward to put the cigarette to the flame, Adrian could see the deep hollow between her breasts. He noticed that although she was heavily built, her legs were long and her ankles unexpectedly slender.

'Phoebe worked in a munitions factory in the war,' went on Daniel. There was no embarrassment as he offered this explanation for her behaviour. He sounded as though he were displaying a new and exotic arrival at a zoo.

'She was a typewritist, weren't you, Phoebe?'

Phoebe blew smoke towards the ceiling in an idle cloud. She was staring at Adrian with a hard, unwavering gaze.

'I must be on my way now, Mr Lester,' said Adrian hurriedly. 'Give some thought to my proposals over the next few days, and then I'll need your signature on some paperwork.'

Daniel looked slyly at his sister, then back to Adrian.

'Happen you need a typewritist, Mr Steele, to help you with all that paperwork. Phoebe here could give you a hand, couldn't you, Phoebe?'

Phoebe's only reply was to drop her cigarette butt onto the kitchen floor and grind it out with the toe of her high-heeled sandal. But her eyes did not leave Adrian's face.

'Do you think he will be all right?'

Jennifer looked doubtfully at her father-in-law. His head was turned slightly to one side. Saliva dribbled out of his mouth and on to the ruff of ginger whiskers, collecting in a pool on the pillowcase.

'Oh yes,' said Lady Henrietta, patting the covers briskly, 'of course he will. He's only had his usual sleeping draught, with some brandy mixed in. And when he wakes up, Deborah will be here with him.'

She continued fussing with the covers, smoothing and straightening them and tidying the medicines on the bedside chest.

'You know, Jennifer . . .' She fixed Jennifer with her glassy blue stare. 'Now that he doesn't recognise me, I've really become quite fond of him. In the way that one would a pet dog, you know. Of course, it's a ghastly inconvenience his being incontinent, but then he didn't ask to be that way, did he? It could happen to you or me, couldn't it? And he's going to have the best possible care from Deborah . . .'

She waited for her daughter-in-law to voice her support.

'Of course,' said Jennifer.

'Good.' Lady Henrietta was comforted by this passive reassurance. 'Right then, let's get on. Is the car out there waiting for us?'

Jennifer glanced out of the window. 'Yes.'

'Very well – onward and upward!' Lady Henrietta pointed to a patch of peeling wallpaper, and laughed. 'I was just about to say that we must get something done about that,' she said gleefully, 'then I remembered that we wouldn't be here to see it. But I've told Deborah she must do something about the rats . . .'

She tripped along the passage to her room, feeling lighthearted as a girl again. At last the moment for the plum gaberdine had arrived! And all the more welcome for having to wait four tedious years! Lady Henrietta hummed a long-forgotten waltz under her breath as she struggled into the suit, oblivious of the fact that it was now extremely dated in style and even more ill-fitting than before. She continued to sing to herself.

She hated what the war had done to England. She had no desire to live in a world where no one had respect for breeding, where the lower classes demanded unheard-of rights and servants charged ridiculous wages. But she need not think about that any longer. She was going to Graylings, and there she could live in a little pre-war world of her own making, creating the sort of life she always *should* have had, if only she had not married out of her class. She felt no pang of regret at abandoning her feeble, demented husband. After all, this was her right. She *deserved* it.

She continued to hum cheerfully and tunelessly as the car that Adrian had sent purred up the high street and into the lane that led to Graylings.

'The motor car is one of the few features of the new age that I am willing to accept,' she said grandly. 'It's so civilized, don't you think, Jennifer?'

Jennifer sat neatly with her feet together and her small, brown hands folded on her lap. She smiled, but offered no comment.

'Now, my dear, we have one or two things to dscuss before we arrive. I hear that Adrian is planning to employ a local girl as a secretary. To help him with the paperwork, apparently. You simply *mustn't* allow it, Jennifer. It's a quite ridiculous expense, and she'll have to work in the house, so she'll be under our feet all day . . .'

Jennifer thought that it would be quite nice to have a girl of her own age in the house, and opened her mouth to say so.

'Now! You're not to worry about telling him. I'll talk to him about it if you like. I know how to deal with him. We're really very close, you know . . . Ah! We're here. Now, don't you worry about anything . . .'

Adrian was waiting for them on the steps.

'I see you decided to accompany Jennifer to her new home, old girl,' he said drily, as he handed Lady Henrietta out of the car.

'Of course.' She frowned at him.

'What's all this?' he asked as her luggage was unloaded by the driver.

'My belongings, what else?' she replied tartly.

The battered morocco, with its gold monogrammed HMD almost rubbed away, was unmistakably hers, a tribute to a former age.

171

'Mama, you seem to be under the impression that you're coming to stay here,' said Adrian coldly.

'But of course! That's what we agreed.' Lady Henrietta's hand flew to her hair, preening it furiously.

'I said nothing of the kind.'

'But Adrian, we always assumed . . . didn't we, Jennifer—'

She looked around wildly for support. Jennifer said nothing.

'Well, in that case, you assumed wrongly. You can't possibly go and leave Father when he's so sick—'

'He'll be perfectly looked after by Deborah!' snapped Lady Henrietta, brushing imaginary dust from a plum gaberdine sleeve. 'And your concern for your father is the most preposterously false thing I've ever heard. You didn't care a fig for him when he was well and you certainly don't now . . .'

Suddenly she felt herself go limp, as though she were very tired. Her lip trembled slightly.

'Adrian . . .,' began Jennifer.

Adrian took her firmly by the elbow and started to lead her up the steps of the portico.

'You'll keep out of this, Jennifer. And you, Mama, will tell Simmonds to put that collection of junk back in the car.'

Jennifer glanced back in sympathy as she went up the steps, and for the remainder of that day she was unable to rid her mind of the image of the frightened face beneath its bedraggled plum-coloured feather.

Jennifer looked down at the tousled red-brown head as it bent over the typewriter. The laborious correction of mistakes was taking place.

'Miss Lester?' she said quietly. 'Phoebe?'

'Oh! Mrs Steele! Well, you didn't half make me jump!'

'Phoebe, there's a cup of tea for you in the upstairs sitting room, if you'd like.'

Phoebe looked surprised. 'Well . . . that's very kind, Mrs Steele. Don't mind if I do . . .' She followed Jennifer upstairs to the small north-facing sitting room. 'Pretty room, this.'

'Yes, it is,' said Jennifer in whole-hearted agreement. She liked coming into this room herself. It had a relaxing feminine air, as though it was meant to be filled with fresh flowers and tinkling tea-cups and whispered confidences. An unknown beauty in a leghorn hat looked down sympathetically from a wall portrait.

She watched Phoebe drain her cup of tea with unselfconscious enjoyment, eventually plucking up the courage to speak.

'Miss Lester . . .'

'Call me Phoebe. Mind if I smoke?' She lit a cigarette without waiting for a reply.

'Phoebe, I hope you don't mind, but I want to ask you something of a rather personal nature . . .' She blushed.

'By all means, Mrs Steele.'

'Jennifer, please.'

'Jennifer.'

'I . . . of course, I used to discuss this sort of thing with my mother, but she passed away several years ago, and there isn't anyone . . . I . . . my husband doesn't seem to be paying very much attention to me.'

'You mean – in the bedroom?'

'In the bedroom, yes.' Jennifer blushed again and smoothed her skirts. 'And I do so long for a baby. I know you're not married yourself, but I wondered if you . . . if there was any advice? . . .'

Phoebe was making sympathetic clucking noises with her tongue. She leaned forward and lowered her voice like a conspirator. 'To my mind, a man's affected in these matters by the smooth running of his domestic arrangements. He wants to be comfortable and well set-up before his mind turns to . . .' She made a veiled gesture. 'What you want to do is to lay on a really first-class dinner, lots of drink and then . . . But you'll need to get a decent cook first. That woman's useless.'

'Are you sure—'

'Look, I'll find one for you, shall I? There's a new employment agency in Wells. I'll telephone them this afternoon. You get your best dress ready.'

Phoebe returned triumphantly a few hours later with the news that a Mrs Rosslyn had been hired. Jennifer almost fainted when she heard what the salary was to be.

'That's awfully expensive. Are you—?'

Phoebe was blasé. 'Well, it's short notice, isn't it? She's going to do you a meal tonight. You see if that doesn't do the trick!'

At eight o'clock, Jennifer bathed and attired herself in a pale green brocade the colour of an icy sea, which gave a flattering warmth to the clay-brown tones of her skin. The dress had a plunging décolletage and clung around her small hips, ending abruptly below the knee. The final touch was a jaunty green headband sewn with dazzling beads that made a ring of light on her smooth dark hair. She sipped a glass of champagne as she dressed and watched it bring a faint glow of pink to her cheeks. She even allowed herself a brief smile at her reflection.

'This is very good, old girl' said Adrian through a mouthful of Mrs Rosslyn's melting fricassee of sweetbreads. 'I take it you've found a new cook? Splendid! What's next on the menu, then?'

He did not venture any comment on his wife's appearance. He complimented her on the venison steaks poached in red wine and praised the meringues with hazelnut and chestnut purée, but, as Jennifer had feared, the quality of the food made him suspicious.

'So, what are we paying this new cook?'

Jennifer told him.

'Bloody hell! We can't afford that! Where did you get her from?'

'It was Phoebe Lester's idea, actually. She telephoned an employment agency.'

'The meddling little harlot! I thought she looked sly. Well, I can't employ both of them, so it will have to be Miss Lester that gets the sack.'

'Oh no, Adrian . . .' Jennifer was mortified. She did not want to lose her new-found confidante. 'She did it with my consent. And apparently they all charge about the same . . .'

Adrian gave way to her pleading, but was silent for the rest of the meal.

Undeterred, Jennifer battled her way through her share of the claret and then led the way into the drawing room.

'I thought we might try a cocktail,' she said, forcing herself to smile at her husband. 'I don't know whether it's fashionable to drink them after dinner, but—'

'Why not!' exclaimed Adrian, his good mood returning, 'Let cocktails be drunk at Graylings! Let's drag it into the modern world!'

His pale skin was flushed and his dark eyes glittered as he drained the glass that Jenifer handed to him. Then he insisted that she make him another. Jennifer was perturbed. The cocktails contained a great deal of gin, and therefore had the potential to sabotage her plan.

'Why don't you go upstairs,' she asked, 'and I'll bring one up to you?'

'I've got a better idea!' Adrain's voice was loud and undisciplined. '*You* go upstairs and I'll bring *you* one.'

Jennifer saw that it was useless to argue. She went up to the bedroom, brushed her hair vigorously, dabbed scent between her breasts and put on her most ravishing nightdress. Then she lay back against the pillows to wait.

Adrian came upstairs at half-past two, blind drunk.

He switched the light on, but did not trouble to find out if Jennifer was asleep. She was not, but she lay with her eyes closed and pretended that she was. Her anger and disappointment kept her awake long after his heavy snores had begun, and his persistent dreams of sleep-tousled hair.

Adrian had a hangover, and he fully intended that his secretary should suffer for it.

Nevertheless, he found himself looking at Phoebe Lester with new curiosity. Why should Jennifer find her so sympathetic? In the two weeks that she had been working for him, she had addressed no more than a few words in his direction.

She stared back at him, and he found himself blushing.

*Damn the presumptuous little slut . . .*

She looked away abruptly. 'I've got some letters for you to sign.'

'Bring them here.'

She swayed across the room towards him. She was wearing a sombre grey suit and a grey blouse that should have made her look like a nun, but made her look like a vamp instead. Her bright brown hair was piled up in a bun. Wisps of it escaped and hung untidily round her neck and temples.

She stood very close to him while he signed the letters. And very still, so that she scarcely seemed to be breathing.

'Miss Lester,' he said coldly, as she returned to her desk, 'I would like to warn you now that I won't have you interfering in my domestic life, or treating my wife with familiarity. And the employment of domestic servants is not your concern.'

She ignored him, crossing her hands on her lap in an oddly demure fashion. 'I've been thinking . . . you haven't changed very much, have you? Haven't done much decorating. I think you wanted it to stay the same, so that you could pretend that you were living here in the old days, you know, like you'd always been here . . .'

'Now look here—'

Adrian moved out from behind the desk in his own corner of the library, which was temporarily serving as an office, and began to walk towards her. But Phoebe only laughed and turned back to her work.

He started to read a book on animal husbandry, but found that he could not sit still. He crossed to the other side of the room where he had left a pile of seed catalogues, and started flicking through them furiously. When he found the one he wanted he paced the room with it, moving his lips impatiently as he read. Then he saw that Phoebe was watching him again.

'Stop behaving like a stage villain,' she said, 'What are you so afraid of?'

He stared at her but did not speak.

'You're afraid of losing this place, aren't you?' she said softly. 'I've been watching you ever since I came here, and I can tell. It doesn't really belong to you. You took it away from those Colby children. I don't know how you did it, but you were clever all right. Only now you're afraid someone's going to try and take it away from you . . .'

As she was speaking, she moved past him to take down a book from the shelf behind him. He could smell her cheap perfume and see the immodestly swelling front of that ridiculously matronly grey suit rising up and down as she breathed.

'Interfering little bitch . . .,' he muttered.

She laughed, brushing against him as she returned to her desk.

Adrian clenched his fists.


*London, 7 June, 1923*

'I'm sorry, I'm afraid I can't help you.'

The manageress of the employment agency avoided looking at Brittany as she spoke. She was a short, fat woman whose powdered neck receded beneath folds of flesh.

'The employment situation is becoming critical. There are many young women looking for jobs now who have already gained some experience during the war. Someone such as yourself, who is

176

untrained and inexperienced . . .'

Go on, say it, thought Brittany. Say that I'm a spoilt, pampered member of the upper classes who has never got her hands dirty and thinks that having a job would be an amusing little game . . .

'Thank you,' she said dully.

She walked back to Park Street at a slow, sullen pace, feeling tempted to break down and cry with exasperation. Perhaps when she first conceived the idea of finding a job, it *had* been just a game, but it wasn't any longer. She did not want to go on living with the Langbournes, and that meant that she had to support herself. If she insisted, Richard would be obliged to release the money he had invested for her, but when it had dwindled away to nothing, then what would she do? The interest it generated would only provide her with the most meagre of livings.

She *had* to find a job. And there was only one day left in which to find one. The Langbournes and George were returning from Dorset the following afternoon, and she did not wish them to find her skulking guiltily in preposterous luxury in Mayfair. She would be forced to make her peace with them and submit herself to Maud's schemes once more.

At all the offices and bureaux she had visited, the response had been the same. They objected to her inexperience, but Brittany sensed that they judged her to be unsuitable. After all, everyone had to start gaining experience somewhere, and she was sure that she could learn as quickly as any. She even went boldly into a costumier's and offered her services as a mannequin, but was politely refused on the grounds that she was not slender enough.

Brittany sat on the edge of her pink and white bed and looked down at her square wrists in despair. Nanny Wynn had spent years forcing large helpings on her with the advice *'It's not nice for a lady to be too thin, dear'*, but she wasn't thin enough. She felt heavy, lumpy.

After a few moments' indecision, she stood up and flung the doors of her wardrobe wide open. The next step was to make sure she was looking her best. If she couldn't find work to do during the day, then she would have to work at night, in a club or a bar.

The idea thrilled and shocked her slightly. She could almost hear Susannah at her most prudishly innocent, saying *'Work in a bar? Oh, but you couldn't . . .'* Brittany thought that it would be fun. She had already tried her hand at mixing cocktails, and there would be plenty of interesting people to see and interesting conversations to overhear. Or perhaps she could work as a dancer. She had received lessons at Graylings, and was a strong, graceful, faultless dancer . .

She took out her best dress from the wardrobe, an expensive creation that Maud had bought for her. 'Sorry, Maud,' she muttered as she pulled the dress over her head. How unseemly to wear such a dress to go touting around bars. It was made of creamy pink chiffon so pale that it was barely pink at all, like the shadow cast at the centre of a rose. It was cut low at the back and had a dropped waist. The hem drifted slightly in thin, delicate layers. She brushed her brazen hair until it shone, and wished she had some rouge for her sallow cheeks. She pinched them hard instead. Finally she hung a pair of diamond teardrops in her earlobes. They had belonged to Maman, and she stared at them for a few moments before she put them on, remembering the way they had caught the light as Maman lifted her black veil on the day of Teddy's funeral . . .

Now only one problem remained. She had never actually been inside a bar, and had no idea where to find one. She wound her way down the silent, thickly carpeted corridors until she came to the cathedral-like servants' hall. Several surprised faces stared at her as she came in.

'John,' she said with relief, spying one of the younger footmen, 'John, I need you to help me.'

Brittany had never lost her childhood affinity with servants, nor her ease of communication with them. She enjoyed stolen conversations with them, well away from Maud's disapproving gaze, and the maids had begun to confide in her. They had divulged that John was quite a swell on his nights off, and the resident expert on London's demi-monde.

'Miss Brittany?'

'John, I want to go to a bar. A good one, where – I mean, could you recommend—'

'Out for a drink are you, Miss? I recommend the Carpetbagger. It's a new jazz club, very popular with the Americans, and they're the ones who invented the thing, aren't they, Miss, the jazz? It's in Half Moon Street, so you could walk it from here . . .'

Ten minutes later, Brittany found herself inside the Carpetbagger Club.

178

She had never before known anything like the wild, uncontrolled shrieking of the music, the smoke and the confusion. At the centre of the low-ceilinged room, young girls in short skirts were dancing wildly. Around the edge of the floor there were circular tables in recessed alcoves, and people were crammed tightly around them, their knees touching. They were talking and laughing. Brittany looked for the bar, but the gloom was so intense and the air so thick with smoke that she could barely see.

'Are you looking for someone?' said a voice at her elbow.

There was a young man sitting alone at one of the tables.

'No, not exactly,' she said. 'I was looking for the manager.'

'Well, sit down, and I'll have him sent over.'

Brittany blinked in the gloom, trying to see her companion more clearly. He had a lot of thick, curling dark hair and a long nose. His teeth were very white and very even. From his accent she guessed that he was American.

'Pleased to meet you.' He introduced himself with a charming smile, and extended a hand.

Brittany sat down at once, anxious to give the impression that she was acquainted with nightclub etiquette.

'I'll call a waiter over,' he said comfortably. 'And then you can tell me why you need to see the manager.'

Brittany peered doubtfully into the darkness.

'You're wondering how the waiter is ever going to see us,' he said quickly, and laughed. 'It's so dark in here the waiters ought to carry lanterns. But don't worry, they'll find us eventually. Is champagne all right?'

A waiter duly appeared and the American ordered a bottle of champagne.

'Now,' he said. 'You've got to keep your side of the deal. Why did you want to see the manager? Have you found a corpse in the ladies' powder room? Of has someone just stolen the family jewels?'

Brittany explained about wanting to find a job. She was not sure whether it was due to the heat and the champagne, or because this nice American was so easy to talk to, but she found that she was telling him a great deal more as well; about living with the Langbournes, and not wanting to marry Witless, and about Papa leaving Graylings, her beautiful Valhalla, home of the heroes, to Adrian Steele.

He nodded sagely and said 'Uh huh' at regular intervals.

When Brittany had finished, he said 'You won't be able to work here. Take a look behind the bar.' Brittany squinted obediently in the right direction. 'You see—' Two men. No women. And they don't have waitresses, only waiters. It's all the same in these places. You very rarely see women working in them, unless they're—' He grinned. 'Anyhow, it's too much trouble for the management. Sometimes customers drink too much, get a little loud, and they need a man to deal with that. Also, they close at all hours in the morning, so if they had women working for them they'd be obliged to provide them with some sort of escort home. It just wouldn't work.'

Seeing Brittany's face, he added, 'But I might be able to help you with getting a job.'

'Why, do you own a bar?'

'Not exactly. A bank. My older brother came over here a few years ago to set up a European branch of my father's bank. And I'm in London to help him for a while before—'

He stopped.

'Before what?'

'Before I go back and settle in New York for good, I guess.'

She asked him to go on, and he began to talk again, about his childhood in a vast, ugly Fifth Avenue mansion, and the games he used to invent to keep boredom at bay. Brittany was delighted to find someone who had shared her childhood contempt for adults. She sipped her champagne very fast and thought how much she liked him. He was cheerful and irreverent and funny. She found herself wondering what colour his eyes were, and whether he was going to ask her to dance.

A large, girl in an orange dress with a mop of curly hair and too much lipstick detached herself from the crowd on the dance floor and hurtled towards Brittany's host, jangling metal bangles in his face.

'Darling, isn't this music *divine*? *'I wish I could shimmy like my sister Kate'* . . . Come on, let's dance!'

She took hold of his wrist with a forwardness that surprised even Brittany, but he shook his head and waved her away.

'Who was that?'

'She says she's my cousin.'

'Isn't she?'

'Not as far as I know.' He laughed again, showing his too-perfect teeth. 'You and I had better dance, or she'll be back again.'

Brittany had no idea how to shimmy, but she quickly learned. Before long she was damp and breathless and laughing with exertion, and it was a relief when the saxaphone broke into a slow, crooning melody and he pulled her into his arms. She floated around the room on a pleasant cloud and Valhalla, home of the heroes, seemed far away. When it was very late, and people were beginning to disappear, he suggested gently that he take her home.

'I can see your eyes beginning to glaze over,' he said, and winked.

She was led outside to a shiny, dark red Lanchester. Beside it stood a big, baby-faced man.

'This is Jack Olsen. My bodyguard. I guess he's the equivalent to your English nanny. Papa's idea, of course. Jack is here to keep me out of trouble.'

Her new friend insisted on driving, so he and Brittany sat together in the front while Jack Olsen crammed his huge frame into the back seat. Brittany was glad of this rather bizarre arrangement, because it gave her a chance to look at the American's eyes as they passed beneath the street lamps. His eyes were a clear, uncompromising green.

'You know, I'd like to help you with your other problem too,' he said as he drove. 'I mean, this Steele guy making off with your home. It doesn't sound right to me. Why on earth would your father want to do that?'

'I suppose he thought Adrian was the best person available to run the estate. He always despised George.'

'But why was it necessary for him to have the house as well? It sounds like the sort of thing that's done under duress. How about extortion?'

Brittany considered the idea for a moment. 'I don't think so.'

'It sounds like a job for Hieronymus Shand to me! Definitely a job for Hieronymus Shand.'

'*Hieronymus Shand?*'

'My *nom de plume*. When I was a kid I was obsessed with detective stories. I wrote a long and ponderous novel called *The Mystery of the Blue Urn*.'

'*The Mystery of the Blue Urn*'? Was it really? Oh no, what a terrible title!'

Brittany burst into gales of uncontrolled laughter, and he joined in.

'I know,' he gasped, when they had recovered their composure and he had narrowly avoided swerving into a lamp-post. 'Isn't it the most terrible thing you ever heard? I thought it was pretty smart at the time, of course.'

They pulled up outside the house in Park Street. He rested his hands on the wheel. There was an expectant silence. Somewhere in the distance a clock chimed two.

'Nobody else home?'

Brittany shook her head.

'Look . . .,' he said slowly, 'you can either go into that cold, empty, lonely house, or you can come back to Grosvenor Square with me, to a warm, cosy apartment, and have a drink. What do you say?'

He gave Brittany an irresistibly boyish smile.

'Yes,' she said.

Jack Olsen stared ahead impassively as though he hadn't heard.

The apartment was spacious and comfortable, with brand-new furniture, conspicuously expensive paintings and a lot of large mirrors.

'Slip your shoes off and make yourself comfortable. I'll pour you a brandy.'

Brittany sank back onto a mountain of plump, luxurious cushions, and suddenly realized how tired she was. She had been walking all day. The last thing she remembered was taking the glass of brandy that was held out to her and thinking that she had already had far too much to drink . . . and wondering vaguely if he was going to try and kiss her . . .

David Stein stood behind the sofa and looked down at Brittany's sleeping figure, feeling a faint thrill of surprise that she had consented to come to his apartment and that she was there now, asleep. Warm and real and breathing; the wronged heroine of a mystery come to life.

The sallowness of her skin reminded him of Dulcibel. He reached out to caress the naked skin of her arm and then withdrew his hand. No, he would not spoil it. He wanted the game to go on a little longer, to study its development. He wanted to delve into her mysterious story.

Instead he pushed back the heavy curtain that obscured the window and looked down onto the moonlit trees in the square below. Thinking of two women: the sleeping heroine on the sofa and the plain, worthy Rebecca, waiting for him to return to New York and claim her as his bride.

When Brittany woke up the next morning, someone was standing over her.

'David?'

It was not David. This man was much taller and his straight hair was nondescript brown. His eyes were colourless.

'I thought you were David,' she said lamely.

He appeared to be embarrassed, pulling his thin lips into a straight line.

'Oh,' she said quickly. 'We didn't . . . we haven't—'

'I'm not interested in my brother's private life.' he said abruptly and walked towards the door.

What a rude, offensive man Brittany was thinking as David bounded into the room in a silk dressing gown.

'I see you two have already met,' he said cheerfully. 'Brittany, this is my brother Jake. Jake, this is Brittany Colby, a friend of mine.'

'Hello,' said Jake.

Brittany nodded curtly and turned away.

'I'd better leave you.' Jake opened the door of the drawing room. 'But in case you hadn't realized, David, it's nearly eleven o'clock. You have a shareholders' meeting in half an hour.'

Brittany frowned at his retreating figure, trying to smooth her hair and the creases in the chiffon dress. She felt dishevelled and out of sorts and her mouth was dry.

'Don't worry about old Jake,' said David airily. 'He takes his responsibility as acting head of the family very seriously. His problem is that he cares too much about everything. Now, we'd better get moving. I'll drop you off in Park Street. And don't forget what I said about finding you a job. The offer still stands.'

Brittany was forced to take up David's offer sooner than she had expected.

When she saw the Langbournes' Daimler parked outside the house, her heart sank. A poker-faced butler was waiting for her, with the message that Maud wished to speak to her at once. A grimfaced Maud was waiting for her in the library.

It transpired that they had terminated their holiday in Dorset a day early, and had arrived home to find Brittany missing. When she failed to return by the small hours of the morning, naturally they had informed the police. A stormy scene ensued with Maud weeping and Brittany protesting her innocence, and Richard pulling his moustache and alluding to 'your poor dear mother's memory'. Then Brittany was accused of ingratitude.

'That's just it!' she shouted. 'That's what you don't seem to understand. I'm sick of being grateful all the time!'

She slammed the door of the library and went straight to the nearest telephone. Unhooking the mouthpiece, she asked to be connected to Stein and Sons, in the City of London.

# 7

## London, 8 June, 1923

David Stein was as good as his word.

'Don't worry,' was the first thing he said when Brittany came through on the telephone and garbled her message about having to pack her bags and leave that very day. 'Jake and I were just going to meet Miriam for lunch. Why don't you join us, then we can discuss everything?'

He named a pretentiously fashionable restaurant in the West End. Brittany agreed to meet him there, wondering who Miriam was.

She ran upstairs to wash her face and exchange the crumpled pink dress for a simple linen suit and a wide-brimmed hat. Then she went in search of George. There had been no sign of him during the morning's débâcle, which was entirely in keeping with his horror of confrontation. But she found herself suddenly overwhelmed with the longing to see him and to know that he was on her side. She needed her old ally.

He was not in his room. She went down to the drawing room.

Through the closed door she could heard voices and a faint, irregular tapping sound. George and Susannah were playing chess together. While they were at Roxton Grange, Susannah had patiently taught George how to play, and once he had mastered the rules he had clamoured to play whenever she had a spare moment. Brittany hestitated, with her hand on the doorknob. There was an outburst of laughter. She turned back to George's meticulously tidy room and left a scribbled note on the pillow: *'George, I desperately need to talk to you. Brittany.'*

*'He cares too much . . .'* Brittany turned David's enigmatic description of his brother over and over in her head as she faced Jake Stein across the restaurant table, examining it from all sides like a prism. She found him disappointing. When David had talked about him at the Carpetbagger he had spoken with awe of his brilliant business acumen and unquenchable ambition. Her imagination had painted a diabolic portrait, executed with sweeping strokes of the brush and coloured black and scarlet. In the smoke and heat of the Carpetbagger Club she had pictured a fusion of Mr Rochester, Count Dracula and the old Jewish moneylender of the fables. The real Jacob Stein was not only ordinary-looking to the point of plainness, he did not even look Jewish. But she noticed that his laugh was unexpectedly vibrant, and that David hung on his every word.

They were four for luncheon: Brittany, David, Jake and Miriam, who turned out to be Jake's wife. Brittany made patterns in the salmon mouse with her fork and stared at Miriam Stein, disliking her instantly. Hers was the darkly fragile and brooding beauty of the well-bred Jewess, redolent of sweet wine, sable and the vast Russian skyline. And she was one of those women who insist on telling other people what they already know.

'Do you like horse racing?' she asked Brittany in her offensive drawl. 'You know they have some races at Ascot real soon. Jake and I were invited but I told him no, not this year, I'd rather be in town than having the heels of my shoes ruined by the turf and watching a bunch of dull old horses running up and down. You going to Ascot?'

She pronounced it 'Ass-cott', with the emphasis on the second syllable.

Brittany smiled wryly. 'I haven't been invited.'

'Oh? That's too bad. Does David know when he's going back to the States yet?'

'I'm afraid I only met him last night.'

'Last night, huh?'

Miriam's spoilt mouth twisted into a knowing smile. Then she caught sight of a plump and painted friend waving to her from the other side of the restaurant. She threw down her napkin and flounced off to speak to the woman, leaving Jake and Brittany eyeing one another cautiously.

Throughout the meal, Jake had been noticeably reticent in making conversation with Brittany. It was also clear that David would be unable to secure her a position at the bank without his brother's approval, so she bestowed her most alluring smile on him and began to question him politely about his work and his stay in London. The more she talked, the more vacuous she heard her remarks become, and the more uncomfortable she felt under his neutral, colourless gaze. Finally her voice trailed away altogether.

'I understand you're about to find yourself out on the street, with no visible means of support, Miss Colby,' he said bluntly.

Brittany felt herself blushing.

'I find that interpretation a little tactless, Mr Stein.'

He raised his eyebrows, unruffled. 'Can you afford to be coy about your predicament? And what do you intend to do about it? Live off charity? Or perhaps marriage is the answer; a nice, lucrative society marriage?'

'Certainly not!' snorted Brittany, aware of her heightened colour as she brought her eyes up to meet Jake's. 'I have no intention of taking that way out. In fact—'

'Good,' said Jake quietly. 'In that case I might be able to help you. I have a proposition to put to you, but this isn't the place to discuss it.'

He took a pen and piece of paper from his pocket and wrote something down.

'This is my address. I'll expect you there at about seven this evening. And bring your brother, will you? I want to meet him.'

Hateful man! thought Brittany as she rattled back to Park Street in a taxi. 'Hateful man!' Irritated, she tried to push all thought of David's brother from her mind.

As she had expected, George was appalled when she told him her plans to leave Park Street straightaway, and even more appalled that she had no intention of leaving Park Street without him. He had wandered vaguely into her room in answer to her summons, only to be bundled into a taxi and whisked off to number fifteen Eaton Place, where Jake Stein lived.

'Are these all right?' George plucked at the dilapidated flannels and well-worn shirt. 'Do you think they're all right, Brittany? Look, I'm not even wearing a tie . . .'

'That doesn't matter. You look all right.' She smiled and squeezed his arm.

George was making a valiant effort to understand the situation he had been thrust into after a rather dozy, uneventful day. 'So whose house are we going to now? Tell me again. David's?'

'No, Jake's. He's the elder of the two.'

'And you've met him before?' The taxi turned sharply round a corner and George slid across the seat.

'Yes, once. But only briefly.'

'So why is he helping you? Giving you a job . . .?'

'George! Are you asking all these questions to annoy me? Because if so—'

'No! No, I'm not. I just don't understand. You've only just met this person called David. And now his brother . . . What's he like? The brother.'

'He is . . .'

Brittany crossed and uncrossed her legs uncomfortably. The taxi turned into Eaton Square, spacious and leafy.

'. . . I don't know. He's American. You know. They're different.'

'David must be very . . . kind.' George had meant to say 'interested in you', but didn't dare.

Brittany laughed and blushed.

'Yes, I think—'

They had arrived. She was grateful that the business of climbing down from the taxi and paying the driver prevented her from completing her reply.

The interior of the house was a surprise. Brittany had expected it to be furnished in a drab, austere style, in sombre colours, but it was not.

She and George were ushered into a large, high-ceilinged room painted in resplendent turquoise, with sea-green drapes and green and yellow cushions. Every conceivable corner was crammed with

187

lurid hot-house flowers. George blinked disbelievingly.

'Was this Miriam's idea?' asked Brittany without preamble.

'No, mine,' said Jake. 'I like colour. Why, how did you expect my house to look?'

'Well, sort of . . . brown.'

'I dislike brown,' he said, with a quick smile.

Brittany could see from his sidelong glance that her reaction amused him. It was as if he had contrived the flamboyant room to compensate for his own plainness. She remembered the way that David had described the Steins' showpiece mansion in New York the night before. Perhaps the colours weren't so surprising, but the homely touches were: a little pile of books, old family photographs, a piano with music sheets open on it.

'I thought you might like to try our native mint julep, Miss Colby, so I've ordered some. I hope that's okay with you? . . .'

The mint juleps were delicious and icy cold, but Brittany was unable to follow George's example and become absorbed in the gradual emptying of the tall glass. She hovered between impatient sips and polite pleasantries.

'Mr Stein, I wonder . . . Would you think me awfully rude . . . Can we talk about the job?'

'Ah yes, the job . . .'

Jake avoided looking at Brittany as he spoke. She watched, fascinated, as he manoeuvred his tall body around the room, stooping to light a cigarette with graceful precision. He sat down so that he was facing Brittany and George, resting his elbows on his knees and blowing smoke carefully up at the ceiling.

'The position is this . . .'

They sat in expectant silence while Jake stared into space.

'David was particularly insistent that I find something for you, but much as I'd like to help, I'm afraid I can't offer you a job, Miss Colby. There's no position at Stein and Sons that would be suitable for a young woman. However, I do need a personal assistant, and I'd like to offer that position to George—'

'But George isn't the one who *wants* a job!' protested Brittany, 'This isn't fair. *I* was the one—'

'Please don't interrupt,' said Jake coolly. 'George's tasks would be quite simple, but he would also have the opportunity to learn a few things about the world of finance. If he became my employee, he would solve the problem of your imminent homelessness, because in addition to a salary, I would provide accommodation. I acquired the lease on a small mews house in Chelsea when I came over here in 1919, and at the moment it's vacant. What do you say, George?'

George smiled shyly and blushed into his glass of mint julep. 'I don't know, I . . . a job . . .'

He looked to Brittany for help. She nodded tersely.

'Yes. I mean, I'd like it.' He took a large gulp of the pale yellow liquid.

'Good.' Jake seemed genuinely pleased. 'That's settled then. If you report to me at our offices in Ironmonger Lane tomorrow morning, I'll arrange for someone to go in and get the house cleaned up, then I'll have the keys sent around to your present address. Does that suit you, Miss Colby?'

Brittany shrugged. 'It seems I don't really have a choice,' she said disagreeably. George looked acutely embarrassed.

Then she pulled herself up short. Why did she resent being beholden to this man? It was as if she was angry with him for being so different from David.

'I'm sorry,' she went on hastily. 'You must think me very bad-mannered. Thank you, Mr Stein.' She extended a cool hand for the briefest of shakes.

Jake's eyes lingered on her face briefly, then he stepped back. 'And now, if you'll excuse me, Miriam and I have a dinner appointment . . .'

George was silent in the taxi on the way home.

'I'm not sure about this,' he blurted out suddenly. 'I'm not sure if it's the right thing to do.'

'You mean, working for Stein and Sons? Didn't you like Jake?'

'Yes, yes, I thought he was very nice. What I meant was, leaving the Langbournes like this, after all they've done . . .'

Brittany felt uneasy. She wanted to keep George with her and besides, she needed him now as her means of escape. She began to cast around in her mind for an incentive to offer him. 'Look,' she said quickly, 'you love Susannah, don't you?'

George's mouth hung open.

'No, don't answer that. I know you do. But she's never going to be able to treat you as anything other than a brother while you're living under the same roof. It wouldn't be proper. Maud wouldn't allow it. But if you have an establishment of your own, she'll have to take you seriously, and you'll be able to pay court to her properly: send her flowers, dine with her. You'd like that, wouldn't you?'

George nodded silently.

'Well, there we are then!' said Brittany brightly.

'What about Richard and Maud? How are we going to tell them?'

'Don't worry about that!' said Brittany, with more confidence than she was feeling. 'I'll do it. I'll talk to them this evening.'

They walked up the stairs in silence and George retreated to his room. Brittany stopped for a moment outside Susannah's door, torn with indecision. Despite her new-found independence, she did not want her old friend thinking ill of her. Should she go in and effect a reconciliation?

She paused for a few seconds, then walked on.


## Somerset, 8 June, 1923

There was an insistent rattling at Lady Henrietta's door.

'*Let me in!*' The voice was urgent. '*Let me in!*'

Lady Henrietta pulled the covers up around her ears and hoped he'd go away. The door handle began to move. She sat bolt upright in bed. This was different from the usual pattern. Usually he shouted in the corridor, and threatened, but he never actually came into the room.

She had slipped from her bed and was fumbling with the sleeves of her peignoir when the door opened.

'Henrietta.'

She stared at him in surprise. She hadn't heard him use her name for months, or even years. The curtains were open slightly, and he staggered into the shaft of moonlight so that his face was illuminated. There was composure in his ragged, features, and for a moment she glimpsed the bluff, athletic young squire who had persuaded her into matrimony.

Then she reproved herself sharply for being sentimental.

'Henrietta . . . must talk to you . . .'

This was even more alarming. He was having one of his lucid spells. They had been so rare of late that she had become accustomed to treating him like a child, or an animal. The idea of

Roland as a *person* was threatening all of a sudden.

'Sit down then, Roland,' she said crisply, 'and tell me what this is all about. There had better be a good reason for this disgraceful intrusion.'

She made no move to light the lamp, as though afraid that direct light would reverse the transformation and turn him back into a dribbling, incontinent beast. He eased his vast body onto the edge of the high, old-fashioned wooden bedstead, and she sat down beside him, pulling her robe around her tightly. Roland seemed unaware that the front of his pyjama trousers was gaping open, and Lady Henrietta looked away in distaste. It was the first time in thirty years that they had been near the same bed.

'Henrietta, I've got to talk to you about it. I keep seeing it, and it was so bloody awful, shocking . . .'

He buried his huge head in his hands and the lank, reddish grey locks tangled through his fingers.

'Talk about what, Roland?' asked Lady Henrietta, enunciating very clearly.

'About Gerald, of course. God, I saw it, it was a dreadful thing. I don't know why he did it but . . . Christ, poor Gerald!'

'*Did what?*' Lady Henrietta was about to ask, but she realized that it was an interrogative approach that was bound to fail.

'But it was a long time ago,' she said quietly, hoping to prompt him.

He looked at her uncomprehendingly. Of course, she thought, the salient feature of insanity is that the past tense had no meaning. Whatever it was that happened is as vivid and alive in his mind as though it took place yesterday, or today even.

And she saw in his face that shock and anguish were being relived even as he spoke.

'. . . I could see it all from where I was standing, because I was low down in the hollow. Anstey and Frederick Colby were above me, and then Gerald was higher still. I'd run out of shot and I was just turning round to shout for my loader, and I saw him. He said he slipped, didn't he, that he'd lost his footing on the scree of the slope, but he didn't, you know, Henrietta. I saw him take aim. He was pointing his gun near Anstey's head. Then Frederick shouted and Anstey moved and . . . Gone.'

He lifted his hands and let them fall back heavily on his thighs.

'I don't know what he meant to do, Henrietta, but Christ, I saw the expression on Gerald's face afterwards and I thought 'Oh, no, poor Gerald'. But he could trust me. I never told anyone until now, and I was the only one who saw. And Adrian, of course—'

'Adrian?' Lady Henrietta whispered softly.

'Yes. Adrian was right at the top of the slope, you see. He wasn't *meant* to be there, but of course he'd hung back to make sheep's eyes at the Colby girl – I always forget her name, something foolish – and they'd all forgotten about him.'

He was staring straight ahead and saliva was beginning to collect at the corner of his mouth.

'Are you *certain* that Adrian saw?' Lady Henrietta asked urgently. 'Did you speak to him about it, discuss it with him . . .?'

But Roland had slipped away again. He was looking about him wildly as though he had just found himself imprisoned in a cell, or alone in an alien landscape, and his eyes were glazed. She took hold of his shoulders, wincing at the touch of his ageing, sweaty flesh beneath her hands, and brought her face close to his. His breath was foul.

*'How much does Adrian know?'*

He pushed her aside and padded over to the fireplace where her collection of miniatures hung. Most of them were family portraits.

'Ah, Bertie!' he said delightedly, catching sight of her brother's moonlit likeness. In reality Robert Dysart had despised his brother-in-law, but in Roland's imagination they were firm friends.

'Bertie, you always were a good sport. Always keen for a game of cricket . . .'

He began to swing with his arms, as though swiping at an imaginary ball. 'Caught in the slips, m'boy '. . .'

The phrase obviously pleased him, for he repeated it as his fist caught the glass dome that covered a valuable pendulum clock and sent it smashing to the floor, splintering into invisible fragments in the darkness.

'Caught in the slips!' he bellowed, and Lady Henrietta pressed herself gingerly against the bedhead as he tossed a marble paperweight through the air. It fell against the curtains and broke a window pane with a resounding crack. Despite the poor light she could see the unnatural darkness of his skin and the dew of sweat on his forehead. She scrambled over the bed and flung open her bedroom door.

192

'*Deborah!*'

Silence.

'*Deborah!*'

Eventually the reassuring footsteps came. Deborah had flung a knitted shawl over her nightdress, but her hair was still tousled.

'Oh no, my lady—'

'Oh yes, I'm afraid. He came in here all docile and, well . . . himself, but he's getting violent. A case of in like the lamb and out like the lion. Help me to get him to his room.'

'It's all right, my lady, I'll deal with him.'

The ever-competent Deborah seized Roland under his armpits and began to pull him from the room.

'Oh, and Deborah—'

'Yes?'

'I'm afraid I'm going to have to ask you to lock him in.'

She closed the door and stepped gingerly back to her bed, avoiding the broken glass. But she knew she would be unable to sleep. The muffled grey light of dawn was beginning to filter into the room. She dressed hastily, pulling her clothes onto the thin body that had never been young and voluptuous and desired, smoothing her faded grey hair into place.

Downstairs, the house was stuffy and unwelcoming, as though reluctant to be roused from its slumber. The revenue from Heathcote's farms had dwindled so much that there was no parlourmaid now, only Deborah and the cook, so Lady Henrietta set about cleaning the grate in the drawing room.

She was troubled with arthritis and had lit a fire the evening before, even though it was a mild summer evening, to warm her bones and dispel some of the damp in the room. In the corner, above her favourite French walnut bureau, the wallpaper was shadowed with mould.

She worked stiffly, but efficiently, sweeping out the old ashes onto a pile of newspaper and brushing the grate clean.

Then she stopped.

She saw with piercing clarity what had happened to her. She saw a picture of herself, an old woman of sixty-five, on her hands and knees, brushing clean a grate in a neglected room, with her hair falling about her face. And superimposed on that, like a faulty photograph, was another picture: the picture of a smart woman with raven hair and a parasol, sitting beside an ivy-clad wall and watching her son master the brutish horse that she had bought for him.

*That she had bought for him . . .*

Why was she allowing Adrian to do this to her? She dropped the hearthbrush as though it had burned her, and sat in a faded chair to think. After all, wasn't Adrian a creature of her own making? She had carved out a path for him and set him down on it, yet . . .

'. . . *There is a way, Mama, I've already found it.*'

Of course she had wondered exactly how Adrian had convinced Gerald Colby to make him heir to Graylings, but had been forced to the conclusion that Gerald had decided he had no better alternative. Now she knew the truth. He had extorted Graylings by threatening to expose Gerald's true role in the shooting 'accident'.

And then he had cast her arrogantly aside, like an old rag he had no further use for. But he would not treat her like that any longer. Not now that she knew . . .

*Five brisk steps up to the top of the portico, a smart rap at the front door, ignore the maid who answers it, breeze straight into the library, removing gloves en route, drop gloves rudely onto his desk . . .*

'Adrian, I have absolutely had enough of this! Your father is beyond my control. He actually became violent last night, and I'm telling you now, I refuse to live there alone with him a minute longer. It just won't do. Now, what have you to say?'

'Mama, we're not alone.' Adrian glanced in the direction of his hoydenish secretary, who was staring down at her typewriter and pretending not to listen.

'Well, tell Miss . . . Thing . . . to leave us.'

'Phoebe . . .' sighed Adrian.

The secretary got up and walked out sulkily, slamming the door behind her.

Adrian's dark eyes gleamed.

'I quite understand, old girl,' he said, smoothing an immaculate white cuff. 'And I intend to remedy the situation at once.'

'You do?'

'Of course. I'll send Jernnifer down to Heathcote for a while. She can help you until . . . a better arrangement can be made.'

Lady Henrietta glanced sharply at her son's face. She was considering trying to penetrate the portals of Graylings irrevocably by revealing what she knew of his methods, but decided against it. It was not the right moment to use such information; her case was too weak. He would only laugh in her face and say she couldn't prove anything. She would wait. And for the moment Jennifer's presence would provide some compensation.

'Very well. Make sure she's at Heathcote within a week, please.'

Jennifer eyed the redoubtable figure of Mrs Rosslyn through the kitchen doorway.

'Is everything all right?' she asked coolly.

'Perfectly, thank you, madam,' said Mrs Rosslyn with an air of dignified martyrdom.

Jennifer stood and watched her as she moulded pastry with her fingers. It seemed remarkable that anything delicate or meltingly fragile should emanate from this woman, but it did. She was a mountain of flesh, a pyramid whose peak was an untidy mop of grizzled hair, and whose base was a vast and ungainly vat of flesh. She had an angry puce complexion and tiny, bleary eyes.

Satisfied that Mrs Rosslyn would again effect this miracle, Jennifer walked away.

Phoebe had told her that she should try again.

After the last occasion, Jennifer had private doubts about her chances of success, but at least Mrs Rosslyn had outlasted her probationary period and had been accepted as a permanent member of the staff. Phoebe insisted that this acquiescence on Adrian's part was a good sign. This evening another elaborate meal was planned. And this time there would be no cocktails to follow.

The dinner passed without a hitch. Adrian complimented the food at length, and even brought a faint blush to Jennifer's clay-pale cheeks by telling her how becoming he found the white gardenias in her smooth, dark hair. When they retired to bed, she managed to ignore the strangely distracted way that he made love to her, and to be thankful for the attention.

As quickly as possible, he rolled off her and mumbled, 'By the way, Jennifer, there's something I meant to tell you earlier . . .'

'Yes?' She smoothed her hair away from her face and straightened her nightgown methodically.

'I want you to go down to Heathcote for a while. Mama's having some difficulties managing Father, and I told her you'd go and help until we could find some better arrangement.'

He waited for her to speak.

All sorts of questions were forming in Jennifer's mind. Why

couldn't Adrian pay someone to go and look after Roland? Why couldn't Lady Henrietta and Roland Steele move up to Graylings together? Why couldn't he be put into a home in Wells?

But she sensed that to demand answers to those questions would undermine what she had achieved so far. So she forced them back, swallowing them and wincing at their bitter taste, and she quelled the thought that if her own parents were alive, then surely her husband wouldn't dare treat her like this. As it was, she had no one to turn to, and Lady Henrietta was her only likely ally. Except for Phoebe, and Adrian would never listen to *her*.

Nevertheless, she could not quell the tremor in her voice as she asked, 'Will I be there long?'

'I shouldn't think so,' said Adrian neutrally. 'I doubt I could tolerate being alone in the house with that trollop for very long.'

He turned his back to her and fell asleep. Jennifer lay awake, listening to his breathing.

The next morning, Jennifer cornered Phoebe in the library and told her the news.

'Oh dear, that's *bad*,' said Phoebe in her broad Somerset accent.

She took a compact from her desk and began to powder her nose, keeping her eyes on the mirror in front of her. 'But look at it this way: if you argue, it will only be worse. Stick it out for a while, I should.'

She snapped the compact shut. 'Anyway, you say that last night he . . .'

Jenifer nodded.

There was a glint in Phoebe's eye. 'Well, you might have done the trick then. Think of that.'

Jennifer thought, *If only there's a baby, then everything will be all right* . . .

## London, 22 June, 1923

Miriam Stein bent close to the telephone.

'All right,' she purred. 'All right, darling, I'll see you very soon. Can't talk now.'

She checked her appearance briefly in the mirror in the hall, licking a finger and smoothing it over her fine, arched brows. A pair of slanting, sloe black eyes looked smugly back at her.

196

Jake appeared on the stairs as she was hurrying to the front door.

'Miriam—'

But she was gone, slamming the door behind her. Jake went to the window and watched her clicking down the street in her ridiculously high heels. He had stopped feeling curious about where she was going. He had certainly stopped caring.

Earlier that day he had stood in the same place and watched David trace a similar course with his habitual exuberance. David had called to inform Jake of his imminent departure for Somerset, with Brittany Colby. David was convinced that if he was *in situ*, he would be able to find the missing piece in the mechanism which had led Brittany to lose her former home; moreover, it would satisfy David's hunger for sleuthing. As far as Jake could tell, Brittany met David's idea with bemused acceptance, but he could sense that she was steeling herself for the disappointment of finding . . . nothing.

Looking out over the empty street, Jake remembered the look on David's face as he had hurried back to Brittany in the waiting car, and felt unaccountably jealous. And then he found himself thinking of Katherine Exley, and he buried his head in his hands, overwhelmed by the blinding pain of irreparable loss.

George tentatively unhooked the telephone receiver, then replaced it. The house was staring at him, dumb, scornful, empty. David and Brittany had just departed for Somerset in a flurry of laughter and hurried arrangements, and now he was left facing the weekend alone.

David had been very excited all week about his attempt to get Graylings back from Adrian Steele. He had talked about his plans incessantly, but George had closed his eyes, not wanting to hear. As far as he could see, everything revolved around an elaborate session of snooping, and asking a lot of people a lot of tedious questions that would probably lead nowhere.

And what if they didn't lead anywhere. George felt very unhappy, angry almost, about what David was doing. David didn't understand what it was like to have all that responsibility, did he? What if Adrian Steele *did* leave Graylings? It would be up to him, George, to go back and take up where Adrian had left off, and he wouldn't be able to do it. It would never be the same without Maman . . .

And if he was to go back there, why should he waste his energy getting used to living in this house? He wondered whether Brittany thought of these things as the reverberations from her life sent him careering hither and thither. He felt confused, cheated, manipulated.

But he was forced to admit that Brittany had done a good job with the house in Cheyne Mews. They had only been there two weeks, but already it felt warm and lived-in and homelike. He wandered around aimlessly, touching things with the regret of a child who has arrived too late and found the fairground closed down and deserted. It was like a doll's house after Park Street. There was a tiny entrance hall with a dining room to the left, a small square drawing room on the right looking out onto the mews and a kitchen no bigger than a cupboard. Upstairs there were two large bedrooms, one with an adjoining dressing room, a bathroom and a maid's room.

It could have been dark and poky, but Brittany had had the whole house painted in delicate, translucent pastel shades: eau-de-Nil, magnolia, café-au-lait, so that it glowed with light like a small, perfect jewel. Furniture salvaged from Graylings had been put to good use, including the ivory-inlaid escritoire, and of course there was the precious gramophone. And all week, David had been arriving with books and expensive Lalique glass and lamps, and pictures for the walls, and banks and banks of exotic flowers. Jake's contribution had been far more useful. She was Florrie, a hard-nosed, cheerful young Cockney, who was employed to cook and clean and play maid to Brittany.

George negotiated his way across the drawing room with a sigh. Florrie did not come in at weekends, and her young mistress was extremely untidy. But at least clearing up after Brittany would delay his having to make a decision about what to do. He picked up several copies of *Vanity Fair* and *Harper's Bazaar* from where they lay in abandoned disarray, with their spines bent and their pages open, on the pale cream carpet. Then he stacked all the romantic *novellas* into a neat pile and put them on a black glass-topped table beneath one of David's more extravagant gifts: a lampshade whose base was a winged sylph. A half-unscrewed bottle of nail varnish and a hair clip were rescued from beneath the sofa. Then he shook out the cushions methodically and opened the window to air the room.

There was nothing more for him to do. He flung himself heavily onto the sofa and tried to think of ways to fill the weekend. Today he could go to Brooks' Club, where he was a member, and stay until late. That would mean sleeping in on Sunday morning. Then perhaps he would be able to pluck up the courage to telephone one of the Nice Young People he had met through Maud Langbourne and arrange a game of tennis or a ride in the Row . . .

And then it would be Monday morning again, and he would have to go back to Stein and Sons. George felt despondent at the prospect. Despite Jake's abundant kindness, he felt ill at ease at the bank. He was slow to learn, and he forgot things, and got into a muddle that had to be sorted out by someone else afterwards. And the offices were hot and stuffy and crowded with people who knew what they were required to be doing at any given time of the day. He supposed he would continue there, for Brittany's sake. His job allowed them to rent this house, and the house allowed her to entertain David Stein, and David Stein seemed to make her happy.

George thought wistfully of the large, mansion in Park Street, and all the activities that Maud would have organized to fill the weekend. He had been back there for tea once or twice, but relations with the Langbournes were now naturally extremely cool. As far as George could see, they had started to deteriorate when Brittany had cut off all her hair, and spiralled rapidly downwards ever after.

He went back into the hall, where the smart white and gold telephone stood beneath a huge mirror, like a prop from a Hollywood film set. Beside the telephone lay a piece of paper. He frowned at it, then picked it up and remembered what it was: a bill from an exclusive Mayfair florist. 'Delivery' it said, in handwritten copperplate. 'To Miss Susannah Langbourne, 8 Park Street. One dozen orchids (white).' Beneath that was his own signature and a figure which indicated the extraordinary number of guineas that George would have to find from his month's salary. He crumpled up the piece of paper and thrust it into his pocket. He did not want Brittany to find it.

Then he picked up the telephone. 'Mayfair 245, please,' he said firmly.

The butler who answered told him for the umpteenth time that day that Miss Susannah was not at home.

George replaced the gold and white receiver and sank further into the gloom of despondency.


## Somerset, 22 June, 1923

The engine of the Lanchester roared expectantly as it was thrust into a lower gear to meet the incline in the lane. They turned sharply to the right.

'Wait, stop here,' said Brittany, reaching out a hand towards the steering wheel. 'There it is, down there.'

Graylings lay below them, cool and milk-white and crystalline in the sunshine, balanced in its green bower as a witness to eighteenth-century man's pact with Nature. The faintest of breezes ruffled the screen of trees behind the house, rippling their leaves from dark green to pale green and back to dark again. Only the dusky cedar stood unmoved on the smooth, green lake of a lawn.

David drew in his breath audibly. 'This place', he declared like a judge pronouncing sentence. 'is worth holding on to.'

He started up the engine and they coasted down the hill, past the place where the steep driveway met the lane, past the beech copse and its strategically placed bench on the left, past . . .

'Wait!' said Brittany again, as they approached the gravelled arc at the front of the house. 'Stop the engine, David. We had better decide on our course of action first. Supposing they're at home?'

'You're right. The question is this – what would Hieronymus Shand have done now?'

Brittany laughed. 'Well, what would he have done?'

'He would have been prepared for any eventuality. So let's think . . . first of all, what if there's no one home? Do you think you can find a way for us to break into the house without causing any damage?'

Brittany nodded.

Now we have to consider what we do if there's someone home. Let's take the wife first. Jennifer. If she's there on her own, we could either come straight out with it and say why we're here, and demand to go through the house as if it's our right. Or we can spin her a tale about you losing some family treasure, or necessary papers, and ask her if we can look for them. What do you think?'

Brittany squinted into the sun. 'I think it's better not to lie,' she said eventually, remembering the look of flagrant calculation on Jennifer Bladon's doll-like face when she first met her future husband. 'She's likely to be suspicious, and even if she's not, she may come with us to look for the fictitious item that I've suddenly come to claim. That could hamper us considerably.'

'I agree,' said David. 'Telling the truth will at least allow us to insist on going through the house on our own. But what about Adrian Steele? He's the one who might be hiding something, so he'll be altogether more difficult to deal with. And he may even refuse to let us in.'

'I doubt that. That would only make *us* more suspicious. My guess is that he'd let us in, but would make sure we weren't left on our own, while doing his best to hide whatever he might have to hide.'

'In that case—'

'In that case,' Brittany put in firmly, 'we'll just have to look out for an opportunity to come back uninvited when he's not here. I'm sure that's what our friend Hieronymus Shand would have done.'

They parked the car in the stableyard and climbed out stiffly, stretching their cramped legs. David leaned against the hot, red flank of the car while Brittany wandered slowly past the loose boxes. She peered inside them but did not recognize any of the horses she saw, except for Adrian's mean-looking dappled grey stallion, who tossed his neck back and bared his ageing teeth in warning. Then she stood immobile in the centre of the yard with the silence roaring in her ears. The metallic rays of early afternoon sun bathed everything in a blinding white light, and if she half-closed her eyes, the air quivered and jumped before them and the cobblestones, the brick walls of the stable and the sky itself were as white as the shimmering walls of Graylings.

She shuddered.

'No sign of life here, David. Adrian's horse is in its box, but it's getting so long in the tooth that he probably uses another. I expect he's out on the estate somewhere, ordering his tenants about. Let's go to the front.'

As they waited for an answer to their peal on the front-door bell, Brittany looked long and hard at David and herself, trying to picture them as the person on the other side of the door might see them, as a couple. They looked out of place here: too smart, too urbane. David was wearing a pale linen suit and a soft collar. His skin, where it showed at his neck and his wrists, was deeply tanned and his black curls made him look foreign. Her own dress of cream silk tussore was painfully fashionable, her silk stockings and glacé kid button shoes shamelessly new and unmarked and the pale cream Mary Pickford hat, whose wide brim folded up at the front to frame her face, altogether too theatrical.

She positioned her gleaming feet together neatly and stared self-consciously ahead.

No one came.

She rang again, and again the peal went unanswered. She coughed nervously.

'Try the door,' said David.

The house was as silent as its surroundings. Blinds had been drawn over most of the windows, and although the air was cool and clean, the house seemed drowsy, as though they had half awakened it from its slumber by opening the front door. Brittany took the precaution of tugging on the bell pull, but still no one came.

'It must be the servants' half day,' said Brittany, instinctively lowering her voice to a whisper. 'But I wonder where Jennifer is . . .'

She drifted through the rooms with David a respectful few paces behind like a consort, touching the paraphernalia of her former home, touching the shape of her childhood.

'Is it very different?' asked David.

'No, it's not. It's not really different at all. But that's all part of the game that Adrian's playing. I think he wants to pretend that it has always belonged to him. If it were all new and shiny and pin-neat, then he wouldn't be able to, would he?'

She started to laugh suddenly, catching sight of the automatic gas-lamps with their dainty chain switches. 'Look, he even instal-led these ghastly things. I remember hearing him recommend them to Maman, and wondering what on earth could have been going through his head. Now I know. I'll have them all ripped out and electrification installed when—'

She broke off and continued hastily towards the library. 'Hadn't we better start looking now, David? Remind me what I'm supposed to be scenting out.'

'Anything,' said David. 'Anything and everything. Since we don't know for sure what happened between your father and Adrian, the only chance we stand is by turning up some piece of evidence of . . . unorthodoxy. So we need to go through accounts, books, letters, legal documents . . .'

He glanced up at an automatic gaslight, grotesque symbol of Brittany's hope.

'. . . And even then, we've got to prepare ourselves for the possibility of finding nothing at all.'

'I know,' sighed Brittany.

The library produced nothing. The table with the typewriter on it ('I might have known *he* would employ a secretary,' muttered Brittany) had a pile of badly typed letters on it, waiting to be signed, and a few crumpled-up first attempts. All related to current estate management. The desk in the corner was piled high with seed catalogues and farming manuals. There was an ashtray overflowing with cigar butts and a notepad with abrupt sentences pencilled in Adrian's hand. *'Speak to fencer re Home Farm paddock.' 'J. Waite – 22s. credit.'* and *'Kale?'*

The study was next, and at first seemed more promising, but apart from correspondence with the Colby solicitors which revealed nothing irregular and – as David was quick to point out – would probably have been made available to Brittany by Mr Gamp, the only papers in the desk drawer related to Roland Steele's overdraft and the financial position of the meagre Heathcote estate.

Brittany sighed in exasperation. 'This was where Papa used to keep his correspondence, I'm sure of it. Whatever was left when Mr Gamp had finished winding up Maman's affairs must have been burnt or thrown away. And anyway, Adrian would hardly leave an incriminating piece of paper lying around, would he? He would have destroyed it, or hidden it. And we certainly don't have time to search the whole house from top to bottom . . .'

Her voice began to rise, in her anxiety.

'Don't worry,' said David calmly. He was sitting on the edge of the desk, one thigh slung casually over its leather surface, an incongruously modern figure among the gloomy eighteenth-century oil paintings of prize cattle.

'I admit we're not getting very far. But I think Hieronymus would have given it one more try. Now, think. Where in the house would old, unused junk be stored? Photographs, document cases, suitcases . . .'

'The attic.'

'Right, lead me to the attic.'

'We'll have to be very quiet if we go upstairs,' whispered Brittany as they mounted the marble staircase. 'It's quite possible that Jennifer might be up there, resting.'

She paused vigilantly on the grandiose first-floor landing. 'Did you hear that, David?' she hissed.

'What?'

'Voices from . . .'

She followed the noise and stopped still in her tracks.

The sounds were coming from Maman's room.

She could distinguish Adrian's voice and that of a woman.

A bed-spring creaked. She narrowed her eyes angrily and her hand reached instinctively for the doorknob.

David's fingers closed on her wrist and pulled her roughly away.

'What the hell do you think you're doing?' he hissed.

'My God!' she spluttered. 'My God, David, they're in *there* – in my *mother's room*!'

Her voice crackled in the silence.

Tightening his hold on her wrist, David dragged her back to the top of the stairwell.

'You little idiot! You almost threw away the last chance you have of . . . *this*!'

He gesticulated silently towards the perfect dome, with its Cyclops-eye of blue heaven.

'He's in bed with his wife – so what? Now for heaven's sake let's get up to that attic before they come out here and find us!'

The windows in the attic had not been opened for years, and the atmosphere was hot and choking. Dust and age crept into eyes and nostrils and throat. Here were no seed catalogues, no automatic gaslights. Time had not moved forward; it had merely sat down tired, and rested.

David began to search at once, methodically opening drawers and cupboard doors. Brittany fingered her way dreamily through a box of toys. Her china dolls were there with their rattling eyes, and an old musical box, in the shape of a house, that played 'The Bluebells of Scotland'. She wound it up and placed it on an empty packing case. Mournful, tinny notes dropped hesitantly into the musty air.

'What's in there?' asked David, pointing to a large brown paper parcel in one corner.

Brittany bent down to look at it more closely.

'Papa's uniform,' she said bluntly. 'It's customary for their belongings to be sent back afterwards, mud, blood and all. They imagine the grieving loved ones will want to shed tears over it.'

'But you never opened it?' David asked incredulously.

'Maman didn't want to. She had it taken up here straightaway. I suppose she thought it was too grisly . . '

While she was speaking, David had begun to rip the grimy string and the brown paper away: thick paper and several layers of it. The uniform lay there, compressed into a sad cube of khaki.

'What are you doing that for?' asked Brittany.

'Do you think this would fit me?' David held the polished Sam Browne belt against his chest. 'You know, I've always wondered what I'd look like in uniform . . . It occurs to me that your father might have kept some sort of evidence with him, just in case . . . It's not inconceivable that he took important papers to France, and they might have sent him back with the uniform . . .'

Brittany removed her hat carefully and knelt on the floor beside him, realizing too late that she was leaving grey-brown stripes of dust on her cream dress.

'It doesn't look as though there are any papers,' she said doubtfully, lifting the jacket. 'Just clothes, I'm afraid.'

David took the jacket from her and began to search the pockets. 'See!' he said triumphantly, holding up a battered and stained brown package.

Brittany snatched it from him, and her hands trembled as she began to read. Someone had scrawled in pencil on the outside of the envelope, in an irregular, childish hand.

'TO WHOM IT MAY CONCERN. URGENT. THIS PACKET CONTAINES THE LAST WILL AND TESTERMENT OF MAJ. G. R. COLBY AND SHOULD BE CONSIDERED BINDING ABOVE ALL OTHER SUCH DOCUMENTS. SIGNED E. HAYNES (CORPORAL) 2 APRIL 1918.'

Brittany took out the papers in silence. 'The Bluebells of Scotland' ground stiffly towards its end. Dying strains, dying wishes . . . 'It is my last wish . . .' she read . . .

'I don't believe it,' she whispered, 'I don't believe it. He made another will . . .'

David took the paper from her hand and began to read out loud.

'*It is my last wish that the instructions of my will of January 1913 be set aside, and that the following bequests be enstated. I bequeath my house, Graylings, of Nether Aston, Somerset, and the estate of the same name to—*'

He frowned at the page.

'Go on.'

'*. . . to Evelyn Margaret Colby*', Who's that? A cousin or something?'

'The Bluebells of Scotland' expired abruptly in the middle of a bar.

'No,' said Brittany quietly. 'It's me.'

David stared at her in surprise.

'Brittany isn't my real name,' she explained. 'It's like a nickname. I was christened Evelyn. No one but Papa and Aunt Georgina ever called me that.'

She laughed disbelievingly.

'Wait,' said David, 'there's more. "*. . . to Evelyn Margaret Colby, in atonement for my part in the death of her father, Charles Anstey, Earl of Teasdale.*" "*Her father*"? Wait a minute . . .'

Brittany reached out and took the paper back from him. She sat down on top of the packing case, next to the musical box in the shape of a house, and stared at the words on the page for a long time, without speaking. The packing case stood in a shaft of dusty sunlight and now she too became part of that blinding patch of light so that David could see only her body in silhouette. The fine, short wisps of her hair seemed caught up in a blaze of golden fire.

Finally she turned to face him and her strange, slanting blue eyes were sparkling with tears of shock.

'There's something else that I have to find,' she whispered.

She began to search frantically through cupboards and drawers, until finally she found a small brown leather suitcase. Inside was a sheaf of old photographs. She flicked through them, pausing every now and then to smile at one of the small, sepia faces: a studio portrait of Maman that imitated the famous Gibson girl commercial, Frederick, George and herself wearing sailor suits, posed stiffly in the dogcart, a formal group photograph of a weekend shooting party . . . and there it was.

She had once seen Maman take it out of the box of photographs and stare at it. A photo of Teddy. He was young and smiling and handsome, dressed in a cricket jersey, and had signed himself 'All the best, Teddy'. She needed no colour in the photograph to see the brilliant blue of those laughing eyes and the Saxon gold of his hair. Looking down at those half-familiar features she saw her own face, and her own life, and she smiled.

'*Because of him,*' she said out loud, '*all of this is mine.*'

'Here, put this on. I don't want to have a baby, do I?'

Lucienne Colby's magnificent bed creaked and heaved beneath its apricot satin polonaise. Naked limbs tangled impatiently in a surf of Nottingham lace. The afternoon sun slanted sharply through the half-drawn curtains, bathing the room with filtered light.

'Shhh!' Adrian sat up suddenly.

'What is it?'

'I thought I just heard something. Someone going downstairs.'

'Hearing things now, are you? Got a guilty conscience?'

Phoebe jumped down off the bed and sauntered over to the dressing table, singing softly under her breath, 'Home in Pasadena, Home, where grass is greener . . .'

Adrian's quick, bright eyes watched her appreciatively, taking in the full, heavy hips, long thighs and slender ankles.

'Come back here.'

She ignored him, picking up one of Lucienne Colby's perfume sprays and squeezing it idly in the direction of her neck. It was empty, and blew out nothing but a puff of dust.

'Come back to bed.'

She laughed again. The first time he had made love to her – the culmination of weeks of tension between his anger and her smirking – he had expected her to say something conventional like 'Whatever must you think of me?' But she hadn't. She had just laughed. And afterwards she had refused to lie down next to him and be embraced, but had sat at the end of the bed like a large, blowsy pixie, with her arms wrapped around her knees, watching him . . .

Phoebe started to walk back towards the bed, standing still a few feet away from it. Her hands were on her lips and her attractions displayed with flagrant immodesty. Adrian reached out to her, but she had deliberately chosen her distance so that he could not touch her without moving from the bed.

She looked in the direction of the door. 'And what about those noises you heard, Mr Steele? Hadn't you better go and see who it is? It might be your poor little wife—'

Adrian lunged across the bed and grabbed hold of Phoebe's thigh, using the hold to steady his weight, so that his fingers dug in hard and left purple marks in her white flesh. She clawed at him, tiger-like, with a flurry of white limbs and rusty hair, but he pulled her roughly onto the bed and covered her limbs with his own, holding fast until the wild flailing of her arms had stopped and her resistance ended.

'I know it sounds naïve,' said Brittany, staring into her glass of claret, 'but I didn't at any time put two and two together.'

They were sitting in the dining room of the Crown hotel in Wells, a haven of hushed voices and provincial respectability. After escaping from Graylings unseen, they had driven to Wells and wandered idly around the shops and the Cathedral Green and the Vicar's Close. They had not spoken much, each engrossed in their own thoughts about the implications of their successful detective work. Brittany had been composed and thoughtful, David had a triumphant gleam in his eye and a self-satisfied smile on his face. As the sun had begun to fade, and Brittany's new kid shoes had begun to pinch, they had decided to go and indulge in the most sumptuous dinner that Wells could offer before they returned to London. It was only then, relaxed by the food and the wine and the reassuring ordinariness about them, that they began to talk.

'. . . I knew that mother and Teddy were in love, and had been for some time. But since no one ever talked about it, I couldn't be sure when they had first met, and I suppose I just took it for granted that it was after I was born. He didn't come into my life until I was five, you see, and . . .'

'But the resemblance,' said David, pausing with a forkful of crown roast of lamb halfway to his mouth. 'You must have noticed. I saw it as soon as you showed me the photograph.'

'It may well seem obvious *now*, but the bar to my understanding was that—' She blushed slightly. 'I didn't know anything about the facts of life. I didn't know where babies came from, how they were made, and therefore the begetting of children was entirely associated with the ritual of marriage. Papa was married to Maman, and Teddy was not, and that was that. Now I can see that it was in my mother's interest to keep me in the dark about sex for as long as possible . . .'

She lowered her voice slightly as the head waiter ushered an elderly parson and his wife to the table next to theirs, making a great show of pulling out the plush chairs from the discreetly candlelit table and standing in a posture of supplication while they ordered two dry sherries and nodded 'good evening' to Brittany and David.

'But later, surely—'

'"Later" might have been different if Teddy hadn't died,' said Brittany sadly, draining her glass of claret. 'But by the time I discovered where babies came from, he had been dead for years, and I had long since stopped wondering about him and Maman. He'd been tidied away in a corner of my mind, like those photographs in the attic.'

'Your poor mother. It must have been—'

'Hell,' cut in Brittany, glancing guiltily in the direction of the vicar. 'It must have been hell. I was thinking about that on our walk this afternoon. I understand everything so much better now: why she kept her distance from me while Papa was around, that guilty look she sometimes wore . . .'

'And Adrian?'

Brittany laughed softly. 'Poor old Adrian,' she said, without malice. 'He's probably sitting down to dinner now, in *my* dining room, in blissful ignorance of what's about to happen. Fancy spending all afternoon in bed with your wife.'

'Yes. Just fancy,' said David, avoiding looking at the vicar as he remembered Dulcibel's warm flesh.

'Adrian was just being clever,' she went on. 'Too clever for his own good, I fear. I don't think we'll ever know exactly what happened. My father's gun was the one that killed—'

She hesitated slightly and gave David a wry smile. 'I suppose I ought to rephrase that. *Gerald's* gun was the one that killed my father, but the verdict was death by misadventure, due to a variety of factors – a sudden commotion, Gerald losing his footing. The wording of this new will suggests that he felt responsible for my father's death, but whether it was only guilty feelings, or whether there had been foul play, it seems possible that Adrian got hold of the fact and used it.'

A waiter arrived, bearing two cut-glass bowls filled with sherry trifle.

'But if Gerald was persuaded to change his will in Adrian's favour . . .' David said reasonably, as he sank his spoon into the custard, 'I think we're left assuming the latter. That Gerald intended to kill your father.'

'Perhaps,' Brittany agreed reluctantly. 'I think he was jealous, but more over the fascination Teddy held for Frederick than over Maman. He worshipped Frederick.' She sighed loudly. 'I still think it's possible that Gerald simply thought Adrian was the best person to have the estate. He did quite like him.'

'Then why the change of heart?'

'I don't know, Davy, I don't think we'll ever know.'

David ordered two brandies and raised one of them in a toast.

'To Graylings,' he said. 'May you live happily ever after there.'

Brittany did not raise her glass. 'It seems a little like tempting fate,' she said soberly. 'After all, this new will hasn't been endorsed by a lawyer, it might—'

'Nonsense! It's been signed by two independent witnesses. I believe there's a law allowing men on active service to draw up their own wills. As long as you're sure it's Gerald's signature?'

'Yes.'

'Well then!'

Brittany lifted her glass. 'To Graylings. May we live happily ever after there!'

She let the incriminating pronoun slip out without noticing, and she was so distracted by the astonished reaction of the vicar that she did not see the shadow that passed over David's face.

'Brittany . . .' said David, as they paid the bill and were ushered from the dining room, 'I thought we would probably finish eating too late to drive up to London, so I took the liberty of booking us in here for the night. Separate rooms, of course.'

'Of course,' replied Brittany, suppressing a smile.

He paused for just a little too long, when they reached her room. Brittany felt reckless and slightly feverish from the combination of strong sun and alcohol and emotional excitement, and when he stepped close to her, she shivered.

'Are you going to come in?' she asked quietly.

'I don't know if I ought—'

210

'What would Hieronymus Shand have done in these circumstances?' She ran her tongue teasingly over her lower lip.

'I'll show you.'

With one swift movement, he opened the door and pushed her into the room. The tips of their fingers brushed, and Brittany gasped with pleasure as David bent his head and pressed his mouth over hers. She received his kiss passively at first, then gave a little cry and locked both her hands behind his head, opening her mouth and letting his tongue explore her lips and gums. His mouth was supple and tasted of the sharp sweetness of brandy. His hands were already straying lower over her body, stroking her buttocks with the lightest of touches and back and forth across her nipples until she groaned out loud.

Then he stopped.

He looked hard at Brittany's face, and she looked back.

'Don't stop,' she whispered, 'Davy, please don't stop.'

Her knees were buckling. He pushed her onto the carpet like a rag doll and rammed his body hard against hers, while she begged him not to stop for a day, a week, a year.

---

# 8

## New York, 1 August, 1923

The new bank building rose cleanly above the crowds on Wall Street, square and massive and faced in white marble. The starkness of its façade was alleviated by a neo-classical porch with pillars which were each as wide as a small house. And there, blazoned across the triangular pediment, complete with Greek 'e's, were the gold letters: 'I. STEIN AND SONS'.

Isaac Stein stood at the window of his fifteenth-floor suite and looked down to the dizzying spectacle of the street below, the trolley buses and cars snaking nose to tail through a seething ribbon of people; busy people, working people clad in dark suits and intent on making money. Isaac found it a very satisfying sight.

The window he was looking through took up the whole of one wall. The other three walls were painted white. Isaac had decided against hanging the portraits of the Jewish elders in his new office. He did not want anything that might remind him, or his visitors, of the Frankfurt ghetto. Instead he had chosen a classical frieze as decoration. It was painted in black and gold and depicted the heroic efforts of some anonymous Olympian athletes. Isaac felt that it made a suitably neutral tribute to the achievement of excellence.

He sat down at his desk, and for the second time that morning picked up a magazine clipping that had been sent to him by Jack Olsen. A condition of Olsen's contract, naturally, had been that his surveillance should extend to discreet spying on David's activities. Isaac told himself that he was only doing it for Hannah's sake, and that it was harmless to take an active interest in the boy's welfare.

The chipping was from a London publication called *Bystander*.

'*Americans are certainly making headlines in London this week,*' the correspondent wrote in a trite and breathy style that Isaac despised. '*. . . On Thursday the Savoy saw a performance by Bert Ralton's Havana Band, who have already caused a sensation with the dancing public. The 'hot' tempo of their delightful music won them warm applause from their audience . . . one prominent American patronizing this musician from his homeland was Mr David Stein, son of Isaac Stein of New York. He has been seen escorting our own Miss Brittany Colby about town recently, and Thursday night was no exception. Miss Colby, formerly the ward of Mr and Mrs Richard Langbourne, one of society's most distinguished couples, was seen dancing well into the night . . .*'

With the cutting, Jack Olsen had sent a brief note saying that David sometimes stopped off at Miss Colby's house after an evening's entertainment, and did not return to Grosvenor Square until the following morning.

Isaac looked down at the cutting with contempt. Thank God Rebecca did not have access to this trash! There was even a photograph, showing David seated next to a dazzling, hot-eyed creature with a beaded helmet on her head and a thin cigarette holder balanced between her fingers. Isaac found himself remembering David's visits to Ginnie Cassidy's, and could not prevent a tug of curiosity. This girl was certainly good-looking . . . He

212

covered the photograph with a plump, freckled hand. He did not want to look at her.

It was definitely time for David to come home. He glanced at his watch, as if to confirm his theory, then he lifted the telephone and called in his secretary to take down a letter to Jake.

## London, 1 August, 1923

The reading room at Brooks' Club contrived to look like the study of a country parson. There were tall, glass-fronted bookcases, discreetly chiming clocks and the creaking of leather furniture, muffled somewhat by the thick, bottle-green carpet.

Adrian Steele sank into a highbacked leather chair, and after ordering a brandy, allowed himself a few moments to savour the irony of his situation. He, Adrian Steele, was a member of this exclusive club because his mother was a Dysart of Castle Cloud, and there had been Dysarts among the original list of members. His membership had even been a present from Mama, for his twenty-first birthday.

And today . . . today was not only the first time he had taken advantage of his mother's generosity by spending the night at his club, but also the day that Mama had revealed her true colours at last. Glancing around the room, and seeing only a few somnolent grey heads, Adrian permitted himself to laugh out loud at the neatness of the coincidence.

He took a large, burning mouthful of brandy and closed his eyes.

*I don't want to think about it. God, I don't want to think about the whole bloody, messy business any more . . .*

But I have to think about it, he told himself, opening his eyes and straightening up his chair. I have to think about it, in order to decide what course is left open to me. The barrister had really been very decent about it, he decided, as he tried to assess the events and place them in their proper order. Really very decent, considering the embarrassing position in which he had been placed.

*But no, that's not the beginning! It doesn't begin with the barrister. Go back to where the story starts and follow it through. That's the only way to work out what to do next . . .*

How far back should he go? It began with Anstey, really, falling to the ground like a dead bird, half his face blown away by shot. Or even earlier. Maman pointing to Graylings with that strange air of suppressed excitement that she sometimes had, and suggesting that he woo Brittany . . .

Begin with Brittany. Brittany inheriting Graylings after all, because of an inappropriate sense of guilt that Gerald Colby had mysteriously discovered in the trenches. Then the inevitable to-ing and fro-ing between lawyers, and an agreed date for his departure; a process rendered doubly humiliating by the arrival of a letter from Brittany, offering him the job of her estate manager. A sneer. An intentional insult. Of course he had declined.

Then there was money. He had invested a great deal of his own money in the estate, even some in the house, and he was determined to get it back somehow.

Enter the barrister. He had tracked down a KC who specialized in such delicate matters, and had written to him explaining the problem. The written reply was full of jargon such as 'equitable interest by way of a resulting trust', but he managed to ascertain that he could apply to the Chancery division of the High Court to reclaim the money he had invested. Furthermore, if the only way that his money could be repaid was by the sale of the estate, then he could 'force an order for sale'. He had become very excited at this news, and arranged to consult the barrister in his London chambers, but then . . .

Adrian took another large mouthful of brandy and pressed his elbows down hard on the arms of the chair. The barrister had greeted him with a long face and had shifted uncomfortably in his chair as he explained that he had just received a letter from someone signing herself Lady Henrietta Steele. The writer declared that she had good reason to believe that his client had obtained the Graylings estate by extortion. Was this true? Of course he had denied it. How could they hope to prove such a thing, after all? Then the barrister had become quite fierce and said, 'Mr Steele, if any such allegations should reach the ears of the High Court, then your application would be suspended pending an inquiry which would seriously damage your chances of success, whatever the outcome, not to mention imposing lengthy and expensive delays. Do you still wish to pursue this?'

Of course he had been forced to say no. He had no idea what Mama might choose to come out with next. He assumed that her new-found temerity stemmed from the fact that she was packing her bags to return to Castle Cloud, her childhood home, and leaving Jennifer to manage Father. Her nephew, the current Earl, had died suddenly without issue and the Castle had been inherited by an elderly first cousin, who had asked Lady Henrietta to go and live there as his companion and hostess. She was returning to her rightful place, and had ensured that her son was back in his. Not Graylings, as she had once so fervently believed, but Heathcote.

Had Adrian believed in God, he would have offered up a hearty prayer of thanks that he had at least retained some prudence during his enthusiastic onslaught on the Graylings estate. He had reduced Gerald Colby's mortgage somewhat with a lump sum, but elected to pay back the remainder in monthly instalments from his own income. So he still had half of his inheritance, and Brittany was left with the problem of the crippling mortgage.

He had money. And he had Phoebe . .

The room was so quiet that he looked up immediately he heard George Colby come into the room.

George's large, slightly pasty face assumed an expression of shock when he saw Adrian. Adrian didn't see why: they had long been members of the same club, so it wasn't really that surprising. The brandy had gone to Adrian's head. He heard his own voice, loud and brash, saying 'George! Sit down and have a drink, old man', and saw George's expression of shock changing to one of absolute horror. It reminded Adrian of the day of Anstey's death, and his attempts to sweeten the lumpish George by offering to teach him about guns.

George sat down on the edge of the chair that faced his own, and ordered a Scotch.

'All packed?' asked Adrian jovially. 'Looking forward to going home? I know I would be.'

George nodded slowly, without taking his large, wet, disbelieving eyes from Adrian's face.

'And your sister—' Adrian gulped at his second brandy. 'She is well?'

'Yes.'

'She must be . . . oh, twenty-five now? Am I right? Surely she'll be thinking of marrying soon?'

'I don't know.'

'But she has an admirer? Someone special?'

'There is someone,' George admitted slowly. 'David Stein. She sees him a lot. I think you could say he was special.'

'David Stein, eh? Jewish, I expect.'

'He's American.'

'Ah. And so, George, what are you going to do when the two of them go off and set up their love-nest in Somerset? Going to stay here in London?'

George looked at him stupidly. 'I don't know. I hadn't thought about that.'

By now the brandy was sending Adrian's blood thumping around his body, and he could control his temper no longer. Afterwards he told himself that it was all George Colby's fault for behaving like a halfwit, a lump of stone. With that face looking so like Frederick's . . .

'Brittany doesn't want you there, you stupid little idiot,' he sneered, incensed at the thought of George wandering idly around the fields that he had sweated for. 'She'll be wanting to go and live there with her lover, and she won't want you getting in the way. You must be mad to think of following her down there like the pathetic little dog you are. And why do you think your father changed the will in her favour rather than yours? Either he assumed you were going to drop down dead of a fit anyway, or he judged you to be too incompetent to take on the responsibility. Neither of those alternatives says much for you, does it?'

Adrian could feel sweat breaking out on his forehead, and there was a hot aching at the back of his throat. Lights flashed vaguely above his eyes. He was about to go on in the same vein, but then he saw Phoebe in his mind's eye, laughing at him for becoming so angry about harmless George Colby, and he managed to control himself.

'I'm sorry,' he muttered, pulling himself abruptly to his feet and draining his glass. 'Shouldn't have said those things. Trying day.'

He walked quickly to the door, leaving a whitefaced George looking the picture of misery.

Brittany decided she had never been so happy.

She and David were at the Savoy, dancing to Nick la Rocca's jazz band without a care in the world. The dancefloor was crowded with people; they brushed against the sedate wallpaper that depicted pastoral scenes in imitation of Watteau, and sent high a babble of laughter, as high as the glorious new electrified chandeliers. On the platform a banjo player strummed jauntily to 'Then I'll be happy'.

Brittany shuffled her feet back and forth on the tiny space allotted to her and sighed with contentment. Graylings was now only days away. Moreover, she had arranged with Jake to continue renting the house in Cheyne Mews at the same modest rate, so that she could come up to London and see David whenever she liked. He, of course, would be able to drive down and see her whenever he liked, and then perhaps . . .

*'If you go North or South, if you go East or West*
*I'll follow you, sweetheart, and share your little love-nest.*
*I wanna go where you go, do what you do,*
*Then I'll be happy . . .'*

David was not happy.

'Would you like to get something to eat?' he asked Brittany.

'No, I'm not hungry, darling. Really.'

Her brightness, her naïvety, her taking for granted things that were not hers, angered David.

'Isn't that Hal Chambers over there?' she was saying, trying to please him by recognizing one of his friends. 'Goodness, isn't he handsome? When you really look at him . . .'

She continued to chatter gaily.

'We've got so much work to do, you and I . . .'

'Work? What work?' David did not conceal his dislike of the word.

'Oh, we'll have to redecorate the whole house, and whitewash the outside walls . . . replant the flower garden. Oh David, I forgot to show you . . . there's a sweet little cottage in the north paddock that we could renovate, and I could paint there. George has still got his oil paints . . . I don't quite know what we're going to do about George . . . How about an orangery? Do you think we could? Do they have them in the States . . .?'

*Stop! Stop this sentimental delusion. I can't give you those things. I can't be the man you want me to be . . .*

David had a sudden picture of himself as a boy, selfishly distracting his mother because he was bored. And later. Visiting Dulcie when it suited him to do so, while Rebecca . . . taking, not giving. He felt profoundly sad.

'Davy, we're so lucky. You know, I really think we're lucky . . . I think I've drunk rather too much . . .'

*If only I could have been more like Jake.*

'David, I don't think you're listening to me!' Brittany was looking at him strangely.

'Sorry. Sorry, honey.' He groped for something to say. 'I was just thinking about Jake.'

'Jake? Why, what . . .? Is it—?'

'Miriam. Medusa. Take your pick.'

'They're not happy, are they?'

'No. No, I don't think you could say they were happy. Not by any standards.'

'Then why did he . . . I mean, Jake seems so sensible—'

'It was one of those things. My father set it up, introduced them—'

'Like an arranged marriage? Davy, how horrid! How ugly.'

'Ugly? Perhaps.' David looked hard into the distance. 'I think maybe at the time people think it's the sensible thing to do. To go with what the family wants. In Jake's case . . . I don't know. He hadn't really got over the Exley girl.'

Brittany waited for an explanation.

'Go on – who was the Exley girl?'

David shrugged. 'Oh, I don't know, maybe I shouldn't be telling you—'

'David, you've got to tell me. We can't have secrets from one another. I couldn't bear it.'

David felt his irritation rising again. 'She was just someone he used to be sweet on. Are you sure you don't want to eat?'

'No, no. I don't want anything. Just to go home, I think.'

Brittany's mood had been thoroughly deflated. She was standing on the Victoria Embankment, shivering as she waited for David to bring the car round. Rows of milky lights rose out of the evening mist and lit the edge of the river like a string of pearls around the neck of some Brobdingnagian empress clothed in the black velvet of the night, while the many-tiered lights that glittered and winked from the tall, square building of the Savoy made up the empress's crown.

It was then that Brittany noticed a large black Daimler parked at the kerb, and a man and a woman climbing out of it. The sleek and pristine condition of the car attracted her first, the polished surface

218

like water in the lamplight. Then her gaze was drawn to the woman's white mink coat, whose dangling ermine trimmings bobbed against her ankles, and by the sharp glitter of jewellery which adorned every visible inch of her body. She thought the man looked like a South American bandit, with his sleek black hair and curling moustache; but there was something about the woman that was more familiar. The lovers clung to one another and kissed, a long, shameless, open-mouthed kiss. As they broke apart the woman turned her face slightly and Brittany finally recognized her.

It was Miriam Stein.

Brittany was lying on the sofa with a biography of Lillie Langtry in her hand, and thinking about Miriam's lover, and the enigmatic Exley girl, when the doorbell rang the following afternoon. Feeling sure it would be David, she flung the book to the floor and ran to the door with childish eagerness.

It was Jake.

Her face fell and she took a step backwards. Jake smiled slightly.

'You gave me a surprise. I was expecting David.'

'David – for once – is in Ironmonger Lane. I just came to make sure that George was here.'

'*George*?' repeated Brittany, and then blushed at her own gaucheness. 'But he's not here, Jake . . .'

'Oh.' Jake frowned.

'I think you'd better come in. Come in, Jake, and sit down.' Brittany led the way into the drawing room and sat down in an armchair. 'Now, what's all this about?' She spoke flippantly, trying to quell a distinct surge of unease.

'We agreed that George would work until the end of this week. He said he'd be happy to do that, even though his contract is about to end. But he hasn't been into Ironmonger Lane at all today, so I thought I'd stop by and make sure he was here with you.'

'He's certainly not here with me. But he didn't say anything. He went out this morning at the usual time and I just assumed that he was with you at the bank.'

They stared at one another blankly.

'I wonder what the hell he's up to!' burst out Brittany eventually.

'Hey, calm down. It's probably something quite simple. Perhaps he had an errand of his own to run.'

'Then why didn't he tell you?'

219

'I don't know. Maybe there's a girl behind it. Is he involved with anyone?'

'No, not really. No.' Brittany decided that Jake would not count George's longstanding infatuation with Susannah as being 'involved'.

'I thought he seemed a little quiet lately. Do you think he's happy about going back to Somerset?'

'I . . . I don't know.'

Brittany reddened guiltily. Was he? She realized that she didn't know. She had been so engrossed in David, and in enjoying herself, that she had scarcely stopped to consider George's feelings.

'Do you want me to talk to him?' Jake asked gently, sensing her agitation.

'Yes. No. I'll talk to him about it when he gets home. No, wait . . .' She performed a hasty mental calculation. 'David and I are going out this evening. If he's still up when we come in, I'll talk to him then.'

'Okay, if you're sure.'

'Quite sure.' She smiled at him warmly. 'But now you're here, will you stay for some tea?'

'Well . . .'

'Oh, go on. Please. I was just about to have some anyway.'

She rang for Florrie to bring them tea.

'Would you like a cigarette?'

She offered him a box of de Reszkes. In the past she had enjoyed watching him smoke, he did it with such deliberation and precision. But this time he declined. She lit one for herself, hoping that he would not notice that she had only just taken up smoking and conclude, correctly, that she was one of that band of young women who just did such things to seem witty and sophisticated and modern.

Jake noticed.

'I wasn't aware that you had taken up smoking, Miss Colby.'

'Oh? I expect there are a lot of things about me that you're not aware of.'

Jake smiled broadly and leaned back in his chair. He ran his hand through his hair, and Brittany noticed for the first time how thick and glossy it was, like the hair of a young boy.

'I happen to know you have a predilection for sliding down banisters.'

She laughed. 'How on earth did you know that?'

'David told me, of course, who else?'

'Well, if you are truly interested, it was once a pastime of mine. But not something that I've indulged in for a while.'

'Ah, but would you like to?'

'Perhaps. Given the right staircase.' She smiled down at the tip of her cigarette, watching it burn.

'You must be looking forward to going home very much.'

'Yes,' She gave him a quick smile. 'But I shall miss London. And David.'

Jake sensed that it would be prudent to change the subject. 'You know, I once slid from top to bottom of our house in Fifth Avenue – down all nine staircases – on a tea-tray.'

Brittany laughed so hard that she dropped her cigarette on the carpet and had to fumble to retrieve it.

'*You* – on a tea-tray? I don't believe it. I always imagined you to be such a good little boy.'

'Quite the opposite. I was extremely naughty. In a quiet, determined sort of way. Until he reached his teens, it was David who was the goody-goody . . .'

Each time he spoke, Brittany watched Jake's face, trying to meet his cloudy eyes, but he kept his eyelids lowered, almost as if he was afraid he meet her piercing gaze. She had grown accustomed to looking for David in his face, but now, with his head turned slightly to one side and the sunlight in his hair, Jake Stein's face had its own atttraction. Brittany wanted him to go on talking, so that she could watch his face. She persuaded him to tell her more about his childhood in New York. The anecdotes he repeated were full of bizarre detail and humorous self-deprecation.

'. . . But,' he finished sadly, 'I'm sure you're finding all this a little dull.'

'Quite the opposite!' said Brittany, and Jake felt a deep thrill of satisfaction when he saw that the pleasure on her face was genuine. She had seemed nervous when he arrived. He lit a cigarette for himself and paused meditatively as he blew out the match.

'I'll tell you something, Brittany – you don't mind my calling you that, I hope – a lot of the things I've just told you are things I never told to anyone before.'

Brittany smiled. 'Tell me some more . . .'

After his third cup of tea, Jake glanced at his watch, sighed and stood up. 'I'm afraid that's enough storytelling for one afternoon. I have to leave now. Let me know if you need any help with George, won't you?'

Brittany sighed and stared at the carpet, fighting back the scorching of remorseful tears. Poor old George. She was letting Maman down, neglecting him like this. Perhaps they should stay in this evening, if George was back . . .

'Won't you?' he persisted, and raised her chin gently with his finger so that her face was on a level with his.

She blinked. 'Yes. And thank you, Jake. You've been very kind.'

She waited until he had reached the front door and then called after him: 'David was right. You *do* care too much.'

'What was that?'

'Nothing.'

George sat down on the edge of the pavement and buried his face in his hands. Nine o'clock, and it had just started to rain. He had been walking about for most of the day, but his exhaustion was dulled by a stupor of misery.

He had been carrying something in his pocket, and now he took it out and looked at it. It was a tiny wooden carving of Barley, the Jack Russell terrier. He turned it over and over in his hands, stroking its surfaces lovingly. Brittany had given it to him on his eleventh birthday, and it had been everywhere with him. He had picked it up as he left Cheyne Mews that morning, knowing that it would comfort him. He had known then that he wasn't going to go into the bank. If only there were somewhere he *could* go.

He was now in an area of London that was unfamiliar to him, somewhere north of Hyde Park, where the streets were dull and narrow and the flat-fronted Georgian houses grimy. Every so often he would pass a bar that spilled a patch of electric light onto the pavement, and hear a burst of saxophone-playing, or a hard, raucous woman's laugh. He had started to feel hungry. The only establishment that seemed certain to offer food was a pub, a depressing Victorian building with peeling brown paint, but as soon as he saw the food that was being served and smelled its sour, stale odour, he felt sick and ordered a Scotch instead. He drank it quickly and ordered another.

All day long he had been thinking about the things that Adrian

Steele had said to him. Brittany had not spoken about the future of her relationship with David, but now that silence seemed ominous. Had she said nothing because she took it for granted that George would follow her down to Somerset anyway? Or because she didn't really want him with her? He had pondered these two possibilities so hard that he had shredded and dissected every conversation he had had with Brittany for the past month, and he only felt further away from the truth than ever.

Perhaps he should go to her and tell her that he didn't really want to live at the big house anyway, and ask her if he could have a cottage on the estate. Then they would both be absolved from the discomfort of a situation in which neither party ever said anything. But if she and David were going to live there, perhaps she wouldn't even want him that close? He must have been a nuisance to her all along, and it must have goaded her to see him going so reluctantly to the job at Stein and Sons, when she wanted to do it herself . . .

By the time he had finished the second Scotch, he had given way to the most negative interpretation of Brittany's behaviour. As he stood up to leave, he knocked against the small, round table, breaking a glass, and the landlord stared at him angrily. He emerged into the street feeling clumsy, useless and ugly.

By now he was crying. *Cry-baby* . . . he said the words out loud as he headed south again towards Hyde Park, but they did not stop the tears welling up so uncontrollably that they blinded him and he stumbled and slipped on pavements greasy with rain. There was only one thought in his mind now, and he walked faster and faster as it took hold of him, discovering a new surge of energy like a dying man groping his way towards an oasis.

Susannah.

Last week she had returned from her trip to the Riviera with Maud, and had at last consented to have dinner with George. What a wonderful evening it had been! It came alive again in his memory, only now it was even lighter, purer and sweeter than the original. They had eaten in a small French restaurant that Jake had recommended, and Susannah had worn a proper evening dress with sequins and fringes, and when he had asked if they could go back to Park Street afterwards and play a game of chess, she had laughed and squeezed his hand. They had won a game apiece. He had felt perfectly happy, and Susannah seemed to be happy too.

When he came to a halt on the doorstep of 8 Park Street, with rain dripping down his nose, he realized that he was drunk. His constant motion had disguised it until now. But it only made what he had to do seem more important.

The butler let him in with a glazed look, pretending not to recognize him or to understand what he was saying, even though he asked quite clearly for Susannah. He was asked to wait in the library, but nothing happened. Then she slid gracefully into the room, beatific in her ruffled white peignoir. Her expression was half puzzled, half amused.

'George, what on earth are you doing here? And look at you – you're soaking wet!'

She touched his damp suit and he was suddenly miserably aware of how dreadful he looked, and of the smell of whisky on his breath.

'I had to see you.'

'I think it might have been better if you'd contented yourself with strumming outside my window. Have you no idea what the time is—?'

Then she saw his stricken eyes, reddened with crying.

'George, what's wrong? You're not ill, are you? Or Brittany?'

He heard his own voice, strange and incoherent, mumbling about Brittany and Graylings, and how he was probably going to die anyway, just like Frederick had. When he was quiet, Susannah crossed slowly to the chair he was sitting in and gently pushed the hair from his damp forehead. Her hands were cool and smooth as marble.

'George, I'm sure none of this is true. Who on earth put such ideas into your head? Of course Brittany wants you with her. She made sure she took you with her when she left here, didn't she?'

'Well, it was different then. That was before she had David. She doesn't need me any more. And I've decided. I'm not going to go with her.'

He reached up and took hold of her narrow wrists, tentatively fingering the gold bracelet, caressing it gently as he had watched her do so many times before.

'Susannah, I do love you,' he said thickly.

She laughed without thinking, and though she checked herself and continued to smile at him, George could still hear an echo of the sound her laughter made: uncertain, brittle.

'I do,' he insisted. Now that the declaration had been made, and the damage done, there was nothing to be gained by retracing his steps.

The laugh came again, a little more nervous this time. 'And of course I love you too, George, but it's not in the way—'

George wasn't listening.

'I'm going to stay here in London with you.'

Susannah's face changed again, and even through the whisky haze there was a warning coldness about his heart as he scanned the perfection of her features.

'Here? I'm sure Mother would be glad to make your room available to you again, if—'

'No. Not here. I mean it would be . . . we'd be married.'

'*Married*?'

'I've just said I love you. I've always loved you. Of course I want to marry you.'

She gave a short, awkward laugh and retreated a few paces, smoothing down the broderie anglaise that trimmed her robe.

'Don't be silly, George, you know that's out of the question. We've practically grown up together, and—'

'That doesn't matter!' he cut in stubbornly. Then he groaned and pressed his hands to his head to dim the roaring in his ears. The lamps blinked and shifted slightly before his eyes. 'Why should something like that matter?'

'Because we've lived under the same roof as brother and sister, and that's what you are to me – a brother. The brother I lost.'

George groped desperately through the fog in his brain.

'Perhaps you only think of me that way because I'm younger than you are. If I were to ask you again in a few years' time—'

'No, George. I couldn't. It's just not the way I . . . feel. I couldn't change my mind about that. Never.'

*Never* . . .

That tiny, condemning word pursued George into the rainwashed streets, where he dropped tears into the gutter to the faint accompaniment of a whore's laughter.

'Are you *sure* you won't come in?'

Brittany bound herself tightly to David's chest, pulling her coat open and wrapping it round them both. Their chins bumped and David covered her lips with his own, exploring them, caressing them.

Brittany raised an eyebrow and drew in closer.

'Perhaps I can interest you in a . . . nightcap?'

David threw up his hands. 'No more drink, please, or I'll dissolve . . .'

Brittany giggled. 'So will I! What were they putting in those cocktails?'

'. . . But I might be persuaded to come in for a while.'

'Good.' Brittany hesitated. 'I wonder if George has come back? Perhaps we should have waited in for him.'

She shrugged off her coat and David took it from her as he followed her into the darkened hallway. 'Don't worry yourself about it, sweetheart. He's probably fast asleep upstairs.'

Brittany broke away from David, and as she reached unsteadily for the light switch, her foot crunched on something. She picked it up and peered at it. It was a small, carved wooden dog. What was it doing on the floor, and . . . something else was different. What was that dark shape, that *thing* dangling from the ceiling? It looked . . .

Brittany took a few steps forward, still puzzled. Then her eyes became accustomed to the half light so that she could see the horribly silent, purple, contorted . . .

. . . And felt the merciless surging of blood in her ears.

She stepped backwards against David, to the sound of her own screams.

The thing was George.


### Somerset, 15 August, 1923

'You're supposed to be out of here by now, aren't you?'

Phoebe rested her tongue on her upper lip and looked up slyly at Adrian.

'The date for Miss Colby's repossession has indeed passed,' said Adrian coolly, running his fingers through Phoebe's tangled, rusty brown hair. 'But as you can see, I'm still here. She's delayed moving down here, due to the sudden death of her brother. But officially it's hers. Which gives me a certain perverted sense of pleasure. Fornicating in one of her beds.' He leaned back against the pillows.

'But how much longer?'

'I shall probably leave tomorrow. Or even tonight.'

'So this is our last time in here, then?' said Phoebe sadly, turning over onto her stomach as she spoke. From this position she could see Lucienne Colby's room better. With the curtains open it looked a little dusty, a little tawdry. There were stains on the satin drapes, and the few bottles that were on the dresser had been left behind in 1922 because they were cracked or empty. 'I really like this room,' she said slowly. 'In fact, I think it's the nicest room I've ever been in.'

Adrian slapped her playfully on the rump. 'How would you like to have another room just like this? All of your own?'

She turned and looked back at him. 'You mean it? Where?'

'I've still got money. You could have an exact replica of this room if you liked. We could even fix you up with one of these ridiculous things.'

He pointed up at the circular Empire polonaise above the bed, whose apricot drapes drifted to each of the four corners of the bed.

Phoebe's lips curled in her clever, cynical smile.

'Listen to the man talk! You want to keep me now, do you, all tidied away in a fancy flat like some tame tart?'

Adrian raised a crooked eyebrow. 'What I had in mind was converting one of the bedrooms at Heathcote House.'

'Heathcote?'

'I do still own it, you know.'

'You're a cool customer, aren't you? What about *her*?'

'My mother? She's leaving for Castle Cloud today.'

'Not *her*, stupid! Your bloody wife!'

'That's why I've stayed here. I didn't want to go back until I'd had a chance to talk to you about it. If you come with me, then she goes.'

'For good?'

'For good.'

Phoebe straightened up on the bed so that she could look at him properly. Her large white breasts shook and she covered them protectively with her hands to still them, narrowing her eyes.

'If only you knew how much I wanted you to be there with me,' Adrian said heavily. 'I need you, Phoebe.'

'I know that,' she purred. 'Don't I know it.'

She leaned towards him and trailed her blood-red painted fingertips over his temples. 'Who's going grey, then?' she teased. 'You old man, you.'

'Well?' said Adrian impatiently. He could see that she was tempted by the idea, and that her playfulness was just a way of stalling for time while she thought about it.

'No,' she said eventually. 'No, I couldn't do it. Not with him there.'

'You mean—?'

'Your loony old father, of course. Even with her gone, he'd still be there, wouldn't he? And I couldn't stick that. I couldn't live under the same roof as him. Makes my flesh creep thinking about it.'

'But Phoebe—'

'No,' she said emphatically. 'The answer's no.'

Lady Henrietta Steele was leaving Heathcote House for good.

Jennifer stood near the window and watched her go. Strangely, she had refused the offer of a lift in the car, even though she claimed greatly to admire its comfort and convenience. Instead she had chosen to take her baggage to the station at Bath in the ancient pony trap. Jennifer deduced that she had deliberately chosen this form of transport – the same that had conveyed her to Nether Aston as a bride – to make a statement, to mark the definitive end of an era.

Lady Henrietta allowed the groom to hand her up, and perched imperiously on the slatted wooden seat, among her assorted belongings: trunks, suitcases and hat-boxes. Several packing cases had already been sent by train to Castle Cloud. Jennifer was tempted to laugh when she caught sight of the frightful plum-coloured gaberdine suit and the tricorne hat, whose feather drooped forward sadly to make its wearer look like a bedraggled parrot. She had grown quite fond of her mother-in-law since her own arrival in Nether Aston as a bride at the end of 1915, but she couldn't feel sorry that she was leaving. It was trying enough to have to supervise her demented father-in-law. She did not want Adrian's unexplained antipathy towards his mother poisoning the atmosphere as well.

Jennifer had been making discreet inquiries about 'rest homes' in the area (no one used the word 'asylum' any more), but so far without satisfactory results. The institutions she approached were either full, with a considerable waiting list, or prohibitively expensive. And the list of possible homes was severely limited in Roland Steele's case because a combination of poor health and violent tendencies necessitated constant surveillance and nursing. 'Why not try a private nurse, madam, at home?' they had all suggested. She had even visited the hospital in Wells to ask doctors their advice, but could not quite bring herself to admit Roland to the geriatric ward, a vile-smelling, room full of drooling, shouting old men. Instead she resolved to discuss the problem with Adrian once he had finally relinquished Graylings.

The pony trap started to move off slowly down the high street, and Lady Henrietta gave a regal smile and a wave to Jennifer. She had regained some of her old spirit in the past few weeks, and Jennifer found herself remembering the first hard look she had received from those blue eyes, cold as marbles. The trap, and the lean angular figure seated in it, disappeared from view, half buried beneath parcels like the conveyance of some aristocratic tinker.

Heathcote was stripped bare. Lady Henrietta had taken all the portraits, all the fine china and all of the valuable antiques that had been part of her dowry. The only thing that she had left was her husband, abandoned like one of the pieces of old furniture that belonged to the house.

Roland Steele was happily unaware of her desertion.

'We'll be ridin' to hounds tomorrow, boy,' he wheezed enthusiastically to Jennifer as he wandered into the empty drawing room, flapping his arms against his sides like a huge ginger crow. In his right hand he was clutching a biscuit, which he waved vaguely in her direction.

'You should have one of these, Bertie, they're delicious! Delicious. De – licious.'

He moved off down the corridor, exclaiming 'De-licious' between every mouthful and sending a shower of crumbs and spittle through the air.

Jennifer stared at the bare walls thoughtfully, and they stared blankly back at her, presaging a new beginning. She felt a little tremor of excitement. The house had been stripped of old memories and it stood waiting, like a hollow shell, for a new life to begin. And tonight her husband was returning.

\*

Adrian returned as the church clock was striking midnight. He had been drinking. Jennifer closed her eyes and waited for him to undress, but he didn't. He sat down heavily on her side of the bed and she could smell him: the faint lime-scent of his hair oil, the smell of horse on his breeches, sour beer on his breath and nicotine on his fingers. She waited for him to touch her, but he did not. Instead he struck a match and lit a candle. There was no electricity in Heathcote House, not even a mains gas supply.

'I need to talk to you.'

She sat up in bed and smoothed her hair back behind her ears with her small fingers.

'You're back here for good, then?'

'Yes.' He still hadn't touched her, or looked at her face. 'I want a divorce.'

'A divorce?'

She could only repeat, stupidly, what he had said, and then wanted to bite her tongue off. She felt the colour rise to her cheeks, and knew an irrepressible urge to take him by the shoulders and shake him so violently that his teeth flew from his skull. A warning bell sounded in her brain. And her dead mother's voice said, *'Keep calm, Jennifer. You'll find a way out of it later. But only if you manage to keep calm now.'*

'I see,' she said levelly. 'And may I inquire what has brought about this decision?'

In her heart, she already knew. She had been doubly betrayed. She pressed her legs down hard beneath the covers to prevent them from trembling.

'Phoebe Lester and I . . .'

He looked up at her. His eyes were so deepset that she could barely see them, just the occasional flicker of reflected candlelight in the recesses.

'. . . are in love.'

The words would have sounded ridiculous had they not been so reproachful, as though he were reminding her that she had forced him to marry her by claiming that she was expecting his child. It was she who was the guilty party, not he.

'I've planned what I want to do,' he said, with some enjoyment. This was the Adrian who had first attracted her: energetic, striving, planning.

'. . . I'm going to use the remainder of Mama's money to renovate this house, and to get the farms ticking over again. Then Phoebe is going to move in here with me. You may stay here until the renovations are finished, by which time we will have had a chance to discuss the details of the divorce settlement.'

*Phoebe. Kindly, sympathetic Phoebe. So that was what she had wanted . . .*

'I see. And your father?'

He appeared to have forgotten about his father. A strange expression crossed his face and his eyes narrowed. 'Father? . . . He'll be all right.'

'He's not all right! He needs—'

'Look, I don't want to discuss it!' Adrian shouted, leaping to his feet and running his hands through his hair until it stood on end. His muscles were stiff with tension.

'Adrian, what's happened to us, why . . .?'

*'What's happened to us? I'll show you what's happened to us!'*

She shrank back, but he pulled back the covers and caught hold of her nightgown. 'I'll show you what's happened to us!'

He dragged her into the gloomy corridor, her bare feet slithering on the floorboards, to where water dripped through a hole in the ceiling. *'This is what's happened to us!'*

He slammed her body against the wall, almost lifting her off the ground, and twisted her head around so that she was forced to look up.

'We're back here again, with all this! I don't want this! And I don't want you either! You trapped me, you—'

His hands twisted the cotton nightdress round her throat until the material started to cut into her. She struggled free and ran into one of the guest bedrooms, slamming the door behind her.

Of course, she did not sleep. The sheets appeared to have been on the bed for several years. They were cold and dank. She sat on the edge of the bed and said to herself over and over again, *'I'm not going to let this happen . . .'*

Perhaps she shouldn't have left their bedroom tonight. Perhaps if she'd stayed, he would have changed his mind. Then she remembered Phoebe Lester's sultry, treacherous charm and decided that it was most unlikely. But at least there might have been a baby.

Footsteps in the corridor. Roland was wandering again. The door was slightly ajar and Jennifer walked across the room to see where he was going, her bare feet making no sound on the wooden floorboards.

But it wasn't Roland. It was Adrian.

She watched him through the crack in the door. He was walking very slowly, very deliberately, to the end of the corridor. To his father's room.

Her instinct was to follow him, and to do so secretly. She waited until he had disappeared from sight and then padded silently down the corridor in her nightdress. She could hear Roland Steele's loud, wheezing snore. Then it stopped.

Adrian had left the door slightly ajar, but his back was towards it, so she could not see the expression on his face as he pressed the pillow down over his father's face and held it there. Instead she found herself counting, just as he was counting, waiting for the breathing to stop. Then the pillow was lifted.

He turned slightly to the left as he looked at his father's dead face, and in the moonlight she could see that Adrian's expression was kindly, and slightly regretful. Was he, like Jennifer, thinking of the suffering that had ended? He lifted the shaggy red head gently and replaced the pillow. Then he said a very strange thing.

'I didn't keep my promise not to say anything about Gerald. Neither did you, did you? And look where it's got the two of us.'

### London, 7 October, 1923

'Surely you must have suspected that this had happened?' the doctor asked.

Brittany shifted uncomfortably on the hard wooden chair. 'No, I . . . I thought it was something to do with the shock of my brother's death.'

'He died recently?'

'Two months ago. He committed suicide . . .'

Suddenly she could hear them again. The dripping leaves. They had buried George in a field and it had rained, so hard that all they could hear was the sound of the drops falling onto the horse-chestnut leaves, and then dripping off again. Suicides could not be buried in consecrated ground, so they had buried him in the field next to the churchyard; and at least the vicar had been sympathetic and had conducted a proper service. As long as it was quiet, he had said, with family and close friends only. The vicar in Nether Aston was personally opposed to the rule about consecrated ground, indignant even. It caused a great deal of suffering to the bereaved, and in his view was not in keeping with the Christian message of forgiveness.

So George had had hymns and flowers, but few mourners. Brittany had told David and Jake that it was too far for them to drive for the afternoon and David had stayed away, but Jake had come, rain dripping onto his black cashmere coat, his head bowed in grief, and she had found his solid presence comforting.

Susannah had come too, and in their mutual guilt they had forgiven one another, clinging together in a single huddle of black crêpe under the green, dripping trees, blaming themselves that George was lying cold and dead beneath the wreath of Arum lilies. In the face of such unparalleled awfulness, Randolph de Beer was insignificant, unworthy.

And then she had walked back alone through the graveyard. Past Maria Padbury's chipped angel. Past Maman's grave, and Frederick's. Wondering what Teddy's resting place looked like. Dead, all dead . . .

'Well, Miss Colby, I can confirm that you are three and a half months pregnant.'

The doctor looked contemptuously at her silk stockings and rope of pearls, her coral painted lips, her kid gloves, and Brittany could tell that he was summing her up as a young society lady who ought to know better: one who ought to know how to avoid a situation like this, and avoid wasting his time.

'Miss Colby, I'm sure I could rely on your discretion if I were to . . . recommend someone.'

He tried to read the expression in her eyes, but only her square chin and full-lipped mouth were visible beneath the brim of her hat.

'Doctor, I have no intention of "using someone". I've now lost my entire family. I want to keep this baby.'

He tapped a pencil impatiently against the edge of his desk. 'I hope you are aware of the seriousness of this step? A child—'

'I will love this child,' she said firmly. 'What's more, I intend to marry the father.'

'Good. Well . . . you're in perfect health in every respect. All I can do is refer you to a Harley Street obstetrician and wish you the best of luck.'

Brittany desperately wanted to tell someone. As she sat in the taxi on the way back from the doctor's, she ran through the list of potential confidants in her mind, dismissing them one by one. Susannah. An obvious choice, yet . . . she remembered Susannah's sweet, innocent prudishness and the glinting crucifix at her throat. No, Susannah wouldn't do. She wouldn't be able to cope with the thought of an illegitimate baby. Jake? No. He was on holiday with Miriam in Nice, and besides, she found it impossible to predict what his reaction might be. That left only David. She had blithely told the doctor that she intended to marry him, but the words had just appeared on the tip of her tongue, uninvited. Was that what she had been hoping for? He had certainly had ample time and opportunity to propose. She would have to tell David about the baby soon, but she wasn't ready just yet. Brittany was, as ever, optimistic. If I wait just a little longer, she told herself, perhaps he'll ask me . . .

She told Florrie.

As soon as she had paid the taxi driver, she ran into the kitchen in Cheyne Mews and crushed the stout young woman in a breathless embrace.

'Florrie! I'm going to have a baby!'

'Very nice, Miss, I'm sure,' said Florrie with a frown. 'You'd better sit down quietly and let me bring you some tea. None of this leaping about. Go on, on that sofa with you.'

As Florrie set the tea-tray down, Brittany ventured cautiously: 'Florrie, if you'd rather not be employed by the mother of an illegitimate child, I'm sure I could arrange—'

'No, thank you, Miss.' She looked at her employer sternly. 'I'm not bothered by what other people think. I'll stop here, if it's all the same with you.' Then she added more gently, 'I should stay in and get some rest if I were you. You're looking a bit pale. Oh, and Mr Jake telephoned to ask if you could have luncheon with him tomorrow. He said to let his secretary know whether the answer was yes or no.'

'Jake? I thought he was in France. Telephone and say "yes" anyway, Florrie. No doubt all will become clear.'

Brittany settled herself to her quiet evening at home with the blissful self-satisfaction of a novice forswearing earthly pleasures for a higher purpose. But by the time it was dark, she had begun to be afraid of the unknown child growing within her. David's son, David's daughter. When the sun was shining it was impossible not to imagine him sharing her joy, but with the fading light the imprint of his face darkened in her fantasy. He would be angry. He would tell her that she should have taken steps to prevent it. That he never wanted to see her again. Perhaps she should tell him now? But much as she wanted to shed the enormous burden of knowing of their child's existence while David was still in ignorance, she also wanted to bind her secret to herself, tightly, chastely; to sanctify it with her own selfishness.

Then, once again, she found herself trying to predict Jake Stein's reaction. What would he think of her now?

She groomed herself with great care for their appointment the next day, anxious that her appearance should betray nothing. That same morning she had had her first attack of morning sickness, retching her way to the bathroom and emerging dizzy and covered in perspiration. She was helped back to bed by Florrie, who sagely brought her sweet tea and water biscuits and advised her to stay in bed until some of the colour had returned to her cheeks.

'. . . You won't want Mr Jake thinking you're poorly, will you?'

After a while, the nausea subsided and Brittany took a long hot bath, girding herself with a dress that David had bought from Worth while he was trying to cheer her up after George's death. The bodice was low cut and fitted closely, but the dropped skirt was as full as a child's and sashed with a bow on her right hip. It was made from crackling organza in swirls of white and a shade of blue that she hoped would draw attention to the blue of her eyes and away from everything else. She stood sideways, frowning, and eyed her stomach critically in front of the full-length mirror. It looked a little plump. Nor had Brittany ever been one of those handmaidens of fashion who defeminized their figures with chest binding, and her newly swollen breasts were accentuated by the line of the bodice.

But Jacob Stein wouldn't notice that sort of thing, Brittany told her reflection with a sphinx-like smile. And in every other respect, the dress was perfect. What a pity David wasn't there to see it.

They had both been delighted with the purchase, but until now there had been no opportunity of wearing it.

She hung her mother's diamond teardrops, clasped in their tiny golden hands, on her earlobes. Her severe shingle had been allowed to grow a little, and it seemed a shame to cover the pretty little curls that were beginning to appear at the back of her neck and over her ears, but this was definitely the sort of dress that required a hat. She chose a white fedora with a wide brim to balance the fluffy skirt, and a white coat to keep off the cold breeze in the dazzling autumn sky. Then she took a taxi to the Ritz Grill.

She saw Jake before he saw her, sitting alone at a corner table, and she was glad of a few seconds' chance to assess his appearance. It quite startled her. He was dressed in a light, stone-coloured suit and his skin was the same nut brown as his hair.

'Well, Brittany,' he said, as she slipped into the seat opposite him, 'you look . . blooming.'

Warm blood flooded her skin and she began to finger the diamond bracelet on her wrist, avoiding his eyes.

'Thank you,' she said at last. 'And you. You look well. But I wasn't expecting you back so soon. Did you have a nice time in . . .?'

'In Nice. Yes, thank you. It was pleasant. And very sunny.'

He proffered a tanned wrist as proof, then beckoned a waiter and ordered Dover sole and a bottle of Pouilly Fumé. Then there was self-conscious smalltalk until the food arrived, and Brittany tried to flirt, but Jake was even more reticent than usual. He offered her a cigarette and looked surprised when she refused.

'I had one just before I came,' she said. In fact the taste now made her queasy, and she had heard that some people believed it might be harmful to the unborn child. She pictured the child now, cocooned in her belly as she sat taking lunch in the Ritz Grill with its unwitting uncle, and the irreverent thought parted her lips in a mischievous smile.

'Something funny?'

'No,' she replied hastily, 'just a thought. How's business?'

Since George's death, Brittany no longer received a daily report on the comings and goings at Stein and Sons. David disliked talking about his work and always brushed her inquiries aside impatiently, so the world of Ironmonger Lane had retreated behind its dark veil of mystique.

'I didn't ask you out to lunch to discuss my financial deals, Brittany, as I'm sure you realize.'

'Is it about the house in Cheyne Mews?'

She feigned innocence, knowing full well that it was not. The details of her lease had been efficiently smoothed out months ago by Stein and Sons' solicitors, and the paperwork was all in order.

Jake was not smiling. It must be about David.

'It's about David.'

'Yes?'

She laid down her fork and he recognized that old defensive look in her strange, immense blue eyes, that 'I'm-Brittany-Colby-and-you-can't-touch-me' look.

'Brittany, will you do me a favour and take your hat off? I can't see you properly.'

She gave an exaggerated sigh and pulled out a long pearl hatpin, placing the fedora on the table beside her.

'Anything you say, Jake . . .'

'For heaven's sake, Brittany, stop treating me like a middle-aged schoolmaster. I'm thirty-five years old. Ten years older than you.' He drained his glass viciously and poured himself more wine. 'David's going back to New York.'

She stared at him, her blood chilling in her veins.

'He hasn't mentioned it to you yet?'

She shook her head slowly.

'I didn't think he had. But you knew his contract here was only temporary?'

'I thought I could persuade him to stay. Perhaps I still can.' She sounded defiant.

Jake shook his head and sighed. 'I doubt that, I'm afraid. You see—'

'So whose idea was this, then? Old Papa Stein's? And you've been in on it all along, I suppose?'

The bitterness in her voice made Jake wince. 'Brittany, please . . .'

He reached tentatively for her hand but she snatched it away and placed it on her lap. Another heart beating there, another pulse. David's child . . .

'. . . You must understand that whatever I say, I'm saying only out of concern for you, and because I don't want to see you hurt. You have to let David go—'

'You don't seem to think I'm in any position to stop him.'

'I mean you must let him go completely, spiritually. Let him out of your life. It's no good deceiving yourself into thinking of it as a separation of a few months, or a few years. When he goes, it will be for good.

*Mr goddamn know-it-all Jake Stein.*

'Of course,' she replied bitchily. 'I had forgotten that you were omniscient, otherwise I'd ask how you can be so sure.'

'I'm afraid you'll just have to take my word for it. I *know*. It's . . . it's a family thing. It's about being Jewish. I can't really explain it any better than that.'

'David doesn't care for all that Jewish nonsense. Surely if we—'

'David's main concern is, and always has been, himself. You think your experience proves otherwise, but I have twenty-eight years experience to go on. He's interested in a good time, but—'

'I'd go with him! I would!'

'I believe you . . .' *She's beautiful* . . . Jake longed to touch the feathery tendrils curling on the nape of her neck. '. . . But what I'm trying to say is, he never intended it to last. It was only ever a short-term thing. He couldn't . . . he couldn't let it be otherwise. I suppose I'd better try and explain—'

'And you're the expert, are you?' Brittany turned her face away from his scornfully, trapping the light in her eyes so that they turned from dull, metallic blue to aquamarine. She was angry because, as ever, she feared that he knew better than she.

He opened his mouth to go on but she cut in hastily.

'Well, Jake,' she said, all spite, pretending to be engrossed in smoothing the toe of her white kid shoe 'How is it that you're so good at running everybody else's life and yet so ineffectual when it comes to your own? If you know so much about lasting love, why does your precious Miriam have to console herself with gigolos?'

She could not resist the final injection of poison. 'She doesn't even respect you enough to be discreet. I saw her myself once, kissing her lover in the street!'

She waited.

Jake lowered his eyes and stared at the tablecloth, drawing his mouth into a thin line. Brittany was stunned by the sudden, raw vulnerability she saw; overawed by the miraculous length of his eyelashes. And she realized with a rush of regret and triumph that she had drawn pleasure from hurting him at last.

238

'I've never wanted to burden you with my private troubles, Brittany,' he said quietly. 'But perhaps you would have made a more sympathetic friend if I had done so. I am seeking a divorce from Miriam. She came with me to France in an attempt to patch things up, but only succeeded in making the situation worse. That's why I returned early. And you—'

He pushed back his chair and stood up.

'– are rude, selfish and immature.'

'Jake!'

She reached blindly for him, almost winded by a childish urge to cry, and caught his sleeve, but he brushed her aside.

'Here—' He threw a banknote onto the table. 'Pay the bill when you're through.'

David arrived at Cheyne Mews that evening to find Brittany tossing clothes half-heartedly into a suitcase.

'Don't look at me!' she shouted as he approached. Her face was red and swollen from crying.

'Brittany, honey, where are you going?'

'Graylings. *Why didn't you tell me?*'

He opened his mouth to protest ignorance, then saw that it was useless. He thrust his hands into his pockets and strolled over to the gable window.

'I was going to.' He pretended to be absorbed in watching a group of fat, noisy pigeons, strutting along the cobbled gully of the mews below.

'When?'

'I don't know, as soon as I found the right moment.'

'No, I mean when are you going?'

'I sail next Saturday. It's your friend Richard Langbourne's new passenger boat. The *Columbine*.'

'Very nice, I'm sure.' Brittany flung herself onto her dressing stool and snatched up a heavy-backed silver brush, delivering punishing strokes as though she still had her long thick tresses of hair. 'So you were intending to go back all along, even after we . . . *this* had started.'

David turned back from the window. 'Brittany, this is just as hard for me. You must believe me when I say that I don't *want* to go back now. I have to. Don't run off to Graylings. Please, let's—'

'I have to go back there before long. The place is deserted and

239

the estate manager keeps writing to say that there are things he needs to discuss with me, and—'

She stopped. David was looking at her curiously.

'Hey, you're wearing the dress. The one I bought. Stand up, let's see how it looks.'

Brittany rose to her feet ungraciously, sniffing.

David moved closer.

'I didn't realize it would fit so tightly. You must have put on weight.'

Very slowly, he ran his eye down over the hard, round ball of her stomach. She felt the veins in her heavy, pregnant breasts pulse angrily. For a moment they both contemplated the truth wordlessly.

'Are you—?'

'Pregnant. Yes.'

David turned and walked back to the window as though he were lost in thought. Brittany sat down on the edge of the bed and clenched her eyes shut. *Please say it. Please say that this changes everything. Please say that you wouldn't dream of leaving me now.*

He swung round.

'You fool! You little fool! Couldn't you have prevented this?'

'David,' she said, trying to force the edge of hysteria out of her voice, 'it's happened now. And this is your child. You can't change that. Now, can we please talk about what we're going to do? Perhaps if marriage—'

'Marriage! That's it, I'm getting married! I'm going back to New York because I'm engaged to be married to someone else!'

She closed her eyes and shuddered as he ran from the room, and as he slammed the front door she recoiled as surely as if he had struck her.

# 9

## *London, 19 October, 1923*

'I don't believe he can have done this to me!'

Brittany rested her hand on the back of a chair, to support a body that was trembling visibly with suppressed anger and shock. It was Sunday. The window overlooking the tiny garden was open, inviting squares of quiet autumn sunlight onto the carpet. In the near distance, dinning bells summoned London's devout and not-so-devout to church. The call of the faithful.

'I wondered whether I ought to come over yesterday evening.' said Jake apologetically, 'but I decided it was better to let you sleep.'

Brittany had not slept. She had lain on her bed thinking of the vast liner embracing the waters of the Atlantic like a lover. Was David standing on the stern of the *Columbine*, looking back to Southampton with regret, or was he lying in bed in his apartment in Grosvenor Square? Angry, but in England?

The suitcase that Brittany had been packing to take to Graylings had remained open and half-filled in a corner of her bedroom. She had not seen David, or heard from him, in the ten days since their quarrel, yet every time she contemplated leaving London, she found she lacked the resolve to do so. *He might change his mind and decide to stay, and I wouldn't be here. He might telephone today*. Or, her thought at the end of a long, empty day: *He might telephone tomorrow* . . .

The tomorrows dwindled. She began to pick up the telephone receiver herself, at regular intervals, but each time a sense of pride overcame her before the operator's voice came crackling onto the line. She would achieve nothing by pestering him. If he stayed, he had to reach his decision unaided.

Then the final Saturday. The day of his sailing. No more 'tomorrows' left, yet still Brittany clung to the wreckage of hope. He might not get onto the boat. He might change his mind at the last minute and be there on her doorstep on Sunday morning, or . . . The whole of that uncomfortable night her wretchedness was turned to a profound, morbid terror that plucked at the nerves of her sweating limbs until all of her was one question:

*What has he done?*

At ten o'clock the next morning, Jake brought the answer.

It was immediately obvious, of course, from his face, but Brittany paid a final homage to self-deception and pretended not to know what Jake was about to say. She even managed to smile at his shy reaction to her changing shape.

'Brittany, I guess you know what I'm here for . . .'

Her eyes wandered over his upright figure. He wore a spotless white polo shirt, unbuttoned at the neck, and pale linen trousers. It was the first time she had been Jake without a suit and tie. How nice he looks, she thought absently.

She nodded slowly and the sunlight quickened, blinding her.

'David sailed for home last night.'

Jake's words floated, hard and hollow, into the room. Into the air which was at first stiflingly hot, then icy cold.

There was an exaggerated silence, during which Brittany remained still. Then the tension left her rigid body with a gasp and she steadied herself against the back of an armchair.

'Jake . . . I don't believe he can have done this to me!'

'He told you about Rebecca?'

'Rebecca? Is that her name? Tell me about her.'

'There's nothing much to say. They were officially engaged years ago. Not exactly a love match. But she's a nice girl: quiet, shy, gentle . . .'

Bland, thought Brittany spitefully, mealy-mouthed . . .

Jake was shaking his head slowly. He looked sad. A sad archangel, Brittany thought. It was a relief to be distracted by the way the sunlight made a halo on his hair.

'I'm sorry. I tried to warn you on that day we had lunch at the Ritz Grill, but it seems I didn't make a very good job of it. I had intended to tell you about Rebecca then.'

'Oh, Jake . . .'

For a moment she was so sorry for him, and so full of remorse, that she forgot her own pain.

'. . . And I was such a pig to you. So stubborn and stupid not to listen.'

'But I'd left it too late anyway. The baby . . .' He glanced self-consciously at the tight front of her dress. 'David told me about it but he didn't say when. When it would be born.'

'In March.'

They both fell silent, and she sensed that he was waiting for her to ask:

'Will you still be in England then?'

Jake nodded. 'But perhaps not for long. I shall worry about you. What will you do?'

'I have Graylings, thank God. I'll go there for a while. I'll be all right.'

*Except that David won't be here to see his firstborn child . . .*

The brightness in her voice rang false and she longed to cry. Jake noticed her frantic blinking and touched her arm with a gentleness that could have felled her.

'I expect you want to be alone for a while,' he said, deftly averting his eyes. Then he pulled an envelope from his pocket and held it out to her. 'I tried to persuade David to come and see you before he left, but he said it would only make things worse. He left this for you, though.'

Brittany did not read David's letter until the following day. She left it unopened on the inlaid escritoire, not because she wished to pretend that all was still well, but because she was afraid of adding disappointment to the burden of despair. David had always avoided talking of his own feelings, hiding them behind studied flippancy, and a letter of explanation seemed likely to be inadequate.

After Jake left, she abandoned herself to torrential weeping for several hours until she felt drained and aching. Then she tidied her hair and changed her clothes and went for a walk along the Embankment, looking out wistfully over the river to the trees of Battersea Park, as if trying to see past it to the ocean and the *Columbine*. By dusk she felt better. The thought of the child was a comfort, an indestructible symbol of her union with David. And even now it was impossible to dampen the embers of hope. *'Not exactly a love match'*, Jake had said. Engagements could be broken. She felt sure he would come back one day.

After breakfast the next day, she went briskly to her desk and tore open the envelope that Jake had given her. The letter was brief, as she had expected it to be.

*'Dear Brittany,'*

The flatness of the opening phrase chilled her. Why not 'Dearest Brittany' or even 'My dear Brittany'?

*I'm sorry about leaving like this. I guess a large part of me wanted to stay and have good times with you for ever. The circumstances in which we are parting make it even harder. I should have told you about*

*Rebecca at the beginning, but it didn't seem important when I cared about you and not about her. Maybe it's for the best that things have turned out this way. I don't know.*

*Perhaps I should have contacted you before I left, but I was angry about the child. We've both been irresponsible, I guess, but I'm glad for you if that's what you wanted. Of course my family will make financial provision for the child, and I'll instruct my lawyers to carry out the necessary arrangements. I shall always think about you. David'*

Brittany looked at the hard, white piece of paper for a few minutes, forcing herself to acknowledge that it did not exactly offer a message of hope. *'The necessary arrangements . . .'*

She screwed it up and tossed it into the grate.

Then she began to make preparations for removing to Graylings, burying the bitterness of disappointment in a frenzy of activity. She called Florrie and told her to prepare to close up the house in Cheyne Mews for a few months. The half-filled suitcase in the corner of her room was now packed, along with several others, the house was cleaned from top to bottom and dust-sheets were draped over the larger pieces of furniture. Brittany was just about to make arrangements for the estate manager to collect her from the station when the telephone rang.

It was Susannah.

'Brittany, I've been meaning to get in touch with you ever since . . .'

She could not quite bring herself to say 'the funeral'.

'. . . How are you?'

Brittany deftly avoided the question. 'I'm just packing my things to go down to Graylings for a while.'

'When are you leaving?'

'Tomorrow morning.'

'Oh no . . .' Susannah sounded genuinely disappointed. 'I was so hoping we could meet. How about this afternoon? Could you come over for tea?'

The interminable tea parties. Brittany hesitated. 'Oh please, Brittany. It would only be you and I. And I'll have the car sent to collect you.'

Brittany gave in. Susannah would have to discover the truth sometime. 'All right. But I won't be able to stay long, Susannah. There's so much to do . . .'

As Brittany stood in front of the perfectly symmetrical façade of

8 Park Street, she experienced an unwonted pang of nostalgia for the days when she and George had lived there. In retrospect, they seemed carefree and innocent.

She was now four months pregnant and her condition was becoming obvious, despite the loose shift dress she was wearing. As she rode up in the thickly carpeted lift with the lugubrious butler, she wondered how long it would be before her hostess was forced to acknowledge the uncomfortable truth.

Susannah was playing the piano. She was dressed very simply in a dark blue dress, and Brittany's first thought was how young she looked. Then she realized with a start that Susannah's hair had been cut. It sat close to her head like a gilded cap, but far from lending an air of sophistication, the effect was to make her extremely childlike. Light from the tall windows behind her was sparkling on the crucifix she wore.

She stopped playing when she saw her visitor, and smiled shyly.

'Brittany! How wonderful to see you!'

She proffered a cool cheek to be kissed, then waved Brittany over to a collection of raspberry-coloured chairs that were grouped formally at one end of the vast drawing room.

'I'll ring for tea.'

Feeling very tiny, Brittany went to sit down. She had forgotten how the towering floor-to-ceiling windows that took up the street side of the room made the inhabitants feel as though they were in a square goldfish bowl. She fumbled nervously for a cigarette but felt queasy as soon as she smelled the smoke, and extinguished it hastily.

Susannah calmly poured two cups of tea from a Georgian silver teapot, smiling into the amber liquid like a blonde geisha girl, then she offered Brittany a plate of *langues de chats* so fragile that they looked as though they might break at the touch of a finger. Throughout the ritual she remained serene, but more than once her eyes strayed to Brittany's thickened waist, and lingered there.

'How's your . . . friend David?' she ventured tentatively.

'He went back to New York on Saturday.' Brittany's voice trembled and she bit viciously into a biscuit.

Susannah looked puzzled.

'But you are getting married?'

Brittany shook her head.

Susannah looked even more puzzled and her hand shook slightly as she returned her fragile porcelain cup to its saucer. 'Forgive me for . . .' she blushed violently. 'I couldn't help noticing, Brittany. I . . . are you—?'

'Expecting a baby. Yes.'

An awkward silence. A maid came in and dawdled over the tea-tray.

After she had gone, Susannah said: 'But I don't understand . . . You said you weren't getting married—'

'Susannah!' Brittany felt the old familiar irritation at Susannah's prudery. 'The is no law of nature by which children are conceived only when one is married or betrothed. It only requires an act of fornication, not a ring and a promise!'

Her voice echoed harshly from the high walls. 'I'm sorry, I didn't mean to shout,' she said, and then found that she was crying uncontrollably.

'Brittany . . .' Susannah reached out a hand, then changed her mind and toyed awkwardly with her gold bracelet.

'Can I get you something?'

'No, no,' said Brittany firmly, 'I'll try to explain. I need to say it out loud, just to convince myself that it's really happened.' She took out a handkerchief and blew her nose noisily. 'David and I got on well from the start, and I was so happy that I just assumed we'd stay together. But it turned out he was engaged to someone else before he even came to England. And now I feel as though the whole thing was just one enormous piece of conceit on my part: never stopping to think that he could prefer someone else, just seeing something and wanting it and reaching out to take it as though it were my right. And God knows what you must think of me now! You must think me the most momumental fool, and worse besides—'

'No, I don't,' said Susannah gently, turning her dark, velvet eyes directly onto Brittany's face. 'I think you've been very brave. I think you've also been . . .' She hesitated. 'I was going to say you'd been unlucky, but the word is so inadequate, it's insulting. I think you know what I mean.'

She took Brittany's hands in hers. 'Brittany . . .'

'Don't, don't . . .'

They groped blindly towards one another, clinging in a tight embrace. When they broke free, Susannah's eyes were shining with tears.

'Let me help you,' she said. 'Please. I want to help. When the baby comes. And before, if you'd like. I've been in agony . . . my conscience has been terrible since . . .'

She stopped, knowing that no further explanation was necessary.

And Brittany knew that they were both thinking of their debt to George.


### Somerset, 21 October, 1923

*Valhalla, home of the heroes . . .*

Brittany looked down on the cool, benign walls of her childhood home and smiled. It hadn't changed. It would never change. It would always be a home worthy of heroes, stepping up between the brave white columns to the sound of trumpets . . .

She had deliberately requested that the small black Austin be brought to a halt at the bend in the lane where Graylings came into view, nestled confidently in its hollow below. Its delights were pointed out to an awestruck Florrie, then they drove on, and down.

They had been met at Bath station by Harry Herbert, the estate manager, the same agent who had managed Graylings during the war and immediately afterwards, until Lucienne Colby's death. He was a large garrulous man who expressed his delight at being reinstated by talking incessantly on the journey between Bath and Nether Aston. Brittany could not help noticing how alarmingly fat he had grown, filling out his voluminous plus fours, and he claimed cheerfully that the purchase of the baby Austin from the estate coffers had been expedient because he was now too heavy to sit a horse comfortably. He volunteered to teach Brittany to drive, so that she could use the car on the occasions when it was free. Brittany thanked him for the offer and, as she contemplated the sight of the enormous body crammed against the steering wheel, made a mental note to acquire another car as soon as possible.

It was not how she had dreamed her homecoming would be.

There was no triumphal music, no row of beaming, welcoming servants, no crowd of cheering estate workers to line the route. But then, what sort of conquering heroine was she? Alone, bereaved and pregnant. The house received her with self-effacing quiet, as though it were aware of her predicament.

Mr Steele – Harry Herbert explained – was loath to lose the services of his excellent cook, Mrs Rosslyn, and had taken her with him when he went 'back down the village'. (Harry Herbert loaded the words with such doom that it seemed as apposite an end as a descent to hell itself.) Another cook had been engaged in her place, and two maids, whose work Florrie sniffed at but pronounced would 'do'.

She and Harry carried the bags and Brittany followed them into the silent hallway. As she looked up into the domed skylight, a cloud passed over it and the glass 'eye' winked at her. It was the only greeting she received.

So began a long dreary autumn, during which Brittany lived as a recluse. When she arrived at Graylings, local society prepared to take her into its bosom again, only to find her growing heavy with an illegitimate child. Local society withdrew, aghast, into provincial prejudice. The flow of invitations dwindled and finally dried up altogether. Her presence in the village drew curious glances, and after a while Brittany rarely ventured further than her beloved graveyard, with its consoling shadows of yew and laurel. It was not that she was ashamed, she told herself, but that she couldn't bear to be stared at as though she were an animal.

She was alone for the first time in her life, and after a few weeks she began to relish her solitude. Even though she was in perfect health, Florrie cosseted her like a favoured invalid, turning the house into a cloister of well-banked fires and wholesome food. In addition to receiving driving lessons from Harry Herbert, she worked closely with him in supervising the estate, noting down queries over financial matters, which were plentiful, in a small notebook so that she could ask Jake's advice when he made one of his frequent telephone calls. She also started a thorough inventory of the contents of the house and spent whole days worrying about whether she had enough linen tablecloths, and how best to protect furniture from woodworm. Plans for the redecoration of the house began to take shape, for instigation after the baby's birth.

In her spare time she would read for hours, painstakingly embroider tiny pillowcases and nightdresses, or simply walk alone through the quiet woods, sifting the hardening leaves with her feet, lost in a reverie about the coming child. Memories of the summer became crystallized like the leaves swirling around her, drifting.

David had no place in the daydreams with which she reinforced her retreat. David had always meant movement: quick humour, mock fights, dancing, strenuous lovemaking. He had no role to play in her slow, heavy-bellied trance. There were slight pangs of trepidation when she imagined the triumph of their child's arrival without David, picturing it like a photograph, with the place of the proud, smiling father a mysterious blank, but she hastily shut her mind to such thoughts.

In October she received a letter that aided this process of self-discipline. It was from Isaac Stein, and stated with a callousness that could only have been deliberate, that if Brittany gave birth to a son, a generous settlement would be made in his name. If the child was a girl, there would be no settlement. Brittany remembered the way that Gerald and Frederick had treated her because she was 'only a girl'. She smarted with fury and indignation on behalf of her unborn daughter, and despatched a reply refusing Isaac Stein's offer outright, whatever the sex of her child. She could only hope that Isaac's letter had been written without David's knowledge.

Susannah was as good as her word.

She was a frequent visitor at Graylings that autumn, arriving in a shining black limousine driven by an impassive chauffeur. She seemed to have become as preoccupied with Britany's state as Brittany herself, a willing handmaiden in the rites of motherhood. She was as ignorant as Brittany of the arcane details of childbirth, but while Brittany was content to remain in the hazy dominion of half-knowledge, Susannah read her way through volumes of medical opinion and almanacs of child-care. And she threw herself with such energy into the task of decorating the nursery that it became sadly obvious that she was missing a nest of her own to feather.

Apart from Susannah and Lucienne's old friend, the witty, worldly Ruth Morgan who had once outlawed herself after a scandalous divorce case, Brittany saw no one. There was no conciliatory call from Jennifer Steele, and as the weeks passed, Brittany's curiosity grew. On her visits to the churchyard she would stare across to the square stone wall that protected Heathcote House from eyes such as hers. Curiosity was fuelled by sympathy. She had heard the maids saying that Adrian Steele had a mistress living on one of the farms on the Graylings estate, and she couldn't help feeling sorry for the tiny, doll-like Jennifer. There were workmen and builders coming in and out of Heathcote constantly, and occasionally she would catch a tantalizing glimpse of movement behind the curtains. But nothing more.

Then came a day, in early December, that saw an intriguing set of coincidences. First, Brittany asked Harry Herbert to give her a lift into the village, as she had an appointment with the village dressmaker to be fitted for some maternity clothes. The dressmaker had tactfully offered to come to Graylings, but Brittany bravely refused the offer, knowing that it would be easier if the fitting took place where all the necessary materials were to hand. Harry dropped her off in the high street and she did not have to walk far. It was the lunch hour, and there were very few people about. As she walked up the left of the street, past the 'Lamb and Child', she saw a horse and rider approaching. Her heart thumped loudly as she recognized the great, thick-necked grey horse and its rider.

Adrian Steele.

He did not speak to her, but he reined in his horse to a slow walk as he passed, staring openly and fixedly at her bulging stomach.

Then he laughed. He laughed a long, sneering laugh and rode on, leaving Brittany rooted to the spot with surprise and indignation.

After she had left the dressmaker's, she went to visit the graveyard. Roland Steele's was one of the newest graves, and she noticed at once that someone had left flowers on it: large, red-brown chrysanthemums. And there, at the far corner, was a small, retreating figure.

'Jennifer!' Brittany called out without quite knowing what prompted her. Jennifer stopped and turned round. She was forced to retrace the tracks she had made across the frosty ground before she could identify the speaker, and Brittany could see how thin and tired she looked. Her smooth, clay-brown skin had a stone-grey pallor. She hesitated, and a look crossed her face that Brittany could not quite identify. It was both angry and wistful. Then she turned and hurried away.

That afternoon Brittany was sitting before the fire, examining Jennifer's plight, when Florrie announced a visitor. She showed in a Junoesque young woman dressed in a dark suit that was tight in all the wrong places, and exposed an indecent amount of cleavage. Her flamboyant chestnut hair was piled in curls on top of her head and she wore the string of cheap glass beds around her neck as though they were diamonds. Her stance, as Brittany struggled to her feet, was a provocative mixture of defiance and embarrassment.

'Miss – er—'

'Lester. Phoebe Lester. My brother Daniel has your Coombe Farm.'

'Ah yes, of course. I believe I have met your brother.'

So this was Adrian's mistress.

'What can I do for you, Miss Lester?'

'I used to work here you know, as Mr Steele's secretary.' Phoebe swung her gaze proprietorially around the room and let it rest on Brittany's figure with a look that said *'And you're no better than you should be either . . .'*

Then embarrassment took the upper hand over defiance. 'I've got a favour to ask you, personal like.'

She flushed so violently that the rouge on her cheeks was no longer discernible. Brittany looked blank.

'It concerns something that I used to see here, when I worked in the house, and I admired it and . . . I wondered if I might take another look at it? It's upstairs.'

'Perhaps you would care to show me?'

Brittany was bemused, but when Phoebe stopped outside the door of Lucienne's room, she felt anger rising within her.

'It's in here.'

'I see,'said Brittany icily.

Phoebe opened the door and sighed deeply as she stepped across the threshold, looking around her reverently. 'It's been cleaned.' It was almost an accusation.

'Yes.'

'That's it.' Phoebe pointed up at the ceiling, at the majestic coronet whose apricot veil draped the bed. 'That thing. I do so want one of my own, only . . .' She blushed crimson again and avoided Brittany's gaze. '. . . I don't know what they're called.'

'It's called a *polonaise*,' said Brittany coldly. 'French. From the time of Napoleon.'

Phoebe took a pencil and a piece of paper from her handbag, but hesitated before she began to write. 'Is that double "l"?'

'p – o – l – o . . . Here, give that to me,' Brittany snapped. She scribbled on the piece of paper and thrust it into the outstretched hand like a formal note of dismissal.

But she could not help smiling as she watched Phoebe Lester teetering down the drive on her pedestal heels.

The third point of the eternal triangle. And all in one day.


## London, 24 December, 1923

Brittany shivered slightly in front of the badly laid fire.

She had given Florrie two days off to spend with her family in Bow, and her absence was obvious from the open curtains through which the hard, dark afternoon stared sullenly. Brittany looked into the drawing room mirrored by the lamplight in the windowpanes, trying to draw comfort from the stirring of the baby under her ribs, but feeling more than a little sorry for herself.

She had decided to spend Christmas in London, rather than at Graylings, but was now regretting the decision. The big house would have seemed empty and lonely, but at least Ruth and Henry Morgan were nearby and had invited her to share their Christmas meal. London had been chosen because of an appointment with her Harley Street obstetrician on the day before Christmas Eve, and so that Florrie would have the opportunity to visit her relations; but certainly not for social reasons. She felt as though she did not know a soul in the city. The Nice Young People she had met through the Langbournes had long since vanished. David's friends had meant no more than an introduction shouted across a crowded dancefloor. And Susannah herself was spending Christmas in the country. The Langbournes had finally bought themselves a country seat: a pile of Victorian Gothic in the heart of Leicestershire.

Eventually she wearied of looking at her fat body reflected against the backdrop of the darkened street, and struggled to her feet to close the curtains. Standing up sharpened her appetite. She lumbered into the kitchen to see what Florrie had left and found an unappealing lamb stew that needed heating up. Would she be able to remember how to light the stove?

The front doorbell rang in the hall.

Brittany opened the door an inch and called out wanly: 'Who is it?'

'It's me.'

Jake was standing on the doorstep, holding an enormous hamper. 'Happy Christmas.'

'How did you know I was here?'

'I had my secretary telephone Graylings, and she was told you were in London. Then I sent her home for the rest of the day, because I thought you might like a picnic.'

Confronted with this briskness, Brittany felt confused and sleepy.

'What time is it?' she mumbled.

'Half-past four.'

She laughed. 'As good a time for a picnic as any. Come in.'

'Perhaps we ought to sing a carol or two,' she said as she led the way into the drawing room, and then corrected herself. 'Of course, I'd forgotten, you're Jewish. You won't know any.'

'We used to sing them in German to impress Papa's Gentile clients when he offered them hospitality at Christmas. Will *Stille nacht* do, or *Es ist ein' Ros' entsprungen?*'

'Very nicely, I'm sure,' she said, smiling at the subconscious echo of Nanny Wynn. 'But there's no piano. We'd better get straight on with the picnic. Unless we employ the gramophone . . .'

'Ah, the gramophone.'

Brittany started her cracked recording of *The Modesty Rag*, then bent down reverently on her hands and knees before the hamper.

'How mysterious it looks. What's in it, Jake?'

'Open it and see.'

She pulled out a half bottle of vintage champagne, a cold roast pheasant, smoked oysters, a terrine of foie gras and a small basket of strawberries.

'Strawberries, in December? Oh Jake, how sinful!'

She fetched plates and glasses and they sat on the hearthrug with the hamper between them, bolstered against the dark and cold by the cheerful crackling of the ragtime rhythm and a rather smoky fire. The champagne seemed to quench Jake's shyness and he helped himself enthusiastically to the food, pausing between mouthfuls to laugh loudly at Brittany's memories of childhood Christmases in Somerset.

'Your poor mother must have had a hell of a time trying to persuade you to go to bed on Christmas Eve.'

'Oh she did, but her problems didn't end there. We used to help Mrs Jennings, our cook, to stir the Christmas puddings and drop the silver charms into the mixture. One year, when Maman had guests, George and I fetched my hoard of milk teeth from the nursery upstairs and dropped those into the bowl when no one was looking. There were some astonished faces on Christmas Day when the guests bit into the pudding and their teeth hit . . . teeth! Poor Maman . . .'

Brittany hiccupped loudly. 'I shouldn't have drunk that champagne.' She fussed over poking the fire, then hauled herself to her feet. Jake averted his eyes politely while she straightened her dress. 'According to Susannah's books of witchcraft, it's not good for the baby, and I'm so prone to indigestion these days.'

She started to move towards the kitchen, and then paused.

'Listen – can you hear that?' There was a faint chiming in the street. 'I think it's carol singers.'

She hurried excitedly to the window and pulled back the curtain enough to allow her to press her face against the glass. 'Yes, it is! Jake, do come and listen. It sounds so pretty.'

The two of them huddled closely at the window, awed into silence as the beautiful sound of human voices in harmony carved the empty air. Jake was so still that Brittany was sure that if she looked closely she would see his heart beating against the wall of his chest. She twisted her body sideways to scrutinize his profile in repose: downcast eyes and calm mouth.

He turned and smiled at her. 'Brittany . . . you're very lovely. I'm glad you didn't have to be alone today.'

'Jake—'

Her rational self fled and she fell against him, pressing herself as close as her swollen figure would allow. His warm, clean, male smell overwhelmed her.

Jake said nothing, but allowed Brittany to cling to him, stroking the hair at the back of her neck with infinite tenderness. He took her hand and led her gently to the sofa, sitting on the arm of the chair opposite her. The record scratched to a halt on the gramophone.

'I'm sorry, Jake—' she began timidly.

'There's no need. I understand already, you know that. It's

Christmas, you're thinking of being at Graylings with your family, you're facing motherhood alone, and you're missing David.'

'Yes, I suppose I am.'

But suddenly she was not sure at all whether she was missing David, and the thought touched her inside like a cold hand.

'You must be feeling rather tired. Would you like to me go now?'

'No, no. Stay a little.'

They sat for a long time before the fire and the remains of their picnic, and there was no sound except for long, heavy sighs from Brittany and the regular hiss–thump of the needle against the label of the record. After a while she reached out cautiously and touched Jake's hand. He did not withdraw it. She stroked it carefully, as a child caresses a frail, baby animal. Then she clasped it boldly in her own, drawing comfort from its strength.

'Brittany, I want to say something to you now, before . . .'

She looked at him questioningly, the blue centres of her enormous eyes burning.

'I know David hasn't contacted you, but you mustn't allow that to persuade you that he doesn't care any more. I've had several letters from him, and I sense that he greatly regrets leaving you. He's arranged to do some work at one of the Boston subsidiaries, which has meant the wedding being delayed until the spring.'

He cleared his throat and stared into the grate, as though waiting for the fire to spring to life. 'It's not like David to be diligent. I think he's procrastinating. What I'm saying is . . .'

He removed his hand from hers and it was his turn to sigh now. The sound was that of deep sadness.

'. . . I don't want you to shut your mind to the possibility that David might come back.'


### Somerset, 24 December, 1923

Adrian Steele carried the Christmas tree into the drawing room and set it down carefully.

He looked around the room thoughtfully, trying to decide on the best site for the tree. Then he started.

Jennifer was sitting in an armchair beside the fire. The seat of the chair was so deep that her legs did not quite reach the floor, and her tiny, daintily-shod feet dangled like a child's. On her lap was a dish of chestnuts, and she was laying them carefully in the embers of the fire, removing them with a pair of heavy brass tongs when they were charred and blackened. She seemed absorbed in her task, and did not look up when her husband came in.

'Jennifer? You're still here? I thought you would be gone by now.'

Jennifer ignored him.

'Speak to me, damn it!'

She looked up and gave Adrian a quick, bright smile. 'Ah, there you are, dear. And you've brought a tree, how splendid! I'll decorate it this afternoon.'

'Shut up!' shouted Adrian. 'Shut up and listen to me! Look at this room. It's finished, isn't it?'

Adrian's grand plan was completed and the last of his money spent. The drawing room had been papered with a tasteful Regency stripe in green and cream, with Chinese rugs in toning colours and fat chintzy furniture that Lady Henrietta would have detested. Hanging from the plaster rose on the ceiling was a chandelier powered by electricity, and there were electric candelabra on the walls.

Jennifer smiled as Adrian gesticulated at the new splendour of the drawing room, and prised open the shell of a roast chestnut with small, immaculate fingernails.

'Do you think we have any candles small enough for the tree?' she asked.

'This tree,' said Adrian, brandishing it at her until the needles spilled onto her lap, and baring his teeth like a fox terrier, 'this tree is for Phoebe and myself. We agreed, didn't we? You would stay here until the work on the house was finished. Now it's finished. And my mother has offered you a home at Castle Cloud. I thought it was all arranged. The divorce—'

'There isn't going to be a divorce.'

Jennifer bit into a chestnut, and the tiny, splintering sound cracked the silence.

Adrian stepped back a few paces and propped the tree against the sofa.

'Would you care to explain yourself?' he asked, brushing the pine needles from his hands.

'I don't wish to divorce you, Adrian. I know I said I was willing to let you trump up some evidence of adultery on my part, but I've changed my mind.'

'How—?'

'I saw what you did to your father, Adrian. You went into his room that night and put the pillow over his head. I was watching. However, since I am . . . *sensitive* to the humane aspects of the killing, I won't mention it as long as you don't mention the word . . .'

She popped a chestnut neatly into her mouth, smiling sweetly.

'. . . divorce.'

Adrian's face whitened slightly, but he managed a smile.

'Come, come, Jennifer, you know that you would never be able to prove it. Hibbert certified death by natural causes.'

'Dr Hibbert is a fool and everyone knows it. I could always arrange for an exhumation and an autopsy. It's a long shot, I agree, but they might just be able to find some evidence of suffocation. Do you want to risk it? Shall I telephone the county coroner, dear?'

Adrian's black eyes darted from side to side as he calculated. A chestnut exploded in the fire.

'All right, no divorce. You can stay here, and continue to be my wife in name, but Phoebe—'

'No. No Phoebe either. I must insist, Adrian.'

'You little bitch . . .' Adrian breathed, stepping nearer. Jennifer gazed back at him boldly, her smooth dun-coloured cheeks blazing from her proximity to the fire.

'You've been saving this up, haven't you? Watching me put this place in order, while all along you had no intention of leaving. You little bitch!'

There was another explosion from the fire, followed by a hard crack as Adrian brought the flat of his hand down on the side of Jennifer's face.

She recoiled in the depths of the armchair and he stood over her, blocking her escape, and struck her repeatedly. When he eventually stepped back and she struggled to her feet, the look on her face was defiant.

'You had better be careful, Adrian Steele. I meant what I said. If I so much as hear that you've been seeing your whore—'

He reached up his hand to strike her again, but this time she caught hold of his wrist and dug her pointed fingernails hard into his flesh. Her eyes were wild and the pins had come loose from her hair, allowing it to tumble around her face.

He laughed softly. 'It's a pity you don't always show such spirit, Jennifer. Then I might not have needed my "whore".'

He used his greater weight to push her backwards, twisting her arm behind her back. Jennifer fell to the ground with her head pressed awkwardly against the stone hearth.

Adrian fumbled with the front of his trousers and sank down on top of her, still laughing.

## London, 29 March, 1924

Brittany glanced at the clock before she started to undress. Half-past eight. In an hour and a half David would see his son.

Brittany had given birth to a healthy boy in the first week of March. Susannah had insisted that she arrange to travel up to London beforehand and be delivered in a small, private nursing home in Marylebone that Maud had recommended, but in the end there was no time. She went into labour two weeks earlier than expected, and although everyone had assured her that it would be a very long and drawn-out affair, the pains were quick and fierce from the start.

'Much better that way,' Florrie said, grunting with exertion as she lifted Brittany onto her bed and stripped away the sheets. 'Get it all over and done with, fast like. I'll go and telephone Dr Hibbert. You'll manage very nicely.'

Florrie had been right. The delivery was quick and easy and Brittany was elated. She knew nothing of babies, and had not expected to find her newborn child either interesting or appealing, but when she saw the tiny flailing limbs and heard the first angry cry, a new excitement beat through her heart and her brain.

She was captivated.

'Don't you think he's the most perfect thing you've ever seen?' she asked Susannah three days later, as she displayed her son's curled fingers and toes.

'He's beautiful,' agreed Susannah, who had seen plenty of babies before. 'What are you going to call him?'

'George. And Theodore, after Maman's father, Armand-Théodore. George Theodore.'

George Theodore Colby, thought Susannah as she studied his sleeping features.

George Theodore Stein, thought Brittany.

Then Jake had telephoned, and learned that he had a nephew. His reaction surprised Brittany.

'A son, a son . . .' he said simply, and she could hear the intense emotion catching in his voice. 'Have you told David yet?'

'No.'

'I think he'd want to know,' said Jake briskly. 'Does he look like his father? . . .'

After Jake had rung off, Brittany sat holding the baby in her arms and looking at his face. Her son, hers and David's. He opened his dark eyes and stared back at her, and for the first time she saw a resemblance to David. She was filled with joy at the discovery. Returning George to his cradle, she called out to Florrie:

'Florrie, do you think you could leave those bottles for a moment? I want you to take a telegram to the post office.'

Snatching up a piece of paper, she scribbled a few lines.

*'Your son arrived safely 6 March. Weighs seven pounds. Called George. Looks like his father. Brittany.'*

Later she had wondered whether the communication had been too curt, but David's reply, brought in by a beaming Florrie two days later, was equally brief.

*'Have broken engagement. Arriving Southampton 29 March. Tell my son I'm coming. David.'*

She had telephoned Jake in Ironmonger Lane straightaway. He listened patiently to Brittany's garbled and breathless explanation, but when he replied, his voice was cold. No, he did not know that David was coming back, but if the cable said so then it was probably true. If she liked, he would check the time of sailing from New York and call her back.

He was as good as his word, confirming within hours that David's boat was due to dock early in the evening on 29 March. He even offered to arrange for a car to be there to meet him, but he sounded displeased.

Brittany pushed the thought of Jake's jealousy from her mind and concentrated on preparing for David's arrival. She took Florrie and George to London with her and, with Susannah's help, transformed the dressing room in Cheyne Mews into a tiny nursery. The three of us will be living together as a family, Brittany had thought, as she cleared drawers and cupboards to make room for David's clothes. It seems odd.

She also wondered whether they would still want each other when he finally arrived, and she was still wondering on the evening of 29 March as she smoothed down her tawny gold hair with scented macassar oil and applied and removed her lipstick over and over again.

The clock above the fireplace said the time was ten-past nine, and when she looked again after what seemed at least half an hour, it said the same. Jake had calculated that David would arrive at about ten o'clock if the driver was urged to hurry and if they did not stop on the way. Brittany was finally ready by half-past nine, but when she contemplated the futile half-hour ahead, she wished desperately that she had left all her preparations until later and had plenty to fill her time.

Florrie had tactfully taken the evening off and George Theodore was fast asleep. She went to stare at his sleeping perfection for a while. He was a model infant. Susannah had suggested that Brittany engage a maternity nurse until a more permanent arrangement could be made, but George was quiet and well-behaved and Brittany recovered her strength quickly, running the nursery quite satisfactorily with only Florrie to help. This evening she found herself wishing that he would sleep a little less and provide her with some distraction.

She decided to wait downstairs.

Every clock in the house seemed to tick loudly and hungrily with expectation as Brittany lowered herself into a chair and carefully arranged her blue and white skirts. She was wearing the Worth gown again, even though the weather was dreary and cold, and hoped the gesture would not be lost on David. Her weight had dropped rapidly since George's birth, and although the thin material fitted smoothly, this time it was not tight.

She looked around the room critically, trying to discern an imperfection that would take time to correct, but the drawing room was unnaturally tidy in preparation for the prodigal's return. The inlaid escritoire and the black glass-topped table glowed dully and emitted a faint smell of the scented polish that Florrie used. Every available vase was overflowing with fragile white narcissi.

There was nothing to do but read or listen to the gramophone, and Brittany decided that the former would be more distracting. She had borrowed some lurid Mabel St John romances from Florrie during her short period of lying-in; tales of working-class viragos who ensnared their employers. She picked one up now, and became so engrossed in the tale of Mabel the plucky mill lass, that when she looked up, the clock's hand had miraculously moved in a near circle. It was twenty-past ten.

She stood by the window for a while, watching the street, but heard Nanny Wynn's voice admonishing 'A watched pot never boils', and knew that the saying was true. For what seemed like hours, her stomach leapt and fell every time a car's wheels growled on the gravel. She went into the spotless kitchen to reassure herself that it was tidy. She went upstairs. She brushed her hair again. She applied more lipstick.

Then she went to the telephone

'Mayfair 245 please, operator.' She clenched her fists. 'Miss Langbourne, please . . . Susannah, it's Brittany . . . No, he hasn't.Not yet . . . Yes . . . No . . . Susannah, I know it's late, but I wondered if you would mind dreadfully coming over here for a while so I can have someone to talk to . . .? Yes, I'm sure he will, but it's so beastly waiting . . . No, Florrie's not here . . . All right. Bless you. Goodbye.

A car. Could it be . . .? Susannah's outline as she stood in the darkened doorway was disappointingly small and blonde. She hugged Brittany tightly.

'My goodness – you're shivering! How awful to have to wait like this! Haven't you lit a fire?'

The soothing voice was Maud's, and she was in Park Street again. Susannah poured her a small glass of brandy and lit the fire.

'Is George all right? Does he need feeding?'

'George – I'd forgotten about him!'

But George was sleeping on, without his father, oblivious.

When the telephone rang just after midnight, Brittany knew that she must let Susannah answer it. Silly to be so superstitious, she told herself, as she strained to hear the conversation. It's probably no more than news of a flat tyre.

Susannah came into the freezing hallway.

'That was Jake.'

Her voice was so still and quiet . . . But it was always quiet, so there wasn't necessarily anything to fear. Yet . . .

'They had an accident. The driver was inexperienced. He was killed.'

The Worth dress grew so tight that it seemed to be choking her. 'But David——?'

'He was killed too.'

The words came from the far end of a darkened tunnel. From somewhere near the end of the tunnel, Brittany could hear herself scream.

Without Jake, it would not have been possible to go on.

Her son was no comfort at first, just a bitter reminder. In the black, early days, Brittany could hardly look at him. A stream of grief erupted against the wall of her chest with primitive violence, escaping now and then into a gasped 'oh' or silent, mouthed scream. The stream ebbed and flowed with the rhythm of a dance and the dance was beaten out in the endless, restless pacing. To stand still was to risk the tide.

And even later, much later on, there were so many moments when she was caught unawares by the aching of her throat and the burning behind her eyes and she had to summon all her strength. With so many of them gone now – Maman, George, David – it was was becoming harder and harder to find that strength. Were it not for Jake, she could have found very little. Perhaps none.

At first Brittany was so stupefied with grief that she forgot Jake had lost a brother, his only brother. She was reminded, with some shock, by the mourning clothes he wore on his first visit to Cheyne Mews after David's burial. She had remained in London since the accident; too grief-stricken and confused to face uprooting herself and returning to Harry Herbert's continual queries about money.

Jake's eyes were instantly on her face when Florrie led him into the drawing room, and she turned it sharply away from him.

'Don't look at me! Please!' she croaked. 'I look so ugly.'

Weeks of crying and sleeplessness had left Brittany's face pale and puffy, and her normally burnished hair dusty looking. She winced when she passed a mirror, and a few seconds' contemplation of her swollen and distorted features was enough to reduce her to tears of self-loathing.

'You look fine,' said Jake quietly. 'Besides, there's no one here to see you except me, and I don't exactly look great either.'

Brittany studied him. 'No, you don't,' she agreed. 'You look very tired. I'm sorry to be so selfish, Jake . . . has it been ghastly for you? Have you seen Miriam?'

'No. The divorce was finalized a few weeks ago. She's in New York apparently, but I didn't see her while I was there.'

'How was it?'

'New York? It was awful. I'm glad to be back.'

Brittany longed to hear something of the funeral, but did not know how to ask.

'Would you like me to tell you about the funeral?'

She nodded.

'It was dignified. Dignified but very bleak. I think it's as well you couldn't go. It wouldn't have helped.'

'And they blame me?'

It was more a statement than a question.

'Outwardly, yes, but they know in their hearts that it's wrong to do so. It was just David; he was like that. Impatient. Selfish, maybe.' He glanced at Brittany and answered the question in her heart. 'Even if he had arrived, he may not have stayed. For a while perhaps, but not for ever.'

Brittany reflected how angry she had become when he had disparaged David's love for her over lunch at the Ritz. She could not feel angry now.

'I know that,' she replied gravely, still looking down. 'I sometimes even feel that it's better he's not here, but still, everything seems so empty. There's a *nothingness* . . .'

'You have a son.'

It was Jake's turn to lower his eyes now, behind their long, fine lashes. 'And you have me.'

'Do I?'

'You know you do.'

The stillness of his face was very beautiful to Brittany at that moment. And the pulling sensation came again as the empty part of her tried to absorb him into her being, all of him. In the distance there was the leaden rumble of a spring storm and rain began to fall in quick, swollen drops.

'I'm glad that you came today.' She smiled at him, a transforming smile. 'You've helped me,' she finished simply.

A slight frown appeared on Jake's face and Brittany thought at first that she had made him angry. He walked to the fireplace and lit a cigarette.

'To be able to help, you have to have felt pain. That's why David was no use to you when George died. He'd never had a day's suffering in his life. I believe he was meant to die in the way he did – instantaneously. Impossible to see him weak or sick.'

Brittany did not want to think about David. 'And your suffering? . . .'

Jake gripped the edge of the mantelpiece, hanging his head so that his voice was muffled. 'I lost . . . I lost the person I loved most in the world.'

Brittany raised her eyebrows in surprise. 'Who was he?'

' "She". A girl.'

Her features relaxed with the dawn of comprehension. 'The Exley girl.'

Now Jake was surprised. 'David told you?'

'He mentioned it once. That's all he said, "The Exley girl".'

'Katherine Exley,' said Jake reverently, and Brittany's breathing became involuntarily jagged at the way he spoke her name. 'I may have been young, but I was in love with her. God, I was in love with her! She had so much life . . .'

The sun blazed suddenly through a gap in the clouds, lighting their faces with brilliant rose and gold.

'What happened? You didn't marry her?'

'Katherine Exley was the daughter of a dyed-in-the-wool New England family. What we Americans call "old stock". An excuse for snobbery. Her people came from Scotland – they were Protestant. So, no question of marriage. Both sides were equally opposed, as you can imagine.'

'How terrible, Jake! What on earth did you do?'

'We had an affair – with difficulty. She was still very young and her parents watched her like a hawk so . . . it was difficult. Then someone told her father. He kept her away from me. She disappeared for a while. And I . .'

The expression that came over Jake's face was so agonized that Brittany started involuntarily towards him.

'You what? Go on.'

'I married Miriam. My family wanted it and I just didn't care any more. Yes, why not, I said. What the hell. Then she got sick. Katherine. I went to her, they couldn't stop me this time. It was meningitis; they said she might get better . . .'

The burst of pink evening sunshine faded abruptly and the rain began to lash the windows again.

'. . . But she died.'

# 10

*Somerset, 20 September, 1924*

Brittany was sitting at the oval table that stood in the window
alcove of the dining room, sipping a cup of tea and reading her
morning mail. One of the letters had a French postmark.

'*Madame . . .*'

She ran her eye quickly over the rest of the letter. On the demise
of Mlle Eugénie de Vesey on 1 July 1924, the whole of her estate
passed to her niece, Miss Evelyn Margaret Colby.

Or so her advocate told Brittany in bland, legalistic French.
Mlle de Vesey was a lady of modest means. Her apartment in St
Germain des Prés was only rented, but the contents – which made
up the bulk of the estate – would fetch something in the region of
£2,000. And the butterfly collection of the late Armand de Vesey
was of considerable value.

Brittany hesitated over the butterflies. She remembered them in
their cases: the strange, salty sweet smell and the rows of merging
colour and descending size. All lying there so still.

'*Pourquoi ne bougent-t-ils pas, Grandpère?*' she had queried in a
squeaky voice as the old count lifted her gently onto her lap so that
she could see better.

He shook his head sadly. '*Ils sont morts, chérie . . .*'

She went into the library. The sunshine that spilled over the
surface of her desk was so bright that she squinted slightly as she
sat down and picked up her pen. In a fit of sentimentality she
instructed Messieurs Lavandin et Belhomert to arrange for the
butterfly collection to be packed up and sent to Graylings, and to
sell the remainder of the estate immediately at the best possible
price. She read it several times, puzzling over her ungrammatical
French, and then altered the wording 'the remainder of the estate'
to 'the remainder of the estate excepting any family portraits'. At
the end of the letter she added that these were to be packed up and
sent to England with the butterflies. After this she was quite
satisfied with the way that she had handled the matter. Maman
would have been pleased.

She sat back in her chair and smiled.

It was now six months since David's death, and Brittany was

265

surprised at the speed with which she had recovered. Having David's child went a little way towards making it all right. Their child, and Jake. Why should it be acceptable for her to have loved David and lost him, all parcelled up as part of her past, just because Jake Stein existed? Was it because he would always take care of her in a way that David never had? Or something more?

She began to know the answer to that, gradually. It began when she realized she was jealous of a dead person. She was jealous of Katherine Exley. But she buried the thought at the back of her mind, dead and buried before it had a chance to live and divert her; and took her son back to Graylings.

After weeks of trying to ignore George Theodore, he gradually became a source of comfort. Part of David was living still and she thanked God for that, but the child was more than a symbol of a dead lover, he was living and he was her responsibility. She spent as much time as possible in his company. He was a well-behaved child and a handsome one. He seldom gave way to either tears or laughter, but applied himself to every task and bodily function with immense seriousness and concentration. Whenever he turned his reproachful blue-green eyes on Brittany and broke into a toothless grin, she felt the soaring thrill of pride. The attitude of her neighbours was still reserved, but now she was no longer pregnant she could go out and about with greater ease, and she spent many happy hours riding around her old haunts on the estate.

Money was a major preoccupation. The remainder of the mortgage that Gerald Colby had acquired before the war entailed an extortionately high rate of interest. And wages had risen sharply over the past few years. Most of the income from the estate was devoured by these two demands, leaving Brittany's domestic budget – which Jake had helped to calculate – very tight. More than once she had had occasion to regret her prompt rejection of the money that Isaac Stein had offered to settle on her child. She had, after all, produced a son.

Tante Eugénie's £2,000 were, therefore, like manna from heaven. Brittany decided that she would put some of the money towards the redecoration of the house, and with the rest she would buy a car. She was so exhilarated at the prospect that she went straight from the library to inform Florrie that they would be leaving for London that same evening. She had some other

266

purchases to make, and London seemed a good place to start looking for the right car.

Their train arrived at Paddington station just before midnight. The next morning she rose early and set out from Chelsea to Mayfair. It was a fine, breezy day and she decided she would walk. The only garage she knew of was in South Audley Street, the one she used to pass when she lived with the Langbournes. She came quickly round the corner, warm and slightly out of breath from her walk across Hyde Park . . .

And there it was.

She found herself face to face with the most perfect car she had ever seen. It was a pale cream sports car with a distinctive radiator like that of a Rolls Royce, dark red seats and gleaming headlamps. And it cried out to Brittany: *Buy me*. There was a neat handwritten notice ticketed on the windscreen. 'For sale. £800.'

There was no one inside the saleroom, but in the forecourt a young mechanic was on his hands and knees, peering underneath a car.

'Excuse me,' said Brittany in a cool, voice. 'That car in the window – I'd like to buy it.'

The man squinted up at her, openmouthed. He had a suntanned face and very large, very even teeth.

'The Sizaire-Berwick, madam? £800. Not new, mind; they cost £1,500 or more new . . .' He hung his head and scratched the gravel with his toe. 'Any road . . . I can't sell it to you. You'll have to wait until the guvnor gets back tomorrow. He handles sales, you see.'

Brittany drooped like a child faced with the postponement of Christmas. 'But I especially wanted to buy it today. I can go to my bank right away and arrange to draw the cheque.'

She saw him hesitating. '*Please*! I'll leave my name and address so that your . . . guvnor . . . can find me if there's any problem.'

He grinned. 'All right, then.'

'You never know – he may be pleased that you've made such an important sale . . .'

Brittany had only ever driven on quiet country lanes, but her nervousness was dispelled after a few minutes behind the wheel, and then driving around London was sheer delight. The veneer of the wood facia, the sparkle of the brass fittings, the knobs and buttons delighted her as the minutiae of her lovingly crafted

Edwardian toys had delighted her years before. It was a car that drew attention, and so did its driver, as she sat straight-backed and pink-cheeked, her short thick hair ruffled by the breeze.

Driving around the streets of London made her think of Jake and how much she had missed him. She could hardly wait to show the car to him, but she would *have* to wait, until that evening at least. At seven o'clock she bathed in liberally perfumed water, applied cosmetics – sparingly, as Jake did not like women to wear too much makeup – and picked out a dress that was exactly the same pale cream as the bodywork of her new car. It was a narrow sheath of crêpe de Chine with a petalled skirt and a low-cut, draped back. Brittany's skin was yellow gold from the sun, and her neck, with its tendrils of tawny hair, rose from the milky folds of the material like the stamen of a lily. She wore no jewellery except for pearls and a pair of pendulous ivory earrings that Lucienne had been given when she was young.

Florrie gave a long, low whistle that would have been judged unacceptable impertinence in any other household.

'You don't 'alf look the thing tonight, Miss. Going somewhere nice?'

'Just out for a drive,' Brittany returned airily as she floated to the front door in a fog of Patou and turned to give Florrie a secretive little smile.

It was a clear late summer evening, but cool, and Brittany shivered as she switched off the engine after the short drive to Eaton Place. Jake answered the door himself, just as she had hoped, and a broad smile rushed to her face.

'Surprise! Look, Jake!'

He squinted, perplexed, into the dusk.

'How do you like my car?'

She danced down the steps and stood next to it, leaning gracefully against the bonnet to create what she hoped would be the most dramatic effect possible. The petals of her skirt fluttered against the running board.

Jake pulled in his narrow lips until they almost disappeared, tightening Brittany's heart with invisible wires.

'You can't afford a car.'

He turned to go back into the house. She followed him lightly up the steps, determined to fend off his disparagement.

'Yes, I can.'

'How much did it cost?' he called over his shoulder as he led the way into the sitting room.

'£800.'

It was not quite dark outside and the lamps had not yet been switched on. The grey light cooled the turquoise walls that had so startled Brittany on her first visit. There was a large vase of yellow carnations on the centre table and she bent to inhale their scent greedily.

Jake glared at her as he raised a match to his cigarette.

'Brittany, what are you trying to prove? You know you have only £200 a month to spend.'

'I inherited some, £2,000 in fact. I haven't received it yet, of course, but when one has expectations . . . Aren't you going to offer me a drink, Jake?'

He waved her sulkily to the tray. 'Help yourself.'

Brittany lost patience. 'Don't be dreary, Jake,' she snapped as she dropped ice cubes into a glass and watched them crack under the Scotch. 'I was so excited at the prospect of showing it off, and naturally I thought you'd—'

'Is that what all this was for?' He frowned in the direction of her half-naked back, a smooth golden V against the cream silk.

She turned.

'I wanted to impress you.'

'Why?'

Jake's question was so stark, so direct, that Brittany jumped slightly and the ice cubes rattled.

'To satisfy my vanity, of course,' she parried quickly, with a slight smile.

She waited for an answering smile, or a compliment, but none came. 'Jake – I've explained about the money for the car. Why are you still cross?'

He sat down heavily, his shoulders bunching in an unJake-like pose of defeat. 'I don't know. I'm on edge, I guess . . . I'm sorry, you look terrific.'

*'Then why don't you want to look at me?'*

He shook his head slowly and rubbed a hand through his thick hair. 'What's the point in pretending any more? You may as well know. Wait there a second—'

He left the room and returned holding a piece of paper which he held out to her. 'I had a letter from my dear papa today. Read it.'

Brittany sat down with the letter in one hand and the glass of Scotch clutched tightly in the other. The letter was typewritten. She was almost sure what it was going to say.

*New York*
*2 September 1924*
'*Dear Son,*
    *I dictated a letter to you last year, outlining my reasons for wanting our beloved David to come home. Now I find myself addressing you on the same subject, and once again I wish to be as direct as possible.*
    '*You are to stay well away from the Colby girl and her bastard. I will not, out of respect for your age, give you a lecture about breaking your mother's heart. But people have heard about it here in New York, and they're talking: like, are you sure it's David's boy and not Jake's? That kind of thing. It's not good for business, Jake, and you know it. Especially so soon after the divorce.*
    '*You've done a lot of good work for the European office, but Bob Easton is well overdue for promotion and I've offered him Ironmonger Lane, which he has accepted. This will mean your relocation to Wall Street before long. Don't let me down, Jake. Your loving Papa.*'

'I'm surprised he doesn't sign it "Isaac Stein"!' exclaimed Brittany in disgust. '*Relocation.* What a horrible word!'

There was a hardness in her eyes that Jake could not quite interpret; a wall behind which unbearable pain and bitterness had been swallowed and shut away. She did not speak for a long time, but sat so rigidly that she scarcely seemed to be breathing. Did he know that she was afraid to look at his face, she wondered?

'Will you want to keep the house in Cheyne Mews?' Jake asked.

'Yes, why not?' she said with enforced cheerfulness. They were silent opposite each other for a while as if both were waiting for a benevolent miracle, for it to be a dream that they could wake from.

'Right . . . well, I'll try and arrange it. But I'm very glad you'll have Graylings too. I know it's what you wanted.'

He stood up to light another cigarette. As he passed her she could scent his warm, clean flesh and she could see the vulnerability of the fine hairs on the back of his neck, could feel her fingers aching to touch them. The ache spread to the back of her throat and then, dully, to the centre of her chest.

'And *you*, Jake. What do *you* want?' The words were meant to be a whisper, but they emerged as a croak.

She walked to him and stood just a few inches away. Their proximity was like an outlawed sea that they had rushed into. Drowning them. With a rush of breath she realized that she had wasted more than a year in avoiding looking at Jake like this: directly, truthfully. For the first time she met his eyes, her long blue eyes looked into his own. And she saw . . . what did she see?

A look of blinding love so pure it terrified her.

She had wanted David continually with the restless urge that finds no true response. But now, finally, answering to the sweetness and savagery of passion, her soul and Jake's were rocked with the same rhythm.

And she was wise at last.

'I want *this*,' he said simply, 'I want *this* so much.'

And he raised his hands so that they were supporting her head, tilting it. Brittany's arms hung submissively by her sides, but her body was tensed, pliant. His lips pressed and moulded hers cruelly, opening them into a soundless gasp and flickering his tongue against the roof of her mouth until her thighs tightened and trembled and her breasts ached hotly against the silk of her dress.

She could not tell whether she was moaning or crying as she placed her hands on his shoulder blades and bent him to her, running her mouth over his sweet-smelling neck and hair, grazing her face on dark stubble, biting his face in desperation. There was a rushing in her mind as she counted the days, the weeks, the months that she had wanted to do this thing, this thing that she had been kept from by the sheer terror of confronting such love.

Jake's mouth found hers again and the deceptive gentleness of the kiss wrung all strength from her. But the movements of his hand between her damp thighs and the pressure from his groin were starkly erotic, primitive, greedy, and he began to push her onto the sofa. Instinct opened her up to him, as wet and hot as fruit in the sun, but her mind snapped shut.

'No, Jake.' Her voice cracked and shook. 'I can't.'

She straightened her dress feebly, eyes downcast, and as she moved, the mingled scent of carnations and cigarette smoke dragged at the back of her nostrils.

Jake's eyes were wild, the eyes of an animal newly caught in a trap.

'I don't believe you don't want it,' he whispered.

'I do, Jake, more than anything, but I couldn't. It's too late now, isn't it?'

'But—'

She remembered David's words as she reached the front door. '*I care too much.*'

She was crying as she ran down the steps to the car, and when Florrie found her parked in Cheyne Mews an hour later, slumped over the steering wheel, she was crying still.

## *Somerset, 20 September, 1924*

Downstairs, Heathcote House was very quiet.

Warm sun reached through the windows, laying its hands in blessing over everything it found, caressing the thin layer of dust that had settled. It chased persistently through empty rooms, penetrating half-open doors and spilling into darkened passageways, polishing the matt surface of the ebony cherubs on the dining room walls.

Upstairs, in one of the bedrooms, sunlight streamed through an open window and onto a large canopied bed. At the centre of the bed, propped up against pillows and partly obscured by the rich satin drapes that billowed from the ornamental polonaise on the ceiling, lay Jennifer Steele. She watched the door expectantly.

Eventually it opened and the village midwife came in, holding a white bundle which she handed to Jennifer.

'Here he is, Mrs Steele, all cleaned up for you. Dr Hibbert's gone home now. Shall I ask your husband to come in?'

'Yes, please,' said Jennifer, without looking up. She was smiling down at the red, creased face of her son.

The midwife returned a few minutes later, alone.

She looked embarrassed.

Jennifer turned and stared out of the window, knowing what the woman was about to say.

'We haven't been able to find Mr Steele, I'm afraid. He appears to be out of the house. But I'm sure he'll be back soon.'

*Soon . . . Out of the house . . .*

Jennifer leaned back heavily on the pillows. How could she explain to the midwife that her husband had been out of the house so long that he wasn't even aware that his wife had gone into labour?

Adrian returned to Heathcote at eleven o'clock.

He knocked aggressively at the bedroom door and opened it without waiting for an answer. Jennifer was sitting up in bed reading a book and the room was lit only by her bedside lamp.

Adrian raised his crooked eyebrows in the direction of the cradle.

'Your son, Adrian,' said Jennifer drily.

He walked to the cradle and carefully lifted the baby into his arms, studying the sleeping face curiously, dispassionately.

'What are you going to call him?' he asked.

'Patrick.'

'Why Patrick?' Adrian put the baby back in his crib and turned away abruptly, as though he had already lost interest.

'I just like the sound of it, that's all. And James, after my father.'

'Patrick James Steele,' intoned Adrian thoughtfully. 'Is he well?'

'Perfectly, thank you.'

*. . . And what about me? What about inquiring how I survived the disgusting, grisly, twenty-hour ordeal of a baby that's too big and a pelvis that's too small? . . .*

Adrian was walking back to the door.

'Are you going? You've only just arrived.'

He did not reply.

'Adrian!'

His hand closed round the doorknob. Jennifer struggled into a sitting position.

'You've got what you wanted now, haven't you?' he asked, inclining his head in the direction of the cradle. 'Now for God's sake, leave me alone!'

The doorknob turned.

'You seem to have forgotten that little episode of *patricide*!' said Jennifer. Her eyes were as bright as candles. 'Shall we talk about it?'

'Jennifer,' sighed Adrian, halfway across the threshold, 'Must we go through this again? Why can't you just get on with being a good mother to our child? I've agreed not to divorce you. And have you stopped to consider what would happen to *you* if I ended my life on

the gallows, or spent the remainder of it in prison? This place
would have to be sold, and you'd be just as you were when you met
me. Homeless.'

'Adrian, where are you going? . . . *I just want you to answer my
question . . .*'

The bedroom door slammed and the sound of brisk, springing
footsteps faded.

In his cradle, Patrick James Steele began to cry fretfully.


*Somerset, 31 January, 1925*

Jake rested his hands self-consciously on the leatherbound steering
wheel.

He was unaccustomed to driving his own car, and sometimes, as
now, when he headed down a steep Somerset lane, he felt it was
trying to run away with him. He checked his own speed as a matter
of habit, never quite able to rid himself of the picture of his brother
lying in the midst of twisted wreckage. And now he was nearing
his destination, surrounded on all sides by the unrelieved browns
and sludgy greys of the English countryside in midwinter and a
blank white sky that pressed down heavily on the landscape.

Jake and Brittany had not met since she had run sobbing down
the steps of 15 Eaton Place, and he had been sealed in confusion
ever since. The next morning she had telephoned to inform him in
a bright and brassily defensive voice that she was returning to
Graylings that morning in her newly purchased car. Jake telephoned her frequently after that, but their passionate embrace on
the night she had bought the cream-coloured car hung between
them, unmentioned.

Sometimes there would be a break or the beginning of a sigh in
Brittany's voice and he expected her to say . . . but it never came.
She behaved with such well-bred sangfroid and formal cheerfulness that Jake was forced to conclude – and the mere shadow of
the thought was enough to drip acid through his heart – that she
was trying to save face after what she saw as an embarassing lapse.
A moment of weakness.

He had looked at his face in the mirror every morning from that
day on, loathing his plainness, and reminding himself that he had
been on the point of asking this woman to marry him, a woman

274

who was searching for the ebullient, charming, dead David in him and who had gone away empty-handed. His heart told him that he had read something different in her yearning eyes that night, but his nondescript reflection told him he was a damn fool. Perhaps it was as well that Isaac Stein was prising him away with Teutonic determination and leaving him no time to find out.

There was a blinding flash of light against the grey-brown trees, like snow on a summer mountain. Jake stopped the car for a while to look down and admire what Brittany had lost and won back. Graylings stood as classically white and clean as a diamond in the mud, its columned porch spreading out from the front of the house like a fan. For as long as he had known Brittany, he had been curious to enter the world she had once left behind. He would see her here at last, in the house where she had been born, and then he would not see her any more.

He had come to say goodbye.

Brittany was wearing riding breeches and a red sweater.

Jake thought she looked wild and exotic like a circus girl. He had never seen her dressed in red before, nor had he seen her wearing trousers, and he averted his eyes from the compelling length of her legs.

Brittany frowned at his dark suit and then laughed when he said he couldn't think what else to wear, and dragged him upstairs to the nursery to see George.

'It's his first birthday soon,' she divulged proudly, as the two of them leaned over the cot and held out their hands for him to grasp. 'And Florrie says he'll soon be able to walk.'

'His eyes are getting greener,' said Jake quietly as she led the way downstairs. 'He's looking more and more like David.'

'Yes, he is,' she agreed, without looking round.

They ate a picnic lunch of cold chicken, cheese and wine on the kitchen table, with the explanation that the dining room was being redecorated, but that it was rather too grand for two anyway. Jake smiled at Brittany's enthusiasm and the total ease with her surroundings that she had never evinced in London. A child absorbed in its favourite game . . .

While they ate she chattered happily to him about her plans for the house, but never quite met his eye, and as soon as he had swallowed his last mouthful she leapt to her feet with a cry of 'And now – the Grand Tour!'

They saw the rooms downstairs first. The ballroom was empty but for a menacingly large chandelier ('I'm not quite sure what to use it for,' Brittany confessed), with walls painted pale duck-egg blue and mirrors gleaming. The formal drawing room had been brightened with décor of china blue, cream and white, cunningly offsetting the blue and gold Sèvres porcelain displayed in cabinets and Armand de Vesey's collection of butterflies framed on the walls ('Though nobody ever comes in here, too grand').

Then upstairs to the little north-facing sitting room, filled with winter light. There was evidence of occupation here: bowls of forsythia and winter jasmine, a handful of novels and a sketchpad on the side table, toys strewn on the ivory-coloured rugs. Jake murmured his appreciation of the clever blend of primrose yellow and apricot and then sat in the window seat to watch the gardener ruthlessly cutting back shrubs in the flowerbed below. He was overwhelmed, seduced by the charm and tranquillity, the *wholeness* of the place and he wanted time to think.

'Brittany—' he began.

Ignoring him, she was on her feet again.

'And now, Jake . . . 'There was a teasing note in her blue eyes and in the twist of her mouth. '. . . I want to show you my bedroom.'

It was beautiful, an extravagant dream of a bedroom.

'Like a movie set,' he said admiringly.

'It used to be my mother's room,' Brittany explained, 'and when I was young I used to think it was the prettiest room in the house. So feminine, so glamorous . . . I swore I would have a room like it one day. And I have.'

She waved her arm like a wand at the enormous canopied bed, a froth of strawberry pink, with ribbons and bows and swagged and draped lace curtains.

'What do you think of it?'

He smiled down at her flushed face and her tawny gold hair, which was thicker and looser now, curling over her forehead.

'I think it's just right.'

They stood still for mere seconds, but the silence of those seconds ached and dragged. But when he looked again at the end of those seconds, marked pointedly by the carriage clock above the

276

fireplace, her eyes had clouded and she was guarding herself again.

They went into the garden next.

Jake looked browner and smaller in a borrowed tweed jacket and walking boots. They sauntered the length of the house, scuffing their feet and studying their white, smoky breath like children.

'I've had the outside of the house whitewashed,' said Brittany. 'It took months and cost an awful lot of money, but I think it was worth it, don't you? The paint was peeling off before, and it looked rather sad.'

She led them down a long path at the back of the house until they came to a tiny, perfect cottage.

'Pretty, isn't it? George and I wanted to make it our own when we were children, but we weren't allowed to play in it. It was almost derelict then, so I suppose they thought it was dangerous. I've had it renovated and I'm using it as a studio. I'm learning how to paint.'

They stopped to discuss the progress of the hardy annuals with the gardener, and finally headed up the steep path to the beech copse.

'You get the best view from up here, in my opinion,' said Brittany as they sat down on the bench.

She sighed as she looked down, but it was a contented sigh. Graylings stood calmly below them, the newly trimmed lawn spreading before it like a smooth, green lake.

'You've done a lot of work, Brittany,' said Jake thoughtfully. 'And I can't help feeling that it cost you a lot of money. I know it's none of my business, but—'

'I've sold some of the estate. Fifteen thousand acres is far too much. The accounts are in a hell of a state too. Adrian Steele employed one system, Harry Herbert another. . . . Then there are the salaries to pay. I still have Florrie with me, to look after George, and I can't manage here with less than two maids, and then there's the cook, and a gardener is an absolute necessity, and the interest on the mortgage is crippling . . .'

She sighed again, and this time the sigh was anxious.

'. . . I've sold 5,000 acres already and I don't see how I'm going to avoid selling the remainder if—'

'Don't do that!' said Jake abruptly.

She turned to look at him curiously. The thin sunshine was making tiny shards of light in his brown hair.

'It would be a great shame to get rid of land that will eventually be capable of providing you with a considerable income, once the effects of the change of ownership have been overcome.'

'What alternative do I have?'

'You're paying far too much interest. I'll put up the money to pay back the original mortgage and then provide you with a new longterm mortgage at a much lower rate of interest. Plus an option to buy the whole thing back at once, in case there's a miraculous change in your fortunes,' he teased.

He looked at the house, then back at her expectantly.

Brittany was grave. 'I don't know, Jake. It sounds like a good idea, but . . . I want to think about it.'

She stood up.

'I'm getting cold. Let's go and have some tea. It'll be dark soon.'

They had tea by the fire in the little sitting room, with George sitting on the hearthrug and staring inscrutably at each one of them in turn.

'Does he always stare like that?' Jake asked, exasperated and amused when his attempts to distract the baby failed.

Brittany laughed.

'He's thinking. Susannah says it indicates strong will and stubbornness – who knows?'

The introduction of a safe, neutral topic of conversation eased the tension and they discussed Susannah's recent engagement to Hugh Stanwycke, eldest son of a Somerset family that Brittany had known as a child. Their farm, Cleveleigh, was about ten miles from Graylings.

'I'm very happy for her,' she told Jake. 'Though it means that I see very little of her now she's so preoccupied with the wedding arrangements . . .'

She fussed over kissing George goodnight and handed him into Florrie's waiting arms.

'. . . and envious?' asked Jake, as Florrie closed the door behind her.

'Envious? No, I don't think so. Hugh's a pleasant enough fellow, but hardly very exciting—'

'I meant envious of her married state.'

She turned her head away sharply. 'Don't, Jake.'

He sat quietly for a moment and did not appear to notice her watching his angelically calm profile with a fierce possessiveness.

278

Then he stood up. The moment that she had been dreading had arrived.

'I must go back now. Have you had any more thoughts about my proposition? You'll have to let me know very soon if you want me to arrange it.'

Brittany picked up the poker and jabbed angrily at the fire. The flames leapt and hissed and filled the room with the warm scent of applewood.

'Yes, Jake, I would like you to arrange the new mortgage for me. But first I must know why. I want to know why you keep on helping me like this. Is it some enduring sense of guilt about what happened to David or . . .?'

'Not at all,' Jake replied, with the coldness that had aroused her of old.

She craned her neck to look up at him from where she crouched on the hearthrug and his tall body seemed to block out all the light except that from the fire.

'George is my brother's son. My flesh and blood. You are his mother and therefore family of a kind. I know you refused financial help from my father, but George's future still concerns me, and that's why I made the offer.'

'For George?'

'Yes, for George.'

A last bold hope withered in Brittany. So that's all I am, she thought, a poor Jewish widow woman. I should be sitting here dressed in black and looking bereaved for the benefit of my self-appointed brother-in-law.

There was one last silence. Then Brittany raised her head and spoke into the fire.

'You're going back soon, aren't you?'

He nodded, then realized that she couldn't see him from where she was sitting. But he also realized that she knew the answer already.

*Do you love me, Jake? . . .*

The words started forward but she bit her tongue to keep them back. 'Will you ever come to England again?'

'Perhaps.'

Neither of them spoke again, but she led Jake to the front door and buried her head against his shoulder when he bent to kiss her. His breath clouded the cold night air and was whipped away by the sharp winter wind. She clung to him and then released her muscles angrily, stepping back and sniffing slightly. He did not turn to wave.

She watched him drive away from the house, and when she saw the wind flutter the hair at the back of his neck, she uttered a great cry of pain and longing and ran into her frivolous strawberries-and-cream sanctuary to weep alone.

The bursting and tearing inside her was deafening, and she wanted no one else to be aware of it.

The bubble of Brittany's domestic peace had been burst.

At the end of February, she received papers to sign relating to the mortgage of the house and the estate, and with them a brief note from Jake saying that he was to sail for New York the following week.

Then silence. And the silence ate into her and gnawed at her insides every night as she lay alone in her perfumed, lace-trimmed bed. It carved its way, shrieking, through the calm of the new life she had created for herself.

When she and David had found Gerald's will in the attic, the discovery that Teddy was her father had relieved and comforted her. She still took out his photograph and looked at it sometimes when she was alone: at the bright, golden-blond hair and the eyes that crinkled when he smiled. Once she held it to the green-eyed, dark-haired George and said, 'Look, darling, your grandfather', but he merely gave the picture his impenetrable stare and reached up to curl his fat, sticky fingers round it.

It was a picture that explained so many flickering past images: Maman's distracted, regretful unhappiness, the hardness in Gerald Colby's eyes when he looked at her, his obsessive love for his firstborn son . . . Lucienne, Gerald and Teddy lived with her at Graylings, no longer spectres but familiar household ghosts, and now that she knew them, they let her rest.

But Jake's leaving changed everything.

For a long time they had met infrequently, sporadically, but Jake, like Graylings, was always there. The reassurance of the thought of his tall, dignified figure moving through the City some-where, or sleeping angelic and alone, had always buoyed and comforted her. Jake, kindly Jake, who was always there when she called – she relied on him, she *needed* him. She was a child who had ill-advisedly released its mother's hand and been swallowed up by the crowd.

She waited daily for letters that never came. At the end of April, in desperation, she wrote to Jake. She entertained him with a lavish account of Graylings' refurbishment and with several anecdotes about the progress of George, who was now staggering unsteadily from room to room. She ended the letter: '. . . *do please write soon, Jake, and tell me all about New York and how you are. It all seems so far away. I think about you often and miss you most dreadfully. Yours ever, Brittany.*'

It was five weeks before she received a reply.

By all the outward signs her life progressed smoothly and serenely during those five weeks. She supervised the redecoration of the dining room and the study and the regeneration of the garden, sat for hours in the nursery playing with George and dabbled messily in oil paints at the cottage. She indulged her passion for village gossip with the maids and learned that Jennifer Steele had given birth to a son in the autumn, christened Patrick James for no clear reason. She and Adrian and Phoebe Lester were still, apparently, ensconced in their mysterious triangle.

Ruth and Henry Morgan were still frequent visitors at Graylings, where they made much of George, and Susannah and her new husband came twice to spend the weekend. They were resident in London, but hoped eventually to move back to Cleveleigh. And there was the occasional trip to London to visit old friends and keep appointments with her dressmaker.

Outwardly all was calm. Inwardly, Brittany was in a turmoil.

She progressed through a frieze of tortured attitudes, endless tears in private, dark despairing nights, frustrated rage and overwhelming love for Jake. She hated him for demeaning her in this way and she missed him more than she would have dreamed it possible to miss anyone.

Finally his reply came.

'*My dear Brittany. It was wonderful to receive your letter, and I'm only sorry that I had no opportunity of replying earlier. Papa intervened with an impromptu trip to Chicago, and I have only just returned.*

'*What can I tell you about life in New York? Wall Street is dull, banking and social circles are dull, home is dull. Mother doesn't seem to have adjusted too well to David's death, but two of my sisters have had children recently, so at least she has the grandchildren to distract her.*

*None of my nephews are as handsome as young George. How soon before he can talk? . . .'*

The last paragraph quickened Brittany's heart.

*'I think about you a lot, Brittany, and wonder if you ever slide down the banisters at Graylings. I miss you like crazy. Affectionately, Jake.'*

She took the letter from its envelope and read it at frequent intervals over the next few days, until she knew it by heart.

*'I miss you like crazy . . .'*

She planned her reply carefully.

This time she wrote nostalgically of their time in London together: their meeting over lunch with David and Miriam; the picnic on Christmas Eve; George's birth . . .

*'. . . It all seems so long ago now. To think that I was twenty-seven a few weeks ago! Graylings is beautiful and full of colour now that all the spring flowers are out, but it seems awfully lonely without you. I do so wish you were here with me to see it all. Come back soon. Yours always, Brittany.'*

Several more weeks passed, and then:

*'My dearest Brittany. Since receiving your last letter I've been thinking about you constantly. Those times in London were very special, even if they weren't always happy.*

*'If you think that reaching twenty-seven is a trial, think how I feel at thirty-seven, with both parents pressurizing me to marry as soon as possible.*

*'As for marriage, I don't see how I could right now. It would seem quite wrong, feeling for you as I do. Part of me will always be at Graylings with you. My love to you, Jake.'*

Brittany was on the telephone to Susannah for a long time that morning. Yes, her father's secretary would be able to arrange places on a Langbourne Lines ship at short notice. Of course, Richard Langbourne would never hear of them paying for the passage. Yes, it would be quite all right for her to motor straight down to the docks from Somerset. Susannah woud arrange to have someone pick up the car and take it back to London while Brittany was away.

She rang for Florrie and waited for her in the upstairs sitting room, resplendent in its spring colours.

'Florrie. I have something of an announcement to make. We're going to New York.'

# New York, 8 July, 1925

The first sight was a disappointment.

Brittany strained her neck and her imagination as she pressed against the railings to get a good view of the city, but New York was not as she had wanted it to be. She had pictured glittering columns, fey and dreaming against a pastel sky, but instead there was an ugly and ill-assorted cluster of buildings huddling together behind ferry slips and sloping lofts. It was a cloudy, humid morning.

Reservations had been made at the Waldorf-Astoria on Richard Langbourne's recommendation, and after a few anxious moments on the quayside with a squawking George and an intractable mound of suitcases, they enlisted the services of one of New York's quaint chequered cabs, sporting its ring of black and white squares like a gaudy hatband.

Brittany felt deflated by the foreignness of it all and had expected Florrie to be even more overawed than herself. But Florrie perched George on her knee so that she could point things out to him, chattering volubly all the way to the hotel.

'Blimey, I bet that looks something all lit up!' she cried when she saw the regiment of lamps that guarded the imposing stone arches of the Waldorf-Astoria. 'I've never seen anything as fancy as that at home – look, George!'

She pointed him in the direction of the lamps, each topped with an elaborate wrought-iron structure resembling Cinderella's coach.

Brittany was too hot and anxious to care for the wonders that New York's hotel had to offer. After a cursory inspection of their gleaming and thickly-carpeted suite, she flung herself onto a sofa and asked Florrie to order up some cold lemonade. Her inclination was for something stronger, but she decided that it was too soon to start embroiling herself in the pitfalls of Prohibition. The lemonade trickled in an ice-cold stream through her grateful body, and once it was finished, she fell asleep.

It was early evening when Florrie woke her, and the heat had eased.

'Is George asleep?' she murmured, rubbing her eyes.

'Yes, Miss. I think he'll sleep on through the night now. Shall I order some tea?'

'Yes, that would be lovely.'

Brittany swung her legs off the sofa and fumbled for her shoes. 'It looks as though we'll eat here tonight, Florrie, but I must say the prices in the restaurant seem fearfully high.'

'Yes, Miss, it's the Prohibition,' said Florrie knowledgeably. 'I took the liberty of having a little chat with the bell-captain this afternoon while you were sleeping, and he explained how it's this Prohibition nonsense that's to blame. The hotels used to make all their profits in the bar, see, so they kept the price of dinin' down, but now there's nothing stronger than cat's . . . dishwater – if you'll pardon the expression – well, it goes without saying, doesn't it?

'Anyway . . .' Florrie smiled at her own resourcefulness, 'he's sending one of his boys out for a bottle of gin, but that'll be pricey too, and not what you're used to at home, seeing as how they cook it in the bathtub . . .'

'Quite. Oh, and Florrie—' Brittany beckoned her back again as she moved off to the telephone. 'Since it's too early to eat, why don't you and I go and do a spot of sightseeing? If you'd like to, that is. We can arrange for one of the hotel staff to sit and mind George.'

Florrie's eyes lit up. 'I'd love to, Miss,' she said, and then added sternly, 'but only if it's proper, mind.'

'Well, I've no one else to show me New York, so I think we British ought to stick together.'


'This is my best hat,' Florrie announced as they set out along the street. 'I thought it seemed the right occasion.'

Beneath the confection of straw and tea roses, her head bobbed rapturously. She was delighted with everything she saw, exclaiming 'Oh, it's grand to be in a city again.'

It occurred to Brittany that she had selfishly failed to realize how strange it must have been for Florrie to be uprooted from London, where she had always lived, and deposited in rural Somerset. She felt a pang of guilty appreciation.

Florrie clearly revelled in the crowds that flocked down Broadway, but Brittany was disconcerted by people passing so close to her that she could hear them breathing.

Commerce was encroaching everywhere. 'Even in a church-yard!' hissed a scandalized Florrie, crossing herself for good measure as they stopped to inspect the beginnings of an eight-storey office block springing up on the Broadway frontage of Christ Church.

Movie theatres had long enjoyed healthy growth and now blossomed, with billboards advertising the latest motion pictures ('we'll go tomorrow,' said Brittany when she saw Florrie's dreamy expression). Hoardings proclaimed their messages from all angles, exhorting them to buy ginger ale, or five-cent cigars, or HO oatmeal, or to shop at Bloomingdales for 'everything under the sun'.

'It's a right old jumble, isn't it?' commented Florrie as they passed a chemist advertising in English and Italian.

Brittany agreed. 'You only have to look at the architecture.'

As they wandered in circles, trying to find their way back to the hotel, they turned it into a game, cataloguing the bizarre and outlandish styles with the avidity of seasoned collectors.

The Temple Emanu-El, with its twin Moorish towers and the Tiffany building masquerading as an Italian palazzo were extraordinary, but they found private residences even more extravagant: hulking Herculean edifices like displaced illustrations from a child's storybook. The ugliness of the romanesque Tiffany residence fascinated them, with its pointed roofs and tiny gingerbread balconies and windowpanes, but Andrew Carnegie's home bought gasps of disbelief.

Florrie took one look at the crenellated towers of dark brick, and the slit windows, and shuddered.

'Looks more like a prison!'

Or one of the Langbournes' holiday homes, thought Brittany.

They scuttled past endless stone pillars that were planted on the streets like the legs of vast, mythical beasts and stumbled gratefully on the Waldorf-Astoria as it was growing dark.

When she woke in the night Brittany could not understand why the muscles in her neck and shoulders were screaming in agony, and then she remembered.

Everything in New York pointed skywards.

The next afternoon, Brittany dressed in a primrose silk shift that balanced sobriety of line with delicacy of colour, pinned her hair neatly in place with pearl and diamond clasps that Susannah had given her for Christmas, and set off down the wide, tree-lined pavement of Lower Fifth Avenue. To make the scene more real, she decided as she walked how she would describe it all to Florrie.

Even the street lamps in this part of town were decidedly larger than life, with their twin double-drop globes, much taller and grander than anything in London.

She paused briefly outside the Steins' house, assessing it with her newly acquired expertise.

It was a four-storey mansion with a mansard roof and palladian steps, and not a Bavarian castle as she had half expected. It seemed unlikely that Jake would be at the house at this hour, but she was aching with curiosity to see his childhood home and perhaps to assess from the reactions of his family how Jake would receive her. If she went straight to see him at his office, he would certainly not bring her here.

She was ushered into a gloomy, cavernous hallway by a footman in a quaintly old-fashioned uniform who slunk away to announce that a Miss Brittany Colby from London was here. The pompous hunting scenes on the crimson walls made Brittany laugh.

*They've never hunted anything bigger than a mouse* . . .

The footman returned and could not conceal his glee at the stunned reaction that Brittany's visit had provoked. Mrs Stein was taking tea with her daughters in the parlour, and Miss Colby would be permitted to join them if she wished.

They're obviously dying to take a look at me, thought Brittany. Funny, I keep thinking of them as strangers, but they're George Theodore's relations . . . She wondered why the girls were there if they were all married, and then remembered Jake telling her that it was customary for Jewish daughters to spend the afternoons at their mother's house.

George's grandmother was serving tea in a parlour so vast that at first it was hard to find her. Her surroundings were an astonishing combination of gaudiness and gloom. The walls were panelled in the same rose brocade that covered the gilt-painted Louis XVI chairs. Rose damask drapes hung beneath a high, vaulted ceiling, cloudless blue and overpopulated with cupids. Curio cabinets were everywhere, crammed to bursting with German porcelain – Meissen and Fulda figurines – and gilded Venetian glass.

Four teacups were lowered carefully, and four pairs of eyes were fixed on Brittany.

The green ones, David's eyes, belonged to Mrs Stein, and she had Jake's smooth, thick, brown hair. She was very handsome and sat very erect.

The other three pairs of eyes were light blue. One of the daughters – the middle one, perhaps – was plump and freckled; the remaining two were strikingly sallow skinned, with dark glossy hair and haughty noses. Brittany stared at them. They were silent as they assessed this tall, fair English girl who held herself as straight as an arrow and dazzled them with her eyes.

'Miss Colby,' said Mrs Stein in a mellow, musical voice, 'do come and sit down. I'm Hannah Stein, and these are my daughters: Leah, Rachel and Sarah.'

The daughters said nothing, but watched Brittany as though she were a property they were considering buying.

'Tea? Milk, cream or lemon?'

*Jersey, Hereford or Shorthorn?* . . . Brittany recited to herself and felt her throat tighten with rising laughter.

'And what brings you to New York? Are you touring America?'

Hannah Stein's tone was so smooth that Brittany was dumbfounded with a sort of admiration. To think that she was blamed for the death of the favourite son . . .

'I'm here to see Jake,' she said as conversationally as she could, smiling at them over her teacup.

'Oh . . .'

Mrs Stein looked confused. She glanced quickly at the eldest of her daughters, who gave the slightest shake of her sleek head.

'. . . Er, I'm afraid you will be disappointed, Miss Colby. Jacob's not in New York. He's . . . away on business.'

From the way her voice trailed off, Brittany knew she was lying.

She lifted her cup tentatively. Four pairs of eyes, three blue and one green, were fixed on her face.

She smiled slightly and began to calculate the minimum number of minutes that etiquette demanded. Cups were lifted to lips with wooden rhythm, and the stark silence was punctuated only by staccato comments on the weather. Finally Brittany's cup came to rest on its saucer.

'Mrs Stein, I really mustn't keep you any longer. Good afternoon.'

She gave the stuffy museum of a room one last sweeping examination before she walked out. David's ghost, wherever it was, was not here. She could not imagine him alive in the room either, with his irresistible smile. Or Jake's buoyant shouts of laughter.

As she went slowly down the endless staircase, she remembered Jake descending on his tea-tray, and smiled to herself.

Isaac Stein's secretary told Brittany to wait, but she was not in the mood to be kept waiting.

She had slept little the night before, returning late from the promised trip to the cinemascope.

It seemed quite normal here in New York, going to see a film with her maid. In London she would never have dreamed of perplexing Florrie by asking her, nor would Florrie have dreamed of accepting for fear of being seen to have forgotten her place. But in New York it was different. Their shared sense of nationality gave way to equality between them, though they both knew that it was temporary.

Florrie had wanted to see Valentino, but when they failed to find an establishment showing his pictures ('He's losing popularity over here – getting too paunchy,' Brittany noted unsympathetically), she happily fell in with the suggestion that they see the torrid *Three Weeks*.

The novel had excited and mystified Brittany when she was sixteen, but now she found the plot rather silly, and was tempted to giggle as Conrad Nagel made cow's eyes at Aileen Pringle.

Florrie, on the other hand, was entirely satisfied with the experience, and her pleasure warmed Brittany's heart. She wept copiously over the fate of the Tiger Queen and gasped with astonishment at the size of the console that bore the organist upward like a gladiator in his chariot; white-gloved hands poised. And when the film was over, he played 'The End of a Perfect Day'.

But the day had been far from perfect, nor had it ended.

Brittany lay awake for hours, questions turning in her mind like an organ-grinder's tune while the rough, starched hotel sheets scratched her skin.

Mrs Stein did not want her to see Jake, any fool could guess that, but it did not necessarily mean he was out of town. It would be sheer stupidity to take the mother's word for it and leave, and she could not afford to languish in a hotel either, while waiting for him to return. Perhaps he had been at his office in Wall Street all along, and if so, he would be there tomorrow. She finally fell asleep deciding that she would call at the headquarters of Stein and Sons in the morning. If Jake was not there, at least Isaac Stein would be a man to deal with her plainly.

She took George with her as her stake in the Stein dynasty, but regretted it during the long wait in the reception lounge. He was hot and irritable, wriggling out of her arms to go to a neat stack of magazines on the low marble table.

The receptionist had said no, Mr Jacob was out of New York, but she would ask Mr Isaac Stein's secretary if he was free for a few minutes.

Mr Stein's secretary revealed that Isaac Stein would be delighted to see Miss Colby, if she did not mind waiting for a while. She waited for an hour and a half. He's trying to demoralize me, thought Brittany, angrily wishing she had worn something cooler than her lilac shantung coat and shirt. To hell with looking the demure young matron.

He was squatting like a speckled toad behind an unnecessarily large desk.

They faced each other at last, old enemies.

Could this small, ugly man with his sandy hair, freckles and protruding eyes *really* have fathered the vibrant David and the enigmatic Jake?

'I thought you might like to see your grandson,' she said without preamble, lifting David Stein's flesh and blood high in her arms so that he could be seen above the top of the desk.

'A fine boy.'

He pretended not to look at George, but Brittany saw his pale eyes shift slightly. 'Won't you take a seat, Miss Colby?'

She chose a leather club chair that sighed beneath her weight.

'Perhaps you would care for a drink? Some iced tea?'

Brittany looked surprised, and then nodded.

'I won't have alcohol served on the premises, you see, Miss Colby. It doesn't look good, the rich drinking as though it were their right. As thought there were no benefit to the poor in Prohibition. Don't you agree, Miss Colby?'

His accent sounded strange to her ears, even after her becoming accustomed to the speech of New Yorkers. It had a Teutonic thread that grated.

She replied smoothly, 'I tend to side with George Bernard Shaw, Mr Stein. He believes in leaving the people free to choose between drunkenness and sobriety.'

He looked at her directly this time. 'You've come a long way for Jake, Miss Colby. Would you have done the same for David?'

His effortless juxtaposition of the two names was calculated to make Brittany look cheap and fickle. Her face grew hot, but she knew she must not appear flustered.

'Naturally Jake and I have become close over the past year . . . And there's something that I particularly wanted to speak to him about. I understand that he's not in New York at the moment.'

'And so you brought your little bastard to try and blackmail me into letting you satisfy your whim with another of my sons?'

The civilized Wall Street potentate was gone, leaving only rasping Germanic ugliness.

There was a knock at the door and they sat in hostile silence while the secretary served them with tall frosted glasses of iced tea and stopped to beam at George, who was banging an ashtray rhythmically on the carpet.

'Mr Stein . . . if you will just tell me where I can find Jake, and then I won't trouble you further. I'm assuming you *know* where he is, of course.'

Isaac Stein laughed, showing yellowed teeth.

'We have a maxim in our Gemorrah, Miss Colby. It reads "Hide not thyself from thy kinsfolk." You didn't think Jake would run off without telling me where he was going, do you? He's thirty-seven, not seventeen. Let's just say he's got a lot to think over at the moment. And now I must bid you good-day, as I have another appointment.'

'You mean—?'

'I have no intention of telling you Jake's whereabouts this time.'

Isaac Stein stood up. Brittany did not move.

'You really are very stubborn, aren't you, Miss Colby? Let me show you something . . .'

He pointed out of the window at another large, white palatial building.

'Look – Kühn, Loeb and Co. Solly Loeb has a lovely grand-daughter. Any day now, she's going to be announcing her engagement to Jacob Stein. End of story.'

He called out to her as she reached the door.

'You're wasting your time staying in New York one minute longer.'

290

She turned back and met his milky blue eyes, and she thought she saw fear in them. And then comprehension hit her like a stone.

*He doesn't know where Jake is.*

If Florrie was disappointed that their trip had come to an end, she had the tact to conceal it.

Brittany left her repacking a suitcase that had only been half-unpacked anyway, and took a cab to the office of Langbourne Lines' New York agent. They were unhelpful at first, uncivil even, but then she showed them the letter Richard Langbourne had written in case she needed to rearrange her return passage at short notice, and they informed her with a surfeit of apology and politeness that there was a ship sailing that evening on which two first-class cabins could be set aside.

Brittany sat wearily through the interminable phone calls and then, thanking them with as much grace as she could muster, she returned to the Waldorf-Astoria to pay the bill.

They had been in New York only three days.

Brittany watched from the stern as they left the harbour and this time, lit up against the night sky, New York did look beautiful and magical. The shores of America receded. Where, at what exact point on that vast continent, was Jake? Her misery was dull and hard and resigned. Jake would find her eventually, or write to her, but perhaps it would only be to tell her that he had decided to marry his second Jewish 'princess' after all.

She stood on the deck for what seemed like hours but was probably only minutes, watching for something that was not there. A man came and stood beside her, wrinkling his eyes companionably and trying to assess her mood. He was plump and round and elderly, with a friendly face that reminded Brittany of a dog her brother George had had once, years ago.

'You over for long?'

The accent was New York with mid-European overtones.

'Three days.'

He looked straight ahead in sympathetic contemplation.

'So . . . you didn't find what you were looking for, huh?'

She shook her head.

'Well, here goes.'

He lifted the light straw Panama hat from his head and cast it vigorously over the side of the railings so that it twisted and spun and landed, a patch of white, on the dark night sea.

Brittany raised her eyebrows quizzically.

'It's tradition, you know. When the boat pulls out of the port you throw your hat away and make a wish. You should do it with yours; it'll bring you luck.'

Brittany reached up and fingered her hat doubtfully; the rakishly sloping brim, the three graceful feathers dyed blue, mauve and grey. It was Parisian and very precious.

'No, I don't think so. Not this one.' She gave the little man a regretful smile. 'Next time, perhaps.'

'That's a pity, lady, you look like you could use the luck.'

No journey is as interesting when made for the second time, and the passage from New York to England dragged. Like reading a book backwards, Brittany decided fretfully.

Florrie was distressed by her gloom, but at a loss to know how to relieve it, and besides, she had her hands full with George. If Brittany went on deck she complained bitterly afterwards that it was too windy, reading wearied her and she reviled all the other passengers as senile or just plain dull. By the time they reached Southampton, she had grown bad-tempered, snapping at Florrie and slapping George in irritation if his small hands strayed. She knew she was committing the unforgivable sin of expending her own misery on others, but was unable to stop herself.

A cable to Susannah had ensured that the Sizaire-Berwick was waiting on the quayside for them, its cream outline comforting in the fading light.

Brittany chose to ignore the sensible advice in the note that Susannah had left on the windscreen, suggesting that they spend the night in a local hotel or drive to London where she and her husband would be glad to accommodate them. And Susannah added that she hoped the trip had been 'useful'.

*Useful . . .!*

Brittany muttered the word through gritted teeth as she drove too fast, bouncing George's sleeping head against Florrie's shoulder and making Florrie grip her handbag nervously.

The whole trip had been a waste of time. *A waste, a waste!*

'Oughtn't you to slow down a bit, Miss?' suggested Florrie as they tore over the Wiltshire–Somerset border. 'You might get lost,' she added lamely.

'No, Florrie, I do not intend to slow down, nor am I going to get lost. I'm going to drive and drive until we get home, and when I get there I am never, ever going anywhere again. Do you understand?'

Her knuckles whitened against the steering wheel.

'Yes, Miss,' said Florrie, clutching her handbag more tightly.

It was very late when Brittany reached her home.

As they approached the house, she saw that one of the maids had left a light on in the kitchen. The thin, yellow gleam spilled out into the stableyard, and onto the bonnet of a car, sparkling in its chrome headlamps. It was not Harry's baby Austin, but a large, dark car she did not recognize.

'Damn!' Brittany braked abruptly, and the Sizaire-Berwick screeched to a halt before it reached the curve of the carriage drive. 'Who the hell is that?'

'Looks like you've a visitor.' Florrie was never afraid to state the obvious.

'Well, *I* certainly haven't invited anybody.' Brittany swivelled round in her seat. 'Do *you* know anything about this?' she accused.

Florrie shook her head. 'I do not,' she said vehemently. 'I don't suppose it could be Mr Stanwycke . . . Oh, look!' She pointed at the portico, where a shadowy figure was just visible between the white columns. 'A man, Miss! Over there . . . Oh my goodness, do you think we're being robbed?'

'I doubt that,' said Brittany, easing off the handbrake and letting the car coast down the slope. 'It would be a pretty poor burglar who parked his car in such an obvious place and used the front door. I can't think who it can be, unless . . .'

'It could be the police, perhaps?'

They were nearing the house. The tall, slightly stooping figure in a trilby hat was clearly visible. A half smile crept over Brittany's face.

'Unless . . .'

The hat was removed and Jake's brown hair shone in the glare of the headlamps. Jake's face smiled shyly. Brittany was already out of the car and running over the gravel towards him.

She hesitated a moment and then flung her arms round his neck, laughing and blinking back her tears.

'Jake, what—?'

'I wanted to surprise you,' he said, and shrugged his shoulders in mock defeat.

They stood there on the steps and Brittany hardly dared to breathe, while Florrie, holding George, slipped quietly past them and into the house, closing the front door discreetly behind her.

'And you're not going back again?'

'No, not this time.'

Brittany snatched her precious plumed hat from her head with a wide-eyed shout of delight, holding it at arm's length. Then, with one movement, she hurled it into the darkness of the night.

# EPILOGUE

## *Somerset, August, 1927*

The retiring afternoon sun warmed the grey stone walls of Heathcote House. Ivy leaves trapped the sun in tiny pools, glowed vividly green, then faded to the colour of dust as the sun withdrew into its narrowing sea of glowing crimson.

Tiny, pretty Jennifer Steele paced the small, square lawn with the baby in her arms, trying to calm her indignant cries. Her son, Patrick, hovered closely, snatching impatiently at her skirt, clamouring to be allowed to hold his newborn sister. Their father was nowhere to be seen.

Two miles away, at Graylings, Brittany and Jake stood on the porch and looked out at the garden. The patches of sunlight on the lawn were slowly fading and merging with the dark shadows cast by the cedar tree. A maid collected the tea things onto a tray, weaving her way expertly among the croquet balls that George had left strewn at intervals on the grass.

In the canopied pram lay their sleeping daughter. Brittany went to look at her, to watch the light, regular breathing and to wonder what life had in store for young Nancy Stein. After a while, Florrie appeared, to take her charge back to the nursery and Brittany's gaze followed the retreating figure up the steps of the porch, watching her go a little wistfully. It was very quiet.

She touched Jake's arm then, as the last of the sun's light blazed and sank in a final curtsy, and he smiled down at her, understanding.

'Let's go into the house,' she said, and slowly they moved across the lawn to Graylings.

## Fiction

| | | | |
|---|---|---|---|
| ☐ | **Castle Raven** | Laura Black | £1.75p |
| ☐ | **Options** | Freda Bright | £1.50p |
| ☐ | **Chances** | Jackie Collins | £2.50p |
| ☐ | **Brain** | Robin Cook | £1.95p |
| ☐ | **The Entity** | Frank De Felitta | £2.50p |
| ☐ | **The Dead of Jericho** | Colin Dexter | £1.50p |
| ☐ | **Whip Hand** | Dick Francis | £1.75p |
| ☐ | **Saigon** | Anthony Grey | £2.95p |
| ☐ | **The White Paper Fan** | Unity Hall | £1.95p |
| ☐ | **Solo** | Jack Higgins | £1.95p |
| ☐ | **The Rich are Different** | Susan Howatch | £3.50p |
| ☐ | **Smash** | Garson Kanin | £1.75p |
| ☐ | **Smiley's People** | John le Carré | £2.50p |
| ☐ | **The Conduct of Major Maxim** | Gavin Lyall | £1.75p |
| ☐ | **The Master Mariner Book 1: Running Proud** | Nicholas Monsarrat | £1.50p |
| ☐ | **Fools Die** | Mario Puzo | £2.50p |
| ☐ | **The Throwback** | Tom Sharpe | £1.95p |
| ☐ | **Wild Justice** | Wilbur Smith | £2.50p |
| ☐ | **Cannery Row** | John Steinbeck | £1.95p |
| ☐ | **Caldo Largo** | Earl Thompson | £1.95p |
| ☐ | **Ben Retallick** | E. V. Thompson | £2.50p |

All these books are available at your local bookshop or newsagent, or
can be ordered direct from the publisher. Indicate the number of copies
required and fill in the form below                                                    12

Name_____
(Block letters please)

Address_____

_____

Send to CS Department, Pan Books Ltd, PO Box 40, Basingstoke, Hants
Please enclose remittance to the value of the cover price plus:
35p for the first book plus 15p per copy for each additional book ordered
to a maximum charge of £1.25 to cover postage and packing
Applicable only in the UK

While every effort is made to keep prices low, it is sometimes
necessary to increase prices at short notice. Pan Books reserve
the right to show on covers and charge new retail prices which
may differ from those advertised in the text or elsewhere